S0-EGO-062

Praise for SOVEREIGN SOIL

"Absolute must read for all who love this Country and Freedom. Allen Berberick has nailed it. *Sovereign Soil* is a book that reads more like truth than fiction. An exciting and powerful edge of your seat read."

—Command Sergeant Major Daniel E. Wright
(US Army – CSM of the 4th Infantry Division, Ret.)

"A fiction novel that is based in the reality of our time; a pulse pounding thriller that will leave you wanting more, while stirring the love of God, Country, and Freedom. I look forward to the next in the series."

—First Sergeant Lonnie R. Blevins
(US Army Special Forces, Ret.)

"*Sovereign Soil* is a raw, exciting, action packed, and inspiring story. This work of fiction grapples with the dilemma faced when men find their convictions being compromised. It is eerily prophetic in its message of the times in which we live—I eagerly await the sequel and movie."

—Pastor Steve Turrentine
(Pikes Peak Park Baptist Church – Colorado Springs, CO.)

"This book is the perfect example why we need to put God back into our country, just as our founding forefathers intended this great nation to be governed. The author's profound faith in God and career as a Green Beret were exemplified."

—Sergeant Michael W. Waits
(US Army Infantry)

"*Sovereign Soil* has stunning and realistic action with excellent tradecraft and such a ring of truth that it has obviously been written by a person that has been there and done that! I found this book very hard to put down and I was always looking forward to picking it up again."

—Sergeant, William T. Sofield
(Former, US Marine, Police Officer, and
Overseas Security Contractor)

Author Allen D. Berberick
www.allen-berberick.com
www.tatepublishing.com

SOVEREIGN SOIL

To Mark,

Thank you for supporting
the NRA + our 2ND Amendment
, Allen...

Allen D. Berberick +
"De Oppresso Liber"
NRA Life Member

05/28/16

Jesus Saves   God Bless America
              + Our Troops

SOVEREIGN SOIL
CIVIL WAR IS FORCED AGAIN

AN ALEX BOULDER NOVEL BY
ALLEN D. BERBERICK

TATE PUBLISHING
AND ENTERPRISES, LLC

Sovereign Soil
Copyright © 2014 by Allen D. Berberick. All rights reserved.

No part of this publication may be reproduced, stored in a retrieval system or transmitted in any way by any means, electronic, mechanical, photocopy, recording or otherwise without the prior permission of the author except as provided by USA copyright law.

The opinions expressed by the author are not necessarily those of Tate Publishing, LLC.

This novel is a work of fiction. Names, descriptions, entities, and incidents included in the story are products of the author's imagination. Any resemblance to actual persons, events, and entities is entirely coincidental.

Published by Tate Publishing & Enterprises, LLC
127 E. Trade Center Terrace | Mustang, Oklahoma 73064 USA
1.888.361.9473 | www.tatepublishing.com

Tate Publishing is committed to excellence in the publishing industry. The company reflects the philosophy established by the founders, based on Psalm 68:11,
"The Lord gave the word and great was the company of those who published it."

Book design copyright © 2014 by Tate Publishing, LLC. All rights reserved.
Cover design by Allen Jomoc
Interior design by Joana Quilantang

Published in the United States of America

ISBN: 978-1-63063-280-9
1. Fiction / General
2. Fiction / War & Military
14.02.06

DEDICATION

*In memory of
the United States of America,
the finest nation on Earth.*

We can all remember when America was the greatest nation in the world. Many years ago our forefathers left Europe to escape tyranny and unfair persecution. In 1775 they began to create the foundation for the greatest nation on earth. The strongest cornerstone of this foundation was their strong belief and faith in God. This great nation has believed in and trusted in our Christian God and his beloved son, Jesus Christ since before our founding fathers authored our nation's constitution. They had such faith in God that they even inscribed the words, "*In God We Trust*" on the paper bills and coins that they minted.

There is talk of minting all new currency now that does not have any reference to God on it, because it is offending someone. Our children used to be able to recite the "*Pledge of Allegiance*" in school. Now they can not make any reference to God in school, because it offended someone. It probably offended someone that our children also spoke of allegiance to the flag of their nation, liberty, and justice for all. Two teachers in school were arrested because they were observed in the cafeteria, praying over their own food before they ate. *How absurd has our very own people become?*

The United States has assisted both physically and financially more countries in the world, in need, than all other countries combined. The only thanks we get are other nations casting blame on America for the world's problems. The more Americans take God out of their lives, the more depraved and forsaken this nation becomes. Now half of the Radical Muslims in the world are trying to kill Americans and destroy the United States. With today's current political administration and policies, America's future and existence is in grave peril.

Wake up Americans
Before it's too late…
Freedom Isn't Free.
This is the land of the free;
Because of the Brave!

ACKNOWLEDGMENTS

1. First and foremost, I thank God for giving me the strength and courage to do the things that I have done in my life. I surely could not have done them without Him in my life. I also want to thank God for blessing and protecting America as He has done thus far.

2. I'd like to thank my father, Hank, for being there when I needed him and preparing me for a cruel and harsh world. I inherited my construction and fabrication skills from him. I learned weapons and hunting from him at an early age. I see a lot of him in me. It is true. I am my father's son.

3. My mother, Gloria, has been a large inspiration in my life. She has always been there whenever I needed her. She supported and signed for me to enter the military when I was seventeen years old. Being the fine Christian woman she is, she has always prayed on my behalf when I have been in over thirty countries around the world.

4. My stepfather, Bob, always set a great example for me to follow. He taught me more things than he ever knew. He was a retired US Air Force jet mechanic, whom also supported and signed for me to enter the US Army at age seventeen. He died from lung cancer during my second year in the army. He always swore it was from the Agent Orange that was sprayed on him in the Vietnam War.

5. My brother, Steve, and sister, Becky Jo have also always supported me in whatever endeavors I was involved in. We have always been there for each other. I am truly blessed with a wonderful family.

6. My wife, Lisa, for all of the love and support she has given me. She has sacrificed much, through the years as a contractor's wife. I Love You.

7. My friend, Bill Sofield, for all of his advice and knowledge of fire fighting, airports, air traffic control towers, and aircraft. His knowledge helped promote the realistic accuracy of this book.

8. My friend, SSG Brian Williams, a USAF-PJ (Para-Rescue) airman that died on active duty on 27 March 1990. He was much of my inspiration for going into Army Special Forces in 1987. He was truly the best of the best. Godspeed...

9. Finally, I'd like to thank all of my Special Forces brothers that I have known and served with in Special Forces units and on Special Forces A-teams. We learned together in schools, endured hardships on land, air, and sea together, and completed our missions as a team both in peace time and war. A bond is set for life.

The Green Berets

ABOUT THE AUTHOR

ALLEN D. BERBERICK

A RETIRED, UNITED STATES ARMY SPECIAL FORCES SOLDIER

31 August, 2000

Army Special Forces
The Green Berets

In September 2000, Sergeant First Class Allen Berberick retired after twenty years in the United States Army and Special Forces (the Green Berets). He retired from Special Forces at Fort Bragg, North Carolina, after serving in the 5th SFG, 3rd SFG, USAJFKSWC, and finally the 3rd SFG again. While in Special Forces, he held such MOSs as (18B30W7) Special Operations Weapons Sergeant, (18B40H) Senior Instructor/Writer, (18F40W9) Special Forces Assistant Operations and Intelligences Sergeant, and a secondary MOS of (11B40P) Airborne Infantryman.

Some of the duty positions he held in his unit were SFOD-A Operations Sergeant *as an E-7*, team sniper, combat diver, NCOIC Combat Dive Facility, ASOT operator, HALO parachutist, static line jump master, fast rope master, rappel master, and so on. Sergeant Berberick served in 'Operation Desert Storm' in 1991 as a Special Forces weapons sergeant, where he advised a Kuwaiti commando company on combat tactics and operations.

After retiring from the military, he worked overseas for the US Government for seven years. He provided some special services on hardened US Government structures around the world, in the form of Top Secret security services. The specifics are classified by the Department of State. For 2010, 2011, and 2012 he was a member of the Kabul Embassy Security Force. He protected the American Embassy and its Department of State diplomats in Kabul, Afghanistan—the number one terrorist target in the world. The (KESF) fended off several terrorist attacks during this time frame with no loss of American life. For more about the author, go to www.allen-berberick.com.

CONTENTS

There is a list of Acronyms and Abbreviations
at the back of this book.

EXCERPTS

Pg.-21 A Black Muslim senator from Illinois took up residence in the White House as the forty-fourth president of the United States of America. He was so inexperienced that he never even completed a single term in the senate. However, he was accustomed to conducting politics "the Chicago way". There were people still trying to establish if he was even legal to be the president. Time would tell.

Pg.-61 "I want to use three of your cocaine subs!" Dutch replied. Ethan could tell that Dutch hit a nerve with the general. The general cocked his head and raised his eyebrow. "What are you talking about? I don't have any subs! I use planes to deliver my coke. You know that from the old days."

Pg.-95 The scene degraded until an uneasy demonstration turned into a full-scale riot in the streets of Washington, D.C. The images of Americans rioting hadn't been seen since the 90's L.A. riots over Rodney King and the 60's race riots. Washington's riot police were barely able to contain the violence to a ten block radius.

Pg.-132 As the huge 45 caliber bullets ripped through the inch and a quarter wood deck boards beneath them, the wood splinters flew 20 feet in the air. While the men were frozen in place and time, they seemed to dance in-place. Alex noticed the ceiling was quickly turning red with blood and gray matter.

Pg.-156 These four states are in accord when I say that we can no longer stand idly by and be a part of a federal government that does not uphold our nation's Constitution; of which the Second Amendment is part of. The right of every American to keep and bear arms.

Pg.-167 There were men, women, and children, as well as guardsmen killed in the fighting. This national atrocity would haunt Americans for generations to come. This was even harder to swallow than the nearly 3,000 Americans killed during 9/11, because it was our own government that did the killing.

Pg.-175 "What the hell do you know about ordering men to their deaths, much less ordering them to go against their brothers and sisters? You've never served a day of your life in the military. You wouldn't know the meaning of the words HONOR, DUTY, LOYALITY, COUNTRY, or your brother in arms, if they bit you in the ass!"

Pg.-179 At 2100 EST the 1/75th Ranger Battalion was in the air heading west. Even the pilots thought they were headed for Fort Lewis until they reached Tennessee. Then they received their actual orders for 'OPERATION CONDOR REPO'. The first section on the classified OPORD was for the C-17 crew.

Pg.-187 Major English would command the other half of the Delta Force assault team that would simultaneously take down the RAPCON, next to the ATCT. It was critical that the actual ATCT room and RAPCON room be stormed at exactly the same moment. Otherwise, one could alert the other because they had a symbiotic working relationship. Major English's call sign was War Machine.

Pg.-191 That was one of those things that every man on the team would take to his grave. They all just kind of watched the corps spin around in the chair like a carnival ride. Once he stopped spinning, the closest man checked his pulse. He looked around the room and said, "O yea, he's toast." They all probably realized that very well might have been the first casualties of the next American civil war.

Pg.-205 As soon as Governor Pevey received word that Texas was under attack he called his top naval commander, Admiral Wollard and told him that Dyess Air Force Base was under attack and needed naval air support. The admiral agreed and committed to scramble a squadron of his Naval Reserve F-14s from the Naval Air Station at Fort Worth Joint Reserve Base.

Pg.-222   There were still two AH-64 Apaches in the fight and they were proving hard too kill. Unlike fighter jets that had to keep moving over the battlefield, helos could duck for cover and hide while still covering their assigned sectors. One of those gunships had been hiding behind a stand of trees just northwest of TRP-1. His call sign was Magpie and his mission was to keep the North end of the runway clear so the B-1 Bombers could take off.

PG.-237   One reporter asked the colonel, "Sir, Do you think President Osama has any remorse about sending Americans to kill Americans?" The colonel took off his shades and looked him squar in the eyes. The reporter was a bit intimidated by the colonels rough look and his battle scar that ran down the entire right side of his face.

Pg.-251   The pilot sent out a MAYDAY over the radio and his crew chief started yelling to all of the VIPs to strap in and hang on. That's when Pulaski looked at Senator Josh Kaylee from Massachusetts who was setting beside her and said, "That's military jargon for 'put your head between your legs and kiss yer ass good-bye boy!'" Senator Kaylee started crying like a little girl. Pulaski shook her head in disgust and said, "I always knew you were a big pussy, Kaylee. For once, act like a man. You make me sick!"

Pg.-256   The day that all US American gun owners feared had finally come. This was the day that President Osama's national gun ban would kick in. The only question was how earnestly were the feds prepared to try to enforce it?

Pg.-272   At the conclusion of the FBI's investigation, their findings were that a member of the Hispanic cleaning/moving crew had been able to plant the device under the Vice-President's desk while performing his duties. The man was a deep cover operative for the Zetas cartel out of Mexico.

Pg.-285 Lord, please let our birds fly as swift and as invisible as Your angels. You have given all creatures on Your blessed earth the right to defend themselves from harm from others. Lord, if we should have to defend ourselves on this just mission, please make our shots as straight and powerful as Your lighting bolts.

Pg.-298 Just like Waco and Ruby Ridge, after the miss-handling and over exertion of force on a small group of American citizens in their home, the FBI was called in and took control of the situation. Special Agent Delancy Barns from the Cincinnati office assumed command as the On-Site Commander. He was not well known for his patients or even temperament.

Pg.-302 These people didn't appear to have any special skills or training. They just used some imagination and guts. Think about it. These seven men and women took out 24 highly trained and heavily armed federal agents before they were killed. That's pretty good in my book.

Pg.-330 The two Blackhawks proceeded to follow the two Hueys, while ordering the Hueys to stop and land. As Hades and Zeus continued flying, one of the door gunners in the lead Blackhawk sent a burst of 7.62 tracers across the bow of Damon's bird. Then Damon came over the radio and told Dutch, "Zeus, let's take em out, they're not going to stop!"

Pg.-339 In 2009 FEMA (Federal Emergency Management Agency) had also graduated their first class of 231 recruits. They were all ages 18 to 24 and recruited from the President's AmeriCorps volunteers. They were the first wave of DHS's paid Youth Corp Army across the country. To date they had 5,000 of those brain washed troops. They sort of reminded people of Hitler's Youth Corp, in an eerie sort of way.

Pg.-346 The FSA troops gave several radio calls for the Apaches to cease and desist, with no response. Therefore, the commander of the unit ordered one of his Vulcans to send a hundred round burst of 20 mike mike across their bow. Then Major Dollar, the commander of the Apache attack squadron ordered his birds to open fire upon the FSA troops on the other side of the national boarder. This was the act that started America's second Civil War.

Pg.-357 Meanwhile, while Task Force Titan was sleeping, there were hostile boarder skirmishes all up and down the national boarder. Things were definitely heating up between the USA and FSA. It seemed as though there were plenty of families willing to take the risk to get to the western side of the boarder. Some made it and some didn't.

Pg.-368 Alex said, "Have them land the chopper on our helo pad out by the big metal building. Clint, what does he want?" "Well Alex, all I can say is President Pevey has quite an amazing proposal for you, young man. Be prepared to be shocked!"

THE STAGE IS SET

20 JANUARY 2009
WASHINGTON, D.C.

A Black Muslim senator from Illinois took up residence in the White House as the forty-fourth president of the United States of America. He was so inexperienced that he never even completed a single term in the senate. However, he was accustomed to conducting politics "the Chicago way". There were people still trying to establish if he was even legal to be the president. Time would tell.

09 FEBRUARY 2009
DURANGO, COLORADO

In 2008, Alex met the woman of his dreams, and on February 9, 2009, he married her, and settled down with her in Durango, Colorado. Her name was Leiko. She was a five-feet tall, one hundred pound, full-blooded Japanese woman with no kids or extra baggage. Alex met her during his quest for property in that region of the Rockies. Even though he loved his beloved West Virginia, it was time to move on. The east coast had become far too crowded with all of their anti-gun, panty waist liberals.

With Bakr Houssam Osama in the White House with all of his bogus czars, Alex just wanted to puke. It seemed as though if you weren't politically correct and onboard with Osama, you weren't welcome in the USA anymore. Alex always loved the mountains, any mountains, and he figure that out west was the place for him to live out the rest of his days.

One thing Alex knew about Asians was that they liked to gamble. Leiko and he would go to some of the Indian casinos to have some fun and drop a little coin. Alex truly did enjoy hanging out with that woman. She brought out the best in him. They were destined for interesting times.

Alex never played any kind of lottery games before he met her. Now he was a regular every Wednesday and Saturday, drawing on the Powerball and Colorado Lotto. Hey, you never know.

ONE IN TWO HUNDRED MILLION

31 OCTOBER 2009
DURANGO, COLORADO

Alex always checked his lottery ticket numbers on their official website. He'd seen too many store clerks in the news that had cheated previous winners out of their winnings.

On October 31, 2009, Alex thought Leiko was screwing with him. When he started checking the ticket numbers, they started matching. One then two then three then four. He started looking around for a miniature camera somewhere, thinking he was on one of those punked shows or something. Then five, he started crapping his pants and convulsing on the floor. Then even the Powerball number matched.

Alex always swore he wouldn't get all verbal and excited like those dummies on TV when they won a car, a trip, or something. Well, the fact of the matter was, Leiko had to step on his tong just to see if he was still alive. She yelled, "Come on boy, snap out of it!" After she clamped the car battery charger to his nipples and cranked his heart up again, they began to celebrate.

Like Alex said, "Ya never know." That day, they won the largest Powerball jackpot to date. It was 382.7 million dollars, and they were the single jackpot winners! The magical numbers were 04, 20, 50, 52, 57, and a Powerball number of *12*.

Alex did his research on the smart way to collect the booty. He hired an attorney so they could claim the massive jackpot under anonymity. He conducted all facets of the transaction just as he would conduct a covert mission. No photos, no giant check, and no public knowledge of the real winner's names.

On top of all that, he was able to get all public records concerning their winnings sealed from the public. Alex was able to convince the judge that it was in everyone's best interest for safety and security reasons. After all, if anyone came around their home trying to make an illegal withdraw, he would have to terminate their account. That would make more work for the judge, and we all knew how bogged down our justice system was.

After taxes and taking the one time, lump sum payout, it came out to 193.7 million dollars, clams, buckaroos, or good old American greenbacks. Alex called that the chance of a lifetime or your one lifetime chance to make a difference.

The next step was to segregate the millions. Alex never believed in putting all his eggs in one basket. Just like when his SF team (US Army Special Forces, the Green Berets) would travel in a split team concept on a mission. That way, if one of the two choppers were eliminated, the other half of the team could still arrive and complete the mission.

Well, the way that banks in the US screw you over, they were definitely going to diversify. That one hundred fifty million would go into ten different offshore accounts. The remainder of the lute would go into five different US banks.

The next step in protecting their funds would be to employ the only CPA (Certified Public Accountant) in the world that Alex trusted one hundred percent. His sister, Brook, who had been a senior CPA for eleven years. She also worked in a bank, and she was about to get a new job offer.

Now that Alex didn't have to worry about his next contract, it was time to employ his plan for protecting his family and friends in these very uncertain times. He thought that he would never be able to employ his plan, but he believed God had given him the chance to do so now. He'd have to get on the ball because he was behind the power curve, according to US and world events.

Alex found out very quickly when you were that wealthy the bankers kissed your ass all the way out the door. After an hour briefing from one of his bank presidents, Alex understood how to expedite a multimillion dollar purchase.

The financial attorney that they hired for the lottery transaction was a stand-up kind of guy. After a career in SF, Alex was a quick study of people's character, and he was rarely wrong. Alex told Leiko, "I like him and pretty much trust him, although I know I won't give him too much authority." His name was Clint Stanly, an elderly gentleman in his mid-sixties. To see Mr. Stanly on the street, you would never guess him to be a high-powered attorney in Denver.

He dressed just like he worked in a lumberyard or on a ranch. Blue jeans, flannel shirt, cowboy boots, and a rugged canvas vest. Best of all was his Charlie-one-horse cowboy hat with a horseshoe branded on the front. It had character just like him.

One reason Alex wanted to use him was because he already knew of their wealth. No sense in letting more people know than needed to. Alex told him their first business at hand was to purchase several thousand acres of property probably in Colorado, Wyoming, or Montana. Alex said, "Clint, I'll let you know as soon as I locate it. Then I'll fly you up to see it and start the ball rolling."

With Clint's cheerful smile, he replied, "Yes, sir, I'll be ready."

THE PLAN

After returning from Clint Stanley's office in Denver, Alex and Leiko began preparing for their journey to go and find their property to build their retirement home on. The 2002 Dodge Ram 3500 5.9L diesel 4x4 and thirty-two-foot homemade gooseneck RV (recreational vehicle) that they had just didn't seem to be adequate any more.

The next day, they went to the Ford dealership and bought the truck of Alex's dreams. It was a black Ford F-750 Super Duty with a 7.3L turbo diesel quad cab 6x6 dually that had two brushed aluminum one hundred gallon fuel tanks—one on each side. Of course, this rig had every bell and whistle possible on it.

This truck had a sixteen-foot straight rail frame behind the cab, just the way he wanted it. Then Alex told them to get a sixty-inch double sleeper cab with a TV, frig, and microwave and install it and a standard eight-foot dually bed. Naturally, it all needed to be all flat black to match the truck and be tactical.

For the finishing touches, Alex ordered a sprayed-in Rhino lining and a fifth wheel-hitch for the bed, a custom Road Armor bumper for the front and rear and an eighteen thousand pound Warn winch for a MRAP (Mine Resistant Ambush Protected vehicles) inside both bumpers. He told them they wanted that complete package ready to be picked up in one week. Of course that cost him an extra five thousand. The total package cost was $113,789.

Now it was time for a new RV. That was easier to find than the F-750 was. In Colorado, there was a major RV dealership in every town it seemed. Alex remembered the sight of so many RV storage places everywhere when he first came to Colorado. He attributed that to all of the state and national parks out there. It truly was the land of wide open spaces in the United States.

They ended up deciding on a Gulfstream, Prairie Schooner thirty-eight foot fifth wheel RV. This was one heck of a sweet mobile home. This huge tri-axle rig was as complete and luxurious as most homes. It had every system on it that they could ever want. The only thing was it didn't match the truck. For an extra ten thousand, they were willing to paint it to match the truck. Same deal: Alex told them they wanted the complete package ready to be picked up in one week. Total package cost was $178, 514.

The last thing to buy with wheels for the journey was a Hurricane twenty-four-foot bike trailer, flat black of course. It was plenty large enough to fit the 2003 Harley-Davidson "Screamin' Eagle" Road King and two large 4x4 ATVs (All Terrain Vehicles) in. Total package cost was $9,000.

The three machines would have to come along on the quest for the new property. They would come in handy for conducting recons (Reconnaissance, to look for) both on and off road. The twenty-eight-foot truck, thirty-eight-foot RV, and twenty-four-foot bike trailer made for quite the big rig! What a sight. Ninety-feet of steel rolling down the road, and Alex still didn't need a CDL (Commercial Driver's License) because it was for personal use.

They lived in an apartment when they won the jackpot. Therefore, they didn't have much to do before departing Durango. They sold Leiko's car and Alex's old truck, and the homemade thirty-two-foot RV.

A week and a half later, they were on the road headed east for I-25, RV and bike trailer in tow. Once they hit I-25, they headed north for Fort Collins. At dusk, they pulled into a rest stop near Walsenburg, Colorado. After letting the truck's turbo cool down, Alex shut her off. He checked and prepped everything for a night's stay, fired-up the generator, and conducted a final security check.

Leiko fixed them a fine dinner. She always was a great cook. After dinner while sitting at the table, Alex said to Leiko, "Here's the plan, shorty."

"I've watched this great country steadily going down the crapper for the last twenty years. The last ten were more noticeable than the first ten, and these last three years have been so painfully blatant.

"With the financial meltdown, record unemployment, a national debt the American working people can never pay off, a new national healthcare disaster, wars on two fronts, thirty-one unqualified or criminal czars, and a Muslim president, whose only concern is tearing down this country and appeasing the world's radical Muslim population, America doesn't have a chance!

"Leiko, I really believe with all of my heart that America is headed for another civil war. We're already at fifteen percent unemployment in this country. Osama and his cast of criminals are tearing this country and its people apart.

"In light of this economic meltdown, everything we buy is going up, and the quantity is going down. You know that just from the food you buy. Half of the things that Osama does these days are just to let congress and the senate know that he's not going to ask for their permission to do whatever he wants.

"Like appointing any of his friends he chooses as a czar, even though they are not qualified or are a criminal. They don't even need a resume or vetting process that they have to go through with anyone. He's putting the worst of the worst in there. When you have registered communist and convicted felons in high-paying government jobs in Washington that answer only to Osama, something is seriously wrong with our leadership.

"Our founding forefathers didn't intend for this great nation to be governed in this manner. With four western states claiming they're going to secede from the union, things are going to get much worse than we've ever seen in our generation. And don't forget all of the predictions that the Bible makes concerning one world money, mark of the beast, and the Antichrist."

Alex pointed to the map on the table as he continued, "That's why we're headed for Fort Collins, Colorado. That region is where we will begin our search for several thousand acres of wooded, mountainous, semi-remote land. That much area will support my plan for a safe future for our families and friends. We'll find it in Colorado, Wyoming, or Montana.

"Once we find and buy this land, Leiko, we're going to build a secure and safe community for our families and friends to live on without the threat of civil or government dominance. We'll all live free and have our constitutional rights the way our founding forefathers intended us to.

"After we've decided on the property, I'll fly Clint Stanley up to close the deal. He's already on standby for that notification. Once the property is ours, I'll hire a construction company to come in and erect a guard house and ACF (Access Control Facility) at the main gate. Then a personnel perimeter fence system, a perimeter road on the inside of that, and a perimeter reinforced concrete wall that's five-foot high to keep any vehicles out. That will provide some good layered security obstacles for us.

"They should be able to get that done in about three months. It will be pushing it, but I'll offer the contractor a $50,000 bonus if he gets it completed in that time. While the fence is going up, I'll bring in a team to install an electronic security network integrated within the construction."

Leiko smiled and gazed at Alex as he continued talking. "While that is going up I'll hire, train, and employ a special guard force to man the gates and patrol the grounds. From that point on, our grounds will be fairly secure. Then with security and access control in place, I'll have a paving company begin, laying the driveways and the roads to all of the buildings. While the road construction is ongoing, we'll begin the recruitment phase. We'll go to the areas where our people live and we'll give them the offer of a lifetime.

"I'm telling you, girl, when civil war strikes and this nation is ripped apart, times will be worse that we have ever seen. We'll offer them to come to our secure, self sufficient community, where there's a new three thousand square foot home, a three-car garage, and one hundred acres of land waiting for them.

"I once read a government study that showed 100 acres of land, and two horses can sustain a family of four, indefinitely. We're way beyond that in our community. We have enough property for major farming of crops, sustainment of wildlife for hunting, and we'll have a heard of three hundred horses and five hundred head of cattle.

"It will be theirs for one dollar on a one-hundred-year lease. Even their children and grandchildren will have a home for life. The only catch is that they must work, defend, and contribute to the community. That means working in their areas of expertise.

"When I say defend, I mean just that, to the death if necessary. After all, this will be their homes, their lives, and their community. It will be their best chance at a good and semi-normal life for them and their children.

"The homes will all have the same floor plan; however, the one hundred acres of property will be of various shapes. By then we'll own our own construction company to build any additional structures for anyone such as the community church, barns, equipment buildings, and so on.

"For those that say yes, when the time comes, we will fly by chopper to pick them up and bring them home. We're only making one flight back east for everyone. That will be far enough. Of course, anyone will be welcome to come before that time, if they so choose. Well, baby, that's the plan in a nutshell. What da ya think?"

Leiko was silent for about ten seconds, and then she looked up at Alex with those big brown eyes and said, "I like it! I think it's the best gift we could possibly give our families and friends." Then she gave him a big hug and exclaimed, "That's why I love you, baby, you're always thinking."

INVEST IN THE COMMUNITY

After two weeks of dealing with realtors and looking at property, they finally found what they were looking for. It was 4,738 acres of forest, lakes, meadows, streams, and mountainous high country. Breathtaking! The only catch was that it spanned two states. *No problem, I have it covered*, Alex told himself.

He wanted to be able to take advantage of two different state's laws. This could have its advantages. After flying Clint up to see the property and review the formalities, Alex told him how he wanted to handle the deal.

Alex said, "I want to buy it in two halves. Each half will be in its own state."

Clint questioned, "I don't know if the owner will go for that?"

Alex raised his voice, "For 23.3 million bucks, I'm betting he will. Make the offer and tell him I'm in a hurry! I've got a house to build before this country goes to hell."

The Colorado half was a few miles north of Craig, Colorado. The Wyoming half was about eighty-miles west of the Medicine Bow Mountains, Wyoming. Mr. Thomas Roosevelt agreed to the sale, even the split concept. It only took three days to confirm the surveys and boundaries and finalize the contract.

When Alex and Leiko divided their stateside, $43.7 million, into five US banks, they put twenty-five million in the Wells Fargo bank in Denver because Alex knew they'd find the land in Colorado, Wyoming, or Montana. He anticipated twenty to twenty-five million for the property and didn't want to have to draw from several banks.

13 DECEMBER 2009
DENVER, COLORADO

A deal was struck. At the conclusion of the contract sign-ing Mr. Roosevelt looked at Alex and said, "Congratulations, Alex, you're the proud owner of two states, well, damned near, hahahahahahaaaaa!"

Alex replied, "Yes, sir, and a lot of people thank you," as he stood up and shook his hand with a hardy handshake.

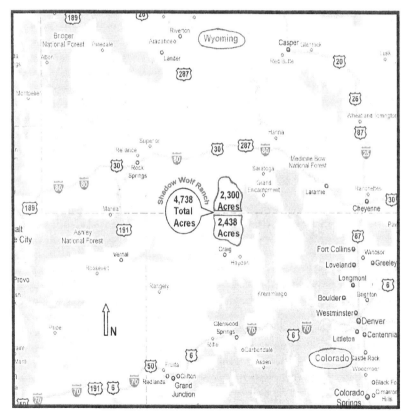

Once Mr. Roosevelt and his attorney left Clint Stanley's con-ference room, Alex collected all of the electronic devices that Clint, Leiko, and he had on their persons and put them in his hat.

He also unplugged the landline that was on the conference table and placed it with his hat and laid them on Clint's secretary's desk. Then Alex closed and locked the door behind him.

The only electronics still in the room was a small radio on the corner of the table. Alex turned the radio on, fairly loud, for cover noise. He told them both, "I don't want anyone hearing what's going to be said between the three of us." Then he started pulling all of the blinds as he thought, *Don't need any lip reading going on either.* Once Alex had all the blinds pulled he muddled, "That should do it."

The three of them all sat and huddled together at the end of the table so they could speak softly. Alex instructed Clint, "No notes" as he began to convey his wishes.

"I'd like you to establish three companies for us, that are so buried under a dozen or so shadow companies that it would take anyone years to trace them back to us. Nothing illegal, just the same thing that the government and these huge corporations do when they don't want anyone to know who really owns them.

"The first company will be used to purchase electronic equipment. The second company will be used to purchase aircraft. The third company will be used to purchase military surplus equipment.

"Next, Clint, I'd like you to establish a straightforward company named Lupus Enterprise, Inc. This company will have four divisions. A construction company, a class three weapons guard force company, a company that buys every day wholesale bulk items, and an airborne wilderness touring company.

"I don't intend to do anything illegal. I just don't want anyone in our business."

Clint assured Alex, "I understand. It should take me about two weeks to accomplish this task."

Alex replied, "Thank you, sir, please give me a call when you're ready, and I'll come in person to learn the details." They all stood, and the two shook hands.

With searching for the land and all, Alex didn't really have time to prep for that sensitive meeting. He wouldn't get caught short again in that department. If there's one thing that he learned in all T/S (Top Secret) environments, it's how to keep from being seen or heard. That even goes for the world's elite.

First task at hand is to construct an electronic free, anti-eaves-dropping, soundproof conference room in his twenty-four-foot bike trailer. That way, he could take it wherever he needed it. Its first meeting would be in two weeks with Clint Stanley. He'd also take it with them on the recruitment drive back east.

The best thing about that rig is no one would ever suspect its true purpose, especially after Alex put a few Harley-Davidson stickers on it. Two guys step in the side door of a bike trailer for fifteen or twenty minutes, and anyone would assume that they were checking out some scooters.

The next day, Leiko and Alex were going shopping. First order of business was to have a company come and install a one-hun-dred-foot wide by three-hundred-foot long by forty-foot tall steel building for their special projects. Next, have a modular house set-up to live in while the hard structures were being built. And finally, have all of the electric, well, and septic systems installed."

Alex told Leiko, "I can get that all accomplished in two weeks. Boy, I like having money."

Alex said, "Man, those two weeks went fast! Clint came through for us just like he said he would." Now that all of the companies were in place, and they knew how to purchase things through them, they'd be busy. Alex always took Leiko to all of their meetings so she was in on everything. That way, she could take over if anything happened to him. She was his right hand man, uh, lady.

During the two weeks that they were waiting for the meet-ing with Clint, Alex was a very busy camper. He took the test in Colorado and Wyoming for his construction contractor's license. Now he was legal to build in both states. Their own construction company would build their community and a heck of a lot cheaper than any other company would. Leiko and Alex laid out the loca-tions of all twenty of the home sites, community buildings, and special structures. The residential section of the community would be located on the Colorado side of the property and most of the covert defense facility will be located on the Wyoming side.

They also bought five concrete trucks and a portable concrete batch plant for $1.7 million. They would be delivered to the property and set up in three days. Alex also hired the batch plant foreman from the company they bought the equipment from. You don't want to screw around with the quality of your concrete, especially if you're being shot at.

15 FEBRUARY 2010
SHADOW WOLF RANCH

Alex walked into the sunken living room and stated to Leiko.

"It's the middle of February, and it's time to bring in Luis Kingston, my cousin from New York. He's an architect and civil engineer. I'm going to give him the recruitment pitch, but I can't wait for him until we drive to New York. We need him here now to draw up all the plans to the buildings, underground facilities, and the underground chopper hangars.

"Plus, I need him to ramrod the above ground construction and roads while we're back east. I'm calling him now to see if he can fly right out here even if it's just for the weekend. If he says yes, he won't have to be worrying about his job next week."

As Alex hung up the phone, he informed Leiko of the following results of his and Luis's conversation. "Good news, baby, Luis will be here Friday afternoon. I'm e-mailing his airline ticket to him tonight. You'll like him. He's a hoot! Luis is the kind guy you want watching your back in a barroom brawl. He's also king of the one-liners. Let's put him up in the bedroom next to the loft. Now let's give Gerard Willard a call and see when he can come see us."

Leiko said, "I've heard you talk about Luis, but who's this Willard guy?"

Alex replied, "He's an old guy I worked with for a year in Kenya. He's a great guy. We can surely use his kind of skills in the community. He used to work for the company before I worked with him in Kenya."

"What company?" "The agency." "What agency?"

He rolled his eyes at her and said, "You know, the one with the initials C-I-A (Central Intelligence Agency)!"

Leiko's eyes got big. "Oh, okay I get it."

Alex continued, "Anyway, shorty, he's a specialist in electronic security. He can install anything and everything we'll ever need on our property. We need him here before the construction starts, so he can have all of his equipment and material here beforehand." "What kind of materials are you talking about?"

"You know, security equipment like CCTV (Closed Circuit Television) cameras, multiplexers, metal detectors, microphone systems, microwave systems, X-ray machines, retina and palm scanners, intrusion detection systems, alarms, special locks, computer systems, and so on. Yup, he can do it all."

After speaking with Gerard he said, "All right girl, Gerard can be here Saturday morning. So I'll get Luis Friday afternoon and then Gerard on Saturday. We'll give Luis the pitch Friday night, after supper. Then we'll give Gerard the pitch Saturday afternoon after lunch."

Then Leiko asked, "Why don't we just wait and give them both the pitch at once, and save our voices?"

Alex answered her question, "Because, my young apprentice, you always want to give a covert recruitment offer to people, one-on-one. That way, they never see anyone else in the organization in case they decline. Also, their decision isn't influenced by anyone else. You stick with me, kiddo, and you'll learn all this secret stuff."

Leiko said, "I've got your back, boy."

"Leiko, lets review our recruitment pitch before Luis and Gerard get here." "Yeah, I want to be straight on this before we get in that cracker box." That's what she called the mobile conference room.

"Okay, my little friend, the pitch goes like this: Before or after the country goes to hell, he and a partner if he likes, can come to the ranch to live the rest of their lives. There will be a new three thousand square foot home, three-car garage, and one hundred acres of land waiting for them. It will be theirs for one dollar on a one-hundred-year lease. Even their children and grandchildren will have a home for life. The only catch is that they must work, defend, and contribute to the community.

"Now, for the older dudes, I'll make it clear that we don't expect them to be out there jumping obstacles with an Uzi and a ruck on their backs. They will be required to work in their area of expertise and maintain OP/SEC (Operational Security) for the community.

"We need these two guys here working ASAP (as soon as possible). Their jobs need to begin yesterday! We will also pay their moving coast and pay them a salary. That's one heck of a good deal if you ask me, don't you think?"

Leiko nodded her head up and down. Then Alex got a very serious look on his face and said, "One last thing. If anyone declines, we'll have to kill them right then and there!" Leiko's eyes got as big as moon pies.

Then he said, "That's why I put floor drains in the cracker box so the blood will drain out." Leiko couldn't even speak. Then Alex busted out laughing and said, "I'm just kidding, baby."

His face went sober again and he continued, "No really, if anyone says no, we will ask them to never speak of the community again. Everyone that I'm considering to ask would honor that request. That's just the kind of people they are. I would be proud to call any of them my neighbor and friend."

✳ ✳ ✳

Alex was at the airport to collect his cousin. "Hey, Luis, how ya doing, cuz? How was your flight?" "Oh, you know me. I don't care much for flying." "Yeah, but ya don't mind riding that Harley all summer, do ya? Did ya have any trouble with that e-ticket that I sent you?"

"No, sir, no trouble at all."

Luis was one of Alex's favorite cousins. He was a husky fellow with a full, light brown beard and a great sense of humor. He always reminded Alex of *Grizzly Adams*—one of his favorite TV shows. "Well, let's grab your bags, and we'll head for the house," Alex suggested.

"Alex, How far is it to your house?"

"About a two-hour drive. You'll see some beautiful country on the way," Alex commented as he piloted the big rig down the road.

Luis exclaimed, "Yeah, I always wanted to get out this way and see the sights." "Well, you're going to get the grand tour and more, my friend. You're finally going to get to meet Leiko. I've told her a lot about you, even the, 'Squirrel Killer' story!"

Luis's left eyebrow raised as his lip curled, and he asked, "Really, what did she think of that?"

Alex chuckled. "Well, as much as she loves animals, she thought it was pretty funny. I told her I remembered that day I was behind you. I almost fell off of my bike I was laughing so hard!" Luis mumbled, "Yeah, all the guys busted a gut on that one that day."

***

After meeting Leiko and having a fine dinner, it was time for the pitch. Alex said, "Hey, Luis, let's step outside and check out my new bike trailer."

"Okay, I haven't seen your Screamin' Eagle in a while anyway."

Alex replied, "I keep it in fine condition as usual."

Once all three of them stepped in the side door of the bike trailer, Alex closed it behind them and locked it. Then he turned the lights on, and they heard Luis blurt out, "What the hell is this?"

Alex said, "Its one sweet custom ride, man." This was the part where people always freaked out.

Alex held his index finger up to his lips, gesturing Luis to keep quiet as Alex turned the stereo on. Then Alex retrieved a single sheet of paper from a concealed location and placed it on a small table about the height of a workbench. Then he placed a box over the paper with a two-inch hole through the top center.

The box had battery-operated LED (Light Emitting Diode) lights mounted on the underside of the top. They provided the required light to read a document within a dark plywood box. Alex pointed to the hole and gestured for Luis to put his eye to the hole and silently read the document. The detailed instructions read as follows:

- Please DO NOT SPEAK and follow all of these instructions to the letter!

- We are about to go into a soundproof conference room where there are NO ELETRONIC DEVICES whatsoever.

- Once we're in the conference room, there will be no chance of being eavesdropped in on either physically or electronically.

- Therefore, I need you to perform a couple of simple task to ensure our complete security.

- Please step into this changing room and take off all of your clothes. Everything. You should be buck-ass naked when you're finished. Not even any watches or jewelry of any kind!

- Then get into the flight suit and slip-on shoes provided for you.

- Leave all of your belongings in the booth and then lock the padlock on the door. You may keep the key around your neck.

- Then you will be ready to step through the metal detector door-way into the secure conference room.

- Once inside, sit down and say nothing until I secure the door and tell you we can speak freely.

- I/we, will also complete the very same security steps that you do.

- This way, we will all be sterile in the secure conference room.

- I will explain everything once we're safely inside. All of your questions will be answered in a few moments.

- Thank you very much for your assistance and cooperation!

They were just as protected as the professionals. Alex not only had the built-in generator running for power, but it also vibrated the entire trailer and gave great external cover noise. Once secured inside the conference room, Alex opened a safe, removed a radio, and cranked some Guns and Roses tunes, more cover noise.

When Alex gave Luis the okay signal to speak, he said, "What the hell was that? Am I being recruited by the CIA? You might want to put some crap paper in here as well!"

Leiko and Alex started laughing their heads off. Alex said, "No, man, that was just to make sure that you don't have any cuddies on ya." Luis started chuckling.

Then Alex's demeanor changed to a serious one as he instructed Luis. "Before we get into our conversation, Luis, I would like you to promise us that you will never discuss this conversation with anyone else, ever!"

Luis said, "I can do that."

Alex continued, "Okay the reason for the entire cloak-and-dagger routine is that we've got some very important, classified subjects to speak to you about."

Luis's face instantly went sober as he blurted out, "I always knew you were into some of that secret spy stuff. That's why you were always working all over the world for the government!"

Alex informed Luis, "Well, you're partially correct my friend, however, this business is not for the government. It's for a bunch of God-fearing American people whom just want to be left alone and be permitted to live out their lives the way God and our founding forefathers meant for them to."

"Luis, the first thing is to inform you of our status."

"Alex, wait a minute. First there's something I've got to ask ya."

Alex consented, "Okay, Luis, what is it?"

"Why did I have to read those instructions through the hole in a box?"

As Alex chuckled, he said, "Well, with no speech and radio music background noise, it prevented any verbal recordings. The only way that I could counter against a miniature camera, that you might unwittingly have on you, was to keep the instructions where it couldn't see it; provided there was one."

"Oh, okay, that makes sense."

"All right then, let's get started," Alex said as he slid a news paper in front of Luis with Powerball headlines plastered all over the front page. "Remember some time back when a guy won the biggest Powerball Jackpot ever? That was 382.7 Million bucks. Well, my friend, that was us, Leiko and I. Presently, no one except our attorney knows that fact. Now that would also be except you! Can you keep your pie hole shut?"

Luis's eyes were as big as buttons. He started laughing and said, "Well, hell yes. what-da-ya think I am, a bucket mouth?"

Alex said, "No, sir, I don't."

"Anyway, that's how we're going to finance the little operation that I'm fix'in to tell ya about."

They proceeded to give Luis the entire recruitment pitch. It took about thirty minutes. He was quite intrigued with their proposition and the entire plan. Alex told him that they could give him the remainder of the weekend to think it over. However, they would need his response one way or the other by then.

Luis stopped Alex right then and told them that he didn't need any longer to think about it. He was in to the end. Alex and Leiko both shook his hand and said they were thrilled that he was the first member of their community. Luis said, "Damn, now I can understand why ya went through the whole stripper routine."

Alex related, "Yeah, tomorrow Leiko and I have to repeat it all over again to a buddy of mine coming in. If he says yes, I'll introduce the two of you later tomorrow. I'll loan you my bike tomorrow so you won't be around until after our meeting." By the way Luis, the name of our ranch is Shadow Wolf Ranch (SWR)."

Luis said, "Cool beans, man. I've always liked wolves." After repeating the stripper routine, Alex re-secured the bike trailer, and they all went back into the house to watch the movie *Red Dawn*. Wolverinesssssssss! That movie really made ya think."

Later the next morning, Alex collected Gerard at the airport and had him to the house by lunch time. Once again, Leiko prepared a tasty meal. She told Alex, in passing in the hall, that she liked Gerard so far. She said, "He's got that old man thing going on."

Alex said, "Yeah, he's a good old boy." Then he proceeded to expound on Gerard's past. "After lunch we'll head to the cracker box. This stuff won't be as much of a shock for him as it was with Luis. Gerard's been around this stuff all of his adult life. He's already lived a full life, kids, exes, and all. I'll bet he's ready to give up that rat race and have a community that he can count on."

The meeting took an hour and a half with Gerard. He voiced his opinion and a lot of concerns plus the fact that he didn't shed clothes as fast as a stripper. Alex said to Leiko, "Maybe we should give classes on that before we put anyone else in the cracker box. Anyway, he's in, and now we're up to two members in our community."

The good news was that they were both able to start work on Monday. Once Luis returned home on Alex's scooter, Alex introduced the two of them, and they hit it off right away. Alex told Leiko, " We'll put these two bachelors up in the two spare bedrooms in our house temporally. Meanwhile, those other two, three-bedroom modular homes will be finished in a day or two for the guys to move into."

The last task at hand before Leiko and Alex could head for the east coast was to recruit two more guys to begin work ASAP. They were Dutch Banner and Ethan Prowler, both former SF brothers. Alex gave Leiko a bit of history on those two.

"Dutch is a retired SF guy that I worked a year contract with in Kenya as I did Gerard. Dutch will be my XO (executive officer or second in charge) and operations chief. There is no one else on earth that I'd trust more with the community than Dutch Banner! I'll also task him with being the special purchasing agent. He'll like that; covert buying trips overseas.

"Ethan Prowler was one of my junior weapons sergeants that really knew his stuff and took pride in being the best in his field. That boy could find or fix any weapons system out there, a damn good skill to have in a pinch when resources are low and bad intentions are high.

"The fact that he was an aircraft weapons munitions specialist before he went into SF didn't hurt matters either. Ethan didn't retire from the military. He just ETSed (Estimated Time of Separation, meaning he got out of the military). He became tired of the fact that SF started becoming more conventionalized than he liked. He should be ready for a UW (Unconventional Warfare) mission by now. I'm betting on it."

✳ ✳ ✳

After Alex confirmed all of the details, he shared them with Leiko. "Hey, Leiko, Dutch and Ethan will both be coming in this coming Saturday. Dutch is driving in from Leadville, Colorado, and will be here in late afternoon. Ethan is flying in from the Bronx, and he'll be here in the morning. I just e-mailed him his ticket.

"I'll have to pick him up at the airport. We'll be back here before Dutch gets in. We'll feed him and give him the pitch. Then once Dutch gets here, we'll do the same. This time, I'll have you wait in the house just incase Dutch arrives early. You can entertain him until we exit the cracker box. I hope we have as good of luck with them as we did Luis and Gerard."

* * *

Ethan was a breeze. He was chomping at the bit to get started. He was the third new member to join the community. "Leiko, has Dutch shown up yet?" "No sign of him yet." "Okay, I'm going to take Ethan to his house and get him settled in. Please, give me a call when Dutch shows up."

In her usual chipper voice Leiko said, "Okay, honey, you got it."

As Alex opened the front door, he told Ethan, "Well, here it is, brother, house number two, your three-bedroom house, and three-car garage. A heck of a lot better that those team houses that we used to have to jam into, huh?"

"You've got that right, man. You're running a first-class operation here, Alex. I'm really going to enjoy working with you again."

Alex replied, "Cool, I think you're also going to enjoy working with the other guys that I'm going to try to bring in." As Alex used his index finger to point, he said, "That phone there is a direct line to all of the other houses. Just use the directory on the map. Give us a call if you need anything."

"Okay, thanks, brother," Ethan replied.

As he closed the front door behind him, Alex said, "I'll return later this evening. I'll have some other community members for you to meet."

* * *

"Okay, Leiko," Alex said, "Ethan is getting settled in. I'd like you to stay in the house while Dutch and I are in the cracker box. That way, if any of the other guys call, you can answer their questions."

"Yes, sir," she said as she snapped him a quick salute.

Alex said, "Thanks, baby. Tomorrow, let's plan on a meeting with all four guys and give them enough details to get them all started in their perspective directions."

Leiko said, "Sounds like a plan. Do you think we need Clint there as well?"

"No ma'am, we have all of the details of the companies for any purchases that they'll be conducting."

Twenty minutes later, Alex said, "Hey, girl, Dutch just pulled in. Crank up the stove." Alex walked out to meet him and said, "Hey, buddy, come on in and let's get you fed."

Dutch saw Leiko standing in the doorway and asked, "Hey, Leiko, how are you? Is this bum treating you okay?"

"Always," she said without hesitation.

At the conclusion of the pitch, Alex said, "Great, Dutch. I'm so glad that you're on board! This is going to be the best thing that we can do for a small group of Americans, our family, and friends. When you and your family move in here, are you still going to live part time in your cabin in Alaska?"

"I don't know right now," Dutch said. "It's still a great hide-a-hole if things really go to hell."

Alex commented, "Let's hope it doesn't come to that. All right, lets stop at the house and get Leiko and a couple of buddies and walk over to house number two."

✳ ✳ ✳

Alex stuck his head into house number two and yelled, "Hey Ethan, ya in here buddy?"

Ethan sounded off, "I'm upstairs. I'm coming right down."

Once Ethan was present, Alex gestured with open hands and started the introductions. "Okay, gents, this is Luis Kingston, my cousin. This is Gerard Willard. This is Ethan Prowler, a former SF teammate. This is Dutch Banner. Gerard, Dutch, and I all worked on a year contract together in Kenya in 2002."

Dutch walked over to Gerard, shook his hand, and said, "How's it going, Pop—long time no see."

"Well, I've been getting along all right. You haven't changed at all I see."

"Oh, I've got a few more aches and pains nowadays."

They both started laughing as Gerard patted Dutch on the back. That seemed to smooth the tension a bit for Luis and Ethan.

Then Alex took the podium again. "Here are the new living arrangements. The three modular homes and three, three-car garages that you see here are the only buildings up right now. Well, except for the one hundred foot by three hundred foot special projects metal building and the concrete batch plant. We're only in these houses temporarily until the secure homes are finished. Later on, I'll assign these houses to our perimeter security guard force. For now though, this is how I would like the housing to go.

"Tomorrow, Luis, Ethan, and Gerard will live in this house—house number two. Gerard, please do me a favor and you move into the downstairs bedroom. Leave the stair climbing to the young studs."

Gerard started laughing and said, "Gladly, I've had my fill of that nonsense."

Then Alex continued, "Dutch's family will be here next week. Therefore, we'll put them into house number three. Leiko and I will continue to keep our two spare bedrooms empty in order to continue to shuffle new community members in and out. Your houses are fully furnished and the kitchens are all fully stocked. Any questions from anyone?"

Luis asked, "Is there a bathroom upstairs? I've got an enlarged prostate, and I piss a lot at night."

As Alex grinned, he answered, "Yes, sir. I made sure that every bedroom has its own attached head. We're all too old to be sharing a bedroom or bathroom with some other dudes." The reason Alex was grinning so hard was because he also had nightly battles with the Piss Monster. On second thought, that was probably also why Gerard was grinning as well.

"Okay then," Alex continued, "There will be a 0800 meeting in the cracker box tomorrow. We'll cover everything that you all need to know to get you rolling. Dress light. All right then, welcome everyone and have a good night. We're really glad to have you all as part of our lives!"

21 FEBRUARY 2010
SHADOW WOLF RANCH

It was 0800 and time for the communities first classified meeting to begin. Alex addressed everyone, "Okay, fellas, you all know the drill for the cracker box. Now let's go. Gerard, there's no stripper pole in there. Keep it moving." Once everyone was seated, Alex began, "First thing at hand, let's cover duty positions."

Alex sat at the head of the four-foot by ten-foot table like the chair of a corporate board meeting, with Leiko at his side, and then began. "I'm the SFCPF Leader. That acronym stands for (Special Forces Citizen Protection Force). I chose that name because as Special Forces warriors, we're responsible for the protection of America's citizens, especially our families and friends.

"I'm responsible for the lives and property of this community in that order. Leiko and I have pledged our entire fortune and our very lives to accomplish this mission. There is no more important task in our lives than the one before us now.

"That mission is to create a safe and secure community that we all may live out our lives as free men and women without the domination of the government or any other group of people, the way that God and our founding forefathers intended for us to live. I mean that as a defensive and offensive mission! We'll do whatever it takes to remain free. And I will say, so help me God!"

Alex stared on in disbelief as everyone at the table gave him a standing ovation including Leiko.

"Well, I guess you all agree and approve."Then Alex continued, "I am the one constant here that links all of you together. All of you already know my skills and qualifications as a Special Forces team sergeant. You don't all know each other yet, but you all know and trust me. Most of you for many years and some of you all your lives. We will all become one body. One for all and all for one."

Then he stated that the following were the formal introductions since they were in the cracker box now, and free from any unwanted eyes or ears.

"Well, you've all met my wonderful wife, Leiko. She's responsible for ensuring that I never forget my compassionate side or sense of humor. She's a RN (Registered Nurse), master of kung fu, and the best cook among us all. She's fluent in Japanese and Korean.

"Luis is my cousin and our architect, civil engineer, and mining expert. He'll be in charge of drawing all classified plans and the construction crew foremen will answer to him. He's fluent in construction jargon and American redneck. He was never in the military, so be gentle with him, boys.

"Gerard is our security chief, electronic install tech (technician), and former case officer. He'll be in charge of all electronic security equipment and its install and upkeep. He used to do this kind of work for the agency, so you can bet he knows his stuff. He's fluent in German, Russian, and Chinese.

"Ethan is our weapons chief, armor, and former 18B (Special Forces Weapons Sergeant (E-6/E-7; trained in small arms, crew serve weapons, heavy weapons, and special tactics). He was also an aircraft weapons munitions specialist before he went into SF. He'll be responsible for all aircraft weaponry and all other weapons. He's fluent in French.

"Dutch is our XO, operations chief, and former 18Z (Special Forces Operations Sergeant E-8; operations sergeant; NCO incharge of a twelve-man army special forces (A) team). He's a retired SF master sergeant. His talents are too vast to list; however, he is also our special purchasing agent. That means, he buys the, hard to get items. He's fluent in German, Spanish, and Russian. Ethan, he'll be assisting you with purchasing some of your weapon systems.

"As you can all see, thus far we have a remarkable group of people assembled here with very specialized sets of work skills. There will be more such people joining us to provide the totality of skills necessary to become a completely self-sufficient community."

Alex challenged them all. "Brothers and sisters, I charge you. Let no one stand between us to prevent us from making a better home for ourselves!"

Now that the formal introductions were complete, Alex continued to brief the group. "In a week or so, Leiko and I are driving back east to begin our major recruitment drive. As additional community members are recruited, they will be integrated here with you, or they will be part of our primary EXFIL (Exfiltration from an area) mission. Okay, let's get down to some specific tasking. By the way, there are some drinks in that ice chest by the door.

"I have a financial attorney in Denver that handled the lotto transaction for us. We've also hired him to be our special financial and legal attorney. I've had him create four companies for me that will enable us to complete our covert and our open business transactions.

"The company in the open is called Lupus Enterprise, Inc. This company has four divisions. A construction company, a class-three weapons (guard force) company, a company that buys everyday wholesale bulk items, and an airborne wilderness touring company.

"Our own construction company will build our community and then continue to make money for the community afterwards. Our own guard force company will protect the outer perimeter and grounds. Remember, we have 4,738 acres to patrol.

"The wholesale bulk company will allow us to stockpile supplies and materials without raising suspicions. Lastly, the airborne wilderness tours company will provide us with reason for flight training and ownership of aircraft. We'll openly register one Huey (UH-1H Iroquois, a single blade, single engine, medium utility or gunship, helicopter with crew of 1 to 4) and one Hughes 500 (A four blade, single engine, light utility or gunship, helicopter with crew of 1 to 2) for this ruse (trick or deception).

"Now for the other three shadow companies, the first is called Bender Inc. This company will be used to purchase our massive amounts of electronic equipment. This is your baby, Gerard."

Gerard gave Alex a nod of conformation as Alex continued, "The second company is called Compton, Inc. This company will be used to purchase aircraft. We will be buying three choppers and possibly, briefly, lease a transcontinental Learjet. This will be you, Dutch." Dutch said, "Copy, got it."

Alex rolled on, "The third company is called Plastic Buttons, Inc. This company will be used to purchase military surplus equipment in bulk. All three of these companies are buried underneath a dozen or so shadow companies that would take anyone years to trace them back to me. I am quite comfortable with this covert conception.

"Now for your particular tasks. Luis, anything underground or unaccountable for will be bought on the sly. We bought our own concrete batch plant so that we don't attract any attention as to the massive amounts of concrete we'll be using on the underground facilities. It's easy. If we don't want to have to answer for an item, buy it through a shadow company."

Luis commented, "I'll have a lot of questions. I haven't done this sneaky stuff before."

Alex assured him, "Well, between Dutch, Gerard, and me, we'll have all of the answers for ya." Alex got back on track with the remainder of his instructions, "Gerard and Dutch, I'll get with you later on the overall prints. Gerard, I want our facility to be as tight as the agency's structures. I'll get with you one on one about some things I'd like here. I also want you to get two dozen encrypted cell phones ASAP. I'll need commo with you guys from the east coast, and I'll need to issue them out to our new community members. Also, we need another cracker box. Would you please build one in the steel building, and teach Luis how to build one."

Gerard assured Alex, "Yes sir, we'll get crankin' on that tomorrow and I'll have those phones loaded and ready for you before you and Leiko depart."

Then Alex addressed Ethan, "I want all basic weapon systems for the guard company bought in the open. All other weapons and aircraft systems, on the sly. I'll give you a list of what I want to start with." Alex saved the hardest task for last. "Dutch, we need two Hueys and a Chinook (CH-47 Chinook, a twin-engine, tandem rotor, heavy-lift helicopter with crew of 2 to 5). We need one Huey ASAP. Make sure you take it for a spin and put it through the paces. The US Army is getting so hard up for funds that they're selling surplus choppers, without the weaponry.

"Once you get it, fly it to within three hundred miles of the ranch and then truck it in covertly and store it in the steel building. Get the pilot a plane ticket back to where he needs to go. After you get the first Huey, start tracking on getting our weapons and ammo.

"Dutch and Ethan, we require ten 7.62 mini guns (rapid fire automatic electric Gatling gun, with 6 ea. barrels that fires three thousand rounds per minute) with about five million rounds, eight 2.75 inch rocket launchers (Mighty Mouse; [FFAR] Forward Firing Aircraft Rockets, 70mm, air-to-ground, speed: 1,500 fps, range: 3,400 meters) with a long term supply of rockets, and eight, 50 cals. (Browning fifty caliber heavy automatic machine gun, belt fed) with a million rounds. I expect that may involve a trip to Nicaragua for you and Ethan. However, we need two mini guns and one 50 cal. ASAP."

Then Alex addressed everyone with guidance concerning security. "That should do it for now to get everyone rolling. Remember your OP/SEC everyone. For you, Luis, that means watch what you say, to whom you speak, and think about everything you do before you do it. When in doubt, ask Dutch or Gerard. Just think of it like James Bond is watching your every move.

Luis responded, "Hey, just 'cause I don't know all yer sneaky ways don't mean I'm a bucket mouth!"

Alex assured him, "I know, Luis, but don't you fret none. When we're finished with you, you'll be so crafty you could steal Osama's job, kinda like he stole it from America."

THE RECRUITMENT AND ARMS DEAL

Now that everyone was tracking on their specific task and Alex had Luis to watch over the construction and Dutch to watch over everything else, Alex and Leiko were ready for their mission back east.

15 MARCH 2010
NEWPORT, VERMONT

After a week on the road with the RV and cracker box in tow, Alex and Leiko arrived in Newport, Vermont, at Leiko's sister's house. Her sister Raku and her husband, Kenley, were blown away to see them. They didn't inform them that they were coming. Kenley said, "We're going to have to rent the state park just so you can park that rig."

It was late in the evening so Alex and Leiko figured they'd give them the pitch tomorrow. They were off on Saturday anyway. They figured they'd spend about a week with them before heading south on their mission.

Their house was right on Lake Memphremagog about forty miles south of the Canadian border and twenty miles west of US Highway 91. Beautiful country! This terrain was as rugged as the wilderness Alex grew up with in the mountains of West Virginia.

Later the next day after lunch, they invited them to see a scooter in the cracker box. After answering many questions about everything, they had one stipulation. Raku and Kenley agreed to come, when the time was right, only if they could bring their daughter and her family as well. Alex and Leiko agreed. It would be great to have children in the community as well. Raku's daughter had too small boys.

The next day, the four of them conducted a map recon in the cracker box and then went on a vehicular recon for suitable PZs (pick-up zone). They needed to be a fair distance away from their home, be open enough for a CH-47 Chinook helicopter to set down, and have two avenues of approach in case one was blocked. They all agreed on too locations that would accommodate all scenarios.

The primary PZ was about ten miles northwest of their house. It was on a secondary road that paralleled the west side of Lake Memphremagog for about eight miles. Then you turned due west and headed about too miles up to the top of a small hill top. There was also another secondary road that lead to North Troy. It was about three miles west of the same hill top. That PZ meet all three of Alex's requirements.

The alternate PZ was about twenty miles southwest of their house. It was on a secondary road that lead to the town of Troy, about too miles south off of the road. There was another secondary road to the southeast that lead to the town of Coventry. That route would be a bit rougher to negotiate than the Troy route. That PZ also meet all of Alex's requirements. It sat in a large open area with prairie grass.

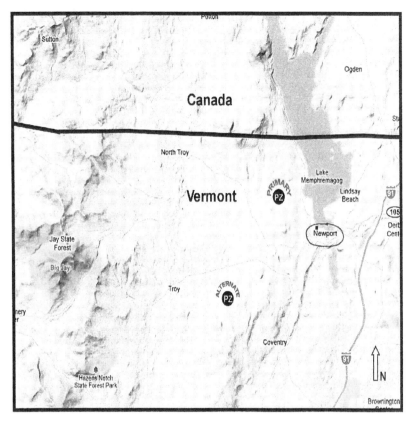

It was some rugged territory and fairly remote country. If any of their birds went down around there, the crew would surely have a harsh E & E (escape and evasion) corridor to run. It's a good thing that they'd have supporting birds for the EXFIL mission. Alex was also glad that all of the SF guys had been through SERE (survival, evasion, resistance, and escape) School. That's one school that no one wants to go to, but you're sure glad to have the training when you find your ass stuck behind enemy lines.

Alex hoped there would be no CSAR (combat search and rescue) mission in their future. They'd prep for the worst and hope for the best. He'd better have Ethan give everyone some survival French lessons anyway. You never know.

Once they all returned to Raku's house, Alex gave Raku and Kenley a class on the specially encrypted cell phone that he was giving them. The most important things were, always keep it charged, turned on and with you, and never use it for any other call than to us for your actual EXFIL.

Their next class was on three different methods to give the chopper a visual conformation from the PZ—IR (inferred) strobe, a unidirectional code letter, or prearranged glint tape. Alex also provided them with a pair of NVG's (night-vision goggles) and all of the necessary equipment for signaling them.

Then he warned them, "You'll hear us, but you won't see us until we're right on top of you. We'll be flying on NVGs and full black-out drive."

Sitting on their front porch, looking northward into Canada, Alex told himself, *This EXFIL could get real hairy real quick.* When you're talking thirty nautical miles from another country's border at night and the aircraft won't respond on the radio, you could be looking at some unwelcome company in the sky. Shoot, for that matter, they won't be responding to US air traffic controllers either. There may be some US aircraft up there as well.

One week was enough with the in-laws. It was time to head their train southward to New Shaefferstown, Pennsylvania, where Alex's mother and sister lived.

Meanwhile, while Leiko and Alex were conducting their recruitment mission in the east, Dutch had just procured their first Huey at Fort Hood, Texas, from a National Guard unit there. He said it went off without a hitch. Tested and true on the test flight, now it's sitting in the steel hangar on the ranch. This is the one they bought in the open. *One down, two to go.*

22 MARCH 2010
THIRTY-THREE THOUSAND FEET
IN THE AIR

Now that Dutch and Ethan were on a plane for Nicaragua, it was time for a clandestine arms deal. Dutch still knew a Sandinistian general down there from where he worked there in the past. General Poncho Sanchez was a greedy man that didn't let his military position get in the way of getting rich; any way he could. Guns, drugs, and corrupt government bribes—it didn't matter.

After stepping out of their motel room in the capital city, Dutch meet a dude in an alley and bought a .32 auto (32 caliber, semi-automatic pistol) from him. Dutch and Ethan were putting in the leg work to set-up their cover story. They were looking for property to purchase.

After three days in Managua and a five-hour jeep ride through the triple canopy jungle that Nicaragua was famous for, Dutch and Ethan arrived at a secret gorilla base camp where they were to meet with General Sanchez. They heard a rough voice from the front seat say in broken English, "Hey, amigos, you take off blindfold. Come this way."

Dutch had worked with General Sanchez when he trained his men on counter-narcotics missions when he was in 7th Special Forces Group in the 80s. That was all part of the heat that Ollie North jumped on the grenade for in the Iran-Contra scandal.

Anyway, the general trusted Dutch and was very pleased to learn that Dutch had a lot of money and wanted to buy some weapons from him. That meant an early Christmas for the general.

The general gave Dutch a big hug and said, "Dutch, how the hell are you my old friend? I see time has treated you very well!"

"Yes, sir, I've been looking forward to seeing you again. I'd like you to meet my weapons sergeant, Tony." No sense in telling him Ethan's real name. After a few shots of tequila and reminiscing some old stories, the general was ready to deal.

"So, Dutch, what is it you need from a poor Nicaraguan soldier that you can't get from your own government?" The general always had a way of indirectly letting you know that he knew what kind of a spot you were in.

Dutch replied, "Well, sir, I'd like to buy some of the armament that we supplied you with for all of the Huey gun ships we gave you."

The general held his open palms upward as he asks, "Why do you need them from me? Your country makes them. Can't you just buy them directly from the factory?"

"Well, let's just say that they need to be unaccountable for," Dutch said with a grin.

General Sanchez leaned in and said, "Before I can sell them to you, I need a guarantee from you that they will never come back to be used against me."

Dutch said, "Yes, sir, I'll bet my life on it."

Then the general asked, "Yes, Dutch, but are you willing to bet your family's lives on it? You know that is what it will come down to if these weapons ever came back here to be used against me!" The good thing about General Poncho Sanchez was you always knew where you stood with him.

The general directed, "Give Captain Ortega here a list of what you need and we will talk about a price and the necessary arrangements."

Dutch suggested, "With a pen and a sheet of paper, Tony will write that out for you."

Five minutes later, Ethan had his list ginned up and said, "Here it is, Captain." As the captain took the list, he immediately began going over it like an accountant at tax time.

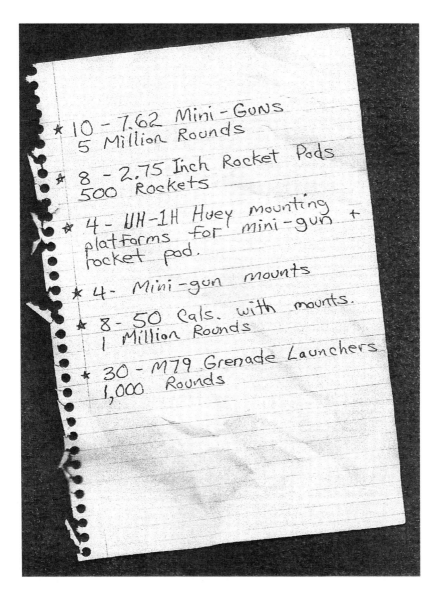

Dutch didn't skip a beat when he said, "General, we're going to require some of your hi-speed transportation assets on this delivery. We can't go by land or air, so we're going to have to go by sea." The general inquired, "Where is it going?"

"We will need it to come ashore at Brownsville, Texas," Dutch replied.

"Yes, I can have my fishing vessel meet your vessel just outside international waters for the transfer," the general assured Dutch.

"Well, sir, I had something a little more hi-speed in mind."

"And what do you have in mind Dutch?"

"I want to use three of your cocaine subs!" Dutch replied. Ethan could tell that Dutch hit a nerve with the general.

The general cocked his head and raised his eyebrow. "What are you talking about? I don't have any subs! I use planes to deliver my coke. You know that from the old days."

Then Dutch called him on it, "General, I also know that you've gotten a whole lot richer and more suffocated in the age of technology. Besides, they were busted out in *Popular Mechanics* magazine last year. The story about the Colombian Cartel and their use of cocaine subs. We both know that you're smarter and better than the Colombians."

The general mean-mugged Dutch for about fifteen seconds and then busted out laughing. "Hahahahaha. You always did know how to save your ass with words, Dutch. It's really going to cost you. Those subs are meant for my dope. We'll do the numbers tonight and talk in the morning. Tonight you have a good time on me!"

The general raised his hand to one of his aids and the man went scurrying off like a chef to prepare a king's meal or fetch his robe. The aid returned with four of the most beautiful Latino women that Dutch or Ethan had ever seen. General Sanchez said, "To keep the snakes away from you tonight. Farewell, amigos, I'll see you in the morning."

Dutch knew the deal. Wild women and plenty of booze all night long would put their heads in the favor of the general for figuring numbers the next morning.

The four *caliente muchachas* led them to jungle bungalows next to each other. When they arrived at their doors Dutch asked Ethan if he thought he was man enough to handle all four. Of course Ethan assured him he was more than UP to the challenge. Dutch said, "Here then, take mine also." That Dutch, he always knew what buttons to push. Besides, he had a lovely wife and baby at home that he loved very much. He wasn't the cheating sort. He knew a single man could appreciate four hammers to hit it on the head.

At 0600, Dutch was beating on Ethan's door to get him up and moving. He knew that the general's strategy would be to get dealing early, the earlier the better for the general. After working in that neck of the woods for ten years, Dutch knew the protocol of a business deal. He was right, General Sanchez sent for them at 0630. Dutch was as sharp and ready for battle as ever. Ethan however, well he was present anyway.

As the two walked up to the general's table, Sanchez rose to bow and extend a sweeping hand of welcomeness. "Welcome, gentlemen, I trust you had a pleasant evening?"

Dutch looked at Ethan and said with a grin, "Very much so, thank you!"

"Very well then, let us get to business" commanded the general.

Dutch could tell that the general was ecstatic with himself because he knew that this deal was going to be 100 percent profit for him. The US government had given his government all of these weapons to begin with. And he knew that the two gringos were going to pay for his three subs. It was all win, win for him.

The general started off the conversation, "You know, it cost me half a million dollars each for those subs." Dutch knew that this was where the general had to feel like he was coming out ahead. After all, those were his dope subs that he really had plans for. The aircraft weaponry wouldn't have made him any money anyway. Dutch said, "Okay, I'll pay you one million each. That's a 1.5 million dollar profit for you right there."

Like he had to remind the general about the numbers. That was Dutch's way of letting the general know that was the last really big *give* he was willing to make. The general said, "For the guns, I need five million."

Dutch countered, "I'll give you four million because they're really worth three."

"Okay, Dutch, you're a good friend to me. And the ammo, I need five million for that."

Dutch offered, "I can only afford three million."

"Okay, Dutch, special price for you is four million."

Dutch hunkered down with, "Well, sir, I've only got ten million for the whole deal. If you can't sell me the ammo for three million, I'll have to get it elsewhere."

The general's final words were, "Well, only because you fought with me in these jungles, Dutch. You've got a deal, my friend."

Dutch recapped, "Ten million for it all delivered to Brownsville, Texas, four months from now. And, General, you guarantee my cargo up to the Brownsville shore."

The general looked as if he had been insulted and replied, "Dutch, you know I always stand by my word, just as you do. If your cargo were to be apprehended twenty miles from delivery, I will send more until you get it."

The two stood and shook on the deal. Dutch said, "I'll have the funds transferred to your account tomorrow. Do you still have your encrypted e-mail system up?"

"Of course Dutch, how else do I get my mail?"

Dutch informed the general, "I'll send you the GPS (Global Positioning System) grid and bona fides (a set of pre-coordinated phrases to confirm a contacts identity) for our linkup."

"One more thing, General, when they load the threes subs, please split the cargo evenly into three groups—both weapons and ammo. That way, if a sub should sink at sea or something, we've still got a proportional amount to deal with."

"No problem, Dutch. Anything for you, my friend," the general said as he patted Dutch on the back.

Dutch suggested, "Now how about a tour of those subs you're so ingenuously manufacturing?"

The general was most accommodating. "Not a problem. We build them here in our warehouse in the jungle. Then we float them down the river to the ocean. We'll see them this afternoon. I think you will be most impressed, Dutch. Now let's have some breakfast."

The general asked, "By the way, Tony, how did you fare against my four muchachas?" The general didn't miss much either.

After chow Dutch told Ethan to ensure he evaluated the cargo space in the three subs to ensure there was enough room for everything and take all of the subs measurements inside and out. "They could probably tell you, down to the gram, how much coke could fit in these subs, however, bulky weaponry and ammo was another matter."

"Will do, Dutch, I've already done my homework."

Then Dutch complemented Ethan, "I figured you did. Alex wouldn't have you here if you were a slacker. He'll be happy we got the deal done for ten million. We won't tell the good general we were prepared to go to fifteen. Well, look at it this way, Ethan. At least we're keeping what would have been three subs full of dope off of American streets."

"Yeah, Dutch, it's a shame we wasted three million bucks to do it."

"Who said we wasted it?" Dutch asked with a devilish grin.

Ethan turned his head and looked Dutch in the eye and said, "You heard what the general does with the subs when the mission is completed, he scuttles them."

Then Dutch proceeded to educate young Ethan, "That's what he does with them. Those subs are ours now. After we off-load the cargo, I'll give the crew fifty thousand dollars each to go back and say they scuttled the subs. I know these guys. They'll do exactly that. They know a sweet deal when they see one. Besides, they know what I'll do to them if they cross me.

"I trained these dudes in this jungle in the 80s. They know exactly what I'm capable of. I guarantee you, they fear me much more than General Sanchez! These subs can be a huge asset to us as INFIL or EXFIL craft. The sweet part is, no one knows they even exist. Let Uncle Sam try to track them down with his high-tech low-jack."

Near the conclusion of their five-hour jeep ride back out of the jungle, they ran into a slight snag. After the jeep had stopped, the man in the passenger seat instructed Dutch, in Spanish, to remove their hoods. Once Dutch told Ethan to take his hood off, they found themselves staring down the barrel of an AK-47 (7.62 mm, shoulder fired, magazine fed, battle rifle).

Dutch asked the big man what the problem was. He proceeded to explain to them that he was working undercover for the Nicaraguan government and he was going to take the gringos back to his HQ (headquarters) for interrogation. Then he threw two sets of hand cuffs in Dutch's lap and instructed them to put them on.

When they removed their hoods they purposely laid them on their laps to cover their groin and waist area. Dutch knew that he had to stall the big man as he slowly retrieved his pistol from his underwear. Meanwhile, Ethan was removing a steel wire garrote (weapon designed for strangulation, constructed of steel wire, filament cord, or high strength fishing line) that he had concealed in his belt.

Dutch told the dude, "General Sanchez will skin you alive for betraying him and kill your entire family as well!"

The fat man yelled, "Not if my government gets him first!" That was all of the time they needed.

Dutch turned his head to Ethan and said, "Well, I guess we better put these cuffs on—now!" At that very moment they sprang into action with the speed of a mongoose striking at a cobra. As Ethan maneuvered his wire toward the driver in front of him, he swung his right hand wide and redirected the AK upward.

Meanwhile, Dutch jammed the 32 auto into the big man's mouth with such force that he knocked half of his teeth out. As he unloaded into the dude's mouth he noticed how completely the windshield was covered with blood and gore. As Dutch was removing his piece from what was left of the big man's head, he looked over at Ethan's handy work.

That's when he realized that Ethan's goal hadn't been to choke the driver to death but to take his damn head off. Well, he came pretty close anyway. Ethan's wire had cut all the way through the man's throat and stopped only after hitting his spine.

From the word go, the deed was done in about three seconds. The two moved with such coordination and precision that one would have thought that they had rehearsed that very scenario as one would rehearse a basic reaction drill.

After they shoved the two bodies out of the seats they took the five gallon water can, which was on the back bumper, and rinsed the mess off. After sterilizing their weapons they left them with the stiffs. Then they only had about a mile of jungle trail to drive before they were back where their rental car had been cached (To hide something or a hiding place). Since they were both behind their targets' seats, neither of them got messy, luckily for them. They weren't forced to resort to their spare clothes in their trunk.

Once they arrived back in Managua at the airport, they were scooped up by six suits driving two black, Chevy suburbans. It's a good thing that Dutch drilled Ethan on their cover story until he was ready to puke. It's also a good thing that they brought along their props, in the trunk of the car.

After a three hour interrogation they walked away smelling like roses, so to speak. Dutch said, "See Ethan, I told you that it would pay off to know your cover story; inside and out."

"Yeah, I guess you were right. I just didn't like the way those agents keep looking at me," Ethan replied.

Dutch smiled and said, "Yeah, I think the little one kinda liked ya!"

Ethan quickly retorted with, "Up yours, man, why did it have to be me anyway? It was your plan."

Dutch replied, "Well, my young apprentice, you're the pretty one." Dutch then commented, "They know something is up, but they can't put their finger on it. They'll settle for our story, for now."

As Dutch and Ethan walked from the building to their car, two of the men in black stood there watching them and talking about the interrogation. The tall one said, "Because I tailed them, I knew they were looking for commercial property to open a business."

Then the little one chimed in, "Yeah, but who would have guessed it was to open a gay club for the young guy!"

The tall agent then came back with, "And what about that pink suitcase full of sex toys in their trunk?"

"Yeah, scary. Let's not talk about it any more!," said the short one as a shiver ran down his spine.

27 MARCH 2010
IN THE AIR: MISSION COMPLETE

Once they were thirty-three thousand feet in the air, Dutch leaned over to Ethan's ear and said, "Always exploit the things that most men don't want to talk about or have anything to do with. Remember, most men won't check your crotch and grab your dick during a search."

Then Dutch said, "I always conceal a knife or small hand gun there when I'm undercover. It's saved my bacon three times now. How do you think I got that piece past the general's, boys?"

Ethan admitted, "Yeah, this time it looks like it saved my bacon as well."

Dutch sighed as he commented, "We got lucky on that one. You pulled your weight as well, brother."

27 MARCH 2010
NEW SHAEFFERSTOWN, PENNSYLVANIA

New Shaefferstown, Pennsylvania was a small all American town where everybody knew everybody. That's where Alex's mother and sister lived now. After his mom and dad split when he was nineteen, his mom remarried and moved there.

After Alex's step-dad Bob died from Agent Orange, his mom never married again. She had a mild stroke while Alex was working in Kenya. She recovered pretty well but still had a slight limp as a reminder. Even though Alex's sister Brooke and James were married, they still lived in his mom's duplex to help her out.

Just as in Vermont, all five of his family folk were up for the relocation. Mom, Brooke, James, and Brook's too kids. They received the same equipment and training that Leiko's kin received. Alex had no problem finding the too required PZ's because he knew the area. The fact that James owned his own farm about ten miles from town also helped. Alex chose one PZ near town and the other near James' farm.

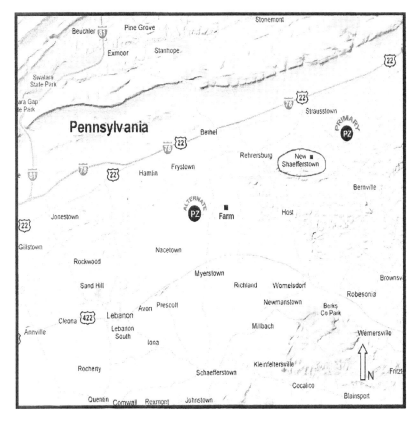

All of their skills would come in most useful on the ranch. Alex's Mom was still one heck of a cook. Brooke accepted that new job as the ranch's CPA and bank president. They figured, why couldn't they start their own private community bank with five million to open it.

James had a green thumb and could grow anything, anywhere, anytime. He could also raise any animal in any region of the country. With nearly five thousand acres, they figured they could have a farm large enough to support the entire community.

And too more kids added to the pot made four. Alex told Leiko, "I think we'll have to build our own school as well. I just happen to know a school teacher whom is on my list to see."

08 APRIL 2010
MORGANTOWN, WEST VIRGINIA

Alex and Leiko were pulling into Morgantown, West Virginia at about 1930. It was a rugged mountain town near his father's cabin where he was born. His father Hunter and his brother Stuart still lived in that same area today. They were just as surprised to see the Colorado couple as everyone else had been.

The recruitment went very well with them. Especially Alex's dad; he stated that he had wanted to get out of that area for years now. He had always wanted to go out west and see how the other Indian tribes had lived, back in the day. He wanted to leave with Alex and Leiko when they left. Alex told him that would be fine. He warned him that he had to travel light with just his RV and his chopper in his enclosed trailer. Hunter was cool with that.

That evening Alex and his Dad sat on the front porch of Hunter's cabin. They were reminiscing about old times there in the mountains. Before Alex knew it, Hunter was telling him how he got his name—the traditional Indian way.

In the still of the night, a child was born in the rugged mountains near Morgantown, West Virginia, former hunting grounds of the Iroquois Indians. He was the son of Hunter and Grace Boulder. Hunter was a full-blooded Iroquois Indian. Therefore, his son was one-half Iroquois Indian, a half-breed to some.

The cold autumn night that he was born in his parent's cabin, his father saw the shadow of a timber wolf being cast on their cabin by the light of the full moon. Right then he knew what his son's middle name was meant to be. He was named, Alex "Shadow Wolf" Boulder. He also knew his son was destined for interesting times.

Hunter said, "I could tell at an early age that you had the spirit of your ancestors in you. By the time you were five, you could identify every kind of animal track and sound found in the woods of these rugged mountains." Then Hunter thought, *It's strange that Alex's elder brother, Stuart, never displayed such a kindred spirit with the land as Alex possessed from near birth.*

Alex said, "Well, Dad, I thank God that I had you to teach me all of that stuff. Most boys aren't so lucky to have a father like you. How did we end up with a last name like Boulder—doesn't sound very Indian to me?"

"Well, son, my father—your grandfather—changed my last name from Running-wolf to Boulder, so that I would fit-in more in the white-man's world. I tell ya son, I'm glad he did, because I saw what he went through, tryin' to fit-in to their society. It was something that no man should have to go through."

Alex replied, "Well, what-da-ya say we turn in now? We've got a busy day ahead of us tomorrow."

They still needed to ID (Identify) the PZs for when they came back for Stuart and his wife Sara. The primary PZ would be very easy since his dad all ready had a helo pad and hangar next to his cabin.

Alex had a pretty good idea for the secondary one as well. It would be on a hill top that he used to hunt bobcat on. It was just southeast of route 19. It was almost at the mouth of his dad's road, Little Indian Creek Rd. That was one of the very few locations suitable for a PZ up there in the mountains.

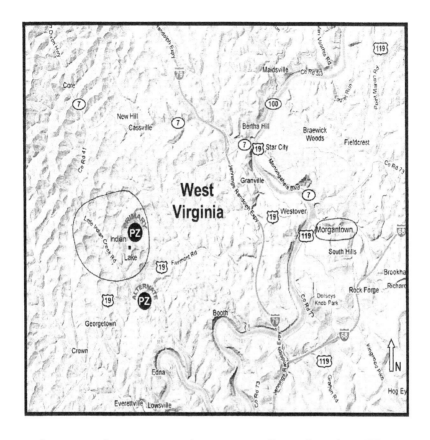

Just to make sure everything was still good with it, Hunter and Alex flew his bird over there to check it out. His dad had a sweet little Hughes 500, like the one on the TV show *Magnum PI*. Only his dad's was better. It was already tactical, for night ops. Just a few mods (modifications) from Ethan and it would make a fine addition to their up-and–coming fleet of birds.

Once the PZ checked out, Alex stayed on the ground and had his dad bring Stuart back to brief and train him up. Forty-five minutes and he was good-to-go. Proper prep always paid off in the long run. Alex learned that lesson early on in SF.

Stuart and Sarah's EXFIL would require a slight modification and extra planning. She was in a wheelchair and, in the middle of the night over rough terrain, might require a special set of wheels. And Alex didn't mean Stuart's sidecar on his Harley.

He was talking about a modified four wheel drive ATV that was especially modified and dedicated for her EXFIL. They'd also have to dedicate a special space on the Chinook for it as well. This way they'd save time by Stuart just driving the ATV right up the ramp and in the bird. Alex had also determined that he had better run the same setup for his mom. The ATV's could double as recon vehicles on the flight back out west.

Alex sited to Leiko some more valuable skills added to the community from their new recruits. "Stuart is one of the best auto mechanics there are. It wouldn't take much training for him to also be able to work on our helos. Sarah is a seasoned computer technician—both software and hardware. Dad brings about as much to the table as Dutch does.

"He's a helo pilot, construction contractor, craftsman, woods-man, gunsmith, and all around Iroquois Indian killing machine when he needs to be. I'm pretty sure that with he and I on each end of a radio speaking our native tongue, not many people can break our code. Kind of like the wind talkers in WWII.

"All right, girl, all of our family members are in, and now it's time for the hard sell. Even though we're talking about eight people, there will still only be one EXFIL at one PZ. That's if everything goes off without a hitch, and it never does. Murphy (Murphy's Law; Anything that can go wrong, will go wrong) always steps in and raises his ugly head. Well, it's off to FayetteNam, North Carolina and Fort Bragg.

"Here's our list of potential recruits, Leiko. This is so you can get familiar with their names and where they live. I've also put their specialties down there as well. All six of these guys are SF."

1. Logan Blayteck, Hope Mills, 18E Como Chief (Special Forces communications sergeant); E-6/E-7—trained in all forms of short and long range communications and Morse code; fabrication technician

2. Dana Blayteck, dentist/oral surgeon

3. Galvin Norstrum, Gray's Creek, 18D (Special Forces medic (E-6/E-7, the most advanced/skilled medics in the US Military with surgical and dental skills) /Combat Helo Crew Chief/EMT (Emergengy Medical Technician)

4. Sue Norstrum, school teacher, grades 1–12

5. John Birch, Rockfish, 18Z/Intel Chief/ASOT (Advanced special operations techniques instructor)

6. Danner Sanderson, Fayetteville, 18C (Special Forces demolitions sergeant/E-6/E-7; trained in explosives and engineering/construction skills) demolitions chief and aircraft mechanic

7. Kendal Howard, Hope Mills, 180A [Special Forces XO (WO-1 and 2; Executive Officer of a 12-man Army Special Forces (A) team)] air traffic controller

8. Tanner Kellerman, Eastover, doctor—General M.D./18D/ Bike Mechanic

Alex went on to explain some of the concerns of the upcoming mission,

> This will be a challenging EXFIL indeed. Our greatest threat will probably be army gunships from Simmons AAF (Army Air field). All they keep there are army helos and their pilots are good; a lot of combat qualified crew from Iraq, and Afghanistan.
>
> Pope Air Force Base no longer keeps fighters there. Just enough transport planes to move the 82nd Airborne and the SF Groups when they need to deploy them. Our greatest asset will be speed and the element of surprise. We'll fly NOE (nap of the earth, flying a very low-level type of flight course used to avoid detection and attack by an enemy when in a high-threat environment—rotary or fixed wing) to avoid their radar. Keeping southeast of I-95 will also help us out. Their military airspace begins just

west of I-95. They won't even send a bird up to challenge an aircraft until it crosses that line.

All of our guys are SF. They know the importance of being on the PZ at the proper time. I'll impress on them the potential problems that will present them selves to us if they're not where they should be, when they should be. This isn't just some training mission. This is the real deal.

By the encrypted call that I received from Dutch this morning, the arms deal with the general was a success. That means we'll at least have the firepower we need if we are fired upon during this mission.

God, I pray that doesn't happen! The last thing I want to do is have to kill my fellow Americans just because Osama is hell bent on tearing our country and its people apart. The Lord has carried us thus far, baby, he's in it with us for the long haul.

13 APRIL 2010
RAVEN ROCK, NORTH CAROLINA

The sun was just setting as Alex, Leiko, and Hunter rolled into Raven Rock state park, in North Carolina. It was near, Sanford, North Carolina, a small town about fifteen miles north of Spring Lake and Fort Bragg. That's where they set up camp. Alex informed Leiko and Hunter how they would operate in and around Bragg.

He said, "I don't want to draw any undue attention with our big RV's and dad's fifty-three-foot enclosed chopper trailer rolling all over the place. We'll take the truck and cracker box and slip in and out of the AO (Area of operation) each day and return to our mobile base camp in the park at night."

✳✳✳

Once they were alone, Alex said, "Leiko, I'm sure that Dad won't mind exploring the state park while we're gone. There probably was an Indian tribe that lived in this area at one time."

Alex figured they would save the good doctor for last. He would probably be the hardest sell and Alex thought that he might need the recruitment of the others to convince him to move out to the country to set up shop. Most doctors worshiped the dollar; however, Dr. Tanner Kellerman wasn't one of them.

He became a doctor because, in his mind, he couldn't do enough for people as a SF 18D, even though he was one of the best. He was one of the kinds of guys that was happy just to be working on or riding one of his seven motorcycles. Yeah, he liked bikes. He had them all before he ever became a doc. His favorite was the BMW with the sidecar on it.

Alex informed Leiko, "In the morning, we'll start calling everyone to check their status and see when we can start linking-up with them. Someone might be on vacation or deployed somewhere. You never know about the nomadic sort that we SF guys are."

By 0800, Alex was making calls. After he got off the phone, he gave Leiko a status report.

"Here's the deal, Leiko. I was able to track everyone down. They're all in town accept for John Birch. He's out in the field instructing an ASOT (Advanced special operations techniques) class. He won't be back in town until Friday. That's okay though, we have plenty to keep us busy until then. The first thing we need to do is ID the three PZs that we need. After people agree to our offer, we'll need to be able to show them the PZs on the map while we're still in the cracker box. We'll take the scooter on those recons."

Leiko's eyes lit up when she heard the word *scooter*. She loved to ride. Then Alex's cell phone rang. "Well, Leiko, here's the update I just received from Luis."

"He says the chain-link fence is up around the entire perimeter of the ranch— north and south. The ACFs are finished and they have hired forty of the sixty local guards, and all of the guard's weapons that Ethan ordered came in yesterday."

She said, "Cool, man, that Luis is a worker."

Then Alex continued, "Now that Ethan and Dutch are back, they're training the guard force up as we speak. Gerard has the first initial security systems in place. The construction crew is working on the five-foot concrete wall around the Colorado side. The blacktop company just finished all of the roads and driveways on the Colorado side as well. And Luis just finished all of the classified plans for all under ground facilities. They've been some busy beavers."

As Alex and Leiko sat on the Harley overlooking an open field, Alex recapped, "All right, baby, that's the last PZ. I think they'll handle just about any contingency that can be thrust at them. I used to live in Rockfish, so I know that the emergency PZ near my old property is solid. With the alternate PZ near the doc's office we've got that end covered. And the primary PZ is centered on the whole AO so that everyone should be able to make it to that one all right."

Just then Leiko kissed the back of Alex's neck, gave him a strong bear hug, and said, "Shut-up and kiss me." What could he do? He dove off the bike—carrying her with him—and then they proceeded to wrestle in the grass. Then he kissed her and said, "I love you, Leiko—don't ever change." Then he told her, "I'll tell ya what, Shorty, by the time our final mission is finished, you'll be qualified to be SF. Of course you'd be the sexiest little green beanie ever!"

She took her right index and middle fingers and gestured as she pointed at her eyes and then pointed them at Alex and said, "Yeah, I got your back, boy."

Then Alex thought to himself, *She's just the one I want covering my back anytime!*

That night, Alex gave his dad the latest update, "After a week, we've recruited the Blaytecks, the Norstrums, and Danner Sanderson. Both couples have two kids each. That brings our total up to eight yard apes now. The good thing is we've got our school teacher onboard. That's another project for Lewis to get started on. At least the driveway is already finished up to it."

Hunter said, "I love it when a plan comes together."

Alex told Hunter, there's more. "Kendal Howard turned us down on our offer. That really blew me away. He was the last guy I expected to say no."

Hunter asked, "What's his problem?"

Alex broke it down for him, "He says he doesn't believe that there will be a civil war in this country. He even said he doesn't think that Osama is doing that bad of a job running this country. Man, that just goes to show you that people can really change, sometimes for the worst. Anyway, he swore that he would never mention the conversation to anyone.

"Just the same, Dad, I want to get finished and headed back west ASAP. If he has a mindset like that now, I don't know if he can be trusted anymore. Once again, that's why we always give a recruitment pitch to people one-on-one. I was just glad that his wife wasn't there with him. That would have been a disaster! That's exactly why I don't take you to these meetings. The less people he knows about, the better.

"For the trip back to Colorado, let's make sure your bird is all prepped for flight and bring a couple hundred extra gallons of fuel. You never know when and where we might just need it.

"Today we're meeting with John Birch. He's back from the field and going to have lunch with us at Cracker Barrel. Then it's off to the cracker box. Tomorrow we're meeting with the doc. After that it's time to take the guys out to see the PZs.

"Dad, I'll need you to come along so you can see them as well. After all, you're going to be flying the Chinook on the mission. I'll be flying cover for you in one of the Hueys. I want Dutch in the other Huey."

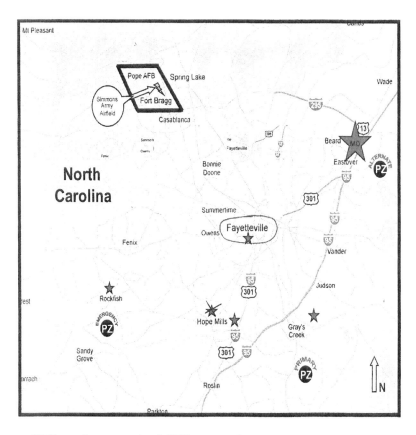

"What about my bird?" Hunter asks.

Alex then explained, "We'll see. We're going to have to crunch some numbers on the fuel consumption for the different types of birds. I'm already considering flying with external fuel cells for the flight here. By only flying and refueling at night, we'd just make it coming. For the return flight, we're going to have to cache our fuel before the mission. Did you find any info on the local Indian tribes around here?"

Hunter replied, "Why yes, I did Shadow Wolf. The Ttuscarora and the Iroquois nations, our own people, were the dominate tribes here. Off to the west was the eastern tribe of Cherokee. You should get into your heritage more often."

Alex took a deep breath before he replied, "I'd love to, Dad, but right now, I'm trying to preserve an existing endangered tribe—the American nation!"

***

The next evening, Alex stated to Leiko and Hunter, "Finally, I'm glad to be finished with the recruitment phase, well, for the most part. I was right, Doc was the hardest sell. It surprised me when he said that it was no surprise to him that Kendal Howard turned us down. That just goes to show ya that he's more in tune with the old teammates than I thought. Anyway, all we have to do here now is to issue the guys their equipment for the EXFIL, give them some refresher training, and physically show them the PZs."

21 APRIL 2010
ON THE ROAD HEADIN' WEST

Alex said to his dad and Leiko, "That all went very well. Thank you both for all of your assistance. What do you guys say about getting this wagon train moving out and heading west?"

Hunter said, "I've been ready for years now."

Leiko jumped up into Alex's arms while she wrapped those sexy little walkin' sticks around him and squealed, "Let's go, big daddy!" He had to give her a big kiss after that. What else could he do?

Alex said, "All right then, let's top off every machine that we've got and hit the road." Then he issued out some instructions for Hunter, "Dad, we'll lead since we know the route. It will take us about a week to get back. We're going to take our time and enjoy the scenery. Remember your Op/Sec, Dad. If you need to, use your encrypted phone."

Hunter shrugged as he said, looking at the phone, "Yeah, okay, I think I've got this thing figured out,"

Now so far, Hunter was the only one in the community to have had any formal training in helos. Once they got back to the ranch and addressed a few issues and put out a few fires, Alex, Dutch, and Hunter were heading to Sanford, Florida for rotary wing flight school. Dutch and Alex would be learning the basics and getting rated up to a Huey. Hunter would be getting additional training and rated up to a Chinook.

Now that money was no longer an issue, they'd be training and flying ten hours a day. They'd be able to be finished in three weeks. Once they were all certified, they'd go back to the ranch and run a train-the-trainer program. Something that SF was famous for. That's mostly what they did in Vietnam.

One of their primary missions was to be a force multiplier. First, Hunter would get Dutch and Alex up to speed on the Chinook and then all three of them would start training the other guys and Leiko. Alex told himself that he couldn't have the disillusion that Leiko would let a homegrown flight school be conducted without her getting in on it. She was a real go-getter for sure.

Alex and Hunter pulled their caravan into a state park near Fort Smith, Arkansas, about halfway to Colorado. As the three of them enjoyed yet another fine meal by Leiko, Hunter and Alex were talking about flying. Hunter said, "There really isn't that much too flying a chopper."

Alex replied, "I think I could just about fly one now with the vast amount of time that I've had in choppers."

"Well, let's test that theory," Hunter said, pointing at his chopper trailer. Then he continued, "It's deserted around here, and I saw a huge, deep, abandoned rock quarry on the way in. Tomorrow, we could slip down there in the bird and be able to hover about fifty feet off the ground without even breaking the plane of the earth. What do ya say, young man?"

Alex got that elfish grin on his face and said, "You're on."

Leiko jumped up and yelled, "Where's the camcorder? I've got to get this on film. Hey ya'all, watch this!"

Alex looked at her and said, "Come on, baby, it's not going to be that bad."

"Oh yeah, I can win ten thousand dollars on stupidest home videos," she assured him.

"You're already a multi-millionaire, how much more do ya want?" Alex questions her.

At 0800, Hunter said, "Well, Alex, you've had the stick for thirty minutes now."

Alex replied, "Yeah, Leiko will be bummed that she can't win her cash."

"That's okay, son. I'd rather have my bird in one piece. You're actually doing pretty well. All except for the part where you almost flew into the side of that cliff."

Alex said, "I wasn't sweating it, Dad, that's what you've got air brakes for."

Hunter countered with, "No, that's what I've got a parachute for. I would have bailed on you boy."

Alex asked, "Oh yeah, how many jumps do you have anyway?"

Hunter said, "Counting this one, one."

"Well, I've got news for ya, Pop, at fifty feet, that chute would have worked about as good as your air brakes." They both started cracking up. Leiko must have thought they were nuts. She could see them up close through her telephoto lens.

Alex was glad he had his dad put that extra two hundred gallons of chopper fuel in his trailer. After topping the bird off, they packed up for the road again. Three more days, and they arrived back at the ranch. Leiko and Alex hardly recognized it.

* * *

What a difference some fencing, roads, and a few buildings can make to a place. Not to mention a butt-load of activity. It was good to be home again with that secure sense that only your own home and friends can bring.

As Alex walked up to his dad still sitting in his RV he said, "Welcome to Shadow Wolf Ranch, Dad, your new home. Why don't you park your whole rig in that huge metal building over there. The access code to the big door is (316-556-762/ God&Guns). Use the letters and numbers. Leave enough room to get your bird out. We'll get Ethan crackin' on it as soon as he gets a chance. When you're finished, come on up to the house, and we'll get ya settled in. You can stay with us until your house is ready. It's good to have you here, Dad."

QUALITY CONTROL

05 MAY 2010
SHADOW WOLF RANCH

Alex greeted Luis, "Good morning, Luis."

"Hey, Alex, how ya doing cuz? It's good to have ya back. They've been running me raged around here since you left."

"Yeah, well, we've got a long way to go and a short time to get there. Get used to it Luis. What do ya say we go look at my scooter?"

"Where is it?" Luis asked. "In your trailer or in the metal building?" Alex looked at Luis and said, "Well, well, I do believe you're picking this stuff up, my friend."

Luis replied with, "Yeah, I've been hanging around Dutch and Gerard for a while now. Those are a couple of smart dudes, man."

"Yes, sir," Alex explained, "That's why they're here. A good leader will always surround him self with good people. That greatly increases his chances of success, and it makes his life a lot easier."

Alex asked Luis, "Do you remember the first time you went through this process?"

He said, "Man, do I ever, and you still don't have any butt wipe in here, do ya?" Alex replied, "Hey, you guys built this one; didn't you put any in here?" Luis said, "I forgot," as he hung his head. As Luis spread his blueprints on the table Alex said, "Anyways, let's see what your prints look like."

"I want to see the main bunker and living quarters first." As Alex examined the prints he said, "Oh yeah, this looks pretty good Luis. How far underground is it?" Luis said, "There will be 100 feet of earth on top of the reinforced ceiling."

Alex replied, "Great, that's plenty for a nuclear blast or a 500 pound bomb. It would even give us plenty of time if some one was just trying to dig down to us to set charges on the structure."

Luis said, "Yeah, that's what I figured to. Dutch kinda helped me out with that one too."

As Alex put on his reading specs, he said, "Let's see what you've put where."

"Okay, Alex, the tour begins now," Luis announced.

- Section 1: On the north end there are fifty sets of sleeping quarters with four bunks each. Enough for the entire community and the local guard force as well.

- Section 2: On the south end are the ACF, DFAC (dining facility), gym, hygiene facilities, and the primary supply storage warehouse, and spring water wells.

- Section 3: On the east side are the tactical briefing room, firing ranges, armory, commo room, and the command and control center.

- Section 4: On the west side is the helo hangar, fuel depot, and the generator rooms.

"This is all on the Wyoming side away from the housing area on the Colorado side. Accept for the twin helo hangars. One will also be on the Colorado side. All of the secure houses will have secure tunnels that lead to the underground ACF for a controlled entry into the facility. I also put these self-sealing blast doors every one hundred horizontal feet, just like you said.

"The X pattern of the facility provides the maximum amount of compartmental security according to Dutch and Gerard. Each of the two hangars can park a Chinook, Huey, and a Hughes 500. You told me we'd always keep one Huey in the metal building on the Colorado side."

Alex nodded his head north to south as he said, "Well, Luis, you have outdone yourself, my friend. Did Gerard say that he can support this plan with all of his electronic installs?"

"Yes, sir, he's already ordered all of his materials."

Then Alex instructed Luis, "Great, tell him that he'll use only our help. No sub-contractors or outside help."

He continued, "Remember Luis, anytime we're building anything underground, I want overhead cover in place first. The ground will also be completely landscaped before removing the overhead. All we need is for some Intel analyst to see this on satellite imagery, and all of our work is for naught."

Alex asked, "How far away is it from the ACF facility on the Colorado side?"

"About five miles."

"Wow," Alex said, "for something that far away, we need to ensure that a pickup truck can fit through the tunnels. That's a long way to hump supplies and materials."

"Tell me, Luis, have you done the math on this entire construction project yet to include the houses?"

"Yes, sir, I have. You're not going to like it. It's pricy. It might put you back in the poor house."

Alex said, "I've got news for you. I've been a working man all of my life, and I'll be that way until the day I die, money or no money."

Then Luis said, "Just remember, Alex, with our own batch plant and own construction company doing all of the work, we're already saving millions. You can even cut my pay if you need to. I can even operate a track-hoe too ya know."

"Lewis, get to the numbers! Are you afraid to tell me?" Alex demanded as he raised his voice.

"Whip it on me, brother, I can take it," Alex reassured him.

Luis said, "About eighty-nine million underground and six million for the twenty homes give or take a million."

"Whooooooooooo, man!," Alex howled.

The room got quiet for about thirty seconds. Then Alex said, "See, that wasn't so bad, was it, Luis?"

Luis said, "Not for me, but I'm not the one that's got to go tell Leiko now."

Alex agreed, "Yeah, that's going to be the dangerous part." Then Alex said, "I think I'll put my body armor on for that meeting."

Luis asked, "Do ya think I need to have Ethan covering your back with his sniper system? Man, I'd tell her from thirty thousand feet. Her on the ground and you in the air."

Alex replied, "Yeah, Luis, but ya gotta come down some time. It's like my ma always used to say. You gotta come home some time, boy."

Alex recalled, "Like the time I streaked at the vo-tech senior graduation, and the school superintendent discovered it was me. She was sitting on the front porch waiting for me."

Luis said, "Yeah, but that was probably the only time in your life you'll ever get a standing ovation from two thousand people while you're buck-ass naked."

Then Alex protested in his defense, "Come on now, I wasn't buck naked. I had a ski mask and a red Dracula cape on. In fact, that cape later became my diaper while I ran through the woods all day, trying to make my link-up (coordinated meeting) point. That actually turned out to be my first tactical operation. I'm glad that none of my military missions ever went that sour. If I'd been SF back then, I could have pulled it off without a hitch. What do they say, live and learn?"

Luis said, "Yeah, or don't and die."

"All right, Luis, let's get back on track," Alex said. "Tell me about the Helo pads."

Then Luis began his brief, "Well, first of all, their both exactly alike. That way we can park the birds in which ever location we need to. We could even use both locations at once.

"They will be like the lifts on aircraft carriers. Kept down at bunker level when not needed and lifted up when prepped for takeoff. There will be a retractable, horizontal blast door at ground level kind of like a sports stadium's retractable roof.

"The deck that they all set on will be large enough for all three birds to have rotors turning at once. That way as soon as the roof door is clear, they can takeoff at once. That will greatly reduce the takeoff exposure time for the birds and time that the blast door is open.

"Here's the kicker, Alex. There will be a huge hangar building above the blast doors. That way when ever the doors are open, no satellite can pick it up. Secondly, if someone ever does see a bird flying out of the hangar, they will assume that it is housed in that above ground hangar."

"Excellent, I like it, I really like it," Alex praised Luis. Then Alex asked, "How far would we have to go to have the tactical facility on the Wyoming side, right in the middle of that property?"

"About fifteen miles total."

"How much would that increase the price-tag?"

Luis responded, "Probably about two or three million for the extra ten miles of tunnel."

Alex then authorized the additional expense, "Good, let's make it happen. That way we'll have fifteen miles of separation between hangars and facilities. That fact alone could give us a huge tactical advantage when needed."

Then Luis asked Alex, "How is it that you know so much about this type of construction?"

Alex proceeded to fill Luis in. One year after retiring in 2000, Alex acquired the perfect job. He was working one year contracts at different locations around the world. He worked for the US government, providing T/S security services at various classified, hardened facilities.

Alex was perfect for the job. With his knowledge of construction and his security skills, he excelled at that profession. He also learned a great deal about constructing hardened structures with superb security measures. He worked in that profession for seven years.

Then Alex shifted gears, "Okay, Luis, it appears that you're tracking very well on the ranch. I have another set of plans that I need you to draw up ASAP. They are to a very special enclosed boat dock with a special purpose in mind. It is to be constructed in Brownsville, Texas. The boat dock needs to be finished in five weeks. We've got ten million dollars and a lot of need riding on this one."

Alex handed Luis some papers, "Here are the rough sketches I've done on it. Before we build, the shore under it needs to be dredged out so that a boat with a draft of twenty feet can pull into it. It's a double-decker boat dock with the top deck being an open-air party deck.

"It needs to be large enough for a boat forty-five feet long by twenty feet wide. The distance between the water's surface and the ceiling needs to be thirty-five feet. There will be a horseshoe-shaped deck ten feet wide around the opening. It needs to be strong enough to support a forklift and twenty tons of cargo.

"Here's the important part. The top structure load bearing beams need to be able to support twenty tons. There will be four fifteen-thousand-pound winches mounted to the support beams in the four corners of the ceiling to hoist boats or subs in and out of the water after we've unloaded their cargo.

"The front of the exterior wall that faces land needs to be able to move like a retractable garage door. I'm guessing a door for a tractor-trailer. The rear of the dock facing the water needs to be the same as the front. And finally, we need retractable, steel I-beams and steel plates to form a temporary floor so that after the front wall is opened up, a trailer can back inside the dock over the water. After all, a man's got to be able to bring his boat in and out of the water. Don't ya think so, Luis?"

"Ah, yeah, man, right," Luis agreed. Luis then stated, "It's pretty clear here from your sketches. Alex, what are the dimensions of these subs?"

Alex said, "Ethan said they are forty-foot long by eight-foot wide by twelve-foot high."

Luis commented, "You should have been a draftsman, Alex."

Alex replied, "I was, just not to your professional degree. Did you like the sketches I did of the underground facilities?"

"Yeah," said Luis, "they were sweet, but I thought Gerard ginned those up."

"No, sir, that was me," Alex confirmed and then concluded, "One more thing about the boat dock, Luis. Once it's completed, we're going to house a forty by eighteen foot pontoon boat in there. It will be our recovery vessel for the subs in the event Murphy intervenes. It will be rigged for subsurface recovery. There will always be six complete sets of dive gear on her at all times. And of course, a dive compressor to re-jam the tanks. All right, do you have anything else for me, Luis?"

Luis said, "Nope, that was all of it. It should take me too or three days on these plans. I'll call ya when they're ready."

Then Luis asked, "Who are ya going to have build it?"

"We are," Alex replied. Then he elaborated, "Well, half of our crew anyway. They can finish it in a week or ten days, excluding driving time. I'll hire a local contractor to build the house and garage. Leiko, Dutch, and I are flying down there tomorrow to purchase the property. I'll get you the address where to have the materials delivered and send the crew to. Thanks, brother."

12 MAY 2010
BROWNSVILLE, TEXAS

Lisa, the real estate agent said, "Well, Mr. Boulder, you've seen all of the seaside properties that my firm has to offer here in Brownsville. Which one can I sell you today?"

Alex looked at Leiko and said, "What do ya think, baby? Which one would you like to have for a summer vacation home?"

"I like this last one right here," Leiko said. "It has the prettiest view, and I like the houses on both sides the best."

Alex looked at Dutch and said, "Well, Dutch, you've been pretty quiet. Which one do you think is the best deal?"

He said, "I'll have to agree with Leiko on this one, brother. She has quite the eye for these things, but you're the one paying for it. I'll rely on your judgment for this one."

That was Dutch's way of telling Alex that tactically, he thought this was the best location to recover the subs from. He was also saying that since Alex was the SF combat diver (Underwater Combat Diver; SCUBA, and Closed Circuit (Oxygen Re-breather; INFIL/EXFIL) and had all of the subsurface experience, he was probably in a better position to make the call. In SF, you got really good at reading between the lines in a mixed conversation.

"Well, there you have it, Lisa. I guess we're getting this one," Alex said. "What did you say the price tag on this one was again?"

She glanced at her papers and said, "Let's see here. This one is $1.3 million." "Okay," Alex directed, "just give, Mr. Stanley, my attorney a call, and he'll close the deal today. We'll sign the papers when we get back up to Denver."

"Yes, sir, I'll give him a call as soon as I get back to the office," Lisa assured him.

Then she asked, "When do you think you'll start building your house?"

"Priorities first, Lisa. I'll build my boat dock before the house. The fishing comes first," Alex reminded her.

"Oh yes, of course. I don't know what I was thinking." Lisa looked at Leiko and rolled her eyes as they both started laughing. In closing, Lisa said, "Thank you very much for your business, and have a good day ya' all."

While Lisa was walking off to her car, Dutch pulled out his cell phone and recorded the GPS grid for the good general. Then they all started walking toward their rental car.

Then Dutch blurted out, "Wow, man, I figured that you would have at least haggled her down to an even million."

Alex replied, "That would have required offers and counter offers for a week or too with the owners. We don't have that kind of time to waste. An offer for the full requested price is always processed immediately. A little useful info a bank president once told me."

Then Dutch muttered, "Yeah, I guess they're good for something."

Alex replied, "The funny thing is, they never helped me before I won the lotto. Well, anyway, I know one bank president that will never fit into that mold—my little sis."

Leiko said, "Yeah, we've got to come up with a name for our bank."

Alex quickly responded, "I already have, girl, the Free People's Bank. Under the name of the bank, an inscription will read, 'By the people and for the people. In God we trust.'"

Dutch and Leiko both looked at Alex at the same time and said, "I like it."

"Yeah, me too. That's the way a bank should be run," Alex concluded.

13 MAY 2010
DENVER, COLORADO

The next day, they flew into Denver so they could sign the property papers with Clint. They had Luis meet them there with the F-750 quad cab. On the way back to the ranch, Alex gave Luis all of the info that he needed to launch the construction crew the next day.

Alex began with the details, "Luis I want you and Gerard to drive down to the dock a day or too before they're finished with it. Make sure it's built to your specs and done right. Take this truck and Dad's helo trailer. The roof on his trailer completely retracts. Put twenty tons of steel I-beams in the trailer and have it all prepped with chains for one single load.

"I'd like you to back the trailer into the dock and test the winches, doors, walls, steel floor, and entire system. Lifting the load up, pulling the trailer out, and then lowering the load into the water should do it. The most important thing to remember here is to always close the trailer roof before you drive it out of the boat dock! Remember the eye in the sky.

"Meanwhile, I want Gerard filming all four angles simultaneously during the entire operation. The goal here is to only be able to see an enclosed trailer back into an enclosed boat dock and then, some time later, pull back out. Nothing more, nothing less."

Luis replied, "I think we can handle that one, Alex."

Then Alex relayed his concerns to Luis, "I don't want any surprises while we're lifting ten million bucks worth of cargo out of there! No satellite or ground imagery capable of seeing anything!

"Luis, while you and Gerard are handling that, Dad, Dutch, and I will be down in Sanford, Florida, in flight school."

Luis commented, "Cool. I want to learn to fly one of those whirly birds when ya get back."

Alex assured him, "You'll get your chance. There will be five of you learning to fly them."

Then Alex asked, "You're not afraid of heights, are ya, Luis?"

He said, "No, just falling from them."

Alex tried to keep a straight face as he said, "Okay, well, ya know the choppers have air brakes, don't ya?"

Luis said, "Don't even try it, man. Leiko showed me the video."

Alex exclaimed, "Man, that girl gets me every time! She leaned forward and reached up from the backseat and jabbed her index finger in Alex's lower rib cage, just above his left kidney and said, "Yeah, I've got my eye on you, boy."

Alex got on the cell to his dad. "Hey, Dad, did you get everything squared away for our trip?"

Hunter replied, "Yeah, I did. They remembered me and said they would be glad to have the three of us down there. They're pretty slow down there right now. It's probably this crappy economy. The school, hotel, car rental, plane tickets, and chopper rentals are all reserved."

Alex said, "Cool, it sounds like you've got everything covered. We'll be back to the ranch in about two hours. See ya then."

Hunter informed Alex, "Hey, when you get back, Gerard's got something to show ya."

"Okay, I'll see him when I get back. All right then, out here." Alex terminated his commo link. Once they arrived at the ranch,

Alex saw Gerard waiting by the driveway and could tell that he was concerned about something and chomping at the bit. While everyone was pouring out of the big rig, Leiko yelled, "Everybody, up to my house in one hour for supper." Hoops and hollers were heard from all, for they knew what awaited them.

Gerard said to Alex, "Come on to the commo room. I've got something to show you."

"Yes, sir, I'm on yer heals," Alex replied.

Gerard's commo room was constructed just as securely as the cracker boxes. It had to be, with everything that was discussed in there. Gerard said, "Look at this clip that I recorded off of *FOX News* three hours ago."

Alex explained, "Yeah, we've been on the road and haven't gotten any news since this morning." The recorded, special live report was showing a huge demonstration in front of the US Capital building that was quickly turning uneasy. With America's unemployment reaching 18.3 percent and still fighting wars on too fronts, American's had had enough.

Osama's approval rating was at an all time low of thirty-two percent. The American people were finally accepting the fact that he had lied about everything he said and promised during the elections, just to get elected. After he and his cronies jammed the health care farce down the public's throat, they even had the balls to rub it in by letting it be known that it didn't even apply to them—the elite, Osama, the senate, or the congress.

The TV screen started off with showing a fairly peaceful demonstration that led right up to the steps of the Capital Building. It was estimated that there were at least a quarter of a million people at the protest. There was another image that showed a huge banner of the Holocaust victims' bodies in a huge pile and compared it to Osama's current National Socialist Health Care plan.

Yes, these people were feed up with the lies and corruption and weren't going to stand for any more. They were going to be heard and hopefully force some level of government reform, even if it killed some of them.

The scene degraded until an uneasy demonstration turned into a full-scale riot in the streets of Washington, D.C. The images of Americans rioting hadn't been seen since the 90's L.A. riots over Rodney King and the 60s race riots. Washington's riot police were barely able to contain the violence to a ten block radius. Alex looked at Gerard and said, "It's starting sooner that I thought it would."

Once Alex was caught-up on the recording, they switched over to the live coverage. The name calling and threats later turned into rock throwing and window smashing. The people's frustrations soon led to full-scale mob mentality. Groups of people over turning cars and setting a blaze to them. Eventually, the firefighters couldn't keep up with the auto fires and just concentrated on the building fires.

The D.C. riot and duty police were barely holding their own. Scenes of police loading hundreds of people into caged buses and Para-medics treating the wounded looked like the streets of Beirut or Lebanon. It was heart breaking for Alex; seeing his fellow Americans having to use such extremes to wake up their own government. He kept waiting to see where Osama had called in the National Guard, but it didn't happen; this time.

By morning, all demonstrators had dispersed and the thirteen thousand arrested were being processed. The fire fighters still had their hands full with many vehicle and building fires. All local hospitals were reporting hundreds of wounded.

The National Guard was never called in; however, the D.C. mayor had implemented a night curfew from 2100 until 0500 for the next three days. His intent was to give the people time enough to simmer down and give the police and fire fighters a chance to catch up with the vast aftermath of the people's outrage. He couldn't realize that these rioting people were from all over the nation, not just D.C. *How naïve.*

OFF TO FLIGHT SCHOOL

28 MAY 2010
SANFORD, FLORIDA

When Alex, Dutch, and Hunter stepped off of the plane, the AIRTEK flight school had a limo there to pick them up. The company's president was even there to greet them. He realized that they were some big spenders the way they even rented their own Huey and Chinook. Most people just learned on the basic trainer helos that the school offered.

As the three of them walked toward the limo, the dude in the suit intercepted them with a big smile on his face. He said, "You must be Mr. Boulder," as he held out his hand to Dutch. It seemed as though Dutch looked more the distinguished, rich type than Alex or Hunter.

"No, sir, I'm Dutch Banner. This is Alex Boulder," he said as he gestured toward Alex. As Alex shook his hand, he introduced him to Hunter as well.

Then Alex said, "Mr. Bell, it's kind of unusual for the school's president to greet its students at the airport, with a limo, isn't it?"

He replied, "Well, perhaps, sir, but it's kind of unusual for new students to rent their own special helicopters as well."

"Yes, well, we're in a bit of a hurry and on a crash course, figuratively speaking of course," Alex admitted.

He continued, "You see, sir, we own our own wilderness touring company out west, and we need to get flying customers ASAP to start paying off the too birds we have. We have a Hughes 500 and a UH-1H Huey."

Mr. Bell said, "Yes, of course, I see, kind of like the cart before the horse."

Hunter's bird had been registered publicly to him for years. The community intentionally bought one Huey publicly as not to raise any suspicions. Alex also had Clint Stanley create a public company for airborne wilderness tours. They just didn't advertise to get any business. After all, they couldn't have any pesky public civilians pestering them for a tour when they were trying to prep for their mission.

Then Alex replied, "You could say that, Mr. Bell, but actually, Dad's had his bird for years, and he's already a pilot. That's why he'll only be getting certified on the Chinook just in case we ever expand our company large enough to buy one. Dutch and I will just be getting certified on the Huey. I hope that pretty much maps it out for you, sir?"

"Yes, sir," Mr. Bell replied. "I'm sure my school can accommodate all of your needs."

"Great," Alex said. "How long do you think it will take us all to get certified?" Mr. Bell answered, "Well, that really depends on you guys and your aptitude for flying. Your father's already proven his abilities and should progress nicely.

"I wouldn't think any more than too weeks for him and three or four for you and Dutch."

Alex smiled and said, "Sounds good. We're all looking forward to working with your flight instructors."

"Well, Alex, they're all ready to start in the morning," Mr. Bell replied.

The two shook hands as Alex said, "Well, thank you, sir, sounds like you've got everything ready for us."

The first week was all classroom instruction and simulator training for Dutch and Alex. Hunter, however, was up in the Chinook in three days. His instructor was quite impressed with his skills and the speed at which he could absorb new information and apply it in practical application. That's just the way he was. If he saw something just once, he could pick it up.

Alex and Dutch both had so much time in helos that they both took to it like fish in water. They started out in the school's small (Schweizer 300) two-man trainers for the first three days. Then they were ready for bigger fish. Alex's instructor put him on the Huey while Dutch started out on a Hughes 500, like Hunter's. After lunch they switched birds and all went up for the afternoon. At the end of the day they were feeling pretty good about their skills.

They continued that pattern for ten more days. They were each logging ten hours a day; five in each type of bird. Hunter was getting in eight hours a day on the Chinook. He was lovin' it; like a beaver in a sawmill.

After too weeks in the air they started night ops. Alex told Mr. Bell that they all needed to be certified on NVG's as well as day flight. That was no problem, for an extra 50K. Hunter was digging all this flight time; all at once. Back when he was taking his flight training, he had to complete it in four different phases. The cost of rotary wing flight school wasn't cheap. Alex knew he appreciated the ability to get it all knocked out in one wack.

Once the three of them had completed the required training and flight time for their certifications, Alex told Mr. Bell that he wanted them to be able to be trained on actual auto-rotations. Mr. Bell tilted his head upward and produced a concerned look on his face. He said, "We've already trained you on that. Do you mean actually doing it all the way to the ground?"

Then he swallowed hard like he had a big turd in his throat. Alex grinned and said, "Yes, sir, that's exactly what I mean."

With Mr. Bell's voice quivering, he said, "That can be dangerous and very hard on the chopper skids."

Then Alex explained himself, "I'm aware of that. I've spoken with our instructors, and they're prepared to conduct the drills with us if you authorize it. They said it would be excellent training for them as well. You see, where we fly at higher altitudes in rugged mountain terrain, we need to be ready for any emergency. This additional training could save our lives and the lives of our clients as well.

"I will personally pay for any damages to the aircraft. I'll even give you a one hundred thousand dollars retainer toward any damages to your birds before we conduct the maneuvers. Your instructors and we will sign wavers for any injuries against your school."

"I want to speak with my staff on this issue. I'll give you an answer by COB (close of business) today," Mr. Bell said, ringing his hands.

Alex closed with, "All right, thank you, sir."

That night Alex, Dutch, and Hunter took all of their flight instructors out for dinner and a little bar hoppin'. They figured if they did the extra training or not, they'd be leaving tomorrow anyway. Two of their five instructors were Vietnam veterans. They both flew Hueys for Uncle Sam in that hellhole.

Gabriel Nightingale flew a med-evac bird. His was a mission of saving lives. Damon Dragoon flew a gunship in the 1st Air Cav. His was a mission of taking lives. He gave Charlie the maximum opportunity to give his live for his country. Not the sort of man used to failing, at anything.

The students found out that night that Damon was the one responsible for convincing Mr. Bell to let them conduct the actual auto-rotation training the next day. Alex liked his style. He was the kind of man that you either liked or hated the first time you met him. The kind of man that said what he meant and meant what he said. He should have been SF in Nam. He surly had the will to be if he had wanted to.

Dutch and Alex had drug Gabriel and Damon over to a corner table where they could try to get some war stories out of them. Meanwhile, Hunter had challenged the other three instructors to join the pool tournament with him. That night there was a doubles tournament with a grand prize of $1,500 bucks. He told them if they won he'd match the prize money and they'd all take home a grand. That would give Alex and Dutch enough time to elicit enough information from their fellow vets to determine if they were good candidates for community recruitment.

Once the stories and beers started flying, everybody loosened up a great deal. They could all sense that they were all in the company of combat veteran brethren. After several mission stories from everyone, the two Nam vets began expressing their intense displeasure with the way the American people and their government had treated them after the war.

They were sure to let Alex and Dutch know that they were fed up with the way that all combat veterans since Vietnam had been treated as well. In light of the present condition of the country and the corrupt government, several comments were made in reference to a better way of life and taking care of their own. At that point Dutch and Alex knew that they had to make their pitch. Through much preparation, the stage was set.

It was no coincidence that they happen to be in that particular bar that night, or that there happened to be a doubles pool tournament that night. For two weeks they'd been cultivating Gabriel and Damon for that night. Ever since they relayed their combat experience and displeasure with the direction that their great nation has taken; especially since Osama stole their nation's highest office with his illegal ACORN (Association of Community Organization for Reform Now) votes and forged birth certificate.

They were also sure to elaborate on all of the illegal funds that Osama accepted from his Syrian born slum-lord buddy and his terrorist friend that bombed the Pentagon, also aided his election campaign. Since the guys flew there from Colorado, they weren't able to bring the cracker box for their recruitment pitch. Therefore, they'd have to do it the old fashioned way; a barroom meeting with lots of loud cover noise.

Alex texted Hunter (number 1) on his phone while he and the three instructors were in the pool tournament. That was his signal to have to take a dump. Therefore, he would have to come and get Gabriel to fill-in for him. That would give Dutch and Alex enough time to give Damon the pitch. It also left Dutch on-deck to play interception if any of the other guys came back early. They approached Damon first because they thought he had more chance of saying yes. Their analysis of his discontentment with America's present state-of-mind was correct. He jumped all over their offer with both feet.

Just then one of the other guys started puking over by the pool table. Damon went over to check him out. After a couple of minutes Damon came back to their table and said, "Ron isn't feeling well and he is calling it a night. He feels bad about screwing his fellow instructors out of the thousand bucks that Hunter was going to match." After all, the fly boys were in the running for the prize money.

That's when Damon volunteered to take his place and told Ron that if they won he'd give him his share tomorrow. Damon said, "You better take your ass home and sober up! You don't want to miss that good training we're going to be doing tomorrow. It's not every day the boss lets us slam multi-million dollar birds into the ground in the name of training."

That's when Dutch looked at Alex and said, "We'd better hurry-up and finish Gabriel's pitch before anything else happens." Alex nodded and texted Hunter again (1 Down). That was his signal to come back into the game and relieve Gabriel.

Once Hunter replaced Gabriel at the pool table, Gabriel went back to their table and Dutch said, "Where were we, brother? O yeah, talking about how dicked-up this country has gotten since we got a criminal in the White House."

Gabriel said, "Yeah, boys, don't get me started!"

Meanwhile at the pool table, Hunter leaned over to Damon and said, "Glad to have ya aboard, brother. I hope Gabriel likes our offer as much as you did." At that very moment Damon got that "deer in the headlights look."

He looked at Hunter and said, "Don't tell me they're going to ask him to join their unit as well! He works for ATF (Federal Bureau of Alcohol, Tobacco, and Fircarms)!"

Just then Alex happened to look over Gabriel's shoulder at his dad, and he saw that crazed look in his eyes that he's only seen when Hunter's had a charging grizzly or mountain lion quickly bearing down on him, or he's been ready to take another man's life.

Just as he had taught Alex to draw a tomahawk from its sheath on his right shoulder blade, Alex saw Hunter reach back-handed beside him and pluck Damon's long-neck *Coors* beer bottle from his hand. Alex knew at that very moment, for some reason, Hunter was going on the warpath. He also knew there would be a very good reason for it, when ever he got the chance to hear it. From the stance he took and the direction his feet were facing Alex knew there was about to be incoming glass in his direction in a heart beat.

It only took the blink of an eye until the *Coors* beer bottle was splattering all over the back of a dude's head. Just as quickly, the man at the table next to them had hit the floor. Well, his five buddies with him didn't seem to appreciate the fact that Hunter had just bagged and tagged their redneck friend.

If that guy wasn't inbred, he sure looked the part now. That's all it took for the entire joint to explode into a free-for-all and Hunter was Florida's most wanted at the moment.

Alex yelled to Dutch and Gabriel, "Follow me to rally with the other guys!" They mustered at the pool table and made their stand there. This would be a good audition for the fly boys.

They were not just fighting the unconscious fellow's five friends, but it seems the other eleven were also his buddies. Alex knew the defensive skills of Dutch, Hunter, and himself. He was also fairly confident of the two Nam vets skills. However, he didn't have a clue about the other two fly boys? Either way, he'd find out in a matter of moments. Alex issued a directive to his guys, "Don't kill anyone. They're all our American brothers!"

The biggest boy among them was wearing bibbed overalls and a leather jacket as he weighed in at about 325 lbs. at six foot nine; quite the mountain of a man. He seemed to be the leader of the pack. The big man yelled at the pilots, "Who threw the damn beer bottle?"

Alex's dad stepped forward and said, "I did ya big tub of S#!T. I'm really sorry about hitting your redneck lover there on the floor. I was really aiming for you ass wipe!" That was all it took. Game on.

As usual, the big man in the pack made the first move. They always assume that their sheer size will give them a decisive victory over the smaller man. They never factor in for training and experience on the battlefield. As he descended on Hunter, Alex could tell the mountain man was planning on splattering him against the pool table.

One step away from contact, Hunter sidestepped the huge gorilla and took his legs out from under him while he simultaneously placed his right palm on the back of the man's head and drove his face into the rail of the pool table with the force of a battering ram. Sweet, now their leader and their courage was out of the fight.

Just after ass wipe swallowed all of his teeth, Alex saw two dudes each grab an arm that Dutch presented to them. In a heart beat they were both down with crushed nuts and splattered noses.

As Alex was partial to a staff, he picked up a pool que and went to work. As he worked his way from the front of the crowd to the rear, taking out knees, nuts, and hands, he looked back to see the two flyboys in question, double teaming a big biker looking dude. They were holding their own.

Once Alex reached the rear of their unorganized formation of injured bodies, he came along their left flank and went to take up a position to cover Dutch and Hunter's rear. He knew they would be going through the crowd capitalizing on the injuries that he had just inflicted.

Once Alex reached their rear, he saw Gabriel and Damon punishing the three dudes that were attempting to take them out. He realized that Damon had kept very fit as he saw him grab a guy by the throat, lift him up, and body slam him onto the pool table. Then he proceeded to break a pool que across the back of the head of one of the two that was on Gabriel. Alex told himself that he should have told those guys not to kill any one.

Within three minutes of ass wipe's lights going out, all sixteen locals had sustained sufficient injuries to take their will to fight. Just about when they had all given up the fight, Alex saw something that he had never seen before. He saw a guy land a punch square on his dad's jaw. Then Hunter went down like a ton of bricks.

That's when Alex introduced his right cowboy boot to the left side of the man's jaw that had clocked Hunter. Then he went out like a light. Then Alex thought, *now let's see what's wrong with dad.* He knelt down beside him and couldn't figure it out. He wasn't unconscious. Shoot, he wasn't even bleeding. He put his ear near Hunter's mouth to try and hear what he was trying to say.

Hunter whispered, "Gabriel's ATF! I started the fight and faked the punch so I could tell you. Now slide me your wallet. Did you make the offer?"

Alex shook his head no, saying aloud, "Leave it to you to catch the last punch of the fight." Alex then instructed the other guys to get out of there ASAP. They had broken the people's will to fight and wouldn't have any further resistance from them. It was time to break contact. Besides the cops would be coming soon enough. They didn't want to be there when they arrived.

Alex slid the owner ten grand in hundreds and asked him if they were squared. He looked hard at him for a couple of seconds and said, "Yeah, man, we're squared."

Alex replied, "Thank you, sir, I'm deeply sorry about busting up your livelihood but we can't tolerate thieves in our society."

He looked Alex in the eye and said, "I'd probably have done the same thing in your shoes. Now go on, get outta here before the cops get here!" They all escaped with only minor cuts and bruises and a few swollen knuckles. Not enough to interfere with tomorrows training anyway.

Once they were all in the limo, Hunter knew that he had to cover his tracks with the other guys, especially Gabriel. So he immediately offered his explanation to all. He said, "Hey, guys, I apologize for getting you all in a barroom brawl, but I just saw that guy lift Alex's wallet."

Then Hunter said, "Here ya go, son," as he handed Alex back his wallet. Then Hunter elaborated, "That's why I sent that Coors tomahawk into his head, and ya might have seen me over there delivering a kick or two to his ribs. I had to go recover Alex's wallet. Anyways, men, I had fun dancing with ass wipe ! How about you, guys?"

Everyone chimed in together. They were all fairly pleased with the activities and the outcome. Alex heard Damon direct a comment toward Hunter. He said, "When you snatched that beer bottle from my hand and pitched it into that dude's head, I thought you were going on the warpath. I didn't know weather to run or cover your back."

Hunter replied, "I'm glad that you chose the latter of the two."

* * *

The next morning, Alex looked surprised as he said, "Well, good morning, Mr. Bell. I didn't expect to see you out here this morning."

"Well, Alex," he said, "I wanted to observe this training that you're so determined to conduct. Besides, this could very well be the only time my staff will ever conduct this drill, all the way to the ground."

Mr. Bell continued, "I've even set up a film crew to capture it all on tape. It will be some valuable insight for future students."

"Well, sir," Alex replied, "I'm glad that you've recognized this opportunity and are taking full advantage of it. I hate to ever see good training opportunities go to waste."

Alex looked at Damon and said, "Damon, may I fly with you today? There are some things I need to speak with you about."

He said, "Sure, Alex, I'm still pumped from last night."

"Great, first just let me speak to my guys before we get started," Alex requested. "Dutch, Hunter, let me speak to you guys for a second," as Alex motioned them to step away from the school staff.

"Listen," Alex informed them, "Mr. Bell is taping this entire training session. Therefore, I want us all to keep our tinted visors down the entire time we're in the birds. We don't need our faces turning up on *CNN* (Cable News Network or the Communist News Network) or in *Aviation Weekly*."

At the trainings conclusion, Damon said, "Well, gentlemen, I can honestly say after conducting three emergency auto rotations in Vietnam myself and seeing a couple more since then, you guys did all right."

Hunter said, "Well, Damon, at least we all walked away from both birds."

Then Alex said, "I know I'll be buying a new pair of skids for the Huey that I rented. However, I think the school's Schweizer is going to require a little more attention." The last autorotation had struck the ground so hard that it spread the skids and snapped the main rotor off.

Mr. Bell jumped in, "Well, as you said, Alex, at least everyone walked away under their own power. Don't worry, we'll send you the bill."

Alex replied, "Okay, and thank you for everything, Mr. Bell. You've been most accommodating. And thanks for the use of your limo last night."

28 JUNE 2010
SANFORD, FLORIDA

Their training was complete, and they were all ready to go home. Damon asked Mr. Bell, "Do you mind if I ride with the guys in the limo to the airport? I've got a war story to finish from last night."

Mr. Bell replied, "Yes, Damon, that's fine. I was going to ask you if you wouldn't mind doing that anyway. I have a meeting to attend and after all you are their lead instructor."

Once everyone was in the limo, Alex said, "Okay, fellas, we've got about thirty minutes to the airport, and the driver can't hear us through the glass. I've got the intercom turned off. Here's the deal, Damon. After one month, you'll give Mr. Bell your resignation. The reasons you stated earlier are sound and viable. After you visit your sister in Ohio, then you'll drive your RV out to our ranch in Colorado. We'll have your place all ready and waiting for ya. By then we should have the rest of our birds, and be ready for our homegrown flight school."

Damon replied, "That sounds great, Alex. Boy, if Mr. Bell knew the real deal, he'd flip his lid."

Alex assured him, "Yeah, well that's why we're handling this the way we are.

Damon, do you think that Gabriel has a clue about last night?"

"No, sir, Damon stated. "You guys really covered all your bases last night. I know I wouldn't have thought any thing of it other than that was one hell of a fun night."

Alex said, "All right, we'll see you in about two months."

"Yes, sir, you guys have a good flight back home. I'll be along shortly," Damon assured them.

Once they were all in the airport at their departure gate, they all felt a little more at ease. Alex addressed Hunter and Dutch, "Well, men, that went much better than I ever could have hoped for. We were all certified on our target aircraft. We had the opportunity to practice our trade craft in offensive and defensive combative skills. We gained one combat pilot instructor. And we managed to do it all by only paying extra for one barroom and two sets of chopper repairs. I would call that a very successful business trip."

Alex inquired, "Tell me, Dutch, was that more fun than you and Ethan had in Nicaragua?"

He said, "Well, it was for me, but I think Ethan would beg to differ. Well, except for the pink suitcase part with the suits."

Alex said, "I agree. We'll never let him live that one down."

Hunter said, "Quick, Alex, look at this!" As Alex turned to his dad and quickly shuffled over to the TV monitor, to his surprise, he saw an old familiar face—his own!

Alex muttered, "I'll be dammed. The bar owner had a CCTV in there that we didn't catch on our initial assessment of the joint."

Right there on the local news was a black-and-white still photo of Alex kicking one of ass wipe's buddy's asses. Alex said, "Well, at least the news media has blocked out our identities."

As Alex was in a good horse stance about to dislocate that fellow's left shoulder, he was sounding off with his Iroquois battle cry. In Dutch's attempt to bust Alex's balls he asked, "What song were you singing to your girlfriend there that you were dancing with?"

Alex replied, "I was singing to his girlfriend over in the corner who was kickin' yer ass."

Hunter threw the general question out there, "Do ya think that the bar owner will talk?"

Alex answered that question, "No, I don't think he'll talk or even press charges. I could tell the way that he acted, he didn't like what we did, but he was okay with the way that I dealt with him. Besides, I saw his photos on the walls. He was a Nam SF vet and POW (prisoner of war). He struck me as still being proud of the fact that he still had his honor."

Alex stated, "Once he opens those hundreds, he'll find the ivory SF coin that I slipped in between the bills."

Dutch insinuated, "You talking about the one that the locals presented you with in Benin?"

Alex muttered, "Yeah, that will probably mean more to him than the cash."

Then Alex said, "Come on, fellas, we're out of here in fifteen minutes. We won't be around here for anyone to see our mugs anyway."

07 JULY 2010
MOJAVE DESERT, CALIFORNIA

After a few days of rest for the whole crew, it was time to get crackin' again. Dutch had been sent to California on another procurement mission. At 0930, Alex got a call on his encrypted cell phone. He said, "That's the best news I gotten all month, Dutch."

"What was the total damage on the bill?"

"Five and a half million."

Alex admitted, "Well, there was no way around it because we couldn't do without it. I'll go give Dad and Leiko the good news. When will you have it here?"

Dutch guessed, "Tomorrow night sometime."

"That sounds good, brother. Good job, Dutch." Hunter was sitting in the kitchen chewing the fat with Leiko as she prepared lunch. Alex slipped in through the back door of the house to surprise her. Just outside of the kitchen, he made eye contact with his dad and gestured for him to keep quiet.

Then he snuck in at her six o'clock as she stood at the sink, washing carrots. Just as he was about to grab her by the ribs, she spun around one hundred eighty degrees and had her left foot resting squarely against his nose and a carrot pointed at his gut as if it were a knife. Alex stood there for a second and looked over at his dad, and Hunter's eyes were big as saucers.

He looked at Alex and said, "I wouldn't if I were you, boy!" So then, Alex grabbed the carrot and started tickling her stomach. Then they both lost their balance and fell on the hardwood floor, laughing hysterically. Even Hunter was cracking up.

After regaining their composure, Alex proceeded to tell them that they had the Chinook secured, and Dutch was in route with it from California. Same deal as last time. He would set down about three hundred miles out and truck it in under cover of nightfall. Then they'd cache it in the steel building first and then put it in the bunker on the Wyoming side. That's where they'll be conducting all of their flight training.

09 JULY 2010
SHADOW WOLF RANCH

As all the guys stood in the special projects building Alex said, "See, boys, I told yas there'd be plenty of room in here. With Dad's rig, the Huey, and the Chinook, there's still plenty of room. Have you locked-in on that last Huey yet, Dutch?"

"Yeah, but this one's coming out of Arkansas from a private owner."

Alex started nodding his head and said, "Good, that's a lot better than from the military."

Luis asked, "Why's that?"

Alex explained, "Because after that guy gets his money he doesn't care what happens to that bird. Even though the military is selling their surplus choppers to civilians now, they still try to track them pretty hard. Isn't that right Gerard?"

"Yes, sir," Gerard confirmed, "I removed three tracking responders and one BFT (Blue Force Tracker) off of the Huey and five from the Chinook along with three concealed BFT units that were tied into the bird's battery system."

Luis asked, "What's a BFT unit?"

Gerard jumped in and educated him, "Well, Luis, that stands for Blue Force Tracker satellite tracking module. Our military has one BFT unit on every soldier and every vehicle on the ground and in the air. That way, when they misplace one, they know where to go to retrieve it. Don't worry, Luis, all of these birds are clean now. I'd stick my reputation on it!"

Then Alex chimed in, "Now that's saying something, Luis, considering who Gerard used to work for."

"Yeah, Alex," Luis admitted. "I feel pretty good about it."

Alex stated to everyone, "Once we get that last Huey, we'll be looking pretty good for our homegrown flight school. The final piece to the puzzle will be having Damon here as our primary flight instructor. We've already got everything else we need for the birds."

LET'S GO FISHING

18 JULY 2010
SHADOW WOLF RANCH

Dutch told Alex, "I just received word from General Sanchez that the fish will be here on the 22nd at 2200."

Alex responded, "That is right on time, Dutch. We just finished the final mods on the three trailers. What do you think? Will they pass a first look?"

"I'll say a first and second look."

"That good, huh?"

"Yeah, man, they look like regular hi-boy triple car haulers with the big words Spitfire Movie Productions on the sides."

Alex admitted, "Yeah, well, they're a lot more than that." Then Alex expounded, "They're extra tall because they're a low-boy configuration. These fifty-three foot trailers have been specially modified with retractable roofs. We gutted everything inside, so they're just empty shells outside. The suspension systems have also been rebuilt to support a twenty ton pay load."

"Well, Alex," Dutch said, "Just like your dad's helo trailer, I can't tell that these have a retractable roof on them either."

Alex nodded his head in approval, "Cool beans, Dutch, that's just what I wanted to hear."

Alex asked Dutch, "How about putting this studio paperwork in all of the glove boxes of the semis? In the event that we get stopped and checked, all those documents make everything appear legit. Thanks, Dutch."

Then Alex told Dutch, "I'm going to get dad and Leiko. Would you please tell the other guys to be in the cracker box by 1700 for the mission brief? By the way, Dutch, did you get any weird vibes from the good general's e-mail?"

"No, sir," Dutch said. "I didn't read anything between the lines."

"Good, we don't need any surprises on this one. This mission has enough moving parts in it as it is," Alex said as he walked off.

Later, Alex opened the briefing with, "All right, men and pretty lady, this is how we're going to conduct 'Operation Barracuda'. Don't worry, Leiko, Luis, Dad, and Gerard. With all of the training we've given you guys on SR (Special Reconnaissance), DA (Direct Actions), UW (Unconventional Warfare), dive ops, and vehicles, you're all ready and prepared to conduct this mission!"

Then Alex read off the roll call for the OPORD (Operations Order, a directive issued by a commander to subordinate commanders for the purpose of effecting the coordinated execution of an operation); Dutch, here; Gerard present; Dad ready; Luis Get-er-done; Leiko, yeah, baby; Ethan, here; and myself. All present. Please write down and hold all of your questions until the end of the brief."

Alex proceeded to read the entire OPORD aloud.

SITUATION

In five days, our three subs full of weapons and ammo will covertly arrive at our boat dock in Brownsville, Texas.

MISSION

We will drive and fly to the vicinity of Brownville, Texas. Once there we will conduct forty-eight hours eyes on the objective, recover the cargo and subs, and return to "Shadow Wolf Ranch" without being detected. If stopped anywhere along the line, we will be prepared to conduct defensive operations as necessary, to evade the authorities, and return back here; un-followed.

EXECUTION

Dad (pilot), Dutch (copilot), and four gunners will fly the Chinook NOE at night, down to the remote LZ that we've established about eighteen miles from our boat dock. They'll depart thirty-six hours after the convoy departs, so they don't sit so long on their first LZ. That will have you guys departing just after dark. Your code word for departing Shadow Wolf Ranch will be *Play Ball*.

They will carry the set of six E & E dirt bikes and one additional Chinook fuel bladder to refuel the bird once they've landed at LZ-1. The code word for that will be *1ˢᵗ Base*. Then they'll be on call to provide over-watch while the cargo is being driven to the PZ. The code word from Gerard for that will be *Guardian Angel*.

Once you're in the air you'll give the code word *Second Base*. Gerard will sound off with the code word *Wal-Mart* once he's prepared to connect the sling load. Once you're at the PZ and in position to retrieve the connex of weapons and ammo, you'll give the code word *Third Base*. Once in the air with the cargo, they'll fly to LZ-2 and cache the bird in the old abandoned hangar until the following nightfall.

When they're in the hangar they'll give the code word *Home Run*. Then after dark they'll fly NOE back to Shadow Wolf Ranch under the cover of darkness. Once they take-off they'll give the code word *Grand Slam*. After they have landed at Shadow Wolf Ranch and have the bird and cargo secured, they will give the code word *Rained Out*.

Alex reminded them, "Everyone, keep in mind our primary mission is to get the weapons and ammo back here! The secondary mission is to get the subs back here."

Then he continued,

Luis, Ethan, and Gerard will drive the three sub-recovery rigs to the staging point at the truck stop, nine miles from the boat dock. On the way down there, you all will stay in a tight convoy. We'll pace it for a two-day drive. After dark, the first night we'll RON (rest overnight stop) at checkpoint *Cougar*. We'll time it so we arrive at checkpoint *Wolverine*, the Brownsville city limits, just after dark on the second night.

Leiko and I will drive the roll back rig with the twenty-foot connex that has the van inside it. On the way down there, we will stay about five miles ahead of the convoy. Once we arrive, we'll park between your three big rigs.

Once all vehicles are positioned, we'll off-load the van. Ethan and Luis will come with Leiko and I in the van to go and post our two LPs/OPs (listening post/observation post). Once Ethan and Luis are in their hide sites, Leiko and I will go to our house. Their code words for emplacement will be *Eagle* for Ethan and *Hawk* for Luis.

While you two are pulling forty-eight-hour surveillance on the neighborhood, we'll be prepping the recovery boat and take it out for a test run the first night. Remember, guys, we don't expect you to stay awake for forty-eight hours. Coordinate for six-hour shifts between the two of you. That way, we will have constant coverage. If either of you see any hostile activity advancing on the house or boat dock, sound off with the code word *Dazzler* and send out a SALUTE (size, activity, location, unit, time, and equipment) report.

The second night at 1600, six hours before the link-up time, Leiko will go pick up Ethan and take him back to the house. When you get there, Ethan, you'll go through the house and use the underground corridor to the boat dock. Luis, you'll have the last watch by yourself.

Ethan and I will take the boat out in the harbor and wait for the contact. Fishing will be our cover story. Meanwhile, after Luis is assured there is no one on to us, he'll contact Leiko for a pick-up. Luis, when you get there, you'll drive in the garage, go through the house, and use the concealed corridor to the boat dock. Leiko, you'll stay in the house to handle anyone that might pop up snooping around.

Gerard, when we have the first sub unloaded and suspended, I'll call you to bring the first rig. The code word will be *Pizza*. Back it right in like we practiced. Once you're backed right up to the semi-door, I'll open it so you can back in. Don't worry, brother, we'll have the retractable floor in place by then!

Once you're all the way in, we'll retract your trailer roof. Once you're loaded and your roof is closed again, you'll return to the truck stop. Ethan will ride with you so he can pull security on the other trucks. Then you'll wait there for the call to bring another empty rig and repeat the process.

Gerard, once all three subs are at the truck stop, you'll bring the roll back with the connex. After we've loaded the weapons, ammo, forklift, and all dunage (cargo packing materials (pallets, 4 x 4's, ratchet straps, etc.), you will depart for the PZ about thirty-three miles from the boat dock. That's about twenty-two miles, as the crow flies, from the LZ where the Chinook will be on standby.

As soon as you pass checkpoint *Badger*, the suspended bridge over the inner coastal waterway, you'll call the Chinook to go airborne and assume an over watch pattern over you until you get to the PZ. The code word for that will be *Guardian Angel.*

Once you've sling-loaded the container to the Chinook and they're gone, you'll return to the truck stop and wait for the rest of the team to arrive. Have the vehicles pre-positioned for the return of the van. The Chinook will go to the secondary LZ and cache the bird in the old abandoned hangar until nightfall. Once it's dark again, they'll fly directly back to the ranch.

Luis, once the cargo has departed the boat dock and we have the front door down, you will put the pontoon boat back in the boat dock and secure everything. Once you're finished you'll come back through the house to the van in the garage. You will set in the second seat from the front so you can cover the sub crews. If you should have to blast any of them, Leiko and I won't be in your line of fire.

Simultaneously, Leiko will be in the van putting on her disguise. Then she will get into the driver's seat and wait for her passengers. Simultaneously, I will have the three sub crews of nine men in the house in the cracker box room. I will Take their photos and finish their IDs. Then I'll show them the prerecorded video of Dutch on my laptop.

In that video, he will be giving them a motivational speech on the advantages of taking the fifty grand each and telling General Sanchez that they scuttled the subs after delivery of the cargo. Of course Dutch will also be enlightening them on the disadvantages of crossing him! Especially, after he has their photographs.

After that, I'll give them their cash and bus tickets. Once that is completed and I have sterilized the entire AO, we'll all load up in the van. The only three places that the Latino's will ever see are the inside of the boat dock, inside of the cracker box room, and the van. At all other times, they will all wear these full-headed mask with no eye holes. They will pass for real faces at night time in a dark van.

Leiko, Luis, and I will then drive the nine of them to the alley two hundred meters behind the bus station. They will get out and follow Dutch's instructions to filter to the bus by ones and twos. Meanwhile, we'll observe the bus using stand off to insure that they all get on and depart. The code word for that will be *Road Trip*. Once they're gone, we'll link-up with the team at the truck stop.

Upon link-up at the truck stop, we will load the van on the roll back and prep for the return drive to Shadow Wolf Ranch. At that point, everything thus far will have been conducted under the cover of darkness. Remember that Leiko is a back-up driver for the sub rigs.

Luis, Ethan, and Gerard will drive the three sub recovery rigs spaced about two miles apart from each other. Use your monitors with your satellite vehicle beacons. They will show all four of our vehicles in relation to each other at all times. Don't forget that simple way that Gerard showed us to query the distance between any other vehicles.

You all have the documentation in your glove boxes that can be verified by the authorities—to include DOT (Department of Transportation)—that you are hauling movie props for the Spitfire Movie Production Company.

If they call all of the contact numbers and public listings for this company, they will be confirmed by an operator/representative on the other end of the line. We've had this company in place for two months now as a prop and cover story for this very mission.

Then Alex said, "Remember to wear your uniforms and have your company ID in your wallets. If the law wants to open your trailer and look inside, accommodate them. Open the two eight-foot doors on the side. The angle of view on the subs will make it appear more like a prop and somewhat misrepresent its true size.

"Drop a comment like it's for a second *Miami Vice* or *Perfect Storm* movie or something. If anyone should get pulled over, get on the horn ASAP and let everyone know. The code word for that will be *Hassel*. Every one else will find a place to pull off until you're rolling again. Then we'll pick it up and press on once more.

"Leiko and I will drive the roll back as forward recon. We will stay about five miles ahead of your three rig convoy. We'll send word of anything up ahead out of the ordinary."

Then Alex continued reading the OPORD.

ADMIN AND LOGISTICS VEHICLES

Everyone already knows what vehicles they'll be in or operating. Insure they're topped off, a mechanical pre-inspection is completed, and all of the accompanying paperwork is with the vehicle. Remember to conduct a systems check on all of the CDSs (chase defensive systems) on the trucks. Gerard, please make a final coordination with our people at the Spitfire Movie Production Company.

WEAPONS

All vehicles will carry two MP-5's (9 mm, Shoulder Fired Sub-Machine Gun), two Glock-30's (45 Caliber, Semi-Automatic Pistol), and a double load of ammo for each weapon. Ethan, your truck will have your sniper system, with your suppressor, as well. Gerard, your truck will have a SAW (Squad Automatic Weapon–5.56 mm light machine gun, belt or magazine fed) as well. Luis, your truck will have an M-79 (40 mm, Single Shot, Grenade Launcher) as well. My truck will have an M-60A3 (7.62 mm Medium Machine Gun, Belt Fed, Shortened Length) and a Thompson SMG (45 Caliber, Automatic, magazine or drum fed, Sub-Machine Gun) as well.

Ensure that you keep all of this equipment in the concealed compartments that we fabricated into the cabs. And the Chinook; well let's just say they'll have everything else.

Then Luis pleaded, "Come on, Alex, spill it. What does the Chinook have on it?"

Alex gave in, "Okay, Luis, here ya have it. Since we're trying to keep a very low profile on this one, we're keeping all of the weaponry inside, incase someone does see the bird. But anyway, it will have one ramp mounted 50 Cal. and two 7.62 mm mini guns for the crew chiefs/door gunners. We can thank Ethan for getting the three guns for the bird. They were acquired in the middle of the night; don't ask, we won't tell.

"We're taking our four best local guards that are part of our Special Units Team. They will fly the mission but are not privy to the classified details of the mission. They're already trained on these weapon systems in the Chinook. They will simply be reacting to orders from Dutch. Don't worry, you all know that all of the men from our Special Units Team have actually been recruited as community members and have as much at steak as we do. They'll do us proud."

ELECTRONIC EQUIPMENT

Everyone will carry both their personal, issued encrypted cell phones, and encrypted Motorola radios. Each vehicle will also have a pair of NVG's in it. The SR team will each have their own pair of NVG's with the laser range finders and thermal optics built-in. Ethan, you'll also carry your break-down sniper system with you to your hide site.

Remember that each vehicle has its own police scanner, CB (Citizens Band Radio), and built-in concealed encrypted SAT (Satellite) phone as well. I'll be carrying the laptop with Dutch's encrypted video message for the sub crews. The ID badging machine is already pre-staged in the vault in the cracker box room at the house.

MEDICAL TRAUMA KITS

Ensure all your vehicles have a medical trauma kit onboard. The van will carry a back board, C-collar, and oxygen.

CHOW

Everyone will carry enough chow and water, in their rucks, for seventy-two hours.

COMMAND AND SIGNAL
CHAIN OF COMMAND

- Mission Commander = Dutch, in the CH-47 / Back-up = Alex, in the convoy

- Convoy Commander = Alex, in the rollback truck / Back-up = Gerard, in the number 3 semi

- SR TL (Team Leader) = Ethan

- Contact and Recovery TL = Alex

- Dive Team TL = Ethan

- Medical Support = Leiko

SIGNAL

During Convoy; the primary means of commo for non-mission traffic is personal cell. For all mission traffic, first use radios and then the vehicle encrypted SAT phones. On the Ground; Radios first. Encrypted cells replace vehicle SAT phones. From Ground to Air and Air to Ground. All Encrypted!

CALL SIGNS

CH-47 Chinook = Grasshopper
Dutch = Gordy… Hunter = McSquizzy
Rollback Truck = Nomad
Rollback Truck; Alex = Boog … Leiko = Elliot
Semi number 1 = Rabbit … Gerard = Wennie
Semi number 2 = Tortoise … Ethan = Shaw
Semi number 3 = Slug … Luis = O'Toole

CODE WORDS FROM AIR CREW

Play Ball = CH-47 DEPARTS SWR
1st Base = Landed at LZ-1 (Refueled and On Call)
2nd Base = In air to over watch cargo (Guns Hot)
3rd Base = In position for sling-load hook-up (Cargo)
Home Run = Have Cargo–Landed at LZ-2 (Hide-out)
Grand Slam = Take-off from LZ-2 (In-route to Base)
Rained Out = Air Mission Complete IN HANGER AT SWR
FUBAR = MAYDAY–Going down–Broadcast GPS grid

CODE WORDS FROM GROUND CREW

Busted = Mechanical Problems
Pit Bull = Fuel stop/ Head call
Hassle = Pulled-over by Law
Eagle = LP/OP number 1–Ethan in Position
Hawk = LP/OP number 2–Luis in Position
Dazzler = Hostile activity around house/boat dock
Whopper = Link-up w/1st sub complete
Pizza = Gerard bring 1st Semi
Guardian Angel = Chinook take-off and over watch cargo
Wal-Mart = Cargo at PZ–ready for hook-up
Road Trip = Bus with Latinos has departed
Toast = Convoy on road–Returning to base

CHECKPOINTS

Cougar = RON 1st Night
Wolverine = Exit Ramp–Staging truck stop
Wolf = Strip mall bus stop
Badger = Suspended bridge

PHASE LINES

Grizzly = Halfway point for bird
Kodiak = Halfway point for convoy
Polar Bear = Brownsville city limits

TIME LINE

18 May
1700–Operations Order

19 May
0700–Mission prep
0900–Ground team departs SWR
2000–RON (*Cougar*)

20 May
0800–Prep vehicles
0900–Ground team departs RON
2000–Ground team arrives at truck stop (*Wolverine*)
2100–Air team departs SWR (*Play Ball*)
2200–SR teams in-place (*Eagle/Hawk*)

21 May
1800–Alex and Leiko conduct test run on fishing boat

22 May
0400–CH-47 lands at LZ-1 (*1st Base*)
1600–Leiko recovers Ethan from LP/OP 1
1800–Alex and Ethan go fishing

2200–Link-up with the 1st sub (*Whopper*)
2230–Luis arrives from LP/OP 2
2300–Gerard delivers 1st semi (*Pizza*)

23 May
0230–CH-47 in air for cargo over watch (*2nd Base*)
0300–CH-47 link-up with cargo (*3rd Base*)
0330–CH-47 set down at LZ-2 (*Home Run*)
0330–Sub crews depart on bus (*Road Trip*)
0430–Load van on roll back
0500–Convoy on road for SWR (*Toast*)
2100–CH-47 departs LZ-2 for SWR (*Grand Slam*)

24 May
0400–CH-47 arrives at SWR (*Rained Out*)
0500–Convoy arrives at SWR (*TURN IN*)

————————————End of Mission————————————

Alex wrapped it up, "Okay then, if there are no more questions, we'll assemble here in the hangar at 0700 and the convoy will depart at 0900."

Luis blurted out, "I don't like driving; can I join the air crew?"

Alex jokingly replied, "No, Luis, now shut your pie hole and go get some sleep."

Alex said, "We're all going to need it. We've got a very long and exhausting five days ahead of us."

Finally Alex reassured everyone, "Don't worry, people, we've planned the mission. Now we'll stick to the plan. You'll all do fine, and it'll go off without a hitch." Alex couldn't fool himself. He thought, *This kind of mission never goes off without a hitch.*

20 JULY 2010, BROWNSVILLE, TEXAS
MISSION TIME

At 2000, the convoy reached Brownville, Texas. Leiko put the call out over the radio, "*Polar Bear, Polar Bear.*"

Twenty minutes later, the convoy heard her squawk, "*Pit Bull, Pit Bull.*" They were going to top off the rigs and get the last hot meal they'd all have for the next forty-eight hours. Alex didn't want them eating or fueling at the truck stop where they'd be parked for the mission.

Once all the rigs were topped off and everyone's guts were filled, they headed for checkpoint *Wolverine*, the exit Ramp for the truck stop where they would be staging the vehicles before and after each sub was recovered. After arriving and off-loading the van from the connex, Alex, Leiko, Luis, and Ethan headed for the hide sites and house. Gerard stayed with the four trucks.

21 JULY 2010, TEXAS
'OPERATION BARRACUDA'

It was 1800 by the time Alex and Leiko arrived at their fishing spot in the harbor. The pinger beacon that Leiko lowered into the water was fashioned to resemble a depth finder for fishing. It was quite powerful and capable of sending an omni-directional signal out for three miles. It would be quite proficient in directing the sub crews not only into the harbor, but right up to the boat.

They stayed out fishing until 2230 to test all equipment and reinforce their cover story for the actual sub link-up tomorrow night. Plus they actually caught some fish. Leiko caught several nice flounder and Alex got a 69 pound Yellow Snapper. He couldn't have been happier because he really liked Yellow Snapper. He couldn't get enough of it.

22 JULY 2010, TEXAS
'OPERATION BARRACUDA'

At 0415, Alex received the code word *First Base, First Base* over the radio. The CH-47 was now at their primary LZ in the on-call mode; just incase the generals men were a little ahead of schedule. They still had about twenty-two hours on standby, even if everything went as planned. It was a smooth flight there and the refueling operation went off without a hitch. The six-man crew had nothing to do now but pull 2-man security shifts and get some rack; especially for Dutch and Hunter. It would be a non-stop flight for them back to Shadow Wolf Ranch.

At 1545, Leiko took the van and recovered Ethan from his hide site. After arriving at the house Alex asked Ethan if he saw anything out of the ordinary while in his hide site. That's when he informed Alex that he thought the houses next to them were vacant. Alex said, "I believe they are. They're seasonal vacation homes."

"Yeah," Ethan said, "I didn't even see a mouse stirring anywhere."

Alex replied, "All the better for us. We don't need anyone snooping around tonight when three semis roll in here, one after the other."

By 1745 they had all the gear checked out; even the dive gear, just in case. Alex said, "Come here Leiko and give me some sugar." After a big kiss he said, "All right girl, now after you pick-up Luis and get him back here, keep a good eye out around the house; especially after those big rigs start arriving." She said, "I've got it covered Big Daddy."

At 1800, Alex and Ethan arrived at the primo location for their link-up and dropped anchor. Ethan commented, "Man, I'm so hungry I could eat some of Luis's cooking."

Then Alex chimed in with, "Well, ya know, last night I caught a sixty-nine-pound Yellow Snapper, and it was quite tasty."

Ethan asked, "Did ya save some for me?"

"Oh no, man," Alex exclaimed, "I don't share my snapper with anyone. But I'll tell ya this. It was yummy. Any way, there are some tuna sandwiches in the cooler there for ya."

Ethan said, "Oh yeah, thanks for remembering me."

Alex replied, "Any time, brother," as he chuckled."

Ethan asked, "Well, do you think they'll be on time?"

Alex replied, "Give or take a couple of hours, I'd say so. General Sanchez's sub crews have had a good bit of experience navigating to the US in the past ten years."

Then Ethan asked, "Well, do ya think the three crews will go for the deal?"

"Yes, I do," Alex said, "Especially after they hear my pitch. Either way, those subs are coming with us. If they're willing to throw their lives away trying to scuttle them; well that's their choice."

At 2230, the submerged pinger (underwater hydrophone listening amplifier and acoustic alarm) got a hit. Ten minutes later, it got a lock. That meant that they were less than one click (1 kilometer = 1,000 meters/1,093 yards) out. Ten more minutes and they could actually hear where the sub ran into the submerged pinger. While Ethan had his twenty-foot gaff in his hand to give the sub's hull five pre-coordinated taps, Alex was saying the code word *Mucho Dinero* on the submerged microphone.

Five minutes later, the sub surfaced just enough for the cap tain to opened the hatch to talk to Alex. A very skinny Mexican-looking man popped his head out and said, "Are you Senior Bart Simpson?"

Alex said, "*Si, con mucho dinero!*" That concluded their bona fides, and the man was satisfied that they were his intended contacts.

Alex then asked him if he spoke English and he replied, "*Si, senior.*" Then Alex instructed him to button-up, re-submerge, follow his boat to the boat dock, and then pilot his sub inside.

Alex instructed Ethan, "Leave the pinger on incase the other two subs are closer than they should be." They're supposed to have a two hour separation. After tying their boat off to the exterior of the boat dock, Ethan and Alex went inside to prep for the sub, where they found Luis already waiting for them.

"Ethan," Alex directed, "Hit that red button over there and that will automatically open the sub-surface gate that blocks the entrance into the dock. Once the sub is inside, close the gate behind them."

Alex asked Luis, "Did everything look okay just before you left your hide site?" Luis said, "Yes, sir, everything was all quiet."

"Cool beans, man, we don't need any uninvited company tonight," Alex stated.

Once the sub came to a halt, it surfaced and the hatch popped open again. Alex asked the captain if his men were okay. He said they were, just very tired and hungry. They ran out of food three days ago. Alex asked the captain, "How many men do you have in there?"

"Two more, senior."

"Can they speak English?"

"No, senior."

Alex assured him, "Okay, no problem. We're bringing you some food and drink."

Alex got on the house intercom and asked Leiko to put together about thirty tuna sandwiches, a big pot of pork and beans, and a case of Mountain Dew for the crew. Then he instructed her, "Don't bring it here, I'll send Luis in for it."

As only Leiko could say in her spunky tone, "You got it, baby, comin' up!"

Alex said, "Okay, Captain, I want your men to hand us all of the cargo through that bigger cargo hatch and we'll palletize it here on the dock."

"*Si senior*," he replied. They had large wooden crates already build on pallets to make loading quick and painless. They also had an electric fork-lift on station for loading into the connex, once Gerard delivered it.

They were running a little bit behind schedule, so Alex called Gerard on the radio with, "*Pizza, Pizza,*" to bring the first semi. Alex told the captain that Ethan was a medic, and he was going to get into the sub to make a quick medical check of his men.

However, Ethan's primary purpose was to check to see if they had any of their own weapons that were for ensuring that they accomplished their mission of scuttling the sub. Ethan's report was that the men were healthy and armed with pistols and AK-47s.

23 JULY 2010, TEXAS
'OPERATION BARRACUDA'

Alex was pleasantly surprised that it only took them forty minutes to unload the entire cargo of the first sub. Once they were unloaded and Alex verified it by checking the sub from bow to stern, he instructed the captain to have his men come out and have all they could eat and drink. Once the three men were sitting at the small round table that was set up for them, they were chowing down like a pack of wolves.

Alex had noticed earlier that the captain took careful note that the three of them were armed with side arms and SMGs (Sub-Machine Gun) slung over their backs. The crew had their side arms on as well; however, they left their AK's in the sub when they came out to eat.

That's when Alex walked up to them and pitched his deal, "Captain, I have a deal for you. I paid General Sanchez for this sub, and I want to keep it. I will give each of you men fifty thousand dollars to go back and tell him that you sank this sub to the bottom of the ocean in very deep water. He will never know that you did not! Well, what do you say?"

The captain's eye brows drew down as he mean-mugged Alex. Then the three men whispered amongst themselves as they discussed Alex's offer or to formulate a plan of attack. As Alex,

Ethan, and Luis intensely watched them they saw each of their gun hands creeping toward their *pistolas*.

Out of Alex's peripheral vision he saw Ethan starting to inch his primary weapon from his back. Alex looked at Ethan and he nodded not to. Alex used his eyes to direct Ethan's attention under them, under the dock, in the water.

He looked on in disbelief as he saw Leiko under them with a Thompson SMG with suppressor, trained upward on them. He knew as well as Alex did that if they went for their weapons they would be dead before they hit the deck.

After what seemed like an eternity the captain said, "Okay, Senior Bart Simpson, we take D deal. You pay us dollars now!"

Alex said, "Yes, but first we must help unload another sub."

"More sub, what you talk about?" the captain questioned him. "There is no more sub," he said. Alex knew that the general wouldn't have told each sub captain about the other subs as a security measure. After all, that's how Dutch trained the general.

Then Alex assured him, "Yes, Captain, there is another sub. It should be here soon, and we need your help."

The captain responded, "Okay, *senior*, we help you."

"Good," Alex said. "Now you finish eating, okay?"

"*Si, senior*," the captain said as he stuffed a whole sandwich down his suck.

Then Alex instructed Ethan to go out to the boat and check the pinger for the next sub. Then he used his eyes to recall Leiko back into the house until she was needed for the next crew.

Meanwhile, Alex instructed Luis to get into the sub and start sterilizing it of all evidence that a three man crew had just been in it for a month. After all, if they got stopped on the road they can't have anything illegal found in their movie props. While he was at it, Luis sprayed some industrial strength glue inside to post some bogus movie dialog lines to support their cover story, should they get stopped. The glue would also help to cover up the stench of three dude's man funk for a month.

Ethan came back inside the boat dock and informed Alex that there was nothing yet. Alex instructed him, "Okay, go back out and keep monitoring for them. Let me know as soon as you get anything." Ethan said, "Rodger, WILCO" (Will Comply).

Alex said, "Okay Luis, it's up to you and me and our three friends here to get this vessel hoisted in the air for loading. "Hey Captain," Alex said, "We need your help to get this sub in the air. First we need to have your *pistolas*, because you can't take them on the bus with you." The captain replied, "Okay, I take them for you *senior.*" The captain collected their shootin' irons and gave them to Alex. Luis had already secured their AK's that were in the sub.

Gerard popped his head in the door and asked if they were ready for him yet. Alex said, "No, sir, but you can help us getting this sub up and ready for you."

"Well, Luis," Alex commented, "your design worked as well as it could have. We had her hoisted and ready to lower in fifteen minutes without a hitch."

"Okay, Gerard," Alex directed, "back that trailer in here. Watch me in the mirror." Five minutes later, they had that rig perfectly positioned under the sub. Alex said, "Okay, Gerard shut her down." As Gerard cut the semi off, Luis activated the enclosures that closed tightly around the trailer to prevent anyone from seeing in. Luis told Gerard to go ahead and activate his automatic roof retraction system.

Once the trailer roof was retracted, Luis began to slowly lower the sub into the specially modified trailer. Luis said, "That's it. Now you guys install that dunage so it doesn't shift." After Luis's inspection of all of their dunage support work, he said, "Looks good. We're ready to roll."

Alex said, "Great, Gerard, please close your roof." Once the trailer was as tight as a hooker's pants on Saturday night, Gerard and Ethan headed out for the truck stop to swap out rigs; full for empty. Ethan stayed with the trucks at the truck stop to pull security.

Alex had Luis stay with the first crew while he went out to link-up with the second crew. Luis had to retract the temporary floor system so the next sub could be hoisted. On the way out there Alex called Leiko on his encrypted phone and told her what an excellent job she had done covering their asses.

Then he asked her if she had gotten into some dry clothes yet. She said, "Why did you wanna watch?" Alex started laughing and told her to get her mind out of the gutter and on her next task at hand. She asked, "What's that? Covering your back again? That's getting to be a lift time job for me."

Alex said, "Oh well, baby, that's what you signed up for."

Leiko said, "You got that right, Boog."

The second sub transaction went as smoothly as the first; under Leiko's watchful eye and Thompson 45. Now they had two of the three subs in their trucks sitting back at the truck stop and the third sub transaction was halfway completed.

The only difference between this sub crew and the others was that one of the crew had died during their voyage. So now they had to add body disposal of an illegal alien to the mission. Not a task Alex enjoyed, but a necessary one. They had just finished unloading the cargo from the sub and it was time to offer the last crew the deal.

They were lucky that General Sanchez followed Dutch's instructions and insured that all three sub captains spoke English. Alex said to the two men stuffing their faces with the sandwiches and beans, "Captain, I have a deal for you and your friend there. I paid General Sanchez for this sub, and I want to keep it. I will pay you both fifty thousand US dollars to go back and tell him that you sank the sub deep in the cold ocean. After I pay you cash, we'll take you to the bus station to go to Mexico. What do you say, my friend?"

Wearing the same side arms that the other crews wore, the two men slowly stood with their hands on their pistols. The captain said, "No, *senior*, I will not betray the general! He gave us job when we hungry."

Alex, having sensed that they were ready and prepared to draw down on them, tried to have the other two captains convince him that it was best to take the deal.

After the other two captains tried talking to the two hold outs, it only proved to provoke them even more. They were furious that the other two crews had betrayed the general. The captain yelled in English, "I kill the three of you!" Then the two made the fatal mistake of going for their weapons. Before their hog legs cleared leather, Leiko had opened up with her Tommy gun, and she had a fifty round drum in it to boot.

As Alex yelled, "Hit the deck!" He continued to observe the event for the following ten seconds in slow motion.

As the huge 45 caliber bullets ripped through the inch and a quarter wood deck boards beneath them, the wood splinters flew twenty feet in the air. While the men were frozen in place and time, they seemed to dance in-place. Alex noticed the ceiling was quickly turning red with blood and gray matter.

As he watched the injuries sustained by the men from the swarm of bullets, Alex saw each of them take several rounds through the gut, throat, and lower jaws. Although they never fell to the deck until the last bullet had ripped through them, he knew they were both probably dead within the first eight or ten rounds.

Leiko let'em have the whole fifty, just to make sure they couldn't fire on her man. Just like an ever proficient Japanese ninja or samurai, she could be cold and brutal when she had to. This would also serve as a good example to the other six men not to cross Alex's team.

Once the hail of gunfire had subsided, Alex looked for Leiko and she was already gone. She knew that one of her sub-task was to keep her identity from the sub crews. Therefore, she swam sub-surface back to the three foot drain line that led back to the underground tunnel from the boat dock to the house. Alex really meant it whenever he said she's got my back.

After the shock wore off for the crews, Luis, and Gerard, they started standing up, one by one. The first thing Alex said to both captains was that their two countrymen were going to kill them. He wanted to imprint that thought onto their minds and get them thinking in that manner.

Then Alex said, "That's why my man shot them!"

Both captains turned and looked at him and said, *"Si, senior, mucho gracias, mucho gracias!"* Then Alex told them that he would put their bodies in the ground for them. Not just the two dumb ones but the one that died in the sub from Dengue fever as well.

Once Gerard dropped off the third sub with Ethan at the truck stop he returned with the car-hauler and connex. They loaded all the cargo and dunage into the container with just enough room for the fork-lift and cooler to fit. Then Gerard was on his way to the PZ.

Other than the fact that the deck and ceiling were blasted to hell, all evidence of the night's activities in the boat dock was gone; to include the blood and brains. Alex told Luis to come back in a week and repair the decking. They put the three bodies in a huge 200-gallon cooler that they kept in the boat dock. Then they put the cooler in the connex as well. Alex figured if they got busted with the government weapons and ammo, they were going down anyway.

As Gerard was in route to the PZ, Alex was dealing with the two sub crews in the cracker box room. Luis was securing the boat dock and tunnel while Leiko was getting into her disguise in the garage. Most people would have looked at the loss of the three sub crewman as a gain of $150 grand to them. Not Alex, he used that money to enhance the bond of the deal.

Since General Sanchez made all of his sub crews operate completely sterile of any form of ID or documentation, they needed IDs to get across the border. There's one for the history books. Alex bet a lot of American's would applaud him if they know he was paying for and assisting six illegal aliens to leave the US and go to Mexico. Go figure…

Alex said, "Okay men, first I take your picture, then I make you ID, then I pay you each seventy-five thousand US dollars. I pay you the three dead men's money also. Is that okay?" The two captains stood up and said, "Oh, *si senior, mucho gracias.* We say nothing to General Sanchez!"

"I hope not," Alex reminded them. "Remember your two friends in the boat dock!"

Just then, Alex heard the code word *Guardian Angel, Guardian Angel* come over his hand-held radio. Five minutes later he heard his dad respond with, "*Second Base, Second Base.*" While Alex was making the IDs, he played the prerecorded video that Dutch made for the sub crews. They watched as they changed into their new clothes.

Once they were paid Alex had them loaded in the van with Luis covering them with Leiko's concealed Tommy gun. Alex instructed them, "Okay, men, put these mask on for the ride to the bus stop." They looked at the mask and all started giggling like little schoolgirls. Anyway, they didn't refuse. Twenty minutes later, Alex's ground team was dropping them off behind the bus stop. Then Alex said, "Now for thirty minutes of observation to ensure they all get on the bus."

Meanwhile, the CH-47 was flying over watch above Gerard and the illegal cargo that could send all of them to the big house for a long time. Epically with the three stiffs on ice. They really upped the incentive not to get caught! Dutch and Hunter were following the container while flying in black-out drive on NVG's. They were observing a patrol car that was following about two hundred meters behind Gerard. They informed Gerard via encrypted net that the law dog was on his six.

That's when it happened. They all saw the blue lights come on like a flash-bang grenade in a dark room. At that point they knew they had to stop the law man before he got close enough to get a plate number and call it in. The truck was on a long bridge with water on both sides.

The crew didn't want to kill a cop if they didn't have to. Dutch said to Hunter, "Let's get ahead of them and hold a relative position." Once they were in position, Dutch instructed the tail-gunner on the 50 cal. to open-fire. Dutch said, fire in the water, on each side of the patrol car." These men were going to do everything they could not to have to take the life of an innocent American.

Then the gunner went to town. His Ma Duce (50 cal.) was loaded with four-in-one tracers. Therefore, it made a pretty light show. It looked like a dragon breathing down fire; much like Puff/Specter (C-130 gunship with massive amounts of fire power, for ground support).

Dutch's call was on the money. The two burst of fifty rounds on each side of his car persuaded him to break off his pursuit. There was a reason Dutch directed the gunner to fire into the water, to the sides of the car.

There was virtually no physical evidence to support the officer's claim that he was fired upon from a mysterious aircraft from above that he couldn't even see. No impact zone to show and no video footage from his forward recording camera on his dash board. A play well executed.

Fifteen minutes later, Alex heard, "*Wal-Mart, Wal-Mart*" from Gerard, which was followed by, "*Third Base, Third Base*" from Hunter. The cargo was being extracted.

Dutch had already given Alex a heads-up that Gerard would be taking the alternate route back to *Wolverine* to avoid any possible police or road blocks. Even if the cop had no evidence to show them, one thing was for sure. If he called in for back-up because he was under fire, they would send in the Calvary. Another thing was for sure; the cop probably had to change his drawers and clean out his patrol car before his backup arrived.

Ten minutes later Ethan and the air crew hear Leiko announce, " *Road Trip, Road Trip.*" That meant their six rich friends were on the bus and rolling for Mexico. Since Puff the Magic Dragon had spoken, Dutch and Hunter knew they had to hall-ass to LZ-2 and get the bird in the hangar ASAP. The law dogs might very well dispatch a helo to the scene of the crime. It was far too early in the game to be blasting any aircraft out of the sky.

At 0412, everyone heard the call, "*Home Run, Home Run,*" to their relief.

Alex told Leiko that they weren't too far off of schedule. He said, "The only part of this mission I'm concerned with right now is Gerard getting back to the truck stop undetected." His alternate route back to the truck stop was twice as far as his primary route.

Fifteen minutes later, Alex, Leiko, and Luis were arriving at (checkpoint *Wolverine*). Ethan came up to their van and gave Alex a status report. He said, "Everything's quiet here; nothing to report."

Alex said, "Good, the only missing piece of the puzzle now is Gerard. We'll go ahead and stage the trucks and wait for his arrival."

At 0537, Gerard arrived to join the convoy. Alex asked him if he had any troubles. He said, "No, I just drove under the speed limit all the way, as not to attract any unwanted attention."

"All right, good deal," Alex said with anxiety, "We'll load the van on the rollback and get this circus on the road." Alex briefed the ground team, "All right, everyone, remember, you'll drive the three rigs spaced about two miles apart from each other. Use your monitors with your satellite vehicle beacons. Leiko and I will stay about five miles ahead of you. We'll give everyone a heads up if we see anything.

"If you get pulled over, announce it with *Hassle* and the rest of us will pull over, keeping our relative positions in the convoy. Be polite and present all of your paperwork. All right, now you three get into your driver uniforms. As soon as you're dressed, we'll pull out. And keep your tunes low enough so you can hear your radios and phones."

As the sun started rising over the horizon the first vehicle was pulling out onto the interstate, headed north. Leiko got on the horn and announced, "*Toast, Toast,*" over the net.

Alex looked over at Leiko and said, "It should be smooth sailing from here."

She replied, "Time will tell, tall boy. I'll just be happy if I don't have to wack anyone else!"

He comforted her by saying, "Just remember, my dear, they made their choice. You didn't have one. If you hadn't fired when you did, Luis, Ethan, or I might not be here with you now."

She said, "I know you're right, and I'll get over it, in time."

There was no RON on the way back to Shadow Wolf Ranch. Straight through, stopping only for go-juice and head calls. Whenever at a truck stop, they always left guys with the rigs to pull surveillance for counter-surveillance on them. They stuck to the speed limit all the way back without incident.

At 2100, as they were all rolling down the road, they heard, "*Grand Slam, Grand Slam.*"

Leiko looked at Alex with a big grin on her face and yelled, "All right, you go, McSquizzy!"

Alex picked up the mic and acknowledged, "Copy, *Grand Slam.*" That was the call everyone had been waiting for. The CH-47 was in the air and heading north to Shadow Wolf Ranch. A sigh of relief was felt by all. Alex had never received any additional comms from the air crew; therefore, he knew that they had no contact at PZ-2.

About an hour into their flight they were over a very desolate desert area of Texas. That's when Dutch looked at Hunter and announced over the intercom for the crew chief and load master to open the connex, get the stiffs out, and put them in the ground; as Alex put it to the sub captains.

They knew the chances of those dudes ever getting found, let alone IDed, was astronomical. Between the facts that they were illegal aliens from Nicaragua with no IDs, their bodies were being fed through a portable wood chipper strapped to the ramp, and the critters down there were very hungry; they placed their bets.

At 0118, Hunter got on the radio and announced, " *Grizzly, Grizzly,*" over the net.

Ethan said aloud in the cab of his truck, "Halfway home, boys."

Alex thought to himself, *Did you boys DX* (discard /throw away/exchange) *those stiffs yet?*

Luis was thinking about learning to fly that Chinook when they all got back.

24 JULY 2010, COLORADO 'OPERATION BARRACUDA'

At 0513, as the convoy was about sixty miles east of Shadow Wolf Ranch, they heard, "*Rained Out, Rained Out,*" over the radio. The best news they'd heard all night. Half of the mission was over and the other half was coming to a close.

By the time the convoy pulled through the main ACF gate, the air crew already had the Chinook stowed safely, one hundred feet below the surface, in the helo hangar in the bunker, on the Wyoming side. That was their main priority to secure the bird and cargo in the most secure location on Shadow Wolf Ranch; deep below the ground under three blast doors.

Once all three rigs were parked side-by-side, Alex told Luis to go and prep the Colorado side helo hangar for the three sub trucks. Time to lay low for a while after a mission like that. Alex said to Leiko, "This entire team has earned it's self some R & R. Especially you, my little friend!"

AIR SUPPORT

13 AUGUST 2010
SHADOW WOLF RANCH

Alex was having a meeting with everyone in the cracker box. He started off with, "Now that everyone's had a good rest after 'Operation Barracuda', we're ready to get back to work. Since Dutch has just acquired our second Huey from Arkansas, we're ready to start installing all of the new modifications and weapons systems to the birds. Damon, our flight instructor will be here next week. Ethan and Gerard, will that give us enough time to finish all of the helo mods (modifications)?"

They both gave a north-to-south nod with their heads. Alex said, "Good, I would like all birds to be combat ready when we show them to Damon to include Hunter's 500."

Alex asked Leiko, "Is Damon's house all ready for him?"

"Yes, sir," she confirmed, "I even have the kitchen all stocked for him."

"Cool beans," Alex said, "He already knows that he's going to hit the ground running."

Then Alex gave them a rundown on the upcoming training, "We'll start our flight training the day after Damon arrives. Leiko, Gerard, Ethan, and Luis will be starting in the classroom with Damon. Dutch and I will be working with Hunter to get up to snuff on the Chinook. After you four are certified on the small birds, then Damon will train you on the CH-47. You're going to learn it all from combat strafing runs to refueling ops.

"The only thing we won't do is actual auto rotations all the way to the ground. You'll have to settle for watching the video of us in Florida. We can't afford to trash a bird before 'Operation Freedom Run.'"

22 AUGUST 2010
SHADOW WOLF RANCH

Alex was out at the main ACF waiting for Damon to arrive. At about 1630 he saw an old 1960's looking RV chugging up the road. Alex cracked up as it stopped at the outer gate. Once he was in the vehicle trap Alex walked up and greeted Damon with a solid hand shake and a pat on the shoulder.

Alex said, "Boy, I'm surprised you made it at all!"

Damon replied, "Well, a good RV is like a good chopper, ya know they don't make em like this anymore. I'd take a good old Huey over a fancy Blackhawk any day."

While Alex was laughing he said, "I know what ya mean. Let me get in, and I'll direct ya to your new home. My wife, Leiko, is there waiting for us."

Alex made the introductions, "Damon, this is my wife Leiko. Now she's Japanese, not VC (Viet-Cong). Don't be having any flashbacks and freak out on her because she might take you out." The tension was relieved as all three busted out laughing.

Leiko said to Damon, "That's what we need around here, Damon—a good sense of humor. All these dudes around here are too uptight man. We're glad to have you as part of our family." Then she gave Damon some advice, "I've got to go and get dinner ready. This is taco night for all of the single dudes. Feel free to join them at 1800 if you like. That would be a good chance to meet all the boys. I'll leave you gents alone now."

Alex said, "After supper, I'll show you the raptors of Shadow Wolf Ranch. We've made a few upgrades. I think you'll be impressed."

After Leiko's *Taco Bell* night, Dutch and Alex drove Damon through the tunnel to the underground hangar to show him the Hughes 500, one Huey, and the Chinook. They keep the other

Huey in the hangar on the Colorado side. They kept that one unarmed for the ruse of the tour company.

However, they had equipped it with all of the necessary preparations to be able to arm that bird in thirty minutes. To look at it, as it was, no one would ever know that it was a gunship ready to deal out a whole lot a hurt to the right customer.

Hunter was preparing to conduct a hover test on his 500. The hangar was large enough to get a feel for the additional weight of his new arms, thermals, and upgraded avionics.

After eyeballing the three birds Alex asked Damon, "Well, what-da-ya think of our air fleet? The other Huey looks just like this one when it's fully armored up." Damon admitted, "Well, gentlemen, you have quite a formidable air capability here; that's for certain."

He continued, "I'll save most of my questions for later but the main two are; do we have a chopper mechanic and an aviation weapons specialist?"

"Yes, sir, to both of those questions," Alex assured him.

"We have the weapons guru here with us now. Unfortunately, we won't get the air mechanic until we evac our brothers from the east coast."

Alex admitted, "Until then we have Hunter whom is also an auto mechanic and machinist. He practically rebuilt his Hughes 500 himself."

Damon replied, "Well, Alex, I'm no mechanic but between us all we should be able to keep them in the air until we get your tech with us."

Alex said, "Well, that's enough for tonight, Damon. In the morning, we'll show you the classified classroom and flight simulator."

Damon asked, "Are the troops ready to start class tomorrow?"

Alex replied, "Yes, sir, they're chomping at the bit. Wild Kiger horses couldn't keep them away. You'll have four students, and Hunter will be getting Dutch and I up to speed on the Chinook. We'll start class the day after tomorrow. That will give you a day to get settled in and prep for class.

"One last thing, Damon, I'm going to have the guys de-rig all of the weapons systems on the 500 and the 47. The last thing we need is for someone to report to the authorities of see-ing some armed choppers over our property. After everyone is NVG qualified, we'll rearm them for some night weapons quals (qualifications).

"We'll leave this Huey armed and just use the other one for training right now. Now that they've all been equipped with their quick detachable mounting hardware, we can have all four birds rearmed in about five hours."

As Damon raised an eyebrow he said, "That's pretty impres-sive even by my military standards!"

Then Alex said, "It even gets better. I've had Ethan modify every one of our mini guns so they can be mounted on any of our ground vehicles or even carried in a man-pack configuration."

HOMEGROWN FLIGHT SCHOOL

01 SEPTEMBER 2010, SHADOW WOLF RANCH FLIGHT TRAINING

One week into flight training, and everyone was doing well—all accept Luis. Damon said, "Luis is all over the math and theory, but the simulator is kicking his ass. I'm afraid to put him up in a bird right now."

Alex asked Damon, "Would you mind if Hunter worked with him a little bit? Dad does things the unconventional way. Sometimes two different techniques are better than one."

Damon said, "Okay, but keep him in the simulator for a while longer."

Meanwhile, the rest of Damon's students were ready for the air. They were all solid on the simulator. He conducted his flight school air phase just like high school drivers-ed. One flying while the rest of the class rode along and learned from the mistakes of the person in front of them. Ethan was first to bat with Leiko on deck. Gerard volunteered to keep the bench warm.

They were all starting out in the Huey. Damon said there really wasn't much difference between the 500 and a Huey for classes. The big advantage was that he could get all of his students up in the air at once. Besides, if Luis got ready to go up, the 500 would be perfect for him.

Dutch and Alex had a week in the Chinook with Hunter before he started working with Luis. What that meant was when you take two SF dudes and give them an expensive, dangerous, fun toy, and turn them loose, well, boys will be boys.

Alex said, "Hey, Dutch."

"Yeah, brother," Dutch replied.

Alex said, "Let's see what this tub-a-bolts will do from a four-thousand-foot dive."

Dutch looked at him with a big grin and said, "Yeah, man, ya never know. This maneuver could just save our asses on the mission."

As Alex tightened his harness he said, "Yeah, ya never know." The two looked at each other and busted out laughing.

Alex suggested, "Let's get a good gorilla grip on the collectives and sticks. This puppy could be slow pulling up."

Dutch asked, "What are ya looking around for, Alex? Don't worry, Leiko's not up here with her camcorder."

Alex blurted out, "Yeah, man, ya never know about that girl. She turns up when you least expect it."

The maneuver went off without a hitch. The two mad men were able to level the bird off at three-hundred feet AGL (above ground level). After a couple more hours of flying, they headed back to the Wyoming (north) hangar. As they were setting the big cargo hauler down, they saw that the other students were already back.

After they completed their post flight checks and refueled the bird, they headed for the classroom that the simulator was in. They wanted to cheer Luis on. Luis was just finishing up in the simulator and the other guys were in their seats. Once Luis and Hunter sat down, Damon conducted a recap on the days training.

After an hour of questions and answers from the class, Damon said, "Okay, I just have one more question for the day. Can anyone give me the definition of a controlled decent?"

Luis raised his hand and said, "I can give you the definition of one, although I've never physically preformed one in the air."

Damon said, "Okay, squirrel killer, go ahead."

Luis looked at Alex and blurted out, "You called me a bucket mouth. Who told him the squirrel-killer story?"

Alex had a dumbfounded look on his face as he heard Leiko giggling behind him. Alex mumbled, "She strikes again."

Damon told Luis that he was still waiting for an answer. "Okay, okay," then Luis began, "Autorotation is a complex phenomenon involving the balance of opposing aerodynamic forces along the rotor's blades. Because of the rapidly varying airspeeds, mach numbers, and angles of attack encountered by the blades as they traverse a full rotation, analysis of the aerodynamics of the rotor presents a difficult problem in fluid dynamics.

"Generally, however, it is the portion of the blade nearer the hub that provides the aerodynamic force (torque) tending to increase rotational speed and the portion toward the blade tip that provides the majority of the lifting force.

"The aerodynamic drag produced by this outer blade region opposes the torque from the inner region, and thus, the rotor's speed arrives at an equilibrium point at which these torques balance each other.

"The equilibrium speed depends on a number of factors including the speed of the rotor through the air—the angle between the plane in which the blades move and the incoming air and the collective pitch setting of the rotor."

Damon raised his hands and stepped forward, saying, "Okay, all right, enough, Luis. That's a perfect text book answer for the definition of a helo autorotation. Jees, man, you can quote an entire flight manual, but you can't fly a bird without hittin' the barn. Go figure!

"I was looking for a more down to earth, sensible answer in layman's terms. Alex, how about you. Can you give us the correct answer?"

"Yes, sir, I believe so," Alex said. "A controlled decent is one where the bird is brought in vertically, without power, with the pilot in semi-control."

"Very good answer," Damon commended him. Then he said, "One more question for you then, Alex."

As Damon pulled a poncho liner off of the screen in the front of the class room, he sarcastically asked, "Then what the hell is this, and which one of you astronauts came up with the idea?"

They both sat in dismay as they gawked at the large photo of the Chinook in a full delta maneuver toward the earth.

Alex and Dutch both just sat there with their fly catchers wide open. They both thought that they were far enough away from everyone else that no one would see their maneuver. Then one of Leiko's sinister giggles was heard from the rear of the classroom. Then Alex said, "Oh girl, you're going to pay!" Just then, everyone in the room bust out laughing.

Alex looked at Dutch and said, "See, man, I told you. Ya never know about that girl."

08 SEPTEMBER 2010, SHADOW WOLF RANCH FLIGHT TRAINING

Another week of flying and Damon had a pretty good feeling that Ethan, Leiko, and Gerard had a good grasp on all of the basics of flight. Luis had even come a long way working with Hunter. He was finally ready to go up.

Hunter told Damon, "We'll just keep him over the sticks where there are no barns to fly into."

Damon and Hunter started laughing as Luis said, "That's right. Laugh it up, fellas. Which one of you guys is flying with me?"

Then they both looked and pointed at each other and said, "He is."

Damon gathered the class and told them that they're all pretty good on their basic flight training and they're ready to begin night ops and NVG training. He told Luis that he was still working the day shift with Hunter. Luis mumbled, "Yeah, I saw that coming."

Then Damon instructed them, "We'll all take one day off from training. I want everyone to get a good day's sleep of at least eight hours. We're going on reverse schedule training where we'll sleep during the day and train at night.

"This will be some very important training for everyone especially since we'll be conducting all of 'Operation Freedom Run' at night. That means all flying will be done on nods. I want everyone here tomorrow night at 2000. That will give us enough time to conduct our preflight checks before we take-off at 2100."

Four nights later as Damon was speaking to Alex, Dutch, and Hunter, he said, "Well, after three nights of flying on NVG's, they all have a good taste for them. It took Gerard a while to get adjusted to the depth perception issues associated with NVGs, but he's doing okay now. That's a common occurrence with older guys that wear glasses."

Meanwhile, the rest of the class was seated in the classroom waiting for the four guys out in the hangar to come in and brief them on their night's flying. Gerard's pager went off, and after he checked it, he told Leiko he had to check something out in the commo room. Then he scurried off like a mad scientist rushing to check on the results of an evil experiment.

About fifteen minutes later, the four guys in the hangar had come into the classroom and took their seats —-all except Damon. He was standing in the front of the class ready to start with the evenings wrap up. Leiko announced to Damon that Gerard had to check something out in his commo room.

Just then Gerard appeared and said, "Excuse me, Damon, but I have to speak to Alex and Dutch." Alex told Damon to continue with the class and then dismiss the class for the night. Then Alex and Dutch followed Gerard to the commo room.

Alex asked, "Okay, Gerard, what do we have?"

Then Gerard briefed them on his findings, "Well, gentlemen, as you both know, I've programmed this TV and recorder with a channel hopping program that constantly scans all of the news channels for any live reports. Once it locks in on one, it records it and sends my pager an alert with the topic of the report. Well, twenty minutes ago, my pager went off with the subject of—-President Osama signs his national firearms ban into law!"

As Alex and Dutch both took their seats, Alex said, "Okay, sir. Let's see it from the beginning."

11 SEPTEMBER 2010, WASHINGTON, D.C.

The *NBC News Live Report* started off with Brad Wilson announcing that President Osama has just singed a new firearms ban into effect.

It seems as though this firearms ban bill was slipped in at the last moment and hidden within a major energy, unemployment funding, and social security funding bill. Osama signed the bill into effect at 2359 last night.

Dutch stood up and yelled, "Damn it, we all know how this goat rope goes! Congress waits until five minutes before midnight and then adds on an additional item to a major bill that they know must and will pass. After they sign it in at midnight, then it's too late for anyone to challenge it.

"That's how they always award themselves their pay raises, retirements, and every other crooked thing that they give themselves, but they'll screw the average American over in a heartbeat. That way the public and press never even see it coming, let alone have a chance to confront the issue. This is the underhanded Chicago way of conducting national politics, and it's got to stop."

The short three-minute clip of Osama showed him signing the bill into law. Then he stated that he had signed in a new national firearms ban that would be to the benefit of the American people. He also said that he was glad to do it for America's children and grandchildren. Then he added that he expected America's violent crimes to dramatically drop in a very short time because of his bill.

Once Osama was finished speaking, Brad Wilson picked-up by explaining exactly what the new law consisted of. The law went into effect immediately; on September 11th, the nine year anniversary of the terrorist attacks on America.

All Americans accept (active duty military and law enforcement) had 30 days to turn in all of their firearms to their local law enforcement agencies. After those 30 days, any American found in the possession of any type of firearm would face a felony charge and up to twenty years in prison. If convicted, the criminal would also be officially listed by the FBI (Federal Bureau of Investigations), and DHS (Department of Homeland Security), as a domestic terrorist.

This new law permitted federal and state law officials to conduct personal, vehicle, and home searches of anyone whom they had reason to suspect of having a firearm.

"Alex said, "I knew Osama would target personally owned weapons sooner or later but I didn't think he would ever conduct such a bold or absolute DA (Direct Actions–offensive operations) mission. I always assumed he would try it little by little and just keep chipping away at our rights."

Gerard asked if the Supreme Court would try to overrule him. Alex replied, "I'm sure they will. They'll have no choice. The American outcry will be so great that they will be afraid not to. The only thing is that Osama owns four of the judges now since he appointed them. I saw him stacking the deck with his ringers since he took office."

Dutch said, "It will be an interesting couple of months down the road now."

"You've got that right, brother," Alex agreed. Then Alex said, "Hey, Gerard, I'm sure there will be a lot more live news broadcast in the next couple of weeks. Make sure that this automated alert system of yours is operating at peak proficiency."

"Yes, sir, I was just thinking the same thing."

Alex stretched he suggested that they call it a night. Then he said, "I'll tell everyone tomorrow night what has happened. I'm sure we'll talk about it for an hour or so before everyone's ready to start flying."

Dutch said, "Yeah, good luck with that time frame with Ethan and Leiko. They're going to go ballistic!"

Alex replied, "Well, I'll break it to Leiko tonight. On second thought —-I'll wait until in class. I'd like to get some sleep before we fly all night." They all started chuckling.

The next evening, as the team was assembled in the underground classroom for their flight brief, Alex told them of the underhanded blow delivered by Osama's administration. Later, Alex said in an authoritative voice, "Okay, Ethan, we've all listened to you for fifteen minutes now enough! We feel the same way about this issue as you do. We just have a little more restraint in containing our feelings on it."

Alex then stated, "First of all we don't know yet if this is going to affect corporate security types or not. Secondly, the public outcry is going to be so loud and outspoken on this issue that we know the Supreme Court is going to have to get involved. Lastly, the stronger state governments are going to fight this tooth and nail. Let's just sit back for now and see what happens."

Alex turned the platform over to Damon for the nights training instructions.

"Okay, people, you're all looking good on your NOD's so far and coming along nicely. One more week of flying on NODs, and you'll be certified on them. Then Gerard, Ethan, and Leiko will be ready to transition to the Chinook. Luis is still playing catch up with Hunter. Hopefully when you guys are finishing up on NOD's, Luis will be ready to get started on them."

✳ ✳ ✳

A week later, Damon spoke to Alex, Dutch, and Hunter in the hangar and gave them his take on the class. "Alex, you and Dutch are good to go on everything. Leiko, Gerard, and Ethan are ready for the CH-47, and Luis is coming along nicely and ready for NODs. They're actually a fast-learning bunch of pilots. They'll all do just fine on the mission. Alex, have you decided who will fly what on the mission yet?"

"Yes, sir," Alex said, "I have. I actually just finished this list today. Let's take a look at it." Then Alex proceeded to read it to them.

1. Huey Gunship number 1: Pilot = Damon; copilot = Luis

2. Huey Gunship number 2: Pilot = Dutch; copilot = Gerard

3. CH-47 Gunship: Pilot = Hunter; copilot = Leiko

4. Hughes 500: Pilot = Alex; copilot = Ethan

5. All gunners and crew chiefs would come from our community's Special Units Team. They would consist as follows:

6. Huey Gunship number 1: one M-79 gunner and one sniper

7. Huey Gunship number 2: one M-79 gunner and one sniper

8. CH-47 Gunship: one crew chief and one loadmaster one 50 cal. ramp gunner one M-79 gunner and one sniper

Alex asked Damon, "Well, how do you think I've matched the pilots, skills, and birds?"

"I think you're right on the money," Damon replied.

Then Alex said, "Cool. Well, here's why I placed everyone in the aircraft I did." Then he elaborated, "I put our weakest pilot Luis with our strongest pilot Damon. I put a nonmilitary guy with an SF vet—Gerard with Dutch. I put our EMT/Nurse Leiko with our biggest gunship/med-evac bird as a back up. I put our only formally trained CH-47 pilot Hunter in the Chinook.

"And finally, I put the mission commander, myself, in the one bird that I can go wherever I need to go without drawing the major air assets from the squadron. When things get hairy and I'm tied up with barking out commands, Ethan can take up my slack pulling the trigger."

Dutch chimed in, "Yeah, I'm sure he won't have a problem working out his rage that way epically after that firearms ban." "Don't worry," Alex said, "I'll unleash him when I need to!"

25 SEPTEMBER 2010
SHADOW WOLF RANCH

Damon addressed the class, "Congratulations, everyone, you're all certified on the Hughes 500, UH-1H Huey, CH-47 Chinook, and of course, while on NODs." Then Damon went on to say that there would be no official diplomas handed out, but there would be a party tonight at his house to celebrate.

13 OCTOBER 2010
WASHINGTON, D.C.

Due to the massive scale of protest at many federal and state buildings throughout the country, the Supreme Court had announced that it would convene to determine weather President Osama's national weapons ban was constitutional or not. If they judged it not to be, it would be struck down. However, if they upheld it, it would go into effect immediately upon their ruling. No personal weapons would have to be turned in unless the Supreme Court upheld Osama's ban.

Not only did millions of angered Americans take to the streets of large cities such as Washington, Boston, Atlanta, Huston, Denver, and Seattle, but they were also showing their support in small towns across America.

It was quite clear; a lot of Americans opposed the national firearms ban and they were showing it to the government by the millions. All eyes were on the Supreme Court and waiting for their ruling on that loaded issue.

Meanwhile, Alex was busy celebrating his birthday when his sister Brook called to wish him a happy birthday. They chit-chatted for a while and then she said, "I hope you have as happy a retired life as you had as a boy in the mountains."

He assured her that he would, and they hung up. That made Alex start to reminisce about his youth.

At age ten on his birthday, he had taken his first white tail buck—a large twelve pointer. His first black bear came at age thirteen, a 580 lb. brute. He was quite proficient and versatile with the different weapons that his dad, Hunter had taught him—from pistols, rifles, shotguns, and bows, to edged weapons. There was also no animal that he couldn't trap.

Several months after he took that black bear, his parents had a third child. That one was a girl named Brook. As she grew, Alex and her were very close. He was proud to have a little sister to teach and protect.

Alex was also quick to learn construction skills from his father in his small construction company. By age fifteen, Alex was a skilled woodsman and carpenter. Given the time and material, he possessed the skills to construct an entire house from scratch. With those advanced skills, he informed his parents that for his junior-senior year in school, he wanted to attend the Monongalia County vo-tec (Joint Vocational School) and take carpentry. They supported him with enthusiasm.

For the next two years, Alex excelled to the top of his twenty-man class. In his senior year, he was even elected class president. He was a natural at building things, not just wood, but anything. Alex also picked up the other trades required to complete a house. The only reason he really went to vo-tec was to learn all of the formal terms and get that diploma/certificate.

Halfway through his senior year, he enlisted in the United States Army with the full support of his parents. As Alex considered his likes and skills for an army profession, he decided on the army's Airborne Rangers. With all of his mountaineering and weapons skills, along with the fact of always being outdoors, it sounded like it was right up his alley.

As Alex sat at his kitchen table, looking at the cake that Leiko had made him, all of the sudden, it exploded and covered him. That brought him back to reality and back to celebrating his birthday with Leiko and all of the crew. That was indeed a good birthday.

07 DECEMBER 2010
WASHINGTON, D.C.

The Supreme Court announced its decision on the national gun ban. Gerard had enough time to call Alex and Dutch into the commo room before the live report began on *NBC*. The report began with Brad Wilson announcing the Supreme Court's ruling. The screen also showed Osama making a statement for the record on his historical ruling.

It turned out that it was a very close ruling. In fact it was split four to four between the justices. The Supreme Justice had to break the deadlock. It seemed that the judges that Osama had appointed since he had been in office had all voted for the ban, and the four that had seniority voted against it. Nonetheless, the deed was done and America would pay the price; and it would be dear.

Their ruling upheld President Osama's signing of the national gun ban. However, they attached an unwavering condition to this bill. The bill and the public had 180 days before it would go into affect. President Osama could take it or leave it. He wanted to take American's teeth away from them so badly that he took the deal. D-Day for all legal American gun owners would come on June 7, 2011.

Dutch looked at Alex and asked him what Clint Stanley had said about it. Alex then went over the details, "Well, it's like this, fellas. Any corporation that has a net worth of twenty-five million or more and has a security division with weapons can keep them as long as they pay the government a five hundred thousand dollars per year tax. Any company that doesn't pay the tax by 1

January 2011 will have the ATF pounding on their door. We're going to pay the tax for 2011 and see what happens after that. I have a feeling that it won't matter much after that."

14 DECEMBER 2010
THE ALAMO, TEXAS

In a *CBS* live news brief, the Governors of Texas, Oklahoma, Colorado, and Montana had announced that their four states had succeeded from the union by the authority of their state constitutions. At the conclusion of each governor's speech and conformation that his state had indeed voted unanimously to detach its self from the United States federal government, Governor Rich Pevey from Texas made this statement:

> These four states are in accord when I say that we can no longer stand idly by and be a part of a federal government that does not uphold our nation's Constitution, of which the Second Amendment is part of—- the right of every American to keep and bear arms!
>
> We have stood by and watched the morals and ethics of this great nation fall by the wayside. We are also in one accord when we say that this Osama nation and administration has the explicit agenda of bringing this great nation down, and we will no longer be a part of it.
>
> We are holding this press conference and standing our ground here in the Alamo, this historical battlefield and sacred ground, just as our forefathers did when they had no other choice. May God bless and protect this great nation that he has watched over for so many years. We—Texas, Oklahoma, Colorado, and Montana—extend an open hand to any other state that is tired of this tyranny and wishes to join us as truly Free Americans. God bless Texas!

"Wow," Alex said, "that Governor Pevey sure is fired up!"

Dutch said, "Yeah, it's about time someone with some power and balls put his foot down."

Gerard asked Alex what he thought was going to happen next. This was Alex's take on it, "Well, I would imagine that Congress will meet to decide if they're going to let them succeed. They know that if they don't nip this in the butt now, they may have more states joining them very soon.

"There are a ton of questions to be answered now, such as military assets, financial assets, federal lands, national security, and so on. Also remember, Texas has two living former presidents residing in that enormous state.

"However, my friends, the most pressing question for us right now is: how will the fact that half of our property is in the free America affect us now? I'll get Clint on that issue ASAP!"

Then Dutch said, "This will indeed be an interesting and possibly volatile couple of months to follow. Let's call a community meeting to inform everyone of what's happening."

Alex seconded the motion.

CONGRESS CONVENES

15 DECEMBER 2010
WASHINGTON, D.C.

Congress ordered an emergency session the day after Governor Pevey announced a four state secession from the union. Their first two pressing questions were; could they stop them from seceding and what would they do if they couldn't stop them?

After hours of discussion it was decided that it would take days of deliberation to answer the first question. Meanwhile, they were all in agreement on one issue. They voted unanimously that they had to close all military bases in those states until they had a solid plan. They didn't want any of their military units thinking that they actually belonged to the states they were in. Congress ordered DOD (Department of Defense) to lock-down all military bases in Texas, Oklahoma, Colorado, and Montana, ASAP.

As far as the second question went; that would even take longer. The government's major concern was over Texas because it was so large and housed so many major assets. She contained six AFB (Air Force bases), three Army forts, one Army depot, and four Navel bases.

Colorado was second with three Air Force Bases, NORAD (North American Aerospace Defense Command inside Cheyenne Mountain, the Rockies), The Air Force Academy, and Fort Carson. Oklahoma was third with three Air Force bases, one Army fort, and two Coast Guard training facilities. Lastly, Montana had two Army forts, one Air Force base, two Air Force stations, and three Mini-MUTES (AN/MST-T1 (V) radar sites. None the less, it was a large percentage of America's military might and the federal government wasn't about to loose it to four states.

The orders sent out to all of the bases from DOD via secure sat comm. (Secure Satellite Communications (Encrypted / Decrypted) were short and to the point. One hunfred percent lockdown until further notice. No military personnel out/no civilian personnel in!

09 JANUARY 2011
WASHINGTON, D.C.

Three weeks later, Congress had come to the conclusion that the federal government had no legal right to stop any state from seceding from the union (the United States). At the same time, they concluded that any state that secedes from the federal government had no right to any federal aid or property.

Therefore, they had mandated a relocation plan of all federal installations in Texas, Oklahoma, Colorado, and Montana to be moved to nearby states. One week after the four states were notified of the new federal law, they sent their state senators back to Washington with this, their own message.

> We Texas, Oklahoma, Colorado, and Montana are not now a part of your federal government. Therefore, we no longer fall under the yoke of your laws or rulings. All military personnel are free to depart the military bases of Free America ASAP. However, all real property and military equipment in these states are the property of these Free American States.
>
> Texas is also proclaiming that it's territorial and EEZ (Exclusive Economic Zone) waters consist of two hundred miles off shore and will be patrolled by our vessels to prevent unauthorized craft from entering our waters. We will not tolerate any unauthorized entry of our EEZ or our military bases.

Needless to say, that message created a whirlwind on all of Capitol Hill. The entire Osama administration was foaming at the mouth. They began to plot and scheme in secrecy upon those that they would do harm.

As that transpired in Washington, the Free States of America were making deals of their own. The four states voted and agreed that they would offer all of the military personnel on their bases a one time offer.

Any military member and his family could stay on and serve the state they were in. There would be no rotating to a non-free State as part of their regular military duty anymore. Therefore, anyone that stayed would pretty much be calling one of those states their permanent home until they established a rotation plan for them within the Free States. Anyone whom didn't want that deal would be sent back to wherever Washington wanted them to be sent.

Since the military had pretty much always done what was right and just anyway, a lot of the airmen, soldiers, sailors, marines, and coast guard agreed with what the Free States were doing by breaking off from Osama's military unfriendly administration.

Once it was all tallied up, about one third of all the military in those four states accepted the offer from the Free States. The other two thirds were sent out to various other military bases throughout the country.

The Free States started an immediate military enlistment campaign to fill a lot of empty slots for troops to man equipment. The Free States started basic and AIT (Advanced individual training) training bases for the five services. Texas would have the navy, marines, and coast guard since they had the coast line. Oklahoma would have the army at Fort Sill. Colorado would have the Air Force at the Air Force Academy and Peterson AFB, in Colorado Springs.

There was much to be done, for the officials of the Free States were sure Osama's cronies wouldn't take this lying down as was their usual positions.

25 JANUARY 2011
SHADOW WOLF RANCH

At 0800 Alex was having a classified meeting about everything that had happened since the Supreme Court announced it's ruling on the firearms ban. Alex began with, "Well, people, here's the jist of it. I don't think Osama and DOD are going to let the Free States just keep all of their military hardware. Texas really laid the law down to Congress on what they weren't going to tolerate and Governor Pevey is just mad enough to make good on it."

Gerard asked, "What has Clint found out about the laws, since our property is split within the two?"

Alex proceeded to tell them where they stood, "Well, sir, he said it shouldn't affect us until one side or the other writes some new laws. I'll tell ya people, I think Osama's going to have a lot more to worry about than just these four states.

"Since his firearms ban went into effect, there are going to be a lot more Americans who are going to be willing to do more than just peaceful protesting. I think they'll start using those firearms to keep them.

"The unemployment rate is up to twenty-eight percent now. Americans are fed up with Osama's crap and the way our taxes are going to frivolous spending and politician's pockets while people are homeless and starving. I think the riots we saw eight months ago in Washington will pale in comparison to those soon to come.

"Lastly, I believe there will be more states to succeed from the union. When they do, the government will really start sweating it because they will finally believe that another civil war or revolution could very well happen again. That's the last thing that they want to happen."

"Okay," Alex asked, "who has anything to add or comment on?" Luis raised his hand.

Alex said, "Go ahead Luis," gesturing with his hand.

Luis stated, "Well, if either one of our states restricts state border movement, we can always move unimpeded through our underground tunnel."

Alex said, "Yes, sir, that's true, and thank you for finishing that project. We're looking good in that respect."

Gerard commented that he had noticed a lot of news coverage on the United States, coming in from all over the world. Alex said, "Yes, sir, I expect this is a pretty big shock to the rest of the world that this is all happening in America—the world's most fair and kind super power to ever exists."

"Okay, folks," Alex went on, "I believe the time is soon coming when violent actions will ensue, and we need to be ready to conduct 'Operation Freedom Run'. Now that all of our gunships but one are re-armed, I'd like them loaded with all of our mission equipment and all the ammo they can carry. This national situation could go south in a heartbeat.

"We'll have an aircraft inspection, ammo count, and equipment accountability inspection tomorrow at 0900. Gerard, please stay on those news broadcast. Anything could break out at any time."

"Yes, sir, I'm on it," he replied.

✳ ✳ ✳

The next day at 1330, Alex, Damon, and Dutch had finished up the inspection.

"Damon, you go first concerning the aircraft."

"All right, Alex," Damon replied. "Okay, guys, everything looks good with the birds. Ethan, I want you to install an eight-inch by eight-inch by quarter-inch steel plate on all of the birds. I'll show you the exact location on each bird. Attached to this plate will be two white smoke grenades with a pilot operated activation switch. This is a sneaky little trick I learned in Nam.

"If the pilot can make the enemy believe he has inflicted significant damage to his bird, he will gain the advantage. When the enemy believes this, it gives him overconfidence and can give you the few extra seconds you need to take advantage of your ruse.

"For instance, if you can break his line of sight while he thinks you're going down, you can do a 180 and ambush him when he follows you in. If you're low to the ground, you can always hit your smoke and auto-rotate to the ground. The shooter now thinks that he's shot you down. Well, guess what, my friends, all of your weaponry still works on the ground, and you can still fly again after firing them up.

"The smoke just gives you some options that you wouldn't otherwise have unless you really are hit. Then it sucks to be you."

Then Damon turned the platform back over to Alex. Alex addresses Ethan, "I have one task for you as well on the Chinook. Please tape off two areas on the floor that will be reserved for the two ATVs for Mom and Sarah during the Pennsylvania and West Virginia extractions."

"Yes, sir," he said, "consider it done."

Then Alex asked, "Dutch, do you have anything to put out?"

He said, "Just a couple of things, Alex." Everyone gave their attention to Dutch as he started speaking, "Since the aircraft and equipment will be ready by COB today, everyone's personal equipment also needs to be ready to go on a moment's notice. Consider yourselves all on a one-hour recall status. Certain circumstances could force us to kick off 'Operation Freedom Run' in a mater of hours.

"Even though there's extra food and water on all of the birds, I still want everyone to carry enough food and water in your rucks for five days. Remember your E & E kits, NODs, and commo gear.

"Tonight Alex, Damon, and I are going to start plotting our E & E corridors and RODs (rest over day stop) for the mission. Luis and Hunter, would you please take one last look at those six E & E bikes on the CH-47. I know they're full of fuel, but I want to ensure they're running fine. That's all I've got, Alex."

03 FEBRUARY 2011
SHADOW WOLF RANCH

It was 1530, and Alex was on a vehicular patrol with his guard force on the Wyoming side. They were traveling about 50 mph on the inner perimeter road in three of their FAVs (fast attack vehicles). As Alex discussed perimeter security over the headset with the captain of the day shift, the captain piloted the second vehicle that they're both in.

Alex, Dutch, and Ethan all took frequent active rolls in property patrols with the community's guard force. They had eighteen FAVs for this purpose, not to mention a Huey and Hughes 500 when needed. The FAVs had all the necessary equipment for patrolling. Such as a 50 cal, an M-60A3, two AT-4s (An 84-mm unguided, portable, single-shot recoilless smoothbore weapon), encrypted and sat comm. radios, an ECM (Electronic Counter Measures to jam all radio frequencies of the enemy) unit, and GPS systems. They even had portable, miniature air drones at their disposal if needed.

The unarmed Huey on the Colorado side was always kept in the surface hangar. Just incase the authorities ever showed up wanting to see their company registered Huey. That way it was always on standby and could be called up any time the perimeter patrols needed an intimidating presence in the sky. If they encountered a serious threat, they would bring out the armed raptors.

While on patrol, Alex always had his secure comms on so he could stay in contact with HQ. While he was talking with the captain, he got one of those calls from Gerard. "Yes, sir," Alex asked, "what-da-ya got?"

Gerard said, "You were correct about those riots. They've begun in several major cities and Osama's calling out the National Guard. You better come and check it out when ya get back here."

Alex replied, "Okay, I should be there by 2100 tonight. Please have Dutch, Damon, and Hunter there as well. I'll see ya then, out here."

When Alex came into the commo room, the guys were sitting there, waiting for him. Gerard said, "Okay, let's roll the footage." He recorded the live report on *FOX News*. The brief started off with Caleb Keenhammer announcing huge riots in several major cities throughout America.

Since Osama had done nothing to create all of the new jobs that he promised Americans to get elected, the US unemployment rate had reached 28.7 percent, an all-time high in America's history. The only new jobs that he did create were to make the federal government larger to spend more money.

Gerard commented that he liked that Keenhammer dude since he replaced Brant Hummer as Fox's news anchor. Alex said, "Yeah, when he speaks, everyone listens. They know he says it like it is and remains unbiased on whatever subject he's speaking about. Maybe he ought to run for president?"

The news cast went on to report that there were several large protest with rioting going on in the cities of Chicago, Cincinnati, New York, Washington D.C., Atlanta, Miami, and New Orleans. The report switched to the White House where President Osama was announcing that he was calling out the National Guard in all of the major cities that were rioting and that he was imposing martial law; along with a 9 p.m. to 5 a.m. curfew in those cities. Then he addressed America.

> My fellow, Americans, I know that times are tough right now, and a lot of you are hurting out there. During, these tough times, we've all had to tighten our belts and sacrifice a little. Violence is not the answer for our nation's unemployment problem.
>
> Please stop your rioting and go home. I am about to unveil my new Jobs for America program next week, and we will be able to put some of you back to work again.

In this new program we have also extended the national unemployment benefits up to 365 days.

This major lawlessness cannot be tolerated in our country. I have activated the National Guard and authorized martial law in the cities where this rioting is taking place. I have also emplaced a curfew that is from the hours of 9 p.m. to 5 a.m., until further notice.

Anyone caught out during these hours that can not prove to the authorities that they are going to or coming from work will be arrested and prosecuted to the fullest extent of the law.

Hang in there, America, and times will get better. It is my belief that we will pull through this recession and be stronger Americans for it. I thank you for your time and patients with our economy. Good night, America.

Alex said, "Well, that was one motivational speech from our comrade-in-chief. It sounds like he has everything under control."

Dutch chimed in with, "Yeah, he'd like to think so. That douche bag won't even admit that we're in a full-blown depression, not a recession as he'd like everyone to believe."

07 FEBRUARY 2011
EASTERN AMERICA

After forty-eight hours of fighting with protesters in seven major cities, the National Guard had finally defused the rebellion. Once it was all sorted out, the authorities all sent their body counts to Washington.

It turns out that 539 American civilians and 127 National Guardsmen were killed in the fighting. It was estimated that there were billions of dollars in damages as well. The live news coverage of some of the shootings only added fuel to the fire.

Congress had stated that they wanted a full investigation into the entire rebellion, as they called it. The Governors of Texas, Oklahoma, Colorado, and Montana, as well as several other

Governors of western states held a live news conference. They went on record as publicly and officially demanding the impeachment of President Osama for authorizing military force against American civilians.

One week later there were televised funerals from all of the cities involved in the protest. There were men, women, and children, as well as guardsmen killed in the fighting. This national atrocity would haunt Americans for generations to come. This was even harder to swallow than the nearly three thousand Americans killed during 9/11, because it was our own government that did the killing.

01 APRIL 2011
WASHINGTON, D.C.

At a live press release from the White House, they were about to announced the findings from the congressional investigation on the national riots. Before the briefing began, it was announced that there would be no questions taken at its conclusion.

The White House press secretary announced that President Osama had been in his full and legal right as president and commander-in-chief when he ordered the National Guard to quell the extremely violent, nationwide riots on February 3.

Then he continued,

> The president deeply regrets that he had to make the decision which coast 666 Americans their lives. However, a democracy must exist in a peaceful harmony within itself. Therefore, a president is from time to time forced to become the peacekeeper for the sake of the nation. Even though lives were lost, this nation as a whole will be better in the long run.
>
> President Osama feels deep remorse about each and every American that died in this unlawful uprising. However, if he had to make the same call again to preserve the peace in the streets of America, he would give that order!

Finally, for those whom participated in the violence, bury your dead, rebuild your lives, but do not attempt this unlawful behavior again. The outcome will be much worse the next time. Thank you, and good night, America."

Alex said, "Damn, do you believe that speech? It might as well come from Osama's lips himself. And he doesn't even have the balls to face America, so he pawns that crap off on his press flunkey."

Hunter said, "He's right about one thing. Next time, the outcome will be much worse, for the government!"

"Well, Dutch," Alex asked, "what's your take on all this?"

He said, "I think America has had enough and they're ready to fight back. And I think that Osama has something up his sleeve, and no one's going to like it."

Alex said, "I agree. I still don't think they're going to sit by and let the Free States keep all of their military hardware. That poses too much of a threat to them."

Dutch asked, "What do you think, Damon?"

"I think we should be ready to fly on a moments notice." Everyone just stood there waiting for him to expound on his statement, but he just stood there, looking at us. Then Leiko said, "Is that it, man? Is that all you got?" Everyone cracked up. They could always depend on her to break the tension.

COVERT OPS

15 APRIL 2011
WHITE HOUSE CABINET ROOM

President Osama, Vice President Binder, National Security Advisor Dolan, Secretary of Defense Gants, and the Joint Chiefs of Staff held a classified meeting to formulate a plan to recover one of their most valuable military assets that just happens to be in Texas.

One of only two such types of units. The 7th Bomb Wing at Dyess AFB, Abilene, Texas. This unit housed thirty-six, one half of America's B-1 Bombers (B-1B Lancer; USAF, supersonic, four-engine, variable-sweep wing, long range strategic bomber with a crew of four).

Even though that aircraft was twenty-five years old, it had been continually updated with the latest technology to keep it the most sophisticated strategic bomber in the world, after the B-2 Stealth bomber of course. The men in that secure briefing room thought that asset was worth fighting for, should it come to that.

President Osama opened the meeting by taking the floor. "Gentlemen, we can't afford to let Texas keep these bombers in their possession any longer. First of all, it's a weapons platform that they could use against us if they ever choose to. And we all know that Governor Pevey is just crazy enough to do it, if he feels threatened.

"We can't rely on Texas to launch the bombers in America's defense if another nation were to attack us, especially if they hit the east coast first!"

Mr. Binder and Gants stated for the record that they concurred with the president. Then the COS (Chief-of-staff) for the navy asked how they would go about getting them out of Texas. The admiral added, "The bomber pilots that choose to stay in Texas won't fly them out for us."

Then Osama replied, "The army has come up with a plan for that, Admiral." The president then extended an open hand toward the army for his brief.

The COS of the army took the floor and instructed everyone to open their classified folders and he began,

> Gentlemen, I am about to propose a viable plan to you that can succeed if it is given the required support needed from all of the services.
>
> We will fly the 1/75th Ranger Battalion from Hunter Army Airfield, Savannah, Georgia, in and conduct a combat jump out of ten C-17s (Globemaster III; a large military transport aircraft used for rapid strategic airlift of troops and cargo) from 500 feet AGL.
>
> Gentlemen, that is nearly a thousand storm troopers securing the target. Once on the ground they will conduct an airfield takedown—their specialty. That means they will control the entire airfield section of Dyess Air Force Base's runway, tower and the entire perimeter surrounding the tarmac areas that the bombers and fighters are staged on.
>
> Please refer to the current, detailed overhead photo of the airstrip that was provided by our NASA (National Aeronautics and Space Administration) boys in orbit. This photo is just three hours old.

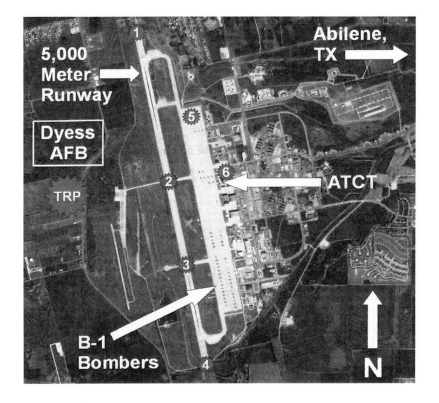

Two hours prior to the rangers hitting the ground, a small unit of Delta Force (a US Army Special Operations force that specializes in counterterrorism and special DA missions) and CCT (Air Force Combat Air Traffic Controllers), from Fort Bragg, North Carolina, will take control of the ATCT (Air Traffic Control Tower) and the RAPCON (Air Force base Radar Approach Control) room.

This team will INFIL by means of self-insertion and clandestine pre-staging. This way, we'll control the tower and their entire radar systems one hour prior to the rangers jumping in. This along with the fact that our C-17s will be flying NOE, they'll never see us coming.

There are thirty-six F-15 (E–Strike Eagle; USAF, supersonic, single seat, twin engine, all weather, tactical fighter) fighters staged on the tarmac along with the thirty-six B1s. Their purpose is to fly escort for the bombers to ensure their safety and completion of their mission.

As soon as the rangers have secured their target, two C-5s (M–Super Galaxie; United States' largest cargo transport plane designed to provide strategic airlift for deployment and supply of combat troops) will land. One with the B-1 and F-15 crews and the other will carry four, ready to fly, Apache gunships (AH-64 Longbow; a four-blade twin-engine attack helicopter with a tandem cockpit for a two-man crew, 30mm chain-gun, 2.75 inch rockets, and Hellfire misslies) for ground and air support.

The C-5 can normally carry six Apaches, if all of their main rotors are off. However, if we take off only two blades per bird, we can fit four birds that can be ready to fly thirty minutes after they're pushed onto the tarmac. We have perfected a special procedure for this quick refit. It's been tested and tried.

Each Apache will have a specific target to protect—one at each end of the runway to keep it open, one on the tarmac to protect the fighters, bombers, and C-5s, until they're all airborne, and lastly, one to hold the control tower.

Once all of the bombers and fighters are in the air, all of our troops will EXFIL on the C-5s. We'll destroy the four Apaches on the air strip at the end of the mission, so we can free-up the C-5 for troops. CCT will call in fire, on the Apaches, from Spectre (AC-130H Pave Spectre; a C-130 gunship with massive amounts of fire power for ground support) once they're in the air.

Each B-1 and F-15 air crew will carry a SAW from the C-5 to their designated aircraft. The bomber crews will take theirs with them and the fighter crews will ditch theirs on the tarmac as they load. They'll melt nicely with a thermite grenade attached to them. We will also have two AC-130H Spectre gunships orbiting for ground support.

The CCT in the control tower will have the best vantage point over the entire airfield. They will be the FOs (Forward Observers that call in fire support from sea, air, or land) for the Spectres. This, gentlemen, will give us the adequate fire support that we'll need if Texas decides to get nasty and mount an offensive.

We'll get all of the fighters in the air first so they can provide fire support while the bombers are getting in the air. Once in the air we'll fly the bombers to Dover Air Force Base in Delaware. That will be their new home.

"Gentlemen," the general said, "that concludes my briefing of 'Operation Condor Repo'. What are your questions?" The COS for the Air Force commented that he had nothing since he helped the army plan the mission, because it was so aircraft dependent.

The COS for the navy then stated that they could provide fire support and fighters from off of the coast if needed. The army then said, "Noted, thank you, sir." Then the COS for the marine corp stated that he thought they have it pretty well covered and he didn't think that they'd need the Corp in this one. Then he mumbled, "I don't want my boys firing on other Americans anyway."

The navy COS then asked, "How do you expect to get enough soldiers and airmen to participate in this mission in the first place? I mean, firing on your fellow countrymen is a line that a lot of men won't cross, no matter the reason."

Then the CJCS (chairman of the joint-chiefs-of-staff) General Demsley addressed the room, "Men, none of you here likes this mission any less than I do. However, it is a mission that must be done. God willing, we'll be able to pull it off without a shot being fired, though I fear not!

"Every one of these soldiers and airmen on this mission is already trained and capable of conducting it without any further training. Therefore, we'll assemble the men with the necessary equipment needed to perform the mission, launch them in the air and then have each aircraft commander brief each bird. We'll send them the mission via secure encrypted text and print one copy for each aircraft commander.

We're going to brief the rangers that they are going to jump into Fort Lewis, Washington, to conduct a live-fire training mission with their second ranger battalion. We'll brief the bomber and fighter crews that they are going on, the first of its kind, training exorcise with their sister unit at Ellsworth AFB in South Dakota. Both of these massive drills will be due to the high tensions between North and South Korea.

"This will serve two purposes. First it will prevent any and all leaks from the troops about their real mission. And a little misinformation won't hurt our cause either. Secondly, it won't give any man the chance to refuse to deploy. Once they're in the air on the way to their target, they'll be easier to manage. This is the same manner that we launched some highly secretive and risky missions during WWII.

"This mission sucks, but I need the full cooperation and support from all of you on this one. This is by far the toughest call I have ever had to make in my entire thirty-three-year military career—to order Americans to fight Americans. Now I know how Mr. Lincoln felt. Curse my soul."

Then President Osama interrupted, "Oh come on, General, stop being so dramatic. I'm sure there are worse things that you've had to do during your career."

Then General Demsley slammed his fist down on the table as he rose to his feet and yelled, "There is, Mr. President, and that's having to call you my commander-in-chief and following your damn orders!" The agitated army general continued to address Osama as though he were one of his privates. "What the hell do you know about ordering men to their deaths, much less ordering them to go against their brothers and sisters? You've never served a day of your life in the military. You wouldn't know the meaning of the words *honor, duty, loyalty,* and *country,* or your *brother in arms* if they bit you in the ass!"

"No, sir, don't ever lecture me about being dramatic. It's called having love and compassion for my fellow Americans. I'll follow your orders as long as they're lawful, but I don't have to like it."

It was so quiet in that room that you could have heard a gnat fart. Osama looked across the table, and every military officer there was glaring at him like they'd all kick his ass if he said another word. He got the hint without even having to read one of his teleprompters.

Then Job Binder broke the silence, "Gentlemen, lets keep this meeting civil. Does anyone have anything constructive to add to this meeting concerning the mission? Mr. Dolan, Mr. Gants, anyone?"

The president finally spoke up after regaining his composure. Osama's voice cracked, "All right then, gentlemen, let's press forward with all necessary preparations for 'Operation Condor Repo'. How soon can we launch this mission?"

The army and air force looked at each other and whisper for a moment, and then they both said, "Five days!"

Then President Osama rose and told the military that he'd be watching the mission from the situation room in the White House, and he expected to have real-time reports on the mission. The air force said, "Spectre will handle that task, sir." Then they convened and all went their separate ways.

RANGERS IN TEXAS

17 APRIL 2011
ABILENE, TEXAS

Just after dusk at 2015 the seventh and final team arrived in Abilene. They all flew into surrounding states, rented cars, and drove in undetected. There were a total of thirty Delta Force operatives and fourteen CCT members.

They had all received their detailed mission brief before leaving Fort Bragg. Now they were all hooched up in seven separate hotels; waiting for their mission time. While in their rooms they continued to receive real-time Intel and satellite imagery. The top four in the COC (Chain-of-Command) for the Delta operatives had adjoining rooms so they could come and go without anyone in the hallway seeing them. The top two were Major English, the RAPCON team leader and Master Sergeant Stevens, the ATCT team leader.

One of the CCT guys had a friend that chose to stay at Dyess AFB after Texas seceded. Those two buddies had kept in touch and according to his Texas classmate; the base hadn't changed their ID card access system for driving on base. One of the Delta boys and one of the CCT guys would attempt to drive on base that night to test it out.

20 APRIL 2011
SHADOW WOLF RANCH

It was 1930, and Alex and Leiko were out feeding their horses in the light of the full moon. The sky was half clear and half clouded.

They had a dozen Quarter horses, four Kiger horses, and six draft horses. Besides the fact that they liked to ride and have horses around, Alex knew how handy they would be if there were ever a massive EMP (Electro Magnetic Pulse; the abrupt pulse of electromagnetic radiation usually results from certain types of high energy explosions) and all vehicles were rendered non-functional. Alex still however stocked many spare vehicle parts in the underground bunkers, just in case.

Gerard walked up and said, "I thought I could find you out here about this time. Alex asked, "What's up?"

Gerard replied, "There's something going on with the military."

"How do you mean?" Alex asked.

Gerard said, "Well, you know how no large unit in the United States can deploy without the locals and news knowing about it."

"Yeah," Alex said, "who's moving?"

Gerard went on, "I just caught a local news report out of Savannah that the 1/75 Ranger Battalion is loading out. The troops were told that they're flying to Fort Luis to jump in and conduct a live fire exercise with their second battalion. They also say there's no scheduled field exercise on the calendar for that training."

Leiko chimed in and said, "I'll leave you boys alone. I'm going to fix supper." Then she sprinted off the 500 meters back to the house.

Alex told Gerard that he'd finish up there and then he'd meet him in the commo room. He asked Gerard to call Dutch, Hunter, and Damon and have them all meet him there as well. Then Alex called Leiko and asked her if she would prepare enough supper for the six of them and bring it to the commo room.

Hunter was the last of them to arrive at the commo room. "Sorry, I'm so dirty," he apologize. "I was machining a part in the shop."

"That's okay, Dad," Alex said, "you might want to wash up a little before supper. Leiko's bringing it here for us so we can track this thing here."

Hunter asked, "What's she fixin'?" as he started lickin' his chops.

Before Alex could reply, Dutch blurted out, "We don't know, but I'll bet its finger lickin'!"

* * *

One day prior to the rangers flying out, the four Task Force 160 Night Stalker Apaches were loaded into a C-5 for the mission. They were fully armed and topped off with fuel —-not a regular HAZ-MAT (hazardous materials such as fuel, ammunition, or chemicals) practice of the air force.

20 APRIL 2011
US AIRSPACE

At 2100 EST (Eastern Standard Time) the 1/75th Ranger Battalion was in the air heading west. Even the pilots thought they were headed for Fort Lewis until they reached Tennessee. Then they received their actual orders for 'Operation Condor Repo'. The first section on the classified OPORD was for the C-17 crew.

The ten C17 crews didn't know it but the Pentagon had arranged it so that the two C5s were trailing the C-17s by about a hundred miles. The C-5 crews as well were receiving a new set of marching orders that would keep them on the trail of the rangers. The two C-130 Spectres would already be in orbit over Dyess airfield when the rangers jumped in.

As soon as the navigations officer printed out the, one and only, hard copy of the OPORD, he said to the pilots, "Damn, boys, you're not going to believe this!"

He handed the orders to the captain of the C-17; Colonel James, as he said, "Check this out sir."

Then Colonel James asked, "Is this for real?"

The NAV (Navigations) officer said, "Yes, sir, it just came in encrypted from the Pentagon."

He then handed it to his copilot. After reading it his copilot asked, "What are we going to do with this sir?" After a brief moment of silence, he looked at his navigator and told him to plot the new course and then call the ranger's airborne commander forward.

"Rodger, sir, will do," the NAV officer said, as he punched in buttons on the NAV control panel like a crazed teenager texting to tell his buddies behind him that there was a DUI check point ahead of them.

Ten minutes later Major Fitzgibbons, the airborne commander for that bird slid into the cockpit. The major asked, "All right, fellas, what's up?"

Colonel James told his copilot to take over for a while. "Well, major, it seems that we're being diverted for a real world mission," Colonel James said with concern in his voice. Then he handed him the OPORD to read.

Then Colonel James said, "Major, after you're finished briefing your men on the mission, I need to get that OPORD back from you."

"Why's that, sir, I was going to keep it so I had the photos of the airfield, tower, and aircraft."

The colonel replied, "I have to collect it because that was our specific instructions from the Pentagon. I don't know why, but that's the way it is."

The major said, "All right, sir, if that's the way they want it. I'll get it back to you just before we bail out."

As Major Fitzgibbons read the OPORD, the colonel heard him mumble, "Damn, there are a lot of call signs and code words in this order."

Once the major finished reading the OPORD, he looked at Colonel James and blurted out, "You gotta be kidding me. Is this for real?"

James replied, "Yes, sir, I'm afraid so."

The major asked, "Well, have you changed course yet?"

"Yes, major, we have, and we'll be there in about ninety-five minutes."

Colonel James asked, "What are you going to do now Ranger?"

After a long pause, he painfully said, "My duty, my damn duty!" Then he asked the colonel to have his loadmaster prep the PA (public address) system so he could read the order to his men.

Major Fitzgibbons got on the PA and started barking out instructions. "All right, men, wake up your buddy next to you and listen up carefully because all of our lives are going to depend on how well you all understand what I'm about to say!"

There were also nine other aircraft/airborne commanders simultaneously giving that same briefing throughout the ten C-17 aircraft strike force bound for Abilene, Texas.

The major began, "Men, we've just received orders for a real world live mission. We're going to Dyess AFB to conduct an airfield takedown against a hostile force. For those of you who don't know, that's in Abilene, Texas."

Just then, you could see some of the men's faces turn white and blank. Then the troops were advised. Now listen up carefully, "We've only got about an hour and a half before we get the green light. That means issuing out orders, mission prep, and in-flight rigging. That's not much time so listen up.

"I'm going to read this unconventional op order to you verbatim. Afterward, I'll draw a sketch of the airfield and tarmac on some butcher block and pass it around. Before I start reading, let me get the CCT and PJ (Air Force Para-Rescue/special operations airman) airmen up here ASAP."

Major Fitzgibbons spoke to them off of the PA. He said, "I brought you guys up here for two reasons. First, so all my men can ID you and keep your asses alive so you can do your jobs. Secondly, you men have very critical and specific tasks during this operation." The airmen assured him that they understood their parts.

Then Major Fitzgibbons got back on the horn. "All right rangers, these two Air Force heroes here are going to be keeping the enemy off our asses by calling down the thunder of Spectre, F-15s, and Apache gunships. So, the better you keep them alive, the better they'll keep us alive. Got it?" Then a thunderous ranger echoed throughout the bird from 102 Airborne Rangers as they shouted and stomped their boots on the deck. Then the major read the OPORD to the troops over the PA:

(Classified)

(Top Secret)

OPORD for 'Operation Condor Repo'

United States Air Force

C-17 Globemaster III Crews

New Destination • NOE to Dyess AFB, Texas • 500 Feet AGL Live Combat Jump • Only one pass over drop zone • Use evasive maneuvers over Texas and return flying at forty thousand feet AGL to HAAF after Airborne Drop complete

(Classified)

(Top Secret)

OPORD for 'Operation Condor Repo'

United States Army

1st Battalion, 75th Ranger Regiment

This operations order is not in standard

US Army OPORD format.

Conduct a combat jump to perform an airfield seizure on Dyess Air Force Base, Abilene, Texas. This is not a training exercise! You will encounter hostile forces that will try to destroy you! The 1/75th Ranger Battalion must not fail.

The security of our nation depends on the successful completion of this urgent and necessary mission.

By order of the president of the United States of America

and Commander-in-Chief of the Armed Forces

04/20/2011, 2000 hrs EST.

Bakr Houssam Osama

- Your unit will jump in at 500 Feet AGL and secure the runway, tarmac, all B-1 Bombers and all F-15 Fighters.

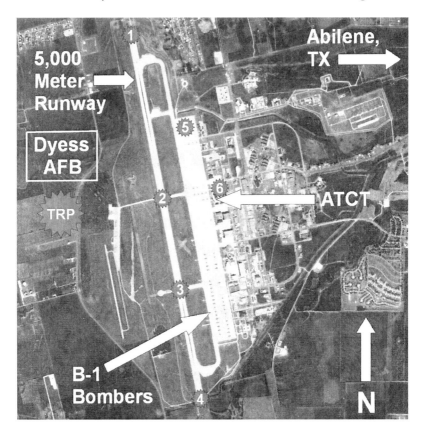

- The ATCT and RAPCON will already be secured by Delta Force and CCT friendlies.

- Once your target is secure, two C-5s will land and crews for the B-1s and F-15s will load their aircraft. The fighters will takeoff first to provide fire support for you. The other C-5 will have four AH-64 Apaches that will be in the air thirty minutes after hitting the ground. There will also be two C-130 Spectre gunships in orbit. This is your fire support package.

- You have sixteen CCT Airmen to direct and control these assets. Four CCT are in the tower, two on the runway, and you have one on each aircraft as well as one PJ on each bird. Safeguard these assets so they can protect you through superior firepower.

- Once the last bomber is in the air, load all wounded, pilots, CCT, Delta Force, and rangers into the two C-5s and takeoff. Once all friendlies are in the air, call Spectre to destroy the four Apaches on the runway. Then return home to HAAF (Hunter Army Air Field) and your families.

Then the major asked, "Everyone trackin' so far?" He received a thunderous AIRBORNE as 102 right boots hit the deck.

Then he said, "Drive on, Rangers!" as he continued reading the order.

SUPPORTING UNITS' CALL SIGNS

- Pentagon TOC = Shield
- Ranger Commander = Hulk
- Delta Force ATCT Assault Team = Iron Man
- Delta Force RAPCON Assault Team = War Machine
- Delta Force ATCT Sniper Team = Zero
- CCT ATCT FOs = Odin

- CCT Airfield FO's = Thor
- C-130H: North-Spectre number 1 = Thunder
- C-130H: South-Spectre number 2 = Lightning
- B-1 Bomber Squadron Commander = Condor-1
- F-15 Fighter Squadron Commander = Raptor-1
- C-5 Commander = Albatross
- Apache number 1: North-Runway = Magpie
- Apache number 2: South-Runway = Blue Jay
- Apache number 3: Tarmac = Crow
- Apache number 4: Tower = Raven

MISSION CODE WORDS

- ATCT and RAPCON Secure = *Dove's Nest*
- ATCT and RAPCON Not Secure = *Bee Hive*
- Air Field Secure = *Serenity*
- Air Field Not Secure = *Havoc*
- C5s are on the ground = *Mother Goose*
- Last Fighter in air = *Formation*
- Last Bomber in air = *Migration*
- All Friendlies in air = *Home Free*
- Apaches Destroyed = *Reservation*
- Mission Complete = *Repo Complete*

YOUR MISSION TRPS (TARGET REFERENCE POINTS)

- TRP-1 = North End Runway: Ele. (elevation) 1,773 Ft. AGL

32° 26′ 17.78′ N / 99° 51′ 30.89′ W

- TRP-2 = 2nd North Taxiway: Ele. 1,782 Ft. AGL
32° 25′ 22.10′ N / 99° 51′ 18.12′ W

- TRP-3 = 3rd North Taxiway: Ele. 1,786 Ft. AGL
32° 24′ 43.59′ N / 99° 51′ 09.61′ W

- TRP-4 = South End Runway: Ele. 1,787 Ft. AGL
32° 24′ 09.97′ N / 99° 51′ 01.40′ W

- TRP-5 = North End Tarmac: Ele. 1,776 Ft. AGL
32° 25′ 40.20′ N / 99° 51′ 06.88′ W

- TRP-6 = ATCT: Ele. 1,775 Ft. AGL
32° 25′ 21.81′ N / 99° 50′ 51.41′ W

—————————————End of Mission—————————

Rangers Lead the Way!!!

(Classified)
(Top Secret)

Five minutes after starting, Major Fitzgibbons finished reading the OPORD. Then he asked his men if any one of them were not willing to follow the orders that came directly from their Commander-in-Chief. Much to Major Fitzgibbons surprise, not one single ranger refused to follow the orders that had been issued. The Rangers had always had an extremely high sense of loyalty and sense of duty. He was proud of his men.

Some of the other airborne commanders weren't so fortunate. About half of the other aircraft had a handful of troops that refused to follow the orders. One bird even had a full squad that refused, even after being told they would be court marshaled. Their squad leader, Staff Sergeant Courtland said, "Wrong is wrong! Besides, I think it's an unlawful order to begin with."

Meanwhile on the ground, the Delta Force/CCT team had successfully infiltrated onto Dyess Air Force Base and was in their staging position to take over the ATCT and the RAPCON. Two of the CCT guys, Doyle and Jenkins, were in position out near the northwest end of the runway where they could laze targets and call for fire, if needed. Their call sign was Thor.

The ATCT Strike Team's team leader was Master Sergeant Stevens. His call sign was Iron Man. Just before they conducted the hit, he instructed his four-man external security team to give him a call if they had any problems at the base of the tower and needed any reinforcements. Their call sign was Saber Tooth.

The gist of their plan was to clear and secure from the ground up. Once they had the actual control room secured, the four CCT airmen, within his element, would continue to handle the regular air traffic radio calls, so as not to alert anyone that the real controllers weren't at the helm anymore. All tower facility personnel would be held in the break room, the next level down, right by the BBQ grill.

There would also be a two-man sniper team, Davis and Donavan, on the roof of the ATCT after they took it. They'd have clear fields of fire to the north, south, and west for three clicks out. Their primary position would be oriented northward with their secondary southward. Their two, M82 Barretts (a recoil-operated, semi-automatic, .50 caliber BMG, sniper system) were just the tools for the job. They were carrying a spare gun as a back-up. A good DDM (Designated Defensive Marksman) and spotter could blast the stink off a buzzard a mile away, easy. They had it down to a science; rocket science actually. Their call sign was Zero.

Major English would command the other half of the Delta Force assault team that would simultaneously take down the RAPCON, next to the ATCT. It was critical that the actual ATCT room and RAPCON room be stormed at exactly the same moment. Otherwise, one could alert the other because they had a symbiotic working relationship. Major English's call sign was War Machine.

Sergeant Stevens was ready to go. "All right, men, the last and most important order I'll give you before we make the hit. Try your damnedest not to kill anyone! They're Americans as well and probably not armed. We can very well beat them into submission instead of shoot them. CCT, once we have both targets in our complete control, I'll instruct you to call Hulk and give him the code word *Doves Nest.*"

"Roger that, we'll be ready," the airmen assured sergeant Stevens. Both of the team's entry/breaching specialists had already by-passed the electronics and opened the locked exterior doors on the ATCT and RAPCON without a sound. As the strike teams were in stacked positions outside both of the entrances, Stevens requested conformation over his encrypted head set that all elements were ready for the strike.

"War Machine ready and set."

Then he heard the exterior RAPCON security team leader sounds off, "Beast in position."

"Thor ready, over."

The exterior tower security team leader sounded off, "Saber Tooth set."

Stevens replied, "Copy all up, on my command."

"Five, four, three, two, one, execute!" as he used his right knee to bump the man in front of him on the ass. Stevens command to move-in was sent forward throughout the stack. That way if someone's coms weren't working or they were droning, they knew they were preparing to move out.

During their mission planning in the hotel, the ATCT assault team had planned to split into two teams. One would take the narrow stair well and the other the elevator. Both teams would stop on each floor and clear and secure it, before moving upward. They were equipped with a full arsenal of non-lethal weapons, in order not to have to kill anyone. However, in the event that became necessary, all of their lethal weapons were fully suppressed.

Once inside, the team split and went around the elevator shaft; which was in the middle of the room. As soon as they had the first floor cleared, the teams split again, leaving a two-man CCT security team at the main entrance.

Seven men went in the elevator and ten went up the stairs. The elevator team had five shooters, one CCT, and one sniper. The stair team had eight shooters up front, one CCT behind them with a sniper bringing up the rear.

Since Major English's objective was at the end of a twenty foot hall way, his team stood fast in their stacked position outside the building until Steven's team was ready to enter the actual ATCT room at the top of the tower. Then both teams would mount a simultaneous assault with precision timing and tactics. Major English waited for Stevens' third command to execute.

The ATCT team cleared the first of four floors with no encounters. Then the second and third floors were just empty landings. While still on the third floor, Stevens prepped his men over his whisper mike. "All right men, time to earn our money."

Like most ATCTs in the world, the elevator shaft stopped on the last floor. That way the shaft didn't extend up into the ATCT room and impede a good 360° view of the airport. This design also lent it's self to more floor space for equipment and desk.

"When we reach the forth floor CCT will hold the stairwell, Up and Down. Sniper team will hold the elevator. Everyone else will stack and take the break room; how copy?" Stevens asks.

"CCT copy."

"Sniper team, copy."

"Elevator team, copy."

"Iron Man, copy all elements. Move out."

As soon as they all entered the forth floor, they all assumed their assigned positions. It only took the team about ten seconds to form the stack with Stevens in the rear. "Okay, on my command, five, four, three, two, one. execute!" Just as the last time, he followed up with his right knee to echo the command of execution forward.

There were three people in the room as the team entered. One airman was at the sink washing some dishes. He was the first to see the team just before the number one man butt stroked him with his weapon. The man that bashed his face kept on moving into the room with lightning speed.

The second person they came upon in the room was an air force staff sergeant. She had been sitting at a table that faced the entrance. As she jumped to her feet the second man through the door hit her with a taser—five hundred thousand volts of shut-its-ville. She never got a word out and started doing the kickin'-chicken on the table. Lucky for her. It broke her fall and saved her pretty face from kissing the tile floor.

The third person in the room had it good. He was an air force captain that was sleeping on the couch. By the time he awoke he had hundred-mile-an-hour tape (Duct Tape) over his pie-hole and flex cuffs on his wrist and ankles. They never knew what hit em'.

Once the other two were bound, Stevens instructed one-man to stay and guard them. The remainder of the team reformed the stack at the base of the stairs. "CCT, hold the stairs and elevator. I'll call you up after it's secure," as Stevens gestured by pointing his index finger upward. Then Stevens called War Machine and told him to standby and wait for his count to kick-off the final assault. They were all too ready...

The assault team inched their way up the stairs until the number one man could see in the room. Then he held up his left fist to halt and gestured with his index and middle fingers that he had eyes on. Now Sergeant Stevens was ready to give the final command.

"Ready, five, four, three, two, one execute! As they stormed the control room they saw two figures silhouetted against the 360-degree windows. The team was wearing their NODs with IR on because they knew that control rooms were inherently dark. However, all equipment there had its own backlighting.

There was one man sitting and one man standing. The sitting man was peering through binos (binoculars). The other man was standing while intently looking at a single suspended monitor hanging from the ceiling. Luckily, both men had their backs to the stairs.

As the team was swooping in on the two unsuspecting men, a team member tripped over an electrical cord on the floor. Just then both men spun around to see what all of the ruckus was about. Just then, the team realizes that they were both wearing headsets and the standing man had a microphone in his left hand. When the two men saw the fast-approaching team, the standing man begun to raise the microphone to his lips.

Stevens said, "Take him out!" Not a split second later, he heard the suppressed sound of two of the teams weapons firing their subsonic ammo. The number one man fired his M-4 (5.56 mm, shoulder fired, magazine fed, select fire rifle) at the man standing. Four rounds of 5.56. Two through the solar plexus and two between the eyes. The air force major was dead before he hit the floor.

The number too man had nailed the man sitting. His MP-5 ripped two holes in his chest and two through the center of his forehead. The impact didn't actually knock him out of his chair. It spun him around about three times before he stopped. Then the number three man sounded off with, "All Clear!"

That was one of those things that every man on the team would take to his grave. They all just kind of watched the corpse spin around in the chair like a carnival ride. Once he stopped spinning, the closest man checked his pulse. He looked around the room and said, "Oh yeah, he's toast." They all probably realized that very well might have been the first casualties of the next American civil war.

Stevens got on his coms and made the call. "War machine, war machine, iron man over."

Major English responded, "Send it."

"All secure, over."

English replied, "Copy, standby, out."

Then Stevens issued commands throughout his team. He sent six of his shooters down to replace the men holding the stairs and elevator. As they were heading down, Stevens said, "Tell Zero and Odin to get up here ASAP!"

In the RAPCON room, the dirty deed was getting done as well. There were five airmen and one civilian that were at the controls in the radar room. When the team had entered the room, the closest airman saw them and ran toward them. Big mistake! The number one man instinctively issued him a palm-heel-strike to the nose. Needless to say that the young man's nose was jammed sufficiently back into his brain to take his life.

The next man, a staff sergeant, jumped to his feet only to eat the butt of the number three man's SCAR (5.56 mm, shoulder fired, magazine fed, SF service rifle, FHN-USA). Judging from the look on his face, he wasn't keen on the taste.

The controller on the far side of biscuit boy was content receiving the 500,000 volt/bolt of lightning; lights out… Then there was a rather large senior airman that resembled a barn door when he stood up. At best guess he was about six foot eight inches and probably 290 pounds.

He was wearing a headset and some sort of 3-D looking glasses, for observing his screen. He stood and assumed a defensive stance just before the number five man gave him a left jab to the throat. A blow that would stop any normal man in his tracks. It didn't even faze Big Foot.

The big man yelled, "I'm gonna tear yer head off boy!"

That's when the number six man put two rounds of 9 mm from his MP-5 right in his brain pan and muttered, "We don't have time for this crap."

The air force major and the civilian dude raised their hands and squealed, "Okay, no problem here fellas!" They didn't move until they were bound and gagged.

Now it was time for Major English's report. He put it out over his encrypted whisper mike. "Iron man, iron man, war machine, over."

"Iron man, go."

"All secure, over."

"Iron man copy, out."

Then Stevens looked at Staff Sergeant Ottis, the CCT team leader, and told him to send Hulk the word. Ottis replied, "Copy, sending now. Hulk, Hulk, Odin over." He waited about ten seconds and repeated. "Hulk, Hulk, Odin over."

"Odin, this is Hulk, send yer traffic, over."

"Hulk, Odin, *Dove's Nest, Dove's Nest*, over."

"Odin, I copy *Dove's Nest*, over."

"Affirmative Hulk, over."

"Good copy and good job, Odin. Hulk out."

Sergeant Stevens then got on the air to his men once more. "Hulk is in route. Stand fast and hold your ground. Report any problems to me ASAP. Zero is now posted to solve any problems out there."

All the CCT were posted; two on the airfield, four in the tower, and eight in the RAPCON. Stevens and English sent all of their extra men outside to strengthen the tight perimeter they held around the ATCT and RAPCON. They were looking pretty good. They also had their sniper team on the top of the ATCT with their two 50 cals. They had nothing left to do but wait for their ride. The Calvary should be there in about an hour.

Back in the air, Major Fitzgibbons called for his primary and assistant jumpmasters and safeties to gather around him. He proceeded to tell them that the birds were only making one pass. He said, "Push everyone out even if they're going on the red light. We need every ranger on the ground to conduct the mission."

One of the assistant jumpmasters said, "Roger, sir."

Fitzgibbons said, "Now let's start the jump commands, and be ready when we get the green light. May God be with us all!"

Four birds behind Major Fitzgibbons lead bird was the bird that Staff Sergeant Courtland and his squad were on. After he and his squad had refused to go on the mission, their company commander had segregated them from the rest of the company. They placed them up front by the cockpit.

Just before they were to begin the jump commands, Captain Johnson, the company commander decided that he had better confiscate the squad's weapons, just to cover his ass. He sent his First Sergeant over to collect them. First Sergeant Lewis said, "Sergeant Courtland, the CO (Commanding Officer) has ordered me to collect your squad's weapons.

"What the hell for?" Sergeant Courtland asked.

Being an experienced and good first sergeant, he knew that his answer shouldn't reflect the fact that his CO no longer trusted the squad. Therefore, he thought quickly and said, "We need them for the mission for spares."

Courtland yelled back, "That's a load-a-bull! Ya'all just don't trust us and think we're a bunch of cowards."

The first sergeant said, "That's not true, ranger. Now just give us your damn weapons!"

The squad leader replied, "I think not. We'll keep them and turn them into the arms room when we get back on Hunter."

Then the first sergeant rushed in close and grabbed Sergeant Courtland's M-4 as the two began to struggle with the weapon. Three other NCOs rushed in as well to assist the first sergeant in taking the squad's weapons. It quickly turned into a brawl 500 feet above the ground. The first sergeant gained the advantage when he worked his way behind Courtland and proceeded to put him into a rear-takedown-strangle-hold.

First Sergeant Lewis's intent was just to apply sufficient pressure to choke him out. That's when Murphy's Law stepped in and things went south real quick. Since the C-17s were flying NOE, they were bucking and bouncing all over the place. Just as Courtland's lights started to go out, the bird bucked so hard that it threw the two men up in the air. When they came down First

Sergeant Lewis' jungle boots slid out from under him on the slippery aluminum deck of the bird.

That unintentionally completed the second lethal half of the choke out/neck breaking hold. It proceeded to snap Sergeant Courtland's neck instantly. All men involved in the scuffle froze in place when they all realized what had happened.

After a moment or two the first sergeant and three other NCOs (Non-Commissioned Officer) realized that now they really had to gain control of the squad's weapons, because they were worried about retribution from Staff Sergeant Courtland's squad. That's when one of Courtland's team leaders butt stroked the first sergeant, stepped back, and yelled back to his squad, "Lock and load!"

The sound of the entire squad's weapons being chambered at once sounded like a drill team on an honor guard detail. The sound was even heard over the sound of the jet engines. The senior NCOs were even more determined at that point to get their weapons.

The first sergeant was so pissed off that an E-5 (Sergeant) butt stroked him that he could only see red. They charged the armed men and First Sergeant Luis dove on the young sergeant and that's when his M-4 selector switch went to auto and 5.56 rounds started flying. The squad had been backing-up from the pressure of the NCOs coming at them. Therefore, by the time the weapon fired, the two men were right behind the crew.

The first sergeant hit the sergeant with such force that his momentum spun them around with the M-4 firing full auto. In one single sweeping motion the entire four-man crew was killed. Once the weapon fired all thirty rounds and stopped firing, First Sergeant Lewis continued fighting with the young ranger.

With the plane only flying at five hundred feet AGL, it was mere seconds before the C-17 slammed into the ground with the force of a freight train hitting a volts wagon. One hundred two rangers and crew went to meet their maker. They didn't even have time to think about bailing out. They never had any chance of survival as the buttoned-up jet erupted into a huge fireball.

Back on the lead bird, Major Fitzgibbons called Captain Harmonski over and told him that he had a weird feeling about the way the air force would only print one hard copy of the T/S OPORD. He looked around to see if any air force dudes were looking at him and then he slipped the OPORD to the captain. He instructed him, "Put this in your ruck and safeguard it with your life! For some reason the Pentagon doesn't want there to be a paper trail of this mission and that doesn't set well with me. As far as they know it's in my possession."

"Roger that, sir," the captain assured the major. "No one will know I have it."

Then the major said, "Captain Harmonski, I'm going to have you and SFC (Sergeant First Class) Sadler each be the number one man out on each door. That way we'll have some leadership on the ground first. I'm going to be the last man out to make sure no one gets cold feet at the last minute."

Harmonski said, "Yes, sir, I'll let Sadler know."

There were many combat veterans in the 1/75th Ranger Battalion. However, there were also a few new cherries in the mix. The fifth man back from the inboard starboard side (Right Side) jump door was just such a cherry named Private First Class Sargent. Now there was a combination for some confusing intro-ductions. He was an M-240 (7.62 mm medium machine gun, belt fed) gunner in 3rd PLT, Co. A.

He had just finished RIP (Ranger Indoctrination Program) and hadn't been to Ranger School yet to receive his Ranger Tab. He had been quite nervous, to say the least, about his first MASS TAC (USAF airborne operation = more than three aircraft), com-bat jump with his new unit. He had been busy thinking about all of that when he heard the jump commands being barked out by the jumpmasters.

"Ten minutes!" barked the jumpmasters over the thunderous drone of the jet engines. All jump commands were always echoed back to the jumpmasters toward the aft (rear) of the aircraft.

"Ten minutes!" the one hundred rangers echoed back with looks of anticipation, wonder, and fear on some of their faces.

What have I gotten myself into? PFC Sargent thought to himself.

"Get ready!" came the next command from the jumpmasters. This was the moment of truth.

"Outboard personnel stand up!" cried the jumpmasters. The soldiers across from PFC Sargent struggled to their feet, encumbered as much by the bulkiness of their parachutes and rucks as by the wild bucking of the aircraft. One of the dudes tumbled forward into the reserve parachute of someone seated to his left.

His squad leader, Staff Sergeant Els seated on his right, turned in his direction and shouted something to him which he couldn't hear over the noise from the plane. From his tone and the look on his face, it was obvious that he was saying some words of encouragement. "Ranger!" The cherry yelled back as enthusiastically as possible, while giving him his most ebullient thumbs up.

"Inboard personnel stand up!" was the next jump command. Because Sargent was sitting in the center section of the aircraft, this was the first command that required him to take action. He, along with the other jumpers of his stick, threw their weight forward in a desperate attempt to shift himself into a more or less standing position.

"Hook up!" they were commanded. They bounced and rolled as the plane bounced and rolled, trying to get the hook on the end of their static line around the anchor line cable. The static line was, fifteen feet long, slender as a whip, bright yellow, and had a tensile strength of six thousand pounds.

By virtue of being connected to the aircraft, via the anchor line cable, it pulled the D-bag off of the parachute, and thence the parachute off of the pack tray and out into the open air. That enabled the parachute to open with no action from the jumper beyond a step into the cold, dark abyss.

The plane bucked and finally click. The snap link closed and Sargent was tethered to the plane. He traced the static line down; making sure it was correctly routed over his shoulder, and finally grasped a four-inch bite in his right hand.

"Check static lines!" they were ordered. He again traced his static line down from the place where it met the anchor line cable, through the four-inch bite, and back toward his shoulder. He then traced the static line of the ranger in front of him, over his shoulder and down.

He continued downward, zig-zagging through the retainer bands on the outside of his parachute pack, and into the center. There, were the four flaps that met and were held closed by a thin line of white cotton string of eighty-pound test. The man behind him proceeded to check his static line in exactly the same manner.

"Check equipment!" the rangers heard, and they did. PFC Sargent traced the chin strap of his Kevlar helmet from left to right, and then the parachute's riser straps, first left, then right, from rear to forward.

Then he inspected both of his leg strap quick releases and his chest strap quick release. Those three clips were all rated above two thousand pounds and they kept his body firmly secured in the parachute harness, during even the most violent opening shock. Lastly, Sargent's weapons container and ruck were both correctly rigged.

"Sound off for equipment check!" bellowed the jumpmasters, their hands behind their ears in a familiar gesture.

"Okay!"

"Okay!"

"Okay!"

"Okay!" the jumpers all called out one after the other.

When the PFC felt a smack on his ass and heard okay, he also called, "Okay!"

The cry went up the line until the number one jumper yelled, "All okay, Jumpmaster!," he said as he gestured with a knife-edged hand and pointed sharply toward the jumpmaster posted at the aft of the aircraft.

The safety shuffled by, rechecking all of their static lines and equipment, and admonishing them to look the jumpmaster in the eyes as they handed him their static lines. Centuries passed. The aircraft was at 500 feet AGL and in its final approach to the drop zone. The jumpmasters waited for the Green Light. The jumpers waited for the command to go from the jumpmasters.

The plane continued to roll and yaw as it encountered choppy air close to the ground. The four engines increased their roar slightly as the pilot inched the throttle forward. The jumper on the opposite side of the aircraft looked at PFC Sargent and their eyes locked for a brief instant. He would be swept out the other jump door within one second of the time when the cherry went out his.

"One minute!" The index fingers of their free hand shot up; a mirror image of the jumpmasters. Sargent felt sweat slide down his face, although the air rushing in through the open jump doors was keeping the cabin cool.

The cool air helped in dealing with the smell of puke in the air, a side effect of flying NOE for ninety minutes. Both jumpmasters leaned out of their doors as they checked for any potential hazards in the sky, identified the DZ, and then leaned back in.

"Thirty seconds," they screamed as the PFC's heart skipped a beat just before it pumped a jolt of adrenaline through his system, just as a 1970s mussel car would receive a shot of nitrous before a drag race.

"Stand by!" Captain Harmonski, the first jumper in line, handed off his static line to the jumpmaster. Then he pivoted to face the jump door and got into a solid position on the jump platform for his exit. The rest of the stick shuffled forward a half step, thus the term; the airborne shuffle. PFC Sargent could hear his own heartbeat over the deafening drone of the engines. They were just then clearing the leading edge of the DZ.

"Green light. Go!" Captain Harmonski disappeared, his static line quivered as it tore the D-bag off of his parachute. A second later, the first jumper on the other side also disappeared. These first two voluntary sacrifices were followed by the rest of the rangers, one at a time.

Sargent shuffled forward until his eyes met those of the jump-master. He handed him his static line, pivoted, stepped forward, and was ripped out of the aircraft by the jet blast. Elbows tucked into his side, chin on his chest, and feet and knees tight together; just the way he had learned in airborne school at Fort Benning.

"One thousand, two thousand!" he counted. "Three thousa—" he felt, more than heard, the loud whump as his parachute filled with air, scattering the cherries limbs every which way. A good thing his main functioned flawlessly because at 500 feet AGL, they weren't jumping any reserve chutes—they wouldn't have had time to even inflate.

Safe! PFC Sargent's parachute had deployed in exactly the same manner as he feared it wouldn't. All fear and nervousness had evaporated. As he quickly drifted across the sky, his mind cleared and he entered an almost meditative state. Then he realized the winds were so high that he was traveling more in a lateral than downward direction. At least with a full moon he could see where he was going.

PFC Sargent was so thrilled that he survived his first combat mass tac as an Airborne Ranger that he didn't even realize that his chute had caught a serious thermal air blast that carried him about fifteen hundred feet up. That along with the high cross winds at altitude had him all jacked-up.

Of course, being the cherry that he was, he ran with the wind. By the time he finally came down he realized that there was no one else around him or even in sight. The fact of the matter was; he had drifted about three clicks away from the DZ. A fact that he wouldn't soon live down.

The last jumper to exit PFC Sargent's bird was Major Fitzgibbons, that bird's Airborne Commander. Just as he was shuffling toward his jump door to exit, the aircraft NAV officer grabbed Major Fitzgibbons by the right arm and said, "Major, I have to get that OPORD back; by order of the Pentagon."

Fitzgibbons quickly and quite aggressively yelled, "There's a crap-load of code words and call signs in that order, captain! If I'm expected to succeed in my mission I've got to have that order on the ground with me. You make the call, Captain. Do you want to explain to the president that the rangers failed their mission because they couldn't effectively communicate on the radio or call for fire using their TRPs? Well, do ya?"

The captain said, "No, sir, I don't."

Then the major said, "All right then, unless you want to come with me, let go of my damn arm!" The captain quickly released his grip on the major's arm and stepped back, and in less time than it took his heart to beat again, he watched the ranger disappear into the black abyss.

With one pass of nine C-17s full of rangers, there were nearly 900 killing machines in the air. At this point in time the element of surprise was gone. It was time to get to work and complete their mission. The one that the president himself had authorized and ordered.

Other than PFC Sargent, the rest of the ranger strike force has landed right where they should have. Most of the men were very experienced and proficient in driving their chutes, in any condition. They were their usual proficiently trained assault force, like clock work. It took them fifteen minutes to stow their chutes and muster in their assembly areas.

Normally they wouldn't roll their chutes and stow them in their kit bags for such an assault; a task that would take an extra three minutes. However, 900 loose chutes blowing around on a windy night could really make for a bad night for an air crew; if they were to get one sucked-up in a jet engine.

DON'T TREAD ON ME

20 APRIL 2011
ABILENE, TEXAS

At 2235 the remainder of the 1/75th Ranger Battalion was on the ground and moving into position to secure the airfield and tarmac where the B-1s and F-15s were staged. By 2300 they were in position to secure and hold their objective.

Lieutenant Colonel Rodgers, the Ranger Battalion Commander, instructed his commo chief to send the Pentagon the code word *Serenity*, that meant his boys had secured the airfield. Colonel Rodgers had been instructed that all of his air traffic for that mission would be piped directly to the Pentagon. From there it was to be relayed directly to the situation room in the White House. There the president and his cabinet would monitor the mission in real time (live) reports and overhead imagery from the Spectre gun ships that would be orbiting above the objective.

Then Colonel Rodgers sent the word up to the two C5s to set down with the air crews and the four Apache gun ships. As soon as the mammoth birds were on the ground the second code word was sent forward. "Shield, Shield, this is Hulk, over."

"Hulk, this is Shield, send your traffic, over."

"Shield, *Mother Goose, Mother Goose,* over."

"Hulk, I copy *Mother Goose,* over."

"Shield, affirmative, out."

Thirty minutes had passed since the second C5 had landed. Three of the four Apache gun ships had been assembled and were going through their preflight checks. All of the B-1 and F-15 crews had arrived at their birds and were conducting their preflight checks when all hell broke loose.

After Texas had broken away from the rest of the United States, they employed some additional Top Secret security measures that only they knew about. They had their best and brightest Lockheed and NASA techs go through all of their B-1 bombers. They removed all of the hardware and software that was required for the president and his cabinet to control the aircraft and their munitions with their NCA (National Command Authority).

Then they installed additional early warning equipment that would alert a special unit on base if they were ever tampered with in an unauthorized manner. As soon as the ranger's first B-1 crew had started their preflight check, the silent alarms were activated and were as effective as Paul Raveer's cry in the night.

The bad thing was, the crews never had a clue what they had done. By then the army had three of their Apaches in the sky and the forth one was nearly ready.

Dyess' security forces had been alerted and scrambled in response to the alarms. This unit was a squadron of the air force's elite Phoenix Raven program which was trained to provide security for AMC (Air Force, Air Mobility Command's) aircraft in high threat areas. The unit was also augmented with PJs and CCT Airmen.

Governor Pevey, along with the base commander had thought that the Osama administration would launch a DA mission against Texas bases, sooner or later. Therefore, they had secretly installed eight each, Phalanxs (MK-15; Close-in weapons system; fires between 3,000-4,500 20mm cannon rounds per minute, either autonomously or under manual command, as a last-ditch defense against incoming missiles and aircraft) within a three click radius of the airfield. Good planning on their part…

Those twenty mike mike Vulcan's had been installed in underground silos that were undetectable by aircraft and satellites, when in their inactive mode. Once those systems would receive a hit on its radar or the gunner would override the automated mode, they were functional. They could fire a solid wall of armor piercing projectiles the diameter of a nickel toward their target. Just like running into a swarm of hornets. A very nasty nest to deal with and no countermeasures available for an incoming pilot flying at 300 mph. The code name for those linked weapon systems was *Death Star*.

The Phoenix Raven Squadron was very well equipped with the very best state-of-the-art equipment available. They had twenty each FAVs, twenty each 650cc scout bikes, ten Avenger Ad Systems (Humvee; 360-degree gunner operated, 50 cal. and 8-pack Stinger FIM-92; [SAM] Surface-to-air missile, short range, heat seeking, speed: Mach 2.2, range: three-miles), and twelve AH-60 Blackhawk gunships (four-bladed, twin turbine, medium helicopter with pilot operated 7.62mm mini guns, 2.75 inch rockets, and Sidewinder: AIM-9X; [Air-to-air missile], medium range, heat seeking, speed: Mach 2.5, range: twenty-two miles) at their disposal and they would be bringing it all to deal with what ever threat they found waiting for them at the airfield. Their advantage; they'd be coming from the north and the south at the same time.

The rangers first three Apaches were in the sky and covering both ends of the runway and the aircraft on the ground. That was when Spectre sent down the first contact report. "Hulk, Hulk, this is Thunder, over."

"Thunder, this is Hulk, go."

"Hulk, you've got six bogies in-bound. Three northbound and three southbound, over."

"Hulk copy, break, Magpie, Magpie, Blue Jay, Blue Jay, did you copy direct, over?"

The Apaches at both ends of the runway had already been scanning their radar for hostile aircraft. Blue Jay, at the south end of the runway, responded to Hulk's warning call. "Copy Hulk, we're dealing with it." Just then Blue Jay saw the incoming Sidewinder missile on his radar and heard his radar warning lock.

The Apache had activated his countermeasures by firing his flairs and chaff to attract the heat seeking missile. Then he conducted a hard portside bank to try to avoid impact.

His tardy maneuver failed as the detonation lit up the sky and gained everyone's attention on or near the airfield. The air force's Blackhawk fired its Sidewinder missile three clicks out as soon as he saw the hostile force holding his air field. Finally, the thought was driven home in every man's mind that they were at war. It was time to fight or die!

Magpie started yelling on the radio, "Raven, Raven, get yer ass up here ASAP. Things are getting hot!"

Raven replied, "Five mikes, give me five mikes!" Meanwhile, the first pair of F-15s just got off the ground.

Colonel Rodgers snatched the radio mic from his commo chief and said, "Raptor-1, get more of your boys in the air, and give me some more fire support! Take out those six bogies!" Colonel Oakley's birds were now on the radar and slated for destruction.

The Sidewinder missile that incinerated the Apache came from Colonel Oakley's AH-60 Blackhawk gunship. He was the commander of the Phoenix Raven Squadron that was tasked with safeguarding the airfield and all of it's aircraft. He was actually piloting the Blackhawk that took out the superior Apache.

Right after he terminated the Apache gunship, he gave the reaminder of his unit a detailed SALUTE report of the enemy forces that he saw around the airfield. His report had also been relayed to the base commander and Governor Pevey.

As soon as Governor Pevey received word that Texas was under attack he called his top naval commander, Admiral Wollard and told him that Dyess Air Force Base was under attack and needed naval air support. The admiral agreed and committed to scramble a squadron of his Naval Reserve F-14s (D – Super Tomcat; USN, supersonic, twin-engine, two-seat, variable-sweep wing fighter) from the Naval Air Station at Fort Worth Joint Reserve Base.

The admiral then told the governor that he also had six F-22 (Raptor; USAF, supersonic, single seat, stealth fighter) Raptors at the base that were there for training new pilots. He promised to get those fighters armed and in the air as well, in the defense of Texas and Free America. The F-22s were the baddest thing in the air with the most sophisticated state-of-the-art avionics and weaponry in the world. He told Governor Pevey, "There's no F-15 in the world that can stand toe-to-toe with my F-22s!"

Governor Pevey asked, "How soon can they be there?"

Then Admiral Wollard explained, "The F-14s are on the deck on standby. I know they're dinosaurs but they're all I've got right now. After making a couple of modifications, they will be in the air in twenty minutes and in the battle fifteen minutes after that.

"We have to make the same modifications and arm the F-22s as well. They should be arriving on scene in about one hour. Our Phoenix Raven unit and the additional airfield security upgrades we installed should be able to hold them until our fighters get there."

Once the admiral was off the phone with the governor, he got on the horn with his base commander, Vice Admiral Sparrow, at the Naval Air Station at Fort Worth. He proceeded to give him his marching orders and he also instructed him to give his ordinance team some special instructions. "Tell them to disarm all of the friend or foe identifiers in the aircraft and the missile laser seeker/sensors. These are F-15 and Apache aircraft that we'll be firing at. If they don't modify those missile seekers we might as well be throwing rocks at them.

"Our systems will be identifying their aircraft as friendly and won't fire on them. Let's just pray that they forgot to disable theirs. That would greatly even the odds, depending on how many of those F-15s they get off the ground. Those birds are combat proven and nothing to sneeze at."

The vice admiral then questioned, "Are we really going to fire on our own US aircraft?"

The admiral sternly rebuked him, "Listen, our boys are dying on Dyess as we speak. We didn't start this war, but we're damn sure going to end it. Got it?"

"Yes, sir, I understand," Sparrow said. "Your aircraft are on the way, sir!"

Meanwhile, on the battlefield things were getting busy. Colonel Oakley activated the Mk-15 Phalanxs with a call back to the Phoenix Raven TOC (Tactical Operations Command). "Raven, Raven, this is Big Daddy, over."

"Big Daddy, this is Raven, go."

"Raven, *Death Star Manual, Death Star Manual,* how copy over?"

"Big Daddy, I copy *Death Star Manual,* over."

"Raven, that's affirmative, out."

The colonel knew that he needed those Vulcan's firing under the command of a human gunner. If they were in the automated mode they would be firing at anything in the air. He didn't need that, especially with their friend or foe identifiers deactivated. He also knew that within forty-five minutes or so he would have some fixed wing support in the air, according to his defensive protocol.

Once his TOC relayed the command for the Phalanxs gunners to go manual, they sprang into action. All eight of the Vulcan systems rose from their silos in unison. Their gunners were also instructed to engage all F-15s and Apaches in the sky. They were also warned not to fire on any F-14s or F-22s.

As soon as Hulk's first pair of F-15s were in the air, they went gunning for the three AH-60s that were coming from the north. Meanwhile, Colonel Oakley's three Blackhawks were still closing from the south.

The three northern Blackhawks had begun to engage the rangers on the ground near the north end of the airstrip. The two F-15s swooped in on the Blackhawks like an eagle lining-up on a rabbit to sink it's talons in deep. Both Strike Eagles fired their Sparrow missiles (AIM-7R: Medium range, semi-active radar homing, [AAM] air-to-air missile, speed: Mach-4, range: thirty-one miles) at the AH-60 gunships.

Both choppers exploded simultaneously. The eighteen-men, on both birds, never had a prayer. By that time Hulk had six of his F-15s in the fight. One of the Phalanxs gunners had a lock on one of the F-15s that had just fired on the Blackhawks. He fired a three hundred round burst of twenty mike mike straight at him. The solid wall of armor piercing ammo cut the fuselage right off the rest of the bird. Only one of the crew members managed to eject before the bird blew.

Meanwhile, on the ground the Phoenix Raven ground units were reaching the FEBA (Forward Edge of Battle Area) where the rangers had laid their linear defense. About the heaviest weaponry that the rangers were carrying were AT-4s and M-203s (40 mm, single shot grenade launcher that mounts under a primary battle rifle), along with their 7.62mm medium machine guns. Their snipers didn't even have any 50 cals. on that mission.

As the FAVs started eating up the rangers with their 50 cals, the ranger's CCT attachments were calling in Puff. "Thunder, Thunder, this is Thor, over."

"Thor, this is Thunder, go."

"Bring down the rain, TRP-1, 225°-300 meters, over."

"Copy, TRP-1, 225°-300 meters, over."

"Affirmative, send it."

"Roger, standby."

About fifteen seconds later the 7.62 rounds came raining down on the FAVs and their 50 cals. While Spectre was firing his solid red tracer wall of lead down on the Air Force defenders, two of the Phalanxs gunners saw the fire coming down and trained their Vulcan chain-guns on the point of origin.

Then they both cut loose with five thousand rounds each. That was all she wrote for one of the orbiting, fire breathing dragons from the east coast. As the fire ball came spiraling down from five thousand feet AGL, it could be seen fifty miles away. Thunder was out of the game.

After seeing the C-130 gunship go down, Hulk ordered Raptor-1 to take out the ground based Vulcans. A pair off F-15s were coming in low and fast headed for one of the Phalanxs that double teamed the Spectre. The Vulcan gunner leveled his cannons and let them have it all, right in the face. He was living on a prayer as he asked the Lord to make his aim straight and true.

By now Hulk had eighteen, F-15s in the air. Between the Phalanxs gunners, Avenger gunners, AH-60 gunships, and the ground troops armed with Stinger surface-to-air missiles, the air force had been holding their own. However, the more F-15s that became airborne, the more Colonel Oakley's assets were being eliminated.

That was all about to change. The first six Navy F-14 Super Tomcats had arrived on the battlefield and had begun acquiring targets. The six naval aviators had broken off in two bird attack teams. Now the F-15s would have to pull double duty and avoid elimination from both the sky and ground forces that would be coming at them.

One of the navy teams was gunning for a pair of F-15s that were three clicks south of the airfield. They came in above them from the rear —- the perfect attack posture. The two Strike Eagles were flying low and coming in from the south to engage some of the Phoenix Raven ground forces and unaware that the navy fighters had arrived over the battlefield.

The Tomcats unleashed their Phoenix missiles (AIM-54C: [AAM]-Air-to-air-missile, long range, radar guided, speed: Mach-5, range: 100 miles) on the distracted F-15s. Outdated ordinance, but as lethal as ever. Once the heat seekers were on their tails they had no reaction time. It was over in a heart beat.

Just as soon as the two fighters flamed to the ground a pair of F-15s were targeting the two F-14s. One Strike Eagle sent a solid stream of lead right up one of their tails. The other Tomcat fired his flairs and headed for the deck. He was hoping if not too shake the eagles in the ground battle, perhaps he could avoid destruction until more of his Navy buddies arrived from their home base.

Just as the air war was being waged, so was the ground war raging on. The Air Force airmen had a platoon of rangers pinned down near the north end of the runway. The airmen were using the bounding over-watch in their FAVs to gain ground on the ranger's linear defense. The rangers were getting their asses handed to them because they were outgunned by the heavy 50 cals. One of Colonel Oakley's Blackhawks was also pounding away at the platoon with his mini guns. The rangers were caught in a wicked crossfire...

Just as the rangers were running out of ammo and about to be overrun, a cherry saved the day. PFC Sargent finally found his squad when they were in a world of hurt. Much to his surprise he found himself just under the Blackhawk gunship that was spanking his platoon's ass with two 7.62 mini guns that were hurdling 3,000 rounds a minute at his brothers.

The lethal air machine was just off the deck at about 50 feet AGL as it fired two solid red streams of lead forward. It looked like it was firing two large lasers like an airship out of a Terminator movie. PFC Sargent leveled his M-240 and fired his entire hundred round belt into the cockpit. Then he reloaded another belt and was ready for the six-man air force strike team that would be coming after him if they survived the crash.

With the hail of gunfire now off their backs the platoon had a chance. Then one of the platoon squad leaders, Staff Sergeant Els yelled at one of the CCT guys, "Hey, man, see if you can get a laze on those FAVs now! If ya can, call in Spectre on them."

"Roger that," yelled the airman.

Then Sergeant Els heard on his squad radio, "Sergeant Els, Sergeant Els, is that you guys over there?"

Sergeant Els questioned, "Is that you, Private Sargent?"

"Yes, Sergeant. I just shot down a chopper! Are you guys the ones they were shooting at?"

Sergeant Els replied, "Affirmative, now get yer ass over here ASAP!"

Then Sergeant Els heard over the radio, "Wait, there's guys coming out of that chopper and shooting at me!"

Sergeant Els yelled into his mic, "Stay where you are, and lay down some suppressive fire. We're coming after you!" He received no reply. He only heard 5.56mm and 7.62mm rounds being fired back and forth.

The rounds from the FAVs 50 cals. still had them pined down. Sergeant Els yelled out, "Airman, I need that spectre now!"

"Roger that. It's on it's way!" Just then, the ceiling fell out with a wall of lead raining down on the three FAVs that had them pined down.

The 50 cal. rounds stopped coming in and Sergeant Els yelled, "All right, first squad B-team, go out and get him."

Once they had PFC Sargent safely back with his squad, there wasn't a man there that wasn't thanking him for saving their bacon. Sergeant Els said to his platoon sergeant, "You know he saved our asses. If he hadn't come along, we'd have all been toast. I'm puttin' him in for the CMH (Congressional Medal of Honor) when we get back."

The E-7 looked at Sergeant Els and said, "You bet your ass. I'll sign the paperwork. What's his first name anyway?"

Sergeant Els replied, "Cody—it's Cody, Sergeant."

Meanwhile, the navy flyboys were out gunned, even with a full 12-bird squadron in the sky now. By then Hulk had over two dozen F-15s in the fight. The stakes just got higher in the battle. The B-1 Bombers were prepped and ready to takeoff, just as soon as Raptor-1 gave the word that he controlled the air space over Texas and it was safe for them to takeoff.

PANIC IN THE WHITE HOUSE

21 APRIL 2011
WASHINGTON, D.C.

Because the C-130 Spectre gunship and three satellites were sending real time imagery to the Pentagon and the White House, President Osama and his cabinet were able to follow the entire battle in the White House situation room; LIVE…

The Secretary of Defense, Roland Gants looked on in disbelief as the destruction and loss of life on both sides continued to mount. Tears could be seen coming from Holly Chilton's eyes as she watched in horror. The occasional expression of disgust could be heard from Job Binder from time to time. The only person in the room, who sat quietly and expressionless was President Osama. It was like he had no emotions as he watched Americans killing Americans. Perhaps that's because he was a Muslim.

Finally Osama asked Mr. Binder, "Job, how do you think the American public is going to react to this little skirmish?"

The vice president's jaw hit the floor as he looked at Osama and barked, "Skirmish, what the hell are you calling a skirmish? You've probably just started another civil war here!"

Osama replied, "Oh come on, it's not that bad. The American public will realize that we had to do this in the interest of national security, right?"

The vice president stood up and said, "I can't believe I actually ran on the same ticket with you. You disgust me, Bakr! I'll be in the bathroom if anyone needs me." Then he walked out of the room. Mr. Gants just sat there, looking at Osama shaking his head in disbelief.

Then Osama asked Holly what she thought about it. She said, "I think you won't have to worry about a reelection. You may have to worry about being lynched by the American public." Once again, the room was so quiet you could hear a pin drop.

The battle was in its third hour now and the local civilians and media around Abilene were aware of the fight and flocking to Dyess Air Force Base to observe. Once the first local affiliate reports went on the airways, the big networks picked it up quickly. *ABC, CBS, CNN, FOX,* and *NBC* were all covering the story of the century, at least for America.

As Harold Rivers reported live on the battle for Dyess Air Force Base, he reviewed the facts. "We don't know exactly what military units there are fighting, but we do know it's a full-scale battle. There seems to be an air war over Dyess Air Force Base as well as an intense battle on the ground. Now we turn you over to our KXVA affiliate out of Abilene, Texas with our on the ground reporter Jack Strong. Jack, if you can hear me, what's the situation there on the ground in Abilene tonight?"

As the reporter covered the earphone in his ear with the palm of his hand, he strained to better hear Harold Rivers' words. "Well, Harlod, let me clarify first that Dyess Air Force Base is not in Abilene. It's about eight miles west of the city. I'm sorry to report that we are unable to transmit any rolling footage of the fighting because our camera was damaged while we were climbing over the base's perimeter fence. The scene here is a lot of heavy air and ground fighting. The fighting here is just as intense as anything I've seen in Iraq or Afghanistan!"

Then Harold Rivers asked, "Jack, can you tell us about the still photo in the studio behind me, of an air explosion?"

Mr. Strong proceeded to give a detailed account of the photo that he and his crew had forwarded on to the *FOX* super station. "Yes, Harold, that was an Apache attack helicopter that seemed to be protecting the airfield here when an air-to-air missile came in from a fighter jet, blew it to pieces, and lit up the sky. Neither of the crew escaped from the chopper. The helmet you see in the lower left corner of the photo is mine. I was watching the air battle when my photographer Les Knowles, kneeling behind me, caught the shot."

FOX LIVE: Attack on Dyess AFB, Texas

Then Harold asked Jack if he could paint a picture for the viewers in regards to the aerial fighting.

"Yes, sir, there are a lot of low-flying attack helicopters in the area, fighting both with ground troops and each other. They're usually flying between fifty and three hundred feet above the ground. Then there are a bunch of fighter jets fighting in dog fights two or three thousand feet up. And as I stated before, some of the jets and helos are attacking each other. Oh, and I even think I saw a Spectre gunship firing down on a position about thirty minutes ago."

21 APRIL 2011
SHADOW WOLF RANCH

By then Gerard's automated notification system had alerted him to the live *FOX News* broadcast with Harold Rivers. Once he

was awake enough to realize what was going on he immediately initiated the alert roster notification system. He called Alex
whom in turn called Dutch whom in turn called Hunter whom
in turn called Damon; all with instructions to assemble in the
commo room.

Alex was the first to arrive in the commo room and started
booting up the systems and put a pot of coffee on. Soon, all of the
senior SFCPF members were all assembled and ready to learn of
the evenings events. Alex asked Gerard, "What was the title of
the alert you received from your system?"

Gerard said, "War in Texas!" No one said anything. They all
just sort of looked at each other and chose their seats to watch
the broadcast.

Alex asked Gerard, "You got your recorder on?"

"Yes, sir," he replied. Alex just issued out pens and clipboards
to take notes and formulate their questions on. Then the men
watched the remainder of the live broadcast with Harold Rivers
and Jack Strong.

✳ ✳ ✳

"Jack, can you describe the ground fighting for us?"

"Yes, sir, there seems to be a perimeter of men around the air strip
in a defensive position with various attacking units hitting them
from all directions. I'm hearing all kinds of small arms and rocket
fire going on. O wait a minute, we just saw a volley of ground
launched rockets takeoff and destroy two low-flying jets. I think
they were F-15s or F-16s." Mr. Strong had a pair of binos in his
hands as he strained to better see the aerial combat above him.
His photographer, Les Knowles was trying to make it out using
a pair of NODs (same as NVGs); however, he quickly discovered
that the aerial explosions he saw only blinded him through the
optics, since they were designed to amplify light.

"Harold, without actually being able to interview anyone
involved in the fighting here and the way things look, I would

guess that the enemy, whoever that is, are trying to hijack or destroy the B-1 Bombers that are sitting here on the runway. We have seen a few pairs of fast movers taking off from the runway. They're probably the jets that are protecting this airbase from the invaders."

Then Harold asked, "Jack, with all of your experience as an embedded reporter in Iraq and Afghanistan with our troops, have you seen any foreign looking vehicles there yet that might give us an indication where these invaders came from?"

"No, sir," the reporter replied. "All I've seen at this point are Apaches, Blackhawks, and either F-15s or F-16s. We're not close enough to see any of the ground troops or their vehicles."

Then Harold said, "Okay, Jack, we'll come back to you a little later on. Keep your head down, buddy."

$$* * *$$

The news anchor started to recap on the story when Alex started to issue out instructions.

> Gerard, please set up your system to record all news channels about this battle. We're bound to gather a little intel there. We'll inform everyone else in the morning. No sense in waking anyone up now.
>
> I want to know more details about this battle before we make any premature decisions. Just the same, we'll conduct a complete mission equipment systems check after our brief tomorrow. We may be executing 'Operation Freedom Run' very soon now. I want to see what happens after the dust settles.

$$* * *$$

As the other men left the room to go back to bed, Alex realized how very soon they could find themselves in battle. As his mind started to drift in that direction, he quickly found himself thinking of his military career that gave him the skills and experience to deal with the impending violence that was headed straight for him.

Having completed six years in the 1/75th Ranger Battalion as a staff sergeant, his combative skills grew much better. Not from the can of whoop-ass to be issued out for the anticipated half-breed comments but from the formal hand-to-hand combat training. Alex's other learned skills and traits included discipline, patience, teambuilding, weapons, tactics, explosives, medical, patrolling, loyalty, honor, and leadership. His combative skills weren't the only thing that grew since Alex went into the service. He gained twenty-five pounds of muscle mass from about a billion push-ups and flutter kicks, not to mention the rest of his intense PT (Physical Training) regiment. Now his frame was six foot one at two hundred pounds—a lean, mean, killing machine.

He liked that unit and that black ranger beret. It set them apart from all of the Legs (Military, Non-Airborne qualified personnel) in the army. The rangers were the most disciplined and conditioned soldiers that he had seen in the army. However, Alex had heard of another special breed of soldier in the US Army.

Now, it was time to reenlist or pack his bags for the block. That decision took him about three seconds to make. Alex went to the re-up NCO and told him that he wanted to volunteer for SF. The recruiter stated that he could re-up for SF; however, there would be a catch. He said, "If you don't pass the Q-Course (Special Forces Qualification Course, same as SFQC), you'll be reassigned according to the army's needs, wherever they need you."

Alex confidently replied, "No problem. I won't fail!"

After completing the SFQC as an 18B, Alex was assigned to the 5th SFG (Special Forces Group) at Fort Bragg, North Carolina.

If one had to make a make a good analogy between Rangers and Special Forces, rangers would be *Star War's* Stormtroopers and SF would be the specially trained, elusive Jedi. Other than being completely the opposite of the rangers, the SF soldiers were taught to be imaginative and creative, as well as totally unconventional and self-sufficient. This SF stuff truly was right up his alley. It also fell in line with his Iroquois Indian heritage.

While in 5th group, Alex was able to get a couple of schools under his belt. Combat Diver and (HALO; High Altitude Low Opening parachute jump). He was starting to acquire some special skills while on his scuba A-team (Army Special Forces, twelve-man team).

Later on, Alex became the 5th SFG, NCOIC (Noncommissioned Officer in Charge) for the Combat Dive Facility, at Bragg. He stayed in 5th group until his 3rd Battalion became the nucleus to reactivate 3rd SFG, which was deactivated after the Vietnam War. The remainder of 5th SFG had been relocated to Fort Campbell, Kentucky.

While in 3rd SFG, First Battalion, Alex was still assigned to a Scuba SFOD-A (Special Forces Operational Detachment—team Alpha (same as A-Team). It was time again for more schools. This time, he attended Sniper and O & I (Special Forces Operations and Intelligence Sergeant 18F; E-7, Trained in intelligence, target and threat analysis, and ID and fingerprinting) school.

The list of deployments and countries that he had worked in was getting longer and longer. After a while, they all seemed to blend into one another, as one long deployment. Alex was honing his skills and trade craft as a quite capable, quiet professional, and warrior.

Between all of the jumping, helo casting, fast roping, SPIES (Special Patrol Infiltration/Exfiltration System), rappelling, INFILs, and EXFILs, he was getting more time in choppers than most conventional crew chiefs and pilots. He was digging it. He was born to soar with eagles.

Well, after thirty minutes of reminiscing, Alex decided to head back to the house for a couple hours of rack time. The trick would be to see if he could slip under the covers without waking the Ninja, Leiko.

Meanwhile, back on the battlefield the ranger unit was starting to loose their foothold on the airfield. By this time four or five of the navy's F-14s had been downed and about a dozen of Hulk's F-15s had been taken out of the fight. The east coast generals certainly hadn't counted on all of the additional security upgrades that the Dyess forces had implemented. The F-15s not only had to deal with the F-22s and the F-14 squadron, but they also had to contend with the ground based Stingers and Phalanxs cannons.

When Colonel Oakley had sent up his initial SALUTE report to the Phoenix Raven TOC, he informed them that from what he saw, he thought the enemy force was trying to take the B-1 Bombers. He was then ordered not too let even one B-1 get off the ground, even if it meant destroying it. That's just what the seasoned war veteran would do, if he had to.

By that time he had lost seven of his twelve AH-60 Blackhawks. He was damned if he was going to loose any more. Just then he had a solid tracer stream of thirty mike mike blow by his cockpit window. That's when his crew chief yelled on his mic, " We've got an Apache on our tail!"

Colonel Oakley instructed everyone, "Hold on, this is going to get harry!"

The Colonel figured if the Apache was firing his chain gun at him, he was probably out of Hellfire missiles (AGM-114; [Air-to-surface missile], semi-active laser homing, speed: Mach 1.3, range: five miles). That meant they still had a chance if he could avoid his line of fire. He got on the radio to one of his southern Phalanxs gunners to set up the kill.

"Death Star-6, Death Star-6, this is Big Daddy, over."

"Big Daddy, this is Death Star-6, go."

"I've got an Apache on my tail, and I'm bringing him straight through your kill zone. Break. He's fifty meters behind me, and my running lights are on, how copy, over?"

"Big Daddy, I copy your Blackhawk lights on, Apache fifty meters in trail, over."

"Affirmative Death Star-6, smoke his ass!"

As Colonel Oakley was jinking his bird left and right to prevent the Apache gunner from lining up his thirty-millimeter chain gun for a kill shot, they were both quickly closing on the ambush kill zone. Just as the Apache pilot heard his gunner say sayonara sucker, the gunner looked out his portside window and saw a solid red wall of twenty mike mike lead about to impact his canopy. A half second later the gunship was a fire ball headed for hell. Colonel Oakley got on the air and said, "Thanks, Death Star, you saved our asses, brother!"

The truth of the matter was; the Apache gunner wasn't out of Hellfire missiles. He saw an outstanding pilot in Colonel Oakley and just wanted to make the kill with his cannons, like the fighters did in WWII. Well, he won't make that mistake again.

The Stinger missile crews, both man-pad and Avenger Ad Systems were getting some F-15 kills as well. However, with their friend or foe identifiers in the missile laser seeker/sensors disabled, there couldn't be any friendly aircraft near the enemy aircraft when they fired. Otherwise, the missile could target either heat source.

There was an air force Stinger man-pad team two clicks west of TRP-2. They had been waiting for the opportunity to fire on a lone team of F-15s ever since they had posted in their bunker. Two strike eagles were swinging wide in a westerly track when the airmen targeted them.

Once fired, the missile was away from the operator before engaging the main two-stage solid-fuel sustainer, which accelerated it to a speed of Mach-2.2.

Even though both birds fired their flairs and chaff, the missile managed to fly right up the tailpipe of the trail F-15. Then the flaming bird's wingman was able to gain a triangulation on the missiles launch site and he targeted it with extreme prejudice. After a sharp 360 the strike eagle was barreling toward the Stinger bunker. Then the bird fired a SLAMER Missile (AIM-120C

[AMR Advanced medium-range air-to-air missiles], semi-active radar guided, speed: Mach 4, range: fifty-seven miles)right on top of their position. There was nothing left but ash and cinder…

As the F-15 crew headed for the ceiling after taking out the missile bunker, they received another shocker. An F-22 Raptor flew right up on their starboard wing and looked them in the eye. The F-15 pilot instinctively performed a hard portside (left side of a water vessel, aircraft, or vehicle) bank to break contact.

Then the weapons officer shouted to the pilot, "Did you see that, a raptor, where did he come from? Is he one of ours? They didn't say anything about F-22s in the brief!" By the time they got their bearings the superior Raptor had vanished in thin air.

"At ease!" the pilot instructed his junior partner.

"Let me call Raptor-1."

"Raptor-1, Raptor-1, this is Tiger-3, over."

"Tiger-3, Raptor-1, send it, over."

"Raptor-1, do we have any friendly F-22 raptors up here, over?"

There was about a five second pause over the radio, and then their answer came. "Tiger-3, negative, negative. They must have come with the tomcats. They are enemy, over."

"Raptor-1, I copy enemy, out."

Then the pilot said to his gunner, "All right, let's find this guy. What da ya got for me?"

His weapons officer said, "Nothin', I got nothin' on radar." Then the pilot tried to calm his frantic partner. "Of course you don't, his bird is a stealth fighter. We've got to find him the old fashioned way, with our eyes."

The long awaited arrival of the six F-22 Raptors had finally come. This should tip the scales in the favor of Dyess Air Force Base. Then the squadron commander called to receive his mission orders. Big Daddy, Big Daddy, this is Eagle Killer, over."

"Eagle Killer, this is Big Daddy, send it, over."

"Big Daddy, you've got six F-22 Raptors at your disposal, where do you need us, over?"

"Eagle Killer, first help your F-14s take out the F-15s and that Spectre C-130 orbiting over the South end of the runway."

"Do not, I say again, do not let any B-1 bombers get in the air, how copy, over?"

"Big Daddy, I copy kill all F-15s and Spooky. No bombers fly, over."

"Eagle Killer, good copy, out."

Then Colonel Oakley put out a net call, "All Phoenix Raven call signs, F-22 Raptors are friendlies. I say again, F-22 Raptors are friendlies, how copy over?" Then all of his unit call signs acknowledged that they heard the call.

There were still two Apaches in the fight and they were proving hard too kill. Unlike fighter jets that had to keep moving over the battlefield, helos could duck for cover and hide while still covering their assigned sectors. One of those gunships had been hiding behind a stand of trees just northwest of TRP-1. His call sign was Magpie and his mission was to keep the North end of the runway clear so the B-1 Bombers could takeoff.

However, his luck was about to run out. One of the Phoenix Raven motorcycle scouts had come up on the lurking gunship and called in for support. He called in a pair of Navy Tomcats to do his bidding. "Tomcat-3, Tomcat-3, this is Rover-5, over."

"Rover-5, Tomcat-3, go."

"Tomcat-3, fire mission, over."

"Rover-5, send it."

"Enemy Apache, hovering twenty feet AGL behind trees; Northwest TRP-1, 350 meters, 290 degrees, over."

After about five seconds the scout received his reply. "Copy Rover-5, Helo, 20 ft. AGL, Northwest TRP-1, 350 meters, 290 degrees, over."

"That's affirmative, Tomcat-3, smoke him."

"Roger Rover-5, standby, out."

About a minute later, the bike scout saw two Tomcats screamin' in on the Apache. That's when the Apache crew realized they were busted and decided to go out shooting. They rose above the tree line and fired every missile they had left. It was a valiant last stand; however, a futile one.

The AH-64 gunship went down in a blaze of glory, the way most American fighting men do. When you've got nothing left to loose, you tend to fight to the end.

Once a pair of F-22s knocked the second C-130 gunship out of the sky, and more F-15s were being taken out, the Pentagon and White House realized that 'Operation Condor Repo' was going to fail. Now, the only eyes they had above the battlefield were in orbit high above the earth.

The only time that an F-22 Raptor could be detected by radar was when it opened the weapons bay doors on its belly to launch its missiles or bombs. Therefore, they had adopted a unique way to avoid being detected. They would roll over upside down while firing their weapons systems. The stealthy curves of the top side of the craft remained facing any radar systems below them.

While the F-15 was still at 10,000 feet AGL looking for the F-22 that had spooked them earlier, they had no luck locating him. That's when the F-22 pilot found them! He flew up from behind them and was about one thousand feet above them. The F-15's radar still had no indication of the deadly Raptor above them.

That's when the F-22 pilot rolled his war-bird over on it's back and unleashed one of his deadly Slamers on him. It was quick to find its target. In mere seconds the F-15 was falling to earth like a fiery meteorite.

When the last pair of F-15s was coming in low and fast to take out Colonel Oakley and another one of his Blackhawks, they caught the attention of one of the Avenger Ad teams in the South. They didn't hesitate to launch their Stinger missiles.

One of the bird's crew managed to eject before the deadly battery of Stinger missiles impacted and destroyed the last of Hulk's fighters. One of the Strike Eagles was unfortunately over the bases main post area when it was hit. The fiery ball of molten metal was headed straight for the base hospital. Thank God it finally impacted on top of the hospital's six story parking garage instead of the patient wards. There were over 800 troops in the military hospital. Many were recovering veterans from Iraq and Afghanistan.

With the last F-15 eliminated, the F-14s and F-22s were freed up to lend a hand toward the ground support role for dealing with the Ranger Battalion. The only enemy aircraft in the sky now was the last Apache gunship and it was preoccupied with trying to gun down one of the Phoenix Raven FAVs. The Airmen were busy firing on the rangers when the Apache picked them up in his sights. Now they were running for their lives at 60 mph.

The 50 cal. gunner in the front was still firing at the rangers, on his starboard side, while the M-60A3 gunner in the rear was firing, point blank, at the gunship on their tail. The Apache gunner had already fired five, 2.75 inch rockets at them and each one had failed to find its mark. While this cat and mouse chase was going on, a pair of F-14s saw it and responded.

Just as the Apache gunner had his 30-millimeter chain gun locked on the FAV and about to squeeze the trigger, the FAV ran into a ditch and stopped the vehicle dead in its tracks. The Apache blew right over them and began to do a 360 to come back around for another strafing run. That's when the pilot and gunner saw the two Phoenix missiles from the two F-14s coming straight for them.

They had no reaction time. They never even activated their flairs or chaff. Their careers were over in a heartbeat. The ditch had saved the airmen's lives from the chopper but the instantaneous stop from 60 mph had however taken all three of their lives.

The rear gunner broke his neck on the roll bar behind him. The front gunner crushed his throat on the butterfly handle of his

50 cal. The driver ripped open his Femoral artery on the underside of the steering column and bleed out in a couple of minutes. Talk about bum luck. The very thing that saved their lives also took them.

By 0430 all of Hulk's aircraft that had gotten off the ground had been destroyed. The Phoenix Raven force once again controlled the air space over Dyess Air Force Base. Colonel Oakley determined it was time to stop the fighting and the killing.

The rangers still loosely held a raged defensive perimeter around the airfield with approximately 300 soldiers. Not one B-1 Bomber ever got off the ground. Still, those brave men were ready to fight to the death, if their commander were but to give the word.

Colonel Oakley and his five remaining Blackhawk gunships had rotated back to the Phoenix Raven air strip and refueled. They all continued to orbit around the enemy forces on their airfield. All of Oakley's ground forces had also encircled the ranger's defensive perimeter.

Colonel Oakley instructed one of his five surviving Blackhawks to prevent the lead B-1 Bomber from trying to take off. As the lead B-1 was sitting on the runway, the crew was discussing weather or not they should attempt a take-off. Just then they saw something directly in front of them. It was about two hundred meters ahead of them while it hovered about fifty feet AGL.

Since it wasn't light out yet, the B-1 crew wasn't entirely sure what they saw up ahead of them. Then the gunship turned-on its running lights and fired a three hundred round burst of 7.62 mm 4-in-1 tracers from their mini guns over the heads of the B-1 crew. The pilot yelled, "Son of a...! That's it boys, we're done—we're not going anywhere! Any gunship that has mini guns has also got rockets and missiles."

Then Colonel Oakley contacted his TOC. "Raven, Raven, this is Big Daddy over."

"Big Daddy, Raven, send yer traffic, over."

"Raven, call the Pentagon and get me the radio frequency of this unit on our airfield. Break."

"I also want the commander's name and call sign so I can talk to him, over."

"Roger that Big Daddy, we're on it, over."

Fifteen minutes later, Colonel Oakley received his info and tried to contact the enemy commander. "Hulk, Hulk, this is Big Daddy, the Phoenix Raven commander, Colonel Oakley, over." He waited for a minute with no response and tried it again. "Hulk, Hulk, this is Big Daddy, the Phoenix Raven commander, Colonel Oakley, over." This time he received a response.

"Big Daddy, this is Hulk. Lieutenant Colonel Rogers, over."

"Colonel Rogers, it's over, you have no more air support, two thirds of your men are dead, you're surrounded by troops and air power, and you have no way out of here." Colonel Oakley paused for a few seconds before he continued. "Please, sir, consider surrendering before any more of our men die!"

A few seconds later Colonel Rogers said, "Colonel Oakley, I'll give you my answer in fifteen mikes (minutes) over."

Colonel Oakley replied, "Fair enough, sir, I'll be here, out."

Then Oakley switched back to his Phoenix Raven net and put out a net call. "All Phoenix Raven call signs, this is Big Daddy, hold your positions and report any enemy movement, how copy over?" Then all his units acknowledged his instructions.

At 0500, Colonel Oakley received his answer. "Big Daddy, Big Daddy, this is Hulk, over."

"Hulk, this is Big Daddy, send your traffic, over."

"Colonel Oakley, I will surrender my command to you, sir, on one condition. That you personally land at my location to accept my conditions, over."

Colonel Oakley replied, "Copy, I'll give you my answer in five mikes, over."

Colonel Rogers acknowledged, "Copy, five mikes, fair enough, out."

Colonel Oakley then ordered his crew chief to hook-up the sixty-foot fast rope that he always kept in his bird. Then he instructed his copilot, Major Burns to take the bird in just over the ranger TOC and issued his directives.

"Don't worry, Tom, they might be thinking they're getting a gunship, but all they're really getting is me. Once you get there, hold a hover at fifty feet AGL. I'll fast rope down and receive the terms for their surrender. I'll be in contact, don't worry. Tom, don't put any scratches on my baby."

Then Colonel Oakley gave Colonel Rogers his answer. "Hulk, Hulk, this is Big Daddy, over."

"Hulk, go."

"I'm coming in. Clear the LZ, over."

"Hulk, Copy, WILCO, Out." Once Major Burns had a solid hover over the ranger TOC, Colonel Oakley deployed his fast rope and descended into the mist of his enemy.

As soon as he hit the ground his crew chief jettisoned the fast rope. After that Major Burns flew Colonel Oakley's bird back to the other four birds and reassumed his orbit around the rangers.

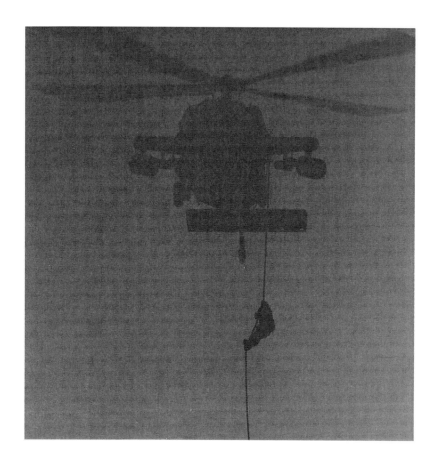

Colonel Rogers walked up to Colonel Oakley and said, "That's pretty good thinking on your part sir." Colonel Oakley replied, "You didn't really think you were going to get control of one of my gunships, did you?" Rogers said, "It was worth a try." Then Oakley said, "I probably would have tried the same thing."

The two started laughing as they shook hands. Colonel Oakley asked, "Where are you from Colonel Rogers?"

He said, "Georgia."

Oakley commented, "I know your unit is in Savannah, but are you actually from Georgia?"

"Yes, sir," he said. "Born and raised in Hinesville, Georgia."

Then Rogers asked Oakley, "What about you, sir?"

He replied, "Colorado Springs."

Rogers replied, "Nice place. I once went there to Fort Carson to train with the 10th Special Forces Group."

After the pleasantries, Colonel Oakley got to the point. "Okay Colonel Rogers, what are the terms of your surrender?"

"It's pretty simple," he said. "I just want to load up all of my dead, wounded, and all of the B-1 Bomber crews and fly out of here on those two C-5s setting on the tarmac.

Colonel Oakley produced a serious frown on his face and said, "You know I can't permit that." Then he continued, "The United States attacked Texas and the Free States in a lethal, unprovoked assault. You've killed innocent civilians and military citizens of another government. We must proceed here just as if you attacked Mexico, Canada, England, or even Russia.

"No, sir, my government will surely use you and your men as a bargaining tool to come to some sort of treaty with Washington. You know I don't have the authority to just release you and send you on your merry way.

"What we will do, sir, is treat you and your men according to the Geneva Convention. You're wounded will be given immediate medical attention. Your healthy men will be fed and placed in detention until our two governments come to some sort of an arrangement.

"And finally, the only way that is going to happen is if all of your men lay down all of their arms. Once that has happened, I will call in my troops to give the aforementioned aid and assistance. I will give you my personal word as a Christian and military officer that your men will be treated as well as I treat my own men. Well, what do you say, Colonel Rogers?"

Colonel Rogers said, "Well, sir, as you well know, I must call my HQ before I can surrender my command and my men to another government."

Colonel Oakley replied, "Fair enough, sir, make your call." Rogers walked away and went to his commo chief. He told him to get the Pentagon on the horn. Then Colonel Rogers proceeded to inform his command of his battlefield situation.

After about ten minutes on the secure sat comm, he came back to Colonel Oakley. He said, "All right, sir, I've been commanded to surrender my command and men to you."

Colonel Oakley replied, "Thank you, sir, I'm glad that no more of our men have to die today. Just as soon as all your weapons are stock piled here, I'll call my medical and security personnel in."

Colonel Rogers told his commo chief to give him the mic. Then he put out a net call to all of his subordinate units. "Attention on the net, attention on the net, this is Hulk *Actual*, Break."

"All Hulk call signs, lay down your weapons and surrender to Dyess troops. I say again, lay down your weapons and surrender to Dyess troops."

"All Hulk call signs acknowledge, over."

After all but one of his call signs acknowledged his instructions. He received the response that every commander dreaded after a battle. "Negative Hulk, this is Iron Man. We will not surrender and be put in a POW camp!" Then Master Sergeant Stevens switched back over to his internal net and issued his sniper a new tasking order.

"Zero, Zero, Iron Man, over."

"Zero, send it, over."

"Zero, do you have eyes on Hulk, over?"

"Affirmative, over."

Sergeant Stevens commanded, "Zero, take out that cowardice bastard. Do you hear me?"

The sniper team replied, "Iron Man, are you sure about this one? Over."

"Zero, do you want to rot in a POW camp or fight our way out of here?"

Zero replied, "Copy, got it, standby for rounds down range."

As Colonel Rogers stood beside Colonel Oakley, they waited for clarification from the Delta Force team commander on what his intentions were. Rogers looked at Oakley and said, "He's hold up in the tower with a thirty-man team." Just then Colonel Rogers head exploded from a 50 cal. round. Then his lifeless body fell to the ground. Colonel Oakley knew exactly where the round came from as he thought to himself, *If this whack job will kill his own commander to prove a point, he'll surely fight my men to the death.*

Then Colonel Oakley grabbed his radio and started barking out orders to his orbiting Blackhawk gunships. "Gunship-1, Big Daddy, take out the control tower with extreme prejudice, how copy, over!"

"Gunship-1, I copy, Over." Just then two Blackhawks broke away from their orbit and went screamin' for the ATCT.

Just prior to firing, Colonel Oakley heard "Rockets Away!" over his radio. A moment later the two gunships unleashed eight 2.75 inch rockets into the top half of the ATCT. Once all of the burning debris had landed, the two birds used their rotor wash to blow the smoke away from the remains to look for any additional threats. Once Major Burns was satisfied that the threat had been neutralized, he sent Colonel Oakley a sit report (Situation Report).

"Big Daddy, Big Daddy, Gunship-1, over."

"Gunship-1, send it, over."

"Big Daddy, threat neutralized, over."

"Gunship-1, good job, reassume orbit, over."

"Gunship-1, copy, out."

About thirty minutes later, there was a huge pile of weapons in the center of the ranger TOC. Then Colonel Oakley called in his troops and they descended on the position like flies on crap. For the first time since the attack began, med-evac helos instead of gunships filled the sky over Dyess Air Force Base.

THE DUST SETTLES

21 APRIL 2011
DYESS AFB, TEXAS

By noon the entire American nation was aware of the fierce fighting that took place in the battle on Texas soil. Once all of the enemy forces were policed up and taken to a hospital, morgue, or detention facility, the clean-up operations began.

Unlike most government and military operations that occur under a darkened cloak of secrecy, Governor Pevey, Admiral Woolard, and Vice Admiral Sparrow all agreed that they wanted the maximum national press coverage possible. They wanted to show America the mass devastation and gain the support of additional western states.

They sent out an open invitation to all of the major US news networks to come to Texas and cover the number one story in the nation's history since the last civil war. Needless to say, they all came, like bees to honey.

21 APRIL 2011
SHADOW WOLF RANCH

The biggest story on the planet was plastered all over the Internet and every TV station in the world. Alex Boulder and his entire crew were all in the ops room watching the live reports. They were watching a *FOX News* (live special report) with Bert Bailer. He went straight to a live press conference that Governor Pevey was holding at Dyess, Air Force Base.

Governor Rich Pevey was furious about this unprovoked attack on his state. It was obvious that he could barely contain his anger as he spoke live to the press and America. He began his speech in a semi calm manner.

By now, America, you and the rest of the world have heard that the great state of Texas was savagely attacked in the still of the night last night. President Osama and the Department of Defense saw fit to order a lethal, unprovoked attack on their fellow Americans at Dyess Air Force Base here in Texas. They ordered the American military to intentionally kill their fellow American citizens—both civilian and military.

On Dec 14, 2010, Texas, Oklahoma, Colorado, and Montana, were all in agreement to secede from Union, and we did so. Since the Osama administration has been in office, they have failed to uphold the Constitution of the United States of America and look out for this nation's best interest at heart.

Now they have tried to start another civil war to further tear this great nation apart. Therefore, we four states, the Free States, extend an open invitation to any other state in the nation that wishes to secede from the union and join us. It is only a matter of time until this mad man turns on your state as he did ours last night.

Now, the press crews that are here on the ground with us in Texas today are going to show you America and the rest of the world the carnage, destruction, and loss of life that Bakr Houssam Osama has inflicted upon his own countrymen. May God have mercy on him because Texas won't! Thank you, and God bless Texas.

Then the network switched back to Bert Bainer as he recapped Governor Pevey's speech. Afterward, they switched to the field crews at Dyess Air Force Base for the images that the Governor had promised the nation and the rest of the world.

One of the first photos they posted was of an F-15 that had been shot down by one of the base's Phalanxs cannons just as it was taking off. The air crew ejected safely only to be captured by

Texas forces. They would be held as POW's along with the other approximate five hundred troops from the east coast.

The tally left about three hundred rangers, 144 B-1 Bomber crewmen, forty Apache technicians, and about fifteen Delta Force and CCT guys that weren't in the ATCT when Colonel Oakley's gunships took it out.

The next photo that they showed was an ARFF (Aircraft Rescue Fire Fighters) team still trying to get many of the aircraft fires under control. That particular fire was the remains of one of the defending Navy F-14 Tomcats that was shot down by a stolen F-15 of the invading military force from the east coast.

Just then the media saw the now famous Colonel Oakley walking toward them. Needless to say, they stormed him like a crowd of bargain shoppers on Black Friday. Little did they know that Governor Pevey had instructed Admiral Wollard and Colonel Oakley to fully cooperate with the press. In fact, the Colonel was to paint a very detailed picture with live graphics for them. Governor Pevey was going to use the press against President Osama, just the way he had so often used them to do his bidding.

Then the barrage of questions began flying from the press. A reporter from channel 25 asked Colonel Oakley what his role in the battle was. Colonel Oakley replied, "I am the Phoenix Raven Unit Commander on Dyess Air Force Base; in charge of defending the airfield and it's aircraft. My unit successfully repelled and captured the attacking force from Georgia in a fierce and deadly battle."

Then another reporter asked, "Can you describe the battle for us. You know, paint a picture for us."

Then the colonel began, "Yes, sir, I can do that. In fact, I need to do that for every American in this country, so they can see just how out of control President Osama and the department of defense really are!

"The main body of the attacking force was the 1/75th Airborne Ranger Battalion out of Savannah, Georgia. Their two air assets were the army's Task Force 160ths Apache attack helicopters from Hunter Army Airfield in Georgia. The second unit was the Air Force's B-1 Bomber and F-15 pilots that flew here in two C-5s from Dover Air Force Base, Maryland.

"The mission that President Osama and the Department of Defense ordered them to execute was capture the airfield, steal the F-15s for air support, and then steal the B-1 Bombers and fly them back to the east coast, where they would have control of the bombers and all of their payload.

"Before they could accomplish that, however, they sent a team of highly trained Delta Force operatives in first to murder the civilian and military personnel that were working in the air traffic control tower and radar room. That way, we wouldn't see them flying in."

Then one of the reporters interrupted Colonel Oakley. "Wait a minute, Colonel, what exactly do you mean by 'murdered'?"

Then Colonel Oakley continued, "I mean exactly that. Murdered! They intentionally executed unarmed civilian and air force airmen that had absolutely no way to defend themselves. That's what I call *murdered*, ladies and gentlemen. Later on, we will show you all on national TV the CCTV coverage from the ATCT that was recorded and piped directly to the RAPCON room.

"Once this unit of killers captured the air traffic control tower and radar room, then the ranger battalion jumped in and took our airfield by force. After that, they stole our F-15s that were parked on the tarmac and got them in the air to attack us when we came to challenge an unknown attacking force in the middle of the night."

Another reporter interrupted again and asked, "Colonel, at this point, you still didn't know who they were?"

Colonel Oakley replied, "Yes, sir, that's correct. As far as we knew, they were Iranians, Russians, or even terrorist like the ones that hit us on 9/11." Then Colonel Oakley resumed his description of the events. "By that time, they also had an unknown number of Apache gunships in the air that were killing us as well. They brought them along with them in one of the C-5s for their deliberate attack. You see, people, they had intentions of killing their fellow Americans all along. You don't bring along gunships armed to the tooth when you don't have ill intentions toward the ones you're going to visit.

"Once my unit arrived on the scene, we determined that a hostile force had killed our people, stolen lethal aircraft to be used against us, and was attempting to steal strategic bombers that could strike any nation in the world. We simply couldn't let that happen, so we defended ourselves and fought back."

One of the female reporters asked him, "Were there any women or children killed in the fighting?"

Oakley replied, "We haven't even begun digging out bodies yet. I would certainly think so because one of their jets that was shot down crashed on top of our military hospital. That hospital has around five hundred to eight hundred beds in it."

As the reporter had a look of disgust and anger on her face, the colonel continued conveying his observations of the battle. "While my forces were engaged with and outgunned by the enemy, Governor Pevey and Admiral Woolard had the foresight to send us some much-needed air support. We were getting pounded by all of the F-15s they were using against us.

"They sent us a squadron of F-14s and some F-22s from the Naval Air Station at Fort Worth Joint Reserve Base. Once those navy fly boys got here, it turned the tide. Between them and our Ad (Air Defense) ground support, we were finally able to knock out all of the enemy's air support to include the two Spectre C-130 gunships they had orbiting over the battlefield.

"This was some of the fiercest combat I'd been in since Iraq and Afghanistan, even more so because at least there, we controlled the air. And just think, people, this was on our own soil, ordered by our own president and government."

One reporter asked the colonel, "Sir, do you think President Osama has any remorse about sending Americans to kill Americans?" The colonel took off his shades and looked him square in the eyes. The reporter was a bit intimidated by the colonel's rough look and his battle scar that ran down the entire right side of his face.

Then Colonel Oakley said, "Absolutely not! There's no doubt in my military mind that he has no feelings of love or concern for his fellow Americans. How did we ever let a man like that become our president and Commander-in-chief?"

In a brief amazing moment, even the people of the press hung their heads in shame. This is the same press that thought Osama could do no wrong as he was campaigning for the highest office in our land. The same press that turned the other way every time Osama was caught keeping the company of criminals, terrorist, communist, thugs, and people whom hated and were ashamed of America.

It seemed as if the press had made an unannounced proclamation that they would do every thing in their power to see to it that he was elected president of the United States of America, even if it meant simply not covering any negative issue concerning him.

Every other presidential candidate in America's history had been toughly crucified by the press for the most miniscule transgression in their past. Perhaps it was time for the press hounds to turn on their master?

Meanwhile, Governor Pevey and Admiral Woolard were in their temporary command center on the edge of the airfield. They were watching Colonel Oakley's live interview on TV. Governor Pevey said to the admiral, "Damn, Joe, we're going to have to put Colonel Oakley in charge of the air force's public affairs unit."

Then Woolard said, "He always was very articulate in the way he spoke."

The governor said, "I believe he just gave the rest of the states the pitch to get them to join us."

After Colonel Oakley put his shades back on, he used his commanding voice to gain the attention of the reporters. "Okay, ladies and gentlemen, if you will walk with me, I'll show you some of the devastation left in the wake of President Osama's attackers." Then he led them to various sites to explain the scene. The first place he took them was to the scene of a fire tanker trying to extinguish an aircraft fire.

Then he proceeded to give the journalist a very descriptive explanation of that particular crash site.

"My friends, I'm going to give you a personal account of this crash site since I was personally involved with it. As you all saw me land my bird before I approached you a while ago, I fly an AH-60 Blackhawk gunship. That's what I fought the duration of this battle in.

"I was flying along when I got an AH-64 Apache gunship, a superior aircraft, on my tail and couldn't shake him. After he began firing his thirty millimeter chain gun at me, I figured that he was out of missiles and we might just have a chance.

"Since I couldn't shake him I set up an ambush for him, and he followed me right into the kill zone. Then one of my ground-based weapon systems knocked him out of the sky, and he impacted right here before you.

"Ladies and gentlemen, I later found out from one of my men on the ground that the hounding Apache did indeed still have an array of Hellfire missiles that he could have fired at us. That pursuing pilot and gunner made a conscious decision not to fire a missile at us and end it quickly.

"The only conclusion that I can come to about them is that they wanted to kill us using their guns, a much more challenging task than unleashing a missile and forgetting about it. To our attacking force, they found some sort of sport and challenge in trying to kill us last night, however, the Lord was on the side of the just last night and helped us prevail over our enemy."

One of the reporters had a condescending look on his face as he asked the colonel and said, "Come on, you don't really believe that God helped you win this battle, do you?"

Then Colonel Oakley continued, "Sir, the army has a saying. 'There are no atheist in foxholes.' If you ever find yourself in combat, you'll see just what that means. We were out gunned in every regard last night—a thousand men against three hundred, superior Apaches against Blackhawks, thirty-six F-15s against twelve, aging F-14s and six F-22s, and two orbiting Spectre C-130 gunships raining down ordinance on my forces.

"Yes, sir, I will certainly say that God was on our side last night! In fact, my copilot's name is Tom, but last night, I would have sworn it was Gabriel. You know, like the archangel."

Then all of the reporters busted out laughing as Colonel Oakley said, "Yes, sir, that's one of the things that are wrong with this great nation of ours. We've taken God out of our lives and country. This country was founded on God and guns!" Much to his surprise, the reporters began clapping after he said that.

Then the colonel suggested that they move on to another site. They were passing a downed F-15 while they were en route to the location where two of his Blackhawks had been shot down. Colonel Oakley had no sooner directed their attention to an F-15 on its belly in the grass, when it burst into flames.

The bird was conducting an emergency landing last night when it struck some unexpected debris on the runway. It snapped his landing gear off, and he slid off the runway and came to a peaceful stop in the grass. The crew didn't even have to eject. They simply got out and ran away.

Something had been smoldering for hours before it finally ignited the jet fuel. Colonel Oakley got on his hand held radio and informed fire control that they had another fire to contend with.

Once Colonel Oakley safely escorted all of the reporters out of the potential blast radius of the F-15, he took them to the next crash site—the place where two entire Blackhawk crews had been killed.

Then Colonel Oakley began to put the pieces together for the media on this tragic crash site. He took off his sun glasses as he spoke, "Ladies and gentlemen, this is where I lost two of my birds and eighteen of my finest men. They were performing their duty while defending their homeland against a hostile force. Their lives were extinguished with extreme prejudice.

"They were blown out of the sky by two enemy F-15s firing their Sparrow missiles on them. My boys never had a chance! It will be quite some time until we can get in there to recover what's left of their bodies."

Just then the woman reporter whom had asked him the question about the women and children looked at Colonel Oakley and saw tears rolling down his face. She asked him, "Are you all right, sir?" Then all the other reporters looked at him and made sure that they caught his emotions on film.

He replied, "Yes, ma'am, I'm just feeling the sorrow that many of America's mothers, fathers, brothers, sisters, and children will feel after we notify them of their losses on both sides." After composing himself, Colonel Oakley continued with the reporters briefing/tour of the battlefield. "All right, people, as you can well guess, there are over eight hundred dead soldiers, airmen, and civilians as a result of this intense battle. As always is the American policy, we will not show you any of the dead bodies. In fact, we're not even going around the locations where they are. Once the medical and identification teams have had a chance to tend to them all, then we'll make a tour available to you all in those areas.

"Now, ladies and gentlemen, we've arranged for you to go to our military hospital and see some of the walking wounded and possibly take some interviews if they are willing."

Then Colonel Oakley got on his radio and called for the two busses that were waiting on the runway to come and pick them up for the short trip.

By 1500, the reporters had wrapped up their interviews and been bussed back to their vehicles. Colonel Oakley thanked all of them for coming and for getting the real story—the truth—out on the air for all Americans to see what horrific results President Osama and the Department of Defense had to be held accountable for.

By 1800, all of the networks had their full stories on the nightly news. Colonel Oakley must have had a profound affect on the reporters because all of their reports were completely factual, unbiased, and accurate, pretty much a first since Osama started his campaign for the presidency.

21 APRIL 2011
SHADOW WOLF RANCH

It was 2100, now and Alex and his team had digested all of the news reports that they had seen. Gerard even managed to record every other news broadcast that they hadn't watched. They would watch them all when time permitted. Alex stood up in front of the room and said, "All right, folks, let's talk about what we think will happen next and what kind of timeline it will happen in. I think there will be more states to secede within a couple of weeks or so. What do ya all think?"

Dutch pretty much agreed with Alex's assessment. Hunter said, "Yeah, but I don't think that any Eastern states will join. Especially those bastards that are in league with the Osama nation!" Gerard seemed to think that the Osama administration wasn't about to let it go, especially since Texas handed them their asses.

Damon said, "I agree with Gerard. They're not going to take that lying down."

Alex asked Damon, "How long do you think it will be before they're bold enough to try something else?"

He replied, "There's no saying, they need enough time to regroup."

Leiko added her two cents worth. "Hey, you guys aren't even thinking about the fact that Congress and the Senate might try to flex their arm against him. They might even try to impeach him after ordering our military to kill Americans. You all know that there are going to be civil uprisings all over the country.

"I think we should just sit back and see what comes down the pike on this one. Hey, if we give it enough time, some concerned citizen might even take care of the problem for the nation."

Alex looked at Ethan and Luis and said, "You guys sure are quiet. What's on your minds?"

Ethan replied, "You askin' for volunteers for that mission? I think we should join forces with Texas and go kick his communist ass! Hey, I'm just sayin'."

Luis said, "I think we should be ready to go on a moments notice."

Alex took the floor again, "Okay, people, how does this sound? As Leiko said, the federal government may act against Osama. Let's face the facts. Nothing is going to happen to the joint chiefs-of-staff. They're probably the ones whom authored the mission plan for Osama's invasion on Texas.

"Governor Pevey is ready to strike at anything that moves after this. I believe he's going to muster much support from the states around him. Like Dad stated though, I don't think any eastern states will rally to his cause.

"I suggest we sit back and wait for now to see what happens. It could strengthen our cause and future mission if more western states secede and join Texas. That will also give Congress and the Senate time to take action if they're going to. One thing's for certain like Luis said, we've got to be ready to execute 'Operation Freedom Run' in a moment's notice.

"From now on, everyone is on lockdown on the ranch. No one goes anywhere without checking with me first. Tomorrow at 0800, let's all conduct another mission equipment check on all vehicles, commo, weapons, chow, and personal gear. Does anyone have any questions or comments?"

Alex looked around at everyone with his eyebrows raised. No one said a thing and then Leiko said, "Okay, boys, breakfast at my house at 0700." Everyone got a grin on their faces and the chatter began.

ALLIANCES ARE MADE

22 APRIL 2011
WASHINGTON, D.C.

President Osama, his cabinet, and the Joint Chiefs-of-Staff knew that they had to address America on the battle in Texas. They had war-gamed it all night as how to present it as a necessary task in the best interest of national security. President Osama wasn't about to face America by himself. He made the Secretary of Defense and the Joint Chiefs-of-Staff stand with him to shoulder the blame. Then he read from his carefully programmed teleprompter. Needless to say, his words fell on deaf ears.

To even show Americans that they were presenting the truth, this national announcement by President Osama, Secretary of Defense Gants, and the Joint Chiefs-of-Staff was broadcast on a *FOX News* (live special report) with Brant Hummer. It aired at 8 a.m. EST. Everyone knew how much Osama disliked the *FOX* network because they weren't his lap-dog like all of the other major networks. They told it like it was and held nothing back, no matter whom it embarrassed or implicated.

President Osama was the sole speaker during the news brief.

> People of America, this is what led up to the battle in Texas. Texas holds one of the nation's most powerful war assets the country has, and those assets need to be under the direct control of the National Command Authority. That asset is one half of our B-1B bombers. When ordered to surrender those assets by the president of the United States, Governor Rich Pevey of Texas blatantly refused.

Therefore, I and the joint chiefs-of-staff had no option but to attempt to take control of those assets. That's when Governor Pevey decided to use physical force to try to keep them. As a result, due to his orders, there was much American loss of life. He apparently has no concern for his fellow Texans or Americans. I condemn his actions and proclaim that he needs to be held accountable for them.

I look to the great people of Texas and the Free States to impeach him and send him to Washington for trial where he can be held accountable for his crimes. Thank you for your support and good night, my fellow Americans.

At the conclusion of the president's speech, the screen switched back to Brant Hummer and he had a stunned look on his face as he said, "Well, folks, I just don't know what to say about that." The real deal was that every viewer knew what to say about it. It was BS from a man trying to cover his own ass by blaming someone else.

The next day, *FOX News* conducted a popularity approval rating for the president and he came even lower than his all time low. He reached an all time bottom of the barrel of eighteen percent. Of course, he was the only US President in history to ever order our military to murder American civilians and service members without cause; much unlike President Lincoln.

28 APRIL 2011
AUSTIN, TEXAS

Governor Rich Pevey was hosting a live news briefing in his office at the state capitol. He had once again invited every local and major news broadcasting station that would entertain him. It seemed that he had a major national announcement to make.

It was 10:30 a.m. CST (Central Standard Time) and Governor Pevey's huge office was packed with the press and seventeen other state governors. He had them all lined up against the wall on his right hand side. They were present to show their solidarity with the first four states that seceded from the union on 14 Dec 2010. Then he began to speak,

> Greetings, ladies and gentlemen of the press and my fellow governors of the FSA (Free States of America), thank you all for coming to show your support for this live, national announcement. This formal announcement goes out to my fellow Americans in both the Free States of America and the United States of America. President Osama and all members of Congress and the Senate of the United States of America; this official notice stands as follows from fourteen of America's western states.
>
> As you can see, the fourteen governors of the following states stand before God, America, and the television audience of the entire world and proclaim that the states of Kansas, Nebraska, South Dakota, North Dakota, Wyoming, New Mexico, Arizona, Utah, Idaho, Washington, Oregon, Nevada, California, and Alaska are all in accord when they seceded from the union to join Texas, Oklahoma, Colorado, and Montana to form our own eighteen-state sovereign nation from this time forward officially known as, "the Free States of America."

At that moment, all of the cameras were panning down the line of state governors as they all gave his noble words a standing ovation. The Oklahoma, Colorado, and Montana governors were also standing with the fourteen joining governors. Even with Governor Pevey's gestures to sit back down, they continued clapping for three more minutes.

Once they took their seats again, he continued to speak,

> Ever since Bakr Houssam Osama took office and assembled a very questionable administration, they have done nothing but bring this great nation down. I refer to everything from employment, national morals, a bogus national

health care plan, gun control, the economy, killing fellow Americans in the streets, and not supporting immigration control to name a few. He has placed such a debt burden on our nation with his frivolous spending that our grandchildren will never recover from it or be able to pay off the multi-trillions that he is needlessly amassing.

However, the inexcusable and unforgivable act that broke this nation's back was when Bakr Houssam Osama authorized and ordered America's own military to turn on its own citizens and murder them. That is the culminating event that has forced this great nation to split in half.

We honest, God fearing, and hardworking people of these eighteen western states refuse to further be a part of a government and nation that will tolerate such unacceptable behavior. For these and many other reasons, we the people of the Free States of America draw the line from Texas to North Dakota. We declare that we are no longer bound by any laws or regulations of the United States of America.

Soon to follow this decree, we will hold free elections for our top political offices to mirror that of our nation's historic positions. We will not, however, have to elect the officials for the offices of congress or the senate since they already exist, just as the gubernatorial officials are already in place.

Our new constitution will mirror that of our nation's historic constitution with the exchange of the phrase, the Free States of America for the United States of America. The majority of our laws and regulations will remain the same as well. The English language will be reclaimed as our only official language. We will also bring our Christian God and religion back into our government and society the way our founding four-fathers meant this land to be governed.

And finally, we will defend this sovereign soil, our citizens, and our way of life against all intruders, both on this continent and off of this continent. After our government is fully established, we will meet with the government of the United States to try to come to an agreement concerning their POWs, commercial industries, and free trade. We will especially address companies that have been split between our two nations.

The other seventeen state governors have voted unanimously that I should hold the position of provisional leader until such time that our free elections have produced an officially elected president and vice president. And by the way, my friends, this is the last time you will see the flag of the United States at an official government meeting of the Free States of America. We're making a new flag to reflect eighteen states.

This, ladies and gentlemen, concludes our official national announcement. Now we eighteen governors are free to answer all of your questions. Please let's just keep this orderly and route all of your questions through me one at a time. We'll set a three hour time limit right now, and then, we'll call an end to this news conference.

Then the existing government of the Free States of America proceeded to answer the questions of the press. There were many to be answered.

WASHINGTON, D.C.
THE WHITE HOUSE

Meanwhile, the Osama administration was having a meeting of their own. They had just finished watching Governor Pevey's announcement to America and the rest of the world on live TV.

After an hour of bickering amongst them selves, the only thing that they agreed upon was that the ten of them alone didn't possess the congressional knowledge to formulate a reactive solution for the bomb that Rich Pevey had just dropped in their laps.

They did however; all agree to summons an emergency meeting with congress, in the morning, to formulate their options.

The next day a nine hour emergency session meeting was held in congress, without the eighteen state representatives that seceded. The only exception in regards to the eighteen state's senators and congressmen/women was Natalie Pulaski the Speaker of the House. She was not willing to give up that position and go back to being just a regular congress woman again. Therefore, a deal was struck.

President Osama signed an Executive Order stating that she could retain her position as the Democratic Leader even if she wasn't a congress woman from California any longer. It was a win / win situation for everyone. Osama kept his lapdog and California, one of the Free States, was rid of her. She was forced to give up her California Congressional Seat and her Free State citizenship. She gladly did both to retain her power over the common people.

The conclusion was reached that they really had no recourse and could not prevent the western states from seceding from the union of the United States of America and establishing their own sovereign nation. They had all agreed that their best course of action was to have formal talks with their leaders and begin addressing some of the pressing issues that came with a nation splitting in half.

One fact that Congress made perfectly clear to the president was that he wasn't to even consider another military action against them without first conferring with them. He was promised that if he did he would be impeached that very day.

21 MAY 2011
FORT LEAVENWORTH, KANSAS

Fort Leavenworth, Kansas was the location agreed upon by both sides to conduct talks concerning civil and commercial reconstitution. Actually, this is the only location that Governor Pevey offered and would accept. He figured that his people wouldn't have to depart their country and Osama's officials wouldn't have to come more than a mile into the Free States of America. A very strategic move on Mr. Pevey's side.

At 2:00 p.m. CST, a total of twenty-three people—congressmen/women, senators, Osama staff members, the US Attorney General Edric Holden and Mirell Osama had just landed in their jet at the Kansas City International Airport. From there a CH-47 would fly them to Sherman Army Airfield on Fort Leavenworth, Kansas.

That Chinook had flown in earlier that week from Fort Rucker, Alabama. Governor Pevey wasn't taking any chances with Osama's staffers being on any Free States birds. After the meeting the US Army flight crew would fly the VIPs back to their jet at the Kansas City Airport.

As the aircrew was sitting the huge, dual engine helo down on Sherman Army Airfield, they noticed an unusually high amount of military armament surrounding the airfield. The military crew knew the deal; however, the state department pukes just thought it was added protection for them. The truth of the matter was, Governor Pevey wasn't taking any chances on another military strike from Osama. In fact, Mr. Pevey and the other Governors had decided to fortify their entire border from Texas to North Dakota.

Much had been accomplished during their meeting, which ended just after dusk. Both sides came to the agreement that no private corporation or industry would be encumbered by the newly established national border. They agreed that in the event of attack from another country, both sides would combine forces to repel the invaders.

They agreed to make Kansas City a National Neutral Zone on the border where both sides could meet freely. It was agreed upon that the West would turn over all POWs from the attack on Dyess Air Force Base within one month's time. The VIPs were even permitted to meet with a dozen of the POWs since they had been moved to Leavenworth prison.

At the conclusion of the meeting, all of the East's statesmen and women loaded aboard the Chinook and took off. Mirell Osama had just gotten off the phone with President Osama. She informed him of all of the progress that they had made and that they were on the chopper headed back to their jet in Kansas City. It was because of her presence that the Secrete Service decided to go very low-key with an unmarked Army bird.

Once they were in the air headed eastward at about 3,500 ft. AGL, the bird developed a critical mechanical emergency. The pilot sent out a mayday over the radio and his crew chief started yelling to all of the VIPs to strap in and hang on.

That's when Pulaski looked at Senator Josh Kaylee from Massachusetts who was setting beside her and said, "That's military jargon for 'put your head between your legs and kiss yer ass good-bye, boy!'"

Senator Kaylee started crying like a little girl. Pulaski shook her head in disgust and said, "I always knew you were a big pussy, Kaylee. For once, act like a man. You make me sick!"

That was when Edric Holden held Mirell's hand and said, "Praise be to Allah. He will keep us safe."

Mrs. Osama said, "He's never let me or Bakr down yet!"

The Chinook started to rapidly loose altitude so the pilot began to apply power to arrest the descent. That's when the in-flight break-up of the helicopter began. The Aft Rotor Blades were then observed departing the airframe. Shortly after the Aft Blades failed, the Aft Rotor Hub, along with half of the Aft Pylon separated from the fuselage. A split second after half of the Aft Pylon separated, the Aft Transmission and the remaining portion of the Aft Pylon began to tear away from the airframe.

The aircraft slowly rolled onto its right side as it continued to fall from the sky at an alarming rate. When the Chinook made contact, the helicopter's right side was in a slightly nose up atti-

tude. Upon impact it burst into a huge fire ball, creating a glow-
ing mushroom cloud above the impact site, on the northbound
lanes of Highway 435.

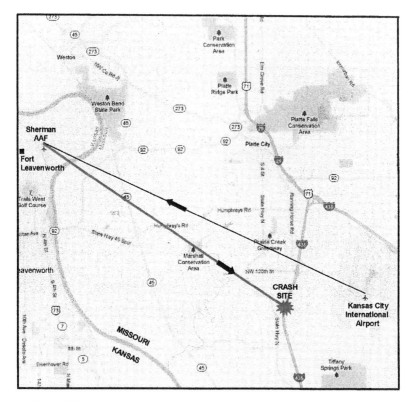

The "G" forces at impact had been estimated at two hundred.
An average 180 pound person aboard the helicopter would have
been subjected to a force of 36,000 pounds. There was no doubt
that death was instantaneous for everyone. Even though fire
fighting crews fought the inferno half the night, the wreckage
was still smoldering when the breaking dawn came.

With the twenty-seven people killed on the bird and many
more dead and injured motorist, it was a major aviation accident
scene that captured all of the headlines. All of the high powered
VIPs didn't help matters much either. All-in-all, there were forty-
three fatalities, thirteen critically injured, and nineteen hospital-

ized with minor injuries. This was the first air crash in US history that ever claimed a member of a Presidential Family.

The two north bound lanes of Hwy 435 remained closed for a week after the crash. The two south bound lanes were split into one lane each direction until the investigation was completed. The FAA (Federal Aviation Administration), US Army, and FBI were all conducting separate investigations. They all wanted to find out why the military helo went down; for different reasons of course.

At the end of the FAA and US Army's investigations, they were both in agreement with each others findings. They concurred that the failure of the Forward Transmission Input Pinion Capsule caused the Number one Synchronized Drive Shaft to rotate eccentric and contact the Forward Pylon structure, causing the shaft to fail, followed by the subsequent de-synchronization of the Forward and Aft Rotor Systems.

The Forward and Aft Rotor Blades meshed causing the Aft Pylon, Aft Transmission and the Aft Rotor System to separate from the helicopter with catastrophic results. The entire crew and all passengers received fatal injuries.

As for the FBI, they were satisfied with their own results. That was to say that, there had been no foul play on the part of the Free States in regards to the Chinooks crash. The Osama administration had also accepted those reports for the time being.

28 MAY 2011
WASHINGTON, D.C.

A week after the deadly crash, President Osama held a national news conference to announce the cause that claimed all twenty-seven people aboard the aircraft. Vice President Binder and Secretary of State Chilton were by his side as he spoke from the White House,

> My fellow, Americans, let me begin by saying that we as a nation suffered a terrible loss the night this helicop-

ter crashed. We not only lost forty-eight American lives that night, but we lost some of the best leadership of this administration.

We lost senators, congressmen and women, members of our military, some of my administration staff, and some civilian motorists that were driving up highway 435 north-bound that night. However, the biggest loss that we have suffered is the loss of our first lady, my wife, Mirell.

The president paused as he removed a handkerchief from his pocket and wiped away a tear. He excused himself and continued,

She has given so much of herself to our nation and helped so many Americans whom couldn't help themselves. She died returning from a mercy mission where she took her life in her own hands as she traveled into enemy territory to visit with our POWs that the Free States still hold against their will.

I have signed into law that from henceforth, every May 21st will be a federal holiday known as First Lady Osama Day. It shall hold the same reverence as Martin Luther King Day and all flags will be flown at half mass.

This day of remembrance will also be to remember the other heroes lost on that tragic night—United States Attorney General Edric Holden, the Democratic Leader Natalie Pulaski, and Senator Josh Kaylee.

The president paused again as he removed his handkerchief from his pocket and blew his nose. Then Mr. Binder handed him his handkerchief. Osama excused himself again and continued speaking:

The FAA and US Army have determined that a catastrophic mechanical failure was the cause for the helicopter's crash that night. Not severe weather or even human error was to blame. This administration's sympathies go out to the rest of the victims of this devastating event. Thank you for your time, America, good night.

That concluded the press briefing. There were no questions taken by anyone. Bewilderment was had by all.

NEW FLAG AND NEW BLOOD

07 JUNE 2011
USA

The day that all US American gun owners feared had finally come. This was the day that President Osama's national gun ban would kick in. The only question was how earnestly were the feds prepared to try to enforce it? Since Osama had lost a few of his top lapdogs, a lot of Americans were betting that he wasn't as prepared to shed blood as he was when he signed the bill on September 11, 2010. That was also before eighteen states seceded from the union.

Time would tell, because according to his original gun ban before it went to the Supreme Court, the public had thirty days before it would have become active. Therefore, the people should have until the seventh of July before they had to decide to give up their guns or use them to keep them.

26 JUNE 2011
DENVER, COLORADO

Right after Governor Pevey's press conference on the 28th of April, the Free States started to entertain the idea of campaigning for a new President and Vice President. Since there were no sitting incumbents, both parties would have to present offerings for election. All states agreed upon a twelve-week total process timeline until election day on July 30. The Free States were in desperate need of an officially elected permanent government.

Those elections would be held in the exact same way that the nation has held presidential elections all along, just on an accelerated time-line. It was also agreed upon that the elected pair would take office immediately after being confirmed. And henceforth, the Free States presidential elections would be held on the odd years, as not to conflict with the US elections.

Denver, Colorado was the Free States National Headquarters for all campaign/election matters. After all, that was the city of their new capital. It was from there that it was announced the winners for the Republican and Democratic Parties.

There were four pairs that ran for the party nominations. The two pairs that won the nominations were Rich Pevey from (Texas) and Sahara Payne of (Alaska) for the Republican Party and Bob Scissor from (Montana) and Charlene Gregtree of (Washington) for the Democratic Party.

26 JUNE 2011
AUSTIN, TEXAS

Governor Pevey, (The Free States Provisional Leader) was making a television announcement on the *FOX News* network. He went on the air to accept the Republican Party's Presidential Nomination and to unveil the nation's new flag that he promised would accompany his next news briefing.

The image on the screen showed a sharply dressed Governor Pevey with the Texas State Capitol Building behind him in Austin, Texas. Over his right shoulder, there was also a photo of the new national flag of the Free States of America.

Governor Pevey began speaking precisely at 8:00 p.m. CST:

> Good evening, my fellow Texans and Americans. Let me begin by saying that I come to you this evening with good news. First, I want to say that I have won the Republican Party's presidential nomination. I accept this great honor with the utmost sincere thanks and humbleness. I will make you a good president, and I will give this great country the very best that I have to offer. We have a lot of work

before us since President Osama ordered America's military might to attack Texas and kill innocent civilians and military personnel six-weeks ago.

Even though I'll be campaigning against the Democratic nominee, I will still be working full time as Texas's governor and the provisional leader of the Free States of America. Secondly, it is my greatest honor to introduce you, my fellow Americans, to our new flag of the Free States of America.

With that introduction, the screen switched to a large image of the new flag that Governor Pevey had previously promised a shocked Texas and Free States of America. As the flag was displayed, Governor Pevey's voice was still being heard as he talked about the nation's new flag and badge of honor.

Gov. Pevey said, "Let me begin by telling you how this flag came to be,

At the conclusion of the press conference on April 28, when fourteen additional western states succeeded from the union, to make a total of eighteen, we governors had a talk. We all agreed that we, as a new nation would need a new national flag. Therefore, we formed a committee of unique individuals to design one.

That committee consisted of we eighteen state governors, a tenth-grade history teacher, a policeman, a soldier, a sailor, an airman, a marine, a firefighter, a preacher, a carpenter, a garbage man, a banker, an artist, a hardware man, a cowboy, and a lumberjack. These people made up the very essence of true America.

The eighteen governors represented their states and the other fifteen Americans represented the average Joe—America's working class. Yes, a very good mix of human beings.

We all agreed on one thing from the get-go. We all loved our flag of the United States of America and wanted to keep as much of it and what it represented as we could. Therefore, we came up with what you see before you tonight, my friends.

As you can see, we kept the red for hardiness, valor, and the blood that was shed on this land; to include the innocent blood on Dyess Air Force Base. We also kept the white for the purity and innocence of our people. And finally, we kept the blue for our vigilance, perseverance, and justice.

We maintained the thirteen horizontal stripes to remember our history of our thirteen original colonies. We added the words, *This We'll Defend. God and Country.* This will always remind us what we honor and will fight for. Then as you can see, we added our most sacred of God's creatures; the American bald eagle.

All thirty-three men and women on this committee agreed that the reason America as a whole has fallen as far as it has since the 1950s is because America has taken so much of God out of this country. After all, this country was founded on God and guns! Without either of them, this country wouldn't have won its freedom and kept it. That is how our founding fore-fathers framed our constitution and meant for this great nation to be governed.

Therefore, we put our Christian God back into this nation like he should be. Just as on all of our currency, we have put the phrase "In God We Trust" on our national flag and symbol to the rest of the world. That's right, the Free States of America is proud of our Christian God, and we won't let anyone ever convince us otherwise again! We are proud of that rugged cross that Jesus freely gave his life on for us.

And lastly, the eighteen stars stand for our eighteen states. We stand united from Texas to North Dakota and from Alaska to California with our national capital nestled safely in the middle in Denver, Colorado.

Then the image on the screen switched back to Governor Pevey as he made his closing statement.

That, my friends, is the history behind our great flag. May God bless and protect this great nation of ours as he did the United States of America before we cut him out and our people's morals and ethics went to pot. Good night, friends and neighbors, and God bless the Free States of America.

With that, the screen went back to the news correspondent whom proceeded to recap what Governor Pevey had just said.

MISSION PREP

26 JUNE 2011
SHADOW WOLF RANCH

Alex, Gerard, Dutch, and Hunter were all in the commo room and had just finished watching Governor Pevey's speech. Dutch looked at Alex and asked, "Well, what did ya think of that little speech?"

Alex replied, "That speech did my heart good. It's about time some national leader in this country grabbed his balls and put God and country first again! Rich Pevey has definitely got my vote."

Hunter said, "Amen to that, son!"

Dutch replied, "Damn straight."

Then Gerard chimed in with, "Yes, sir."

Just then Leiko burst into the room and yelled, "Whooo! Well, did you boys hear that speech by Governor Pevey? That boy was on fire. He's got my vote for sure!"

Alex said, "Simmer down, shorty, we saw it. And, yes, ma'am, he hit the nail on the head."

Then Gerard said to Leiko, "I think he'll be the first president of the Free States of America."

Hunter said, "Yeah, I think he'll get it. After all of Osama's crap, Americans are ready to restore their country to good old-fashioned values again. Well, at least the western half anyway."

Alex looked at Gerard and asked him to send out the code word to Ethan, Luis, and Damon's phones that they were about to have a meeting in the commo room. Within fifteen minutes, everyone was assembled in the commo room and ready for the meeting.

Once everyone was seated, Alex stood before the group and began the meeting. Alex asked the three late comers if they saw

Governor Pevey's speech. None of them had. Therefore, Alex proceeded to fill them in, "Okay, fellas, this is what he said. He won the Republican Party's presidential nomination, and he's accepted it. Then he introduced the new national flag of the Free States of America. If you look at the screen there, you'll see Gerard has an image on the screen for yas. After our meeting, ya' all can watch his entire speech if you like.

"Now that you guys are up to speed, we'll kick off this meeting. We're going to talk about this new turn of events and how you all think we stand in regards to 'Operation Freedom Run'. Dutch, what are your views?"

Dutch stood up and began to address the group, "It's been six weeks since the attack on Texas. We have seen the strengthening of the border from Texas to North Dakota on our side. That could help us or hurt us come time for the mission. It all depends upon how we play it. It's also all about the timing.

"If we wait until hostilities kick off again, we could be perceived at as hostile aircraft by everyone because we won't be responding to challenges over the radio. If we go before then, we can pass as friendlies. There's no doubt in my mind that we should go before any more fighting starts. That's where I stand."

Dutch sat back down and Alex asked Damon a question. "Damon, as far as the air mission goes, how do you feel?"

He replied, "I'm with Dutch on this one. We stand a lot better chance of passing off for friendly or disoriented aircraft before the bullets start flying."

Alex looked at his father and asked, "Dad?"

Hunter replied, "You know, they're right, son. Hell, that's Indian and white man fighting 101 there."

Alex retorted, "Yes, sir, I know. I just wanted to hear it from you." Then Alex said to the group, "Does anyone not feel this way?"

Then Leiko spoke up, "I agree with what you're all saying; I just have one question. Do you think that any of the people we're flying to retrieve will have reservations about coming at the time, if the civil war hasn't actually kicked off yet?"

Then Alex stood and said his piece, "Well, here's the cold hard truth of it. We have to go when we think we have the highest chance of success. We all know that the time is before bullets and threats start flying again. That's also before Governor Pevey locks this border down tighter than a cowboy's jeans on Saturday night. Damon, when do you think is the best time to cross the border?"

Damon looked down for a moment while rubbing his right index finger across his chin. Then he looked up at Alex and said, "Definitely on the weekend. That way, we can pass ourselves off as an Air National Guard unit. Those boys are always misplacing a couple of birds every weekend."

Alex said, "Then it's set. We fly 'Operation Freedom Run' next Friday night. That gives us eleven days to be prepped and make all mission coordinations that need to be done prier. We'll have a meeting in the Ops center at 0800 tomorrow. Then we'll assign everyone their task. Remember, everyone, not a word about this to anyone outside of this room. Everyone's lives depend on it.

The next morning as Alex conducted roll call, everyone was looking at the large map on the wall behind him. It was a new map of America that reflected the new national border between the USA and the FSA. It was time to go over 'Operation Freedom Run'.

Alex said, "Okay, people, this will be the mission in a nutshell. I'll give everyone enough info to get your task completed before mission execution. Please hold all questions until the end."

Then he proceeded,

> You all have probably figured out by now that 'Operation Freedom Run' is about fifty percent flight mission and fifty percent ground mission. That fifty percent ground mission being securing LZs, PZs, refueling, RODs, and loading people into the Chinook. Now don't get me wrong. There is plenty of time on the ground for us to get into trouble.
>
> Especially since we'll only be flying at night and ROD on the ground. Plus we'll have scheduled stops for refueling the birds. You all know the saying, 'You're only as strong as your weakest link.' Well, in our case that is, as strong as our smallest fuel tanks.
>
> The irony of it is that the Hughes 500 has the smallest fuel tanks; however, it doesn't have the shortest flight range. The reason for that is because Hunter and Damon have equipped it with the necessary add-ons to give it an in-flight refueling capability.
>
> Its normal flight range is 225 miles; however, with the two, twenty-five-gallon auxiliary fuel cells they installed, give it an extended range of 375 miles. That means less refueling missions in the air for us.
>
> We have already tested it and we can safely in-flight refuel the Hughes from the ramp of the Chinook. As for the two Hueys, we'll have to set down to refuel them. So that makes the Hueys our weakest link. When they need to refuel, we all need to go to the ground. That's quite all right though; we have a plan for that.

Then Alex asked Gerard to put the Powerpoint slide show on that showed the group how the aircraft would carry auxiliary fuel tanks. Then Alex continued,

> As you all know, the birds will be completely full of fuel on the inbound flight, even the cargo bays. For that reason,

we'll do a lot better on fuel going than coming. It's coming back on the outbound flight that we'll need some frequent fuel caches along the way. That's where Luis comes in. He'll make sure they're there where we need them.

As you all can see by the diagram of the Chinook's cargo bay, we'll be carrying three each, ERFS (Extended Range Fuel Systems) II Robinson Tanks. We'll also be carrying a FARE (Forward Area Refueling Equipment) kit.

These three crashworthy fuel tanks hold 800 gallons each. This gives the Chinook a total of 3,720 gallons of total fuel. That much fuel weighs 19,500 pounds. The total cargo weight capacity for takeoff is 28,000 pounds. Therefore, people, we'll be carrying an extra 8,000 pounds of fuel in a container slung under the bird.

As I said before, the Hueys are our week link. Since we're not equipped to refuel them in flight, they only have a flight range of about 700 miles with the auxiliary fuel cells that they'll be carrying. We have also beefed up their engines so we can squeeze 150 kph (knots per hour) out of them if we need to.

As you can see by the diagram of the Huey's cargo bay, we'll be carrying two each 150 gallon internal fuel tanks. That gives us a total of 523 gallons per bird. Therefore, approximately every 700 miles the squadron will be landing to refuel. In the middle of every 700 miles we'll be conducting one in-flight refueling mission with the Hughes 500.

Alex asked Gerard to put the route map back up on the screen. Then he tossed a US road map to Luis and gave him the following instructions:

Luis, we've marked all of the refueling locations from start to finish on this map. This is where those seven, 5,000 gallon fuel tankers we had you purchase some time ago will come in. The LAT/LONGs (latitude and longitude) is there for your GPS locator.

Each of these concealed locations is on our property in an old warehouse, hangar, or barn complex. They're not only large enough to hide the fuel truck but all four birds as well. Gerard has even set up electronic surveillance on all of these sites. We'll know well in advance if anyone even sets foot around those properties.

This is how you will position them. You will leave from here in a convoy with all seven trucks, topped off with aviation fuel. All of the drivers and TCs (truck commanders) will be guards from our Special Units Team. You will conduct the convoy just as we did for 'Operation Barracuda'. I want you two miles out in the lead in one of the suburbans. Take a driver with you so you can also drive round the clock.

Get with Gerard for all of your comms issue. He's already installed the hidden vehicle tracking systems in the fuel trucks. Get with Ethan for the men's weapons issue. He'll show them where the hidden weapons compartments are in the cabs of the trucks. Have them load enough food and water to last them until we pick them up at the refueling sites.

I also want you to take our diesel mechanic with you in your vehicle. Have him take a butt-load of spare parts incase one of the trucks goes down. Do you have any questions for any of us?

Luis replied, "No, sir, I think I pretty much got it. I just need to know when you want me to go."

Alex said, "Just as soon as your mechanic has all of his spare parts. You need to notify all of your men today so they can prep. Keep it very basic, no specifics."

Luis said, "Okay, if I have any questions I'll ask you or Dutch." Then Alex continued with the rest of the briefing,

Okay, that covers the pre-cached fuel supply. Now, if everyone will direct your attention to the flight route up here on the map. I'm just covering general directions and locations right now. Damon and Gerard have already programmed all of the headings, RPs (Reference Points), LZs, PZs, and targets into the helos onboard navigation systems.

As you can all see here, we'll fly due east. When we get to the new national border, we'll cross it between Omaha, and Sioux City. From there we're headed toward Cleveland, Ohio.

Between Cleveland and Akron we'll assume a new heading that will take us to Newport, Vermont (PZ-11). Once there we'll land and pick-up six pax (personnel).

From there we head to New Shaefferstown, Pennsylvania (PZ-22). Once there we'll land and pick-up five Pax. There will be one ATV four-wheeler as well.

From there we head to Morgantown, West Virginia (PZ-33). Once there we'll land and pick-up two Pax. There will be one ATV four-wheeler as well.

From there we'll head toward Wilmington, North Carolina. Once we've gotten on the east side of I-95, we'll head for Gray's Creek (PZ-44). Once there we'll land and pick-up eleven Pax.

We'll continue on that heading toward Columbia, South Carolina. Just south of Columbia we'll assume a new heading toward Joplin, Missouri. That's near where we'll cross over the border

Once we're over the border, we'll head due west toward Trinidad, Colorado. After we cross over Trinidad we'll cross over the Front Range and head due north right up through the Rocky Mountains. From there it's a straight shot to Shadow Wolf Ranch. That ladies and gentlemen, is the flight route in a nut shell.

Okay, here's your overview. We're going on a mission and picking up twenty-four out-of-state pax. Four of those twenty-four pax will be riding two ATVs into the Chinook. We'll be picking up fourteen of our drivers and TCs at the fuel points. That's a total of thirty-eight pax we'll be flying back here, excluding all of the flight crews.

Remember this; with the fuel bladders in the Chinook inbound, it will be very tight. On the outbound flight it

267

will still be tight with thirty-eight Pax, two ATVs, and six E & E dirt bikes. Here's the bird/aircrew lineup.

Alex looked at Gerard and gestured with his right index finger at the screen. Gerard had the new image on the screen before Alex had his finger back down to his side.

Then Alex read it aloud:

- Huey Gunship number one: pilot = Damon, copilot = Luis

- Huey Gunship number two: pilot = Dutch, copilot = Gerard

- CH-47 Med-Evac/Gunship: pilot = Hunter, copilot = Leiko

- Hughes 500 Scout: pilot = Alex, copilot = Ethan

- All gunners and crew chiefs will come from our communities Special Units Team. They will consist as follows:

- Huey Gunship number 1: one M-79 gunner and one sniper

- Huey Gunship number 2: one M-79 gunner and one sniper

- CH-47 Gunship: one crew chief and one loadmaster, one 50 cal. ramp gunner, one M-79 gunner, one sniper, and two 7.62 mini gun door gunners

Then Alex concluded his briefing and asked, "What are your questions, people?" Everyone just looked at each other as if they had no questions.

Then Gerard spoke up and asked, "What are our actions if we get challenged over the radio while in the air?"

Alex said, "Damon will answer all challenges over the radio. He's much more experienced and knows what would be more plausible for whatever particular circumstance we're in at the moment."

Then Alex looked at Damon with raised eyebrows and asked him if he was cool with that. Damon replied, "I've got it covered."

Alex asked, "Any other questions?"

Ethan asked, "When's our next meeting?"

Alex said, "I'm glad you asked that. We'll all meet here the day that Luis returns from his fuel mission. Then he'll be able to brief us all on their status. Gerard will send out a text to your secure phones as to the time of the meeting." Then Alex asked, "Anything else, anybody?"

No one else had any questions or comments. Then Alex said, "Okay, let's keep prepping and assist Luis so he can deploy ASAP." At the end of the briefing, everyone headed their own directions.

The next morning, Luis met Alex and told him that his diesel mechanic already had all of the spare parts that he might need for the mission. Alex said, "Great, then you can depart in the morning.

Luis said, "Yes, sir, I was hoping you would say that."

Then Alex issued him some final instructions,

> Okay, Luis, just remember that you're not on your own. Any time you have a question or suggestion, we're only a phone call away on your secure phone. Just call me or Dutch and we'll help you out.
>
> Now I want you to inform us right after each fuel truck that you have cached. That way we can track your progress and better estimate your return. If everything goes smoothly, it shouldn't take any more than a week for your round trip.
>
> Just like on 'Operation Barracuda', these trucks all have official documentation for your cover story. They are licensed to the helo fuel company that owns the property that they will be sitting on. Just brief your drivers and TCs and ensure that they all stay in their company uniforms.

The next morning, Alex and Hunter waved Luis on as his convoy of fuel trucks departed through the main ACF sally port (vehicle gate). Hunter looked at Alex and asked, "Well, what da ya think?"

Alex said, "He'll be all right. He's got a good head on his shoulders."

DISASTER IN D.C.

30 JUNE 2011
WASHINGTON, D.C.

9:30 a.m. EST, Vice President Job Binder was in his office in the Dwight D. Eisenhower Executive Office Building next to the White House when a small explosive device detonated, which killed him instantly. By the time D.C. firefighters responded, his entire office was engulfed in smoke and flames.

Once the entire executive office building had been evacuated and all flames were extinguished, the FBI crime scene experts were brought in to figure out exactly what had happened.

President Osama had instructed the Director of the FBI that he was to keep the investigation Top Secret and with as few people as possible. He was also to keep the entire investigation compartmentalized. That way, no one but the director would know the end result of the finding.

The director was also to personally present the findings of the investigation directly to him and only him. Osama told him that he wanted the chance to evaluate the damage before letting the public know the findings. This aroused the director's suspicion and raised a red flag. Nonetheless, he complied with the president's instructions even though he felt there were underhanded reasons for his directives.

The Dwight D. Eisenhower Executive Office Building on Pennsylvania Avenue had been under renovations for several years. At the conclusion of the FBI's investigation, their findings were that a member of the Hispanic cleaning/moving crew had been able to plant the device under the vice president's desk while performing his duties. The man was a deep cover operative for the Zetas cartel out of Mexico.

05 JULY 2011
SHADOW WOLF RANCH

At 1845, Luis, his driver, and their mechanic all came driving in the main gate of Shadow Wolf Ranch on the red-eye express. After a week of driving they were all beat. Their fuel truck mission had gone off without a hitch. Everything was set.

06 JULY 2011
WASHINGTON, D.C.

At 10:30 a.m. EST, FBI Director Robby Miller was meeting with President Osama in one of the secure conference rooms in the White House. Director Miller had just told the president of the FBI's findings.

That's when President Osama stepped closer to Mr. Miller and said, "Rob, that's not how it happened at all. This is how it went down."

Then Osama proceeded, "Ya see, Rob, Job is dead and there's nothing that will bring him back. If we don't acknowledge that we know the Mexican cartel did it, they'll just assume that we never really discovered that it was them.

"Right now, we have a much greater threat knocking at our door. In less than two weeks when we start kicking in doors to confiscate the public's weapons, we're going to need all of the media and public support we can get.

"Now just think how much more support we'll get if the FBI's finding on Job's death points a finger at the NRA (National Rifle Association) and their covert actions. They have the horse power and funding to pull it off. Are ya starting to catch on now?"

Director Miller got a fearful look on his face and said, "I always knew that you were a socialist Muslim, but you're out of your damn mind! There's no way my office will ever back you on this play! This scheme could rip this nation apart, and we just lost half of it as a result of your attack on Texas."

Then Mr. Osama produced a truly evil look on his face and began speaking in a very low voice. "Well, it's like this, Rob. I've got enough serious dirt on you between the FBI's torture techniques, the part you played in the Fast and Furious Program, Guantanamo Bay, and a few other questionable events that you've participated in, that it wouldn't be in your best interest to resist me on this one."

Then Miller got a kick-ass angry look on his face and said, "You arrogant scumbag, you don't have the balls or horsepower to blackmail me!"

Osama's reply was surprising, "You either get on board with this tasking Rob, or I will use every resource at my disposal to burry you. You're a relic from the last administration who doesn't have any comrades in this administration. Don't you want that two-year extension as director of the FBI?

You forget that this is my new administration that I pretty much handpicked from my loyal friends that will do my bidding. And don't forget that I also own half of the Supreme Court as well. You saw how my national gun ban turned out."

Director Miller knew the president had him by the short hairs for the time being. He also knew that he had to go along with this disinformation campaign for now. So Miller asked, "What's the spin you want put on this?"

Osama said, "Now you're talking." He laid it all out, "First we put out a press release that a domestic terrorist group called GOA (Guns of America) has assassinated the vice president in his office. Then we disclose this was retaliation against the new national gun ban. In their letter, they also stated that they will be making more strikes against the federal government in the future.

"This should put the press and about half of the American public on the side of gun control. Then we lock down the entire border with the FSA. This way, the terrorist can't get any assistance or support from them. We already know that Pevey and the whole west support the second amendment.

"Ya know, Rob, this is sheer genius on my part. We can use this fictional terrorist group to make our own hits on our own government officials that don't see things our way. Plus, we can blame anything we want on the GOA and there's no one to deny it."

Then Miller said, "Damn, that sounds like something the CIA would have come up with. Still, I think even they would have used it in some other country, not our own. I'll announce it in a live press conference this afternoon."

The president replied, "Good, I'll be there to back you up."

That same day at 3:00 p.m., EST, President Osama and FBI Director Miller held a live national news conference on *CNN*. The location was the headquarters for the FBI in the J. Edgar Hoover building on Pennsylvania Avenue in Washington D.C. Security was tight to say the least.

The live news brief on *CNN* was so crowded that the press could hardly move in the pit. It started out with President Osama whom stated that the FBI had the findings on the assassination of Vice President Job Binder. Then he turned the podium over to Mr. Miller, director of the FBI.

He spoke with a convincing authority,

> At the conclusion of the FBI's investigation of the assassination of Vice President Binder, we have uncovered a very complex and powerful domestic terrorist group that calls themselves GOA or Guns of America. We have also determined that this terrorist group has ties with the NRA.

> Now we don't know if the NRA has funded them or trained their operatives or exactly what affiliation they have with the GOA terrorist organization. Rest assured, we will ascertain answers to these questions and bring all involved to justice.

> Due to this heightened threat, we will be implementing new security measures in the very near future for the protection of America's citizens. The very first of these coun-

ter measures will be to close and secure the national border between the USA and the FSA. Then this extremely dangerous terrorist origination won't be able to secure arms or support from the western states.

The next step in protecting our citizens will be to start collecting all of the illegal weapons that people still have not turned in yet. The deadline for this is one day away. Therefore, I urge all Americans to turn in any and all illegal weapons that you may have at this time. Remember people, you can surrender those illegal guns at any police, sheriff, highway patrol, or other law enforcement agency anywhere in the country.

It would behoove you to do so before those agencies are knocking on your door. That is all I have for now. The FBI and DHS will be working hand in hand with your local authorities to implement and inform you of all the necessary security measures to be put in place. Thank you, and here is President Osama.

President Osama simply stepped forward and said, "We have already started beefing up the border with the FSA, and all local law enforcement agencies are preparing to collect any illegal guns upon the deadline. We ask for your cooperation in everything we ask you to do to protect you. Thank you, and good day, America."

06 JULY 2011
SHADOW WOLF RANCH

Alex, Dutch, Hunter, Damon, Gerard, and Leiko were all in the ops center making final preparations for 'Operation Freedom Run'. As usual they had seven, forty-two-inch flat screens on for every news station they monitored. When the *CNN* broadcast came on they turned up the volume and everyone took a seat.

At the conclusion of the news cast Gerard told Alex that he would text everyone else to come there ASAP.

Alex said, "Good, but we need to send a runner to check on Luis. He's probably still sleeping from his week of driving."

That's when Leiko said, "I've got it, Big Daddy," and started making a dash for it.

Hunter yelled, "Damn, you might know that bastard would lock down the border a day before our mission!"

Dutch replied, "Yeah, he's famous for his dicked-up timing."

Then Alex reassured them all, "Chill out, people, it's not the end of the world. We'll work our way around it."

An hour later, Luis and everyone else was present. For this meeting, they also had the support members from the special missions unit present, since D-Day was so close.

Then Alex started the meeting and caught all of the other people up to speed. "Okay, now that everyone's up to speed on the current events, I only see a couple of new developments that will affect us on this mission. The first is the border crossings, and the second will be the incursions induced by the weapon's confiscations.

"The border crossings will be handled as planned by Damon posing as air national guard aircraft. Our back-up cover story is that we are all lost Wilderness Tour aircraft. Then it's play it by ear and fly by the seat of our pants. Ya never know, this could work in our favor.

"The weapons confiscations may cause a little or a great bit of trouble for us. All we can do there is handle it on a case by case basis. Remember, folks, the art of deception can take you a long way. We can actually play off our birds as working for either side here.

"The good thing is that Luis has emplaced all of the fuel we need to make the run. Plus we've got eyes and bodies on every refueling point. Needless to say, that goes along with an early warning via secure comms. Okay, who's got any bitches, gripes, or complaints?"

Then Gerard asked, "Are we pushing the mission date back any? You know, to let things cool down."

Dutch spoke up and said, "Things aren't going to cool down. They're only going to get worse, a whole lot worse. The best thing we can do is go on schedule. Friday night."

Alex spoke out and said, "I agree 100 percent with Dutch. Who else has something to voice?"

Leiko asked, "Are we 100 percent ready to kick off?"

Alex replied, "Well, young lady, I was just about to get a status check from every department." Then Alex went down the line.

"Damon, are all the birds ready?"

"Yes, sir, all fueled, armed, programmed, and ready."

Alex replied, "Thank you, sir."

"Ethan, are all weapons systems and ammo ready?"

"Yes, sir," Ethan replied, "All aircraft and personal weapon systems zeroed, qualed, loaded, and ready."

"Thanks, Ethan," Alex replied. "Top of your game as usual."

Then Alex looked at CPT Probts and asked if all of the members of his Special Units Team had qualed and were ready to deploy. He assured Alex that they had and they were. Alex replied, "Thank you, sir, we all really appreciate the work you and your men do around the clock to keep this community safe."

"Gerard," Alex asked, "how do you stand on comms?"

"We're up on everything, Alex. All radios, sat comms, NODs, BFTs, and secure cell phones are programmed and loaded."

"Thank you, Gerard," Alex said. "Leiko, how are you on all of your mass medical supplies in the Chinook?"

"We're complete on that," she said. "And all of the other bird's med kits are topped off as well."

Alex jokingly said, "Thanks, shorty." The two often joked around during meetings.

"Hunter, is all of your mechanic tools and parts loaded in the Chinook?" Alex asked.

"Yup," Hunter replied.

Then Alex said, "Thanks, Dad." And finally Alex asked Luis, "Are all of your supplies loaded into all of the birds?"

Luis said, "Sure enough, food, water, E & E equipment, survival equipment, and all of the cash."

Alex said, "Cool beans. It sounds like everyone is prepped and ready to fly. Does anyone have anything to add to that?" Dutch, do you have anything to add?"

He said, "No, I think everyone's as ready as they'll ever be. Everyone knows the E & E routs and corridors, all of the in-flight contact contingencies, their E & E cover stories, and survival skills. I say let's get a good days rest tomorrow and kick this thing in the ass tomorrow night."

Everyone started clapping and cheering. Hunter said to Alex, "Don't forget your tomahawk, son."

Alex gave his dad a big grin and replied, "It's already packed in my battle gear."

As they all started walking out of the ops center, Leiko yelled, "Cook out at my house." Many whoops and hollers were heard.

MISSION BRIEF

07 JULY 2011
SHADOW WOLF RANCH

1900 MST in the underground hangar on the Wyoming side everyone was assembled for the final mission brief. Dutch read off the roll call for 'Operation Freedom Run'. "Alex, here; Damon, ready to fly; Gerard, present; Hunter, ready; Luis, get-er-done; Leiko, med section ready; Ethan, here; and myself. Captain Probts, are you and your eight men ready?"

Captain Probts responded, "Yes, sir, special units team assembled and ready."

Then Dutch turned it over to Alex for the brief, and he ran with it, "The chain of command is as follows from top to bottom:

- Alex–Hughes 500
- Dutch–Huey number two
- Damon–Huey number one
- Hunter–Chinook
- Ethan–Hughes 500
- Leiko–Chinook
- Gerard–Huey number two
- Luis–Huey number one
- CPT Probts–Chinook

> These positions were chosen not by favorites but for tactical reasons and abilities suitable to this mission. Nothing more, nothing less.

Here are the call signs for the squadron;
Hughes 500 Scout = Cyclops; Alex and Ethan
Huey Gunship number 1 = Hades; Damon and Luis
Huey Gunship number 2 = Zeus; Dutch and Gerard
Chinook/ Med Evac = Pegasus; Hunter and Leiko
My friends, I present to you all, Task Force Titan.

Okay, folks, remember that at the end of this brief the two Huey crews will drive a pickup down the tunnel to the hangar on the Colorado side. From there, you will takeoff and fly to this location and conduct a five-mile security sweep of the area around this hangar, using NODs and thermals.

Upon a clear status you will call us and then provide a 360 over watch while the Chinook and 500 takeoff. Once we're all in the air we'll all fly NOE unless otherwise directed. Assume your preprogrammed flight routes.

On the inbound flight we'll normally fly a standard VEE formation with Cyclops a mile out front on point. In the VEE, Pegasus will be in front with Hades on the portside and Zeus on the starboard side.

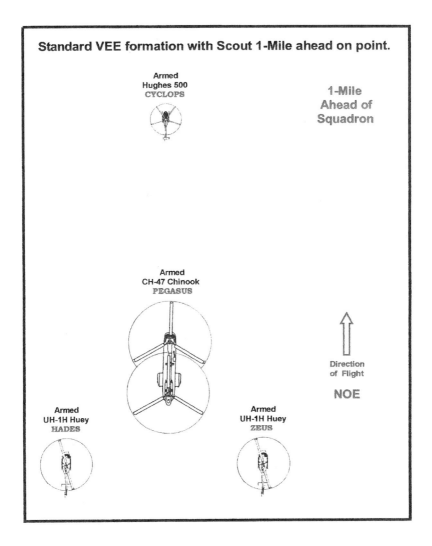

Standard VEE formation with Scout 1-Mile ahead on point.

Armed
Hughes 500
CYCLOPS

1-Mile
Ahead of
Squadron

Armed
CH-47 Chinook
PEGASUS

Direction
of Flight

NOE

Armed
UH-1H Huey
HADES

Armed
UH-1H Huey
ZEUS

On the outbound flight we'll normally fly a Heavy Right formation with Cyclops on point. Hades will be on his port side. Pegasus will be on Cyclops' far starboard side with Zeus on his starboard side.

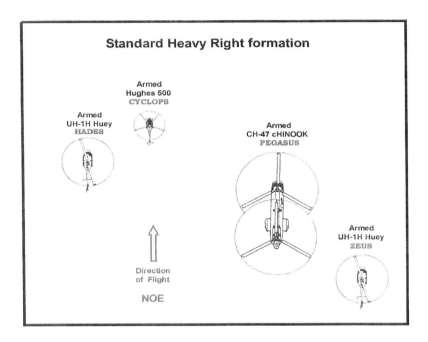

I want all birds close in to protect our precious cargo, thirty-eight pax on the Chinook. Are there any questions thus far?

A few heads were nodding east to west, but no one said a word. Then Alex said, "Okay, good, then I'll keep going." He picked up right where he left off,

Remember, Damon will be handling all radio traffic when challenged by any ground or air authorities. We've also equipped all of our birds with PA loud speakers. They may aid us in our mission by being able to pose as law enforcement or private aircraft. Deception applied at the right time is some times as good as lead flying down range. It all depends on how skillfully it's applied.

On the inbound flight, anytime anyone needs fuel they call to Pegasus and say they need some water. Whenever Cyclops needs fuel, Hades will switch places with him while he in-flight refuels. Then they will swap back. When

Hades and Zeus need to refuel the entire squadron will set down and top off. Remember, the squadron's average range before ground refueling is about 700 miles. Our cruising speed will be 125 knots.

On the outbound flight, we'll still be topping off Cyclops in the air. The rest of us will be landing at our cashed fuel locations. We'll fly all of the two-man fuel crews out with us and leave the fuel trucks in place for possible future missions. After all, they'll be sitting on our property.

Remember, in Pennsylvania and West Virginia we'll be loading two ATVs with us. Every time the Chinook is on the ground picking up pax, the other birds will be in the air providing cover. Keep in mind that some of the people that will be signaling us aren't seasoned pathfinders or SF, but amateurs. Is everyone still tracking with me?

Alex received a room full of north to south nods, therefore, he continued,

One last thing about firing on anyone. If you think you need to fire on someone, please, first call it in through the chain-of-command, and we'll either give you authorization to fire or not. Now let's use some common sense here, people. If you have an aircraft barreling down your throat and posing a threat, by all means, instinctively defend yourselves.

The reason I'm bringing this up is because even when you're being fired upon, sometimes it's better not to return fire than just light 'em up. Here's a scenario for everyone from when we conducted 'Operation Barracuda'.

A law enforcement cruiser was about to pull over our truck full of illegal weapons, ammo, and bodies. At the time we knew he still didn't have the plate number on the truck. Therefore, he still had nothing to call into his HQ that could screw us down the line.

If we had fired him up and they would have found his remains in his car, they could have figured out that he was killed from an aircraft. Then the heat would have really been on us in the air.

We did fire in his general direction though. However, due to Dutch's quick thinking, our ramp gunner fired his 50 cal. warning blast into the waterway beside the cop on the bridge. That served a much better end result than killing the lawman.

Here's why. The cop took the deadly warning to heart and ended his pursuit with no quantifiable information to call his HQ with that could be confirmed. We accomplished our goal of having him cease and desist without having to kill an innocent man.

And because we thought about the way we fired before we fired, there was no physical evidence that the cop could show anyone that he was actually fired upon from above. Not even a shell casing because we use shell collectors on all of our helo guns. So, does everyone get it that there's a time to and a time not to fire on some one?

Dutch could tell that everyone in the hangar appreciated those words of wisdom. Dutch gave Alex a nod to confirm that he agreed with that little speech. Then Alex said, "Well, people, that's about all that I've got to put out. Does anyone have any questions whatsoever that they want to ask before we get into our flight suits and go to get our people?

No one had anything to ask or say so Alex then suggested they say a prayer to God before the mission. Then Alex led them as they all bowed their heads.

Lord, we come to You tonight not as warmongers, but as Christians, Americans, and free men and women. Please watch over us and protect us all as we fight this evil government and oppression of your people, while we try to bring our oppressed loved ones and friends home from a land that was once truly free but is no more.

Lord, please let our birds fly as swift and as invisible as your angels. You have given all creatures on your blessed earth the right to defend themselves from harm from others. Lord, if we should have to defend ourselves on this just mission, please make our shots as straight and powerful as your lighting bolts.

Lord, we give You the honor, praise, and glory that You deserve in everything You do Lord Jesus. Amen.

As everyone raised their heads, Alex noticed there wasn't a dry eye in the house; to include his own. Then Alex voiced one more instruction to Captain Probts. "Captain, keep your eyes pealed, my friend. You're the squadron's primary rear security."

The captain replied, "I won't let you down, Alex."

Alex said, "I know you won't. Just keep your monkey harness hooked up. I wouldn't want to loose you in the heat of battle."

Then Alex thought to himself, *That's it. Nothing left to do but get in, sit down, shut up and fly.* Alex could tell that everyone was tired of all the talk and ready to fly the mission. That went double for him. Once they were all in their birds and on their comms, he said, "*De Oppresso Liber*, Titan Squadron!"

'OPERATION FREEDOM RUN'—INBOUND

07 JULY 2011
1ST NIGHT
HEADING EASTWARD, NOE

Cyclops and Pegasus had rotors turning in their hangar as Hades and Zeus went screamin' over them at fifty feet AGL. Ten minutes later Alex heard the call he'd been waiting for. "Cyclops, Cyclops, this is Zeus, over."

"Zeus, this is Cyclops, send it, over."

"Cyclops, you're clear, over."

"Zeus, copy clear, standby, over."

Moments later everyone heard the call they'd been waiting for. "All Titan call signs, this is Cyclops, I've assumed heading, follow my leader, over." All three of the other birds acknowledged Cyclops's transmission.

Before Task Force Titan reached the new national border they conducted their first in-flight refueling operation with Cyclops near North Platt, Nebraska. It went off without a hitch. It was a good training opportunity before crossing into enemy territory. They were sure to get better and faster at that process as time went on.

Approximately fifty miles west of the new border the Hueys needed some go-go-juice. Therefore, the entire squadron set down and the 500 and both Hueys topped-off. Then the Chinook used the last of the fuel in the slung fuel cell.

They had set down in a deep ravine in a remote location. It was nearing dawn; therefore, they settled in for their first ROD. After they covered the helos with the cammie nets, posted the guards, and got some chow, they all bagged out.

08 JULY 2011
2ND NIGHT
HEADING EASTWARD, NOE

The next evening after dusk, Task Force Titan lifted off and headed east again. The only evidence that they had been there was the empty fuel bladder that the Chinook had slung under its belly. They left it cached in the deep ravine.

Alex had told Hades to take the lead until they crossed the border. It wouldn't hurt any having an old Huey busting the trail for the squadron. After all, the Air National Guard was the only ones still flying the old relics.

Damon really liked it because it gave him the opportunity to be out in the lead, and the opportunity to make first enemy contact. You know the old saying; you can take the dog out of the fight but you can't take the fight out of the dog.

About five miles from the border it happened just like they expected it would. They received a request for clearance over the radio. "Unidentified aircraft on a heading of ninety degrees at seventy-five feet AGL, this is the FSA Border Patrol, identify yourself."

Damon came up on the air and responded. He was using a program that Gerard had installed in all of the birds radios. This program made it sound to the receiving party as if the radio frequency was broken and garbled. However, it was just clear enough to get your point across; kind of.

Damon's response, "FSA Border patrol, this is Air National Guard bird P734ZT in route to Minneapolis with cleared access for this location border crossing, over." About five seconds later they replied. "National Guard helo P73T, we do not have any clearance for you, over."

Damon came back with, "Copy, you have our clearance, over."

After another pause the Border Patrol replied with, "No P7Z4, no clearance, do you copy?"

Just then Luis gestured to Damon to let him talk to them. Damon shook his head no. Then Luis covered up the mike and said, "Let me try, I know this kind-a-guy." Damon thought about it for a second and then he just gestured Luis with a nod yes.

Then Luis came on the air with his best country-boy accent and gave it a shot. "Mr. Border Patrolman, I'm General Walker, and these here birds are a flyin' me and two other generals to Minnesota for a high-powered meatin', and we don't have time to be a fussing, do ya hear me, sir?" After about ten seconds of dead silence on the net, their reply came.

"National Guard bird 73PT, you are not authorized border access, over." By that time, the Hades bird was over the location of the two border agents, and Luis told Damon to assume a hover above them.

Then Luis switched on the spotlight and PA and shouted, "Listen here, boys, get your heads ou-da yer asses, or I'm gonna have ta call my good friend Rich Pevey and have you boys workin' on the border between Alaska and Russia. We got a meetin' to get to, and you two are makin' my balls hurt! Now what's it gonna be, fellas?"

As the rotor wash was beating down on them with that five-million candle power spotlight in their eyes, Luis and Damon saw them simply wave their arms in the direction of the border.

Then they heard over the radio, "General Walker, you have a safe flight and a nice night, sir, and Godspeed, sir."

No sooner than they turned off the spotlight and flew away than the remainder of Task Force Titan came screaming over the two officers heads. Needless to say, those two were going to take the rest of the night off.

Once the air was quiet again one of the guys looked at the other and asked, "Are you going to call the USA border agents on the other side and tell them about General Walker?"

He replied, "The hell with that! As far as I'm concerned, that mad man never came through here."

The squadron was very lucky on that border crossing. There was no USA border patrol presence on the other side at the particular location they crossed. Would they be as lucky on the way back?

As Hades raced forward to reassume his one-mile lead on the squadron, Damon switched to internal comms and said to Luis, "Damn, son, I didn't think you had it in ya. You really pulled that one out of your ass."

Luis said, "Yeah, I'm a quick study and remembered what Alex said about deception at the right time. Anyway, we're over that hurdle for now. We'll still have to deal with it on the rout back."

Just as Damon had switched back to the squadron net, they received a call from Cyclops. "Hades, Hades, this is Cyclops, over."

"Cyclops, send yer traffic, over."

"Any trouble back there? Over."

"Negative. Cyclops. Over."

"Copy Hades. We're coming to your location, over."

"Copy Cyclops. We'll be ready when you get here. Out."

As the Hughes 500 slid up beside the Huey, the Hades crew looked over at them as Damon said to Alex, "Okay, Cyclops, you've got it, we're heading back to the rear with the gear, over."

Alex replied, "Copy, Hades, thanks for the spot."

They flew incident free to the next refueling location for Cyclops, which was about thirty miles southwest of Aurora, Illinois. Once again Hades swapped places with Cyclops as the squadron continued their current speed and heading eastward. Cyclops slid right in behind Pegasus and waited for his unbiblical cord to slowly extend out to him. Then Alex skillfully jinked back and forth until he finally made contact with the fuel nipple.

Then Ethan flipped the switch that sealed the connection. Now it was just a matter of sucking down about a hundred gallons of fuel before they sprinted back up to the front of the squadron to assume their point position again.

The next ROD location for the squadron was about twenty-five miles east of Mansfield, Ohio. This was the first of their cashed fuel locations that Luis had previously emplaced. As they approached the big barns that were to be their home for the day, Gerard accessed his sat comm. CCTVs and conducted a complete IR and thermal scan of the entire property. Once he was finished with his scan, he notified Alex that he only saw their two men on and around the premises.

As the squadron was about twenty miles out, Ethan tried to make contact with the two-man fuel team on the ground. "Digger, Digger, this is Groundhog, over." Ten seconds and nothing was heard. "Digger, Digger, this is Groundhog, over."

"Groundhog, Digger here, go."

"Digger, what's your status, over?"

"Groundhog, my hole is open, over."

"Copy, your hole is open, five mikes out, how copy, over?"

"Digger copy, five mikes out, standing by, over."

Luis had briefed all of his fuel teams that the Chinook would always land first. Then the two Hueys next and finally the 500. This way they could always provide cover from above and each aircraft could have its own ground guide to get it into the tight quarters.

Once all of the birds were safely in their barns, Dutch took a patrol out around the surrounding wood line. The TL of the fuel team was bringing the five-thousand-gallon fuel truck around to all of the birds. While the helos were being topped off, Luis was giving Alex and Ethan a tour of the old farm. Better to know the lay-of-the-land if they had to defend themselves in the middle of the day. After all, none of them would be moving about after the sun came up.

After all necessary tasks were preformed and all sentries were posted, people started chowing down and bagging out. All accept Gerard. He was catching up on the national news in the United States. This was the beginning of the third day of conflict between the federal government and US gun owners.

After scanning several channels he stopped at a sight he couldn't believe. He had to go and get Alex and Dutch to see it as well. Then they watched in sheer disbelief.

09 JULY 2011
SCIOTOVILLE FURNACE, OHIO

It was 7:00 a.m. EST, and the CBS news broadcast was showing a small community in southern Ohio called Sciotoville Furnace. This micro community was off of Hwy 140 and had about seventeen homes in it. It didn't even rate as a village, township, or city; however, it did have its own post office and zip code.

In fact, the only three public structures it possessed was the post office, a small store called Yarboroughs, and a taxidermy outfit called Rolland's. Rolland's was a family owned business that was widely known throughout the county for their fine work. They had a large list of customers that was handed down from generation to generation. That was where the scene was set.

The day before, four sheriff's deputies had gone to Sciotoville Furnace to collect some firearms on record that were never turned-in. All of the legal gun owners had told the lawmen to pack sand and don't come back. The gun owners told them that they were legal, according to the American Constitution.

Then the seven legal gun owners had banded together in Rolland's taxidermy shop because the deputies told them that they would return the following day to execute the warrants. Those good men didn't want any trouble with the law. They simply wanted to continue living the way they and their forefathers had lived for over 230 years.

That was with the God given right to defend them selves, their families, and their communities from anyone whom would do them harm or try to place them under the yoke of a tyrannical government. They believed that the US Constitution was not an instrument for the government to restrain the people; but an instrument for the people to restrain the government.

The images on *FOX News* showed a few people at Rolland's holding up signs about gun control. They were on the front porch waiting for the law, whom they knew were just up the road on HWY 140. Most importantly, they weren't brandishing any weapons.

Then the news images showed the heavy hand of the law coming for them. It showed not only the local armored SWAT (Special Weapons and Tactics) vehicles from the County Sheriff's department, but it also showed the support they had from the state capital in Columbus.

It seemed that the DHS thought it necessary to send additional armored vehicles to Sciotoville Furnace to quell the uprising of seven legal gun owners. They sent in two of their heavily armored, twenty-three ton assault vehicles with medium and heavy machine guns and flame throwers. This was starting to look like the typical federal government siege, such as in Waco and Ruby Ridge. One where the feds had the citizens ridiculously out numbered and out gunned, and spent millions of taxpayer dollars to get a hand full of people.

Between the two sheriff's armored SWAT teams, two DHS armored SRTs (Special Response Teams), two Blackhawk ATF gunships, and about a dozen or so Sheriff and Highway Patrol cars, they had the small community completely cut off from the rest of the world.

Four of the cruisers had all traffic from HWY 140 cut off in both directions; no one in and no one out.

09 JULY 2011
TWENTY-FIVE MILES EAST
OF MANSFIELD, OHIO

As Alex, Dutch, and Gerard watched the broadcast from one of the barns, Gerard asked Alex, "How do you think this is going to go down?"

Alex had a disgusted look on his face as he said, "I think they're going to tell them one time to surrender their weapons and if they don't, they're going to smoke their asses."

Dutch joined in and added, "Ya see, Gerard, this early in the game the feds need to and want to make an example of a group of people who aren't willing to comply with Osama's gun ban. That's why the media is still being permitted to film. Unlike Waco and Ruby Ridge where the media was held a mile away, the feds didn't want the public to see what they were going to do to those people."

Alex then said, "The feds are probably hoping for one or two cocky dudes there to open up on them. That would give them the excuse they're looking for to go in and forcibly take their firearms. That will show the rest of the country what will happen if they don't surrender their firearms."

Then Gerard said, "Look, it's starting. The feds are moving in."

09 JULY 2011
SCIOTOVILLE FURNACE, OHIO

Back in Sciotoville Furnace the feds had just issued their demand over their loud speaker, that any and all citizens of Sciotoville Furnace, Ohio had three minutes to surrender all of their firearms. They were given the ultimatum that if they didn't surrender their guns, they were coming in their homes to take them and arrest all people in violation.

At that point all of the people outside went inside and went into lockdown. At that point the feds started prepping with their breaching teams. At the end of the three minutes the feds could be heard yelling, "Times up. We're coming in!"

With the focal point being on the taxidermist building, that was the one they started with first. The hundred year old building was built like a fortress. It even had functional solid wood shutters over the windows. They prevented the SWAT teams from being able to launch teargas through the windows. After three attempts they stopped firing the CS grenades at the historical site.

A three-man breaching team followed by an entry team headed toward the building under cover of their ballistic shields. Once in position the breaching team blew the double doors off the hinges and the seven-man entry team quickly moved past them and into the first room. Then the breaching team followed them in.

Once inside the room they thought it strange that all of the inner doors were closed and locked. As the team was restacking to breach the chosen door of four, the Team Leader noticed something strange. The entire floor was steel. Just then the overhead sprinkler system came on full blast high pressure and quickly soaked all of the federal agents inside.

That's when the TL realized what the steel floor was for. He started shouting, "Everybody out, get out, everybody g—" That's when they all started dancing in place with fifty thousand volts of electricity flowing through their bodies. After three minutes of cooking in place, the juice was finally cut off and the lifeless charred bodies fell to the floor.

Then Leeroy, the leader of the citizens, yelled out to the feds. "Your ten-man team is toast. Send in your next sacrifice, you spineless bastards!" Just then one of the DDMs fired a shot from his 50 cal. at Leeroy while he was still speaking. He must have had a thermal sight on his weapon to see him through the fourteen-inch thick log wall?

He missed Leeroy by four inches. That was all it took in the people's minds. First they broke in their home, and then they fired on them trying to kill them. Leeroy said to himself, "*Game on, lawman.*" Then he told everyone in the building to prepare for the end game.

Now the ATF mission commander, Major Brewer, told his machine gunners to provide cover fire for the next entry team by firing at all of the windows before they moved. Then he told Captain Max, the site commander for the sheriff's SWAT team to send in an entry team. He said, "Okay, but we won't be so civil about it."

Brewer said, "I don't give a damn. Just get in there and take 'em out!"

Captain Max called his lead explosive breacher over to his location and briefed him, "All right, Jim, this is what I want. I want you to breach a hole through those solid logs large enough for an entry team to enter. We need to go through the south side so we don't come out in that front room where the ATF dudes got fried.

"Now I want you to be as fast as possible and not expose your team to any undue risk. Use your ballistic shields like your lives depended on them because they do. Don't blow it until I give you the word. I've got multiple events taking place at the same time. Got it?"

The demo sergeant said, "Yes, sir!" and went scrambling away. He went back to his trailer and began working with his three-man team. They took a four-by-eight sheet of ¾ inch plywood and basically made a large ring of C-4.

When that was molded they laid another sheet of plywood over the other one and screwed them together. Then he briefed his team on the installation process. "Okay, gents, here's how we're going to do this. All three of us will be in the back of the armored Bearcat. The driver will back up to the breaching point. When we're just far enough away to open the back doors he'll stop. We'll have the plywood C-4 wall on top of the Bearcat. Rick and I will place the wall into position, and, Ronnie, you will use the nail gun to fasten it to the logs. Remember, gents, we've got to get the C-4 above the stone footer.

The last thing is to insert the electrical blasting cap and feed the wire as we drive away. Even if we're being fired at, we can't forget that cap. If we do, this is all for nothing, and we'll have to make another trip up there. Any questions, men?"

Both men shook their heads no. Jim said, "Okay, let's hit it." Then Captain Max told Major Brewer that he wanted one of the Blackhawk gunships also firing upon the roof for a distraction.

Brewer said, "Done, anything else you need, Captain?"

Brewer replied, "No, sir, we're set and ready. As long as those belt feds are firing at the windows and roof, we'll be fine." The major shook the captain's hand and wished him luck.

All agents were listing as Captain Max was in his Bearcat with the breaching team, giving the countdown. "Five, Four, Three, Two, One, gunners open fire." Just then the echo of dueling 7.62 millimeter guns could be heard through the hollers of southern Ohio. As wood chips were flying Jim and his team were getting the job done. One minute and fifteen seconds later the plywood wall was up and the Bearcat was back in position in the security perimeter. Then Captain Max called Major Brewer and said, "I'm set, waiting for your word."

Major Brewer told Captain Max, "Blow it in thirty seconds and send your entry team in. I'll keep the belt feds firing at the windows and roof for cover fire."

Captain Max replied, "Copy, WILCO, out." Then the captain briefed Jim and the entry team that they were about to go hot.

Jim had his hand on his electrical detonator as he counted down over the radio to all agents. "Five, four, three, two, one, fire in the hole, fire in the hole, fire in the hole!" Followed by a large blast and much smoke rolling away from the south side of the log structure was a jagged hole with huge splinters pointed in every direction. Then with their protective mask on, a seven-man entry team entered the splintered hole left by the C-4.

The team soon discovered that they had entered a hallway. The number one man decided to break left and head for the shorter end of the hall. When the team was formed in their stack and ready to breach the locked solid wooden door, they heard a woman's voice on the other side yell, "Hey, boys, I hope ya got yer hip waders on cause yer gonna' fry —-just like yer buddies did! Can ya still smell em? Smells like burnt pig to me. *Hahaha, haaaaaaaa.*"

Yes, there was no doubt about it. The civilians also knew how to effectively use physiological warfare. The door breacher on the team looked back at the TL and asked, "Are you sure we want to go in there, man?"

The TL replied, "She's bluffing. We're going in and taking them out. Now blow that damn door off the hinges and let's go!"

As he used his twelve-gauge pump scatter gun to disintegrate the hinges, the two people in the room prepared for the hellfire, which was about to rain down on them. They each had a one-quarter inch thick plate of steel propped up in front of them. The plates were three foot square, so they afforded them a good amount of cover.

The Sheriff's SWAT team had a mixture of MP-5s and M-4s ; of which, they had directed their entire culmination of fire power upon the two positions. The two civilian defenders were equipped with an M-14 (7.62 mm, Shoulder fired, magazine fed, Semi-auto Rifle) and a Benelli M-1 Super 90 (12 gauge, Shoulder fired, magazine tube fed, Semi-auto shotgun) loaded with three inch magnum sabot slugs, for maximum penetration.

The man and woman liberty fighters pretty much handed the SWAT team their asses before they them selves were killed. Only one man, the breacher, survived the charge. The other six men were directly in the fatal funnel. The lone survivor could be seen on television crawling back to the breach point and rolling out of the hole and falling down three foot to the ground.

Major Brewer yelled over his radio, "Captain Max, get in there and recover that man!" Captain Max was still in his Bearcat and yelled for his medic to get in. Then he instructed his driver to back-up to the breach point, just like he did when they implanted the plywood wall. This time, Captain Max had an M-240 gunner in the cupola, covering the jagged hole in the log wall. He wasn't taking any more chances.

As they were loading the man into the ambulance the Sheriff's medic stated the he was damn lucky. He took hits in all his limbs but not a single round to his torso. Then the bone wagon went screaming' down HWY 140, heading for the hospital in Portsmouth. It seemed as though Major Burns didn't want to loose one of his Blackhawks to fly the man to the hospital. He was thinking that he would need that second bird in a little while.

Just like Waco and Ruby Ridge, after the mishandling and overexertion of force on a small group of American citizens in their home, the FBI was called in and took control of the situation. Special Agent Delancy Barns from the Cincinnati office assumed command as the On-Site Commander. He was not well known for his patience's or even temperament. Of course, with agent Barns came 200 more federal agents and much more logistical support.

The first thing that agent Barns ordered was a simultaneous three-pronged assault on the building. Two additional breach points were blasted through the west side and the roof of the building. Immediately afterward, two, ten-man teams from the FBI entered from the south and west sides. Meanwhile, a seven-man team from the ATF fast roped through the roof.

The press was even permitted to have a helicopter in the air to cover the raid. The average American viewer at home had an extraordinary view of this entire operation. This TV coverage was just as good you would see in an action movie; accept for the indoor coverage. It seemed as though the federal government was indeed using this gun confiscation raid as an example to all Americans, exactly what kind of force would be brought to bear against them if they did not surrender their firearms.

From start to finish, the time it took this third attack on the hand full of civilians was ten minutes. They pumped such fire power into the log building that the people had no chance. In the end, there were seventeen dead civilians. There were seven adults that still maintained their legally purchased firearms, five spouses, and five children. On the feds side there were twenty-four state and federal law officers that were killed.

It had always been the policy of the American news media not to show dead bodies on television. However, someone in the government had instructed them to discard that practice on this particular story. Therefore, this turned out to be a very threatening and disturbing broadcast for most American viewers to swallow.

All of the civilian bodies were dragged out of the building and laid out on the parking lot in a linear formation. As a government double standard, all of the lawmen's bodies were loaded into a U-Hall truck and driven off of the scene. No photo coverage was permitted of the law officers.

Then all of the bodies of the men, women, and children could be seen on television. The camera made a slow sweep from one end to the other. There was a caption above and below their bodies that simply read, Domestic Terrorist. After this horrific display of barbaric journalism, they began to interview Special Agent Barns.

He was still in his battle gear and still amped-up from the mission. He was a straight forward man in his early fifties who got straight to the point. He started off with, "This is not going to be a question and answer interview. I'm going to make a statement on what transpired here today and that will be the end of it." Then he began,

We had some weapons violators here that refused to comply when the proper law officials came to their residence

to serve the warrants on them. They resisted. That was the wrong thing to do. Resistance is futile!

Anyone in this nation that resists the law on this gun ban is going to be dealt with in a just and swift manner. We do not have the time to be dealing with anyone for a period of weeks or months, like in past times.

You will be served an official warrant. If you do not comply with that warrant, we will come in your home or business and arrest you and confiscate your illegal weapons. If you fire upon us you will be killed. End of process.

As agent Barns was speaking, someone yelled, "The building's on fire!" The camera that was fixed on agent Barns panned around to see smoke billowing out of the hole that was earlier blasted through the roof. The reporter asked Barns if he was going to call the fire department in to put it out.

He replied, "No, ma'am, there may be booby traps in there. We'll permit the fire department to contain it, and ensure that it doesn't spread."

Then he said to the cameraman, "Do you wish to continue this interview or not?"

The man panned the camera back around on the FBI agent and the reporter said, "Please continue, sir."

Then he proceeded,

> As the first ten-man assault team entered the building, the terrorist electrocuted them to death and dared us to send more men in. When the second seven-man assault team entered the building, they had such a mass of firepower that they killed all but one of the team.
>
> That's when the FBI was called in and I took command of this operation. Having thousands of similar such gun ban cases to address, we didn't have the time for a lengthy siege. Therefore, I ordered a third assault to be conducted.
>
> We simultaneously entered three separate locations of the building. With superior manpower and firepower, we overtook the terrorist. That was pretty much the entirety

of the operation here today. The FBI would like to thank this county, its informants, and the press for all of your cooperation. Good day.

With that, agent Barns put his left hand over the camera lens and lowered the camera. Then he said, "This interview is over" and walked away. Then the camera panned back to the burning inferno that could have easily been saved. The federal agents had formed a linear barricade to ensure that the firemen couldn't put it out. It was indeed a shameful day in Scioto County, Ohio, that day.

09 JULY 2011
TWENTY-FIVE MILES EAST
OF MANSFIELD, OHIO

Back in the barn, Dutch said to Alex, "Damn, that agent Barns isn't messing around. I bet that SOB was probably at Waco and Ruby Ridge."

Then Gerard cut in and asked Alex, "What was your take on all of this? I mean, was that a standard type of operation for this sort of thing?"

Then Alex unloaded on both of them, "This is what I think, gents. I think this small group of ordinary citizens did an excellent job of defending themselves and making the feds pay a high price to take their guns. However, in the end, it ended as will all small isolated groups against the feds—they died.

"These people didn't appear to have any special skills or training. They just used some imagination and guts. Think about it. These seven men and women took out twenty-four highly trained and heavily armed federal agents before they were killed. That's pretty good in my book.

"The feds defiantly wanted to make an example out of these people. They also set the national standard for dealing with holdouts. Hit them fast and hard and get it finished quickly. That's why there were no negotiations or guest speakers to plead with them to surrender.

"That's why they forced the media to film the dead bodies of the people. That's also why they tagged them as _domestic terrorist_. They're trying to scare all legal gun holders into submission.

"I don't think booby traps were the reason that Barns didn't permit the fire department to extinguish the building. I think that was his way of ensuring that all evidence of what happened to those civilians in there was gone. No evidence, no wrong doing.

"Rest assured, my friends, if they ever try to force their way into our homes and infringe on our constitutional rights, they will pay a much higher price than they did in Ohio today. Now, let's get some shut-eye and we'll brief everyone tonight on what we saw here today."

09 JULY 2011
3RD NIGHT
HEADING NORTHEAST, NOE

At 1900 that evening, Alex was briefing all of the task force members of the atrocities that the three of them had witnessed earlier that day. At the end of his testimony, he could see a tear in Leiko's eye. She always did have a compassionate side for the innocent.

It was 2100 by the time everyone had eaten and prepped the birds for the night's flight. Alex said, "All right everybody, let's have a good flight and pray the Lord watches over us and prepares our way."

With that, everyone loaded up in their perspective birds and cranked those turbines. Cyclops was the first one up into the black, crisp night air. Alex and Ethan conducted a five mile radius recon before the rest of the task force lifted off.

While they were waiting, Hunter asked the crew chief to double check and make sure that the two fuel guys from the barn complex were on his bird. Didn't want anyone left behind. Then everyone received their invitation from Alex. "All task force call signs, this is Cyclops, all clear, follow my leader, over." The other three birds could be heard giving their conformations.

Five minutes later Task Force Titan was flying NOE as they were screamin' northeast at 125 knots per hour. By then all the flight crews were quite accustomed to flying on NODs and full black-out drive. Even though their goal was to stay away from all of the major cities, they still had to fly over some of the smaller ones.

They were forty miles west of Elmira, New York when Cyclops radioed Hades for the refueling switch. Once again the Hughes 500's refueling operation went off without a hitch. Alex said to Ethan, "So far so good. I hope all of these refueling ops go this well."

Ethan started laughing and replied, "Yeah, no kiddin', I'd like to get back to my quad-fifty and see my girlfriend."

Then Alex said, "You've got some strange priorities, Ethan."

Once Cyclops and Hades swapped positions again, the squadron was headed for their next ROD, one hundred miles northeast of Watertown, New York. As they flew invisible to those eyes on the ground, they saw several firefights below them. The same thought crashed through everyone's mind. *They were honest, law abiding American civilians that were forced to fight for their Constitutional rights; the right to keep and bear arms.*

After Gerard gave Alex the call telling him that the LZ was clear, Alex told Ethan to make the call. "Digger, Digger, this is Badger, over."

"Digger, Digger, this is Badger, over."

"Badger, this is Digger, go."

"Digger, what's your status, over?"

"Badger, my hole is open, over."

"Copy, your hole is open, we're five mikes out, how copy, over?"

"Digger copy, five mikes out, we're standing-by, over."

It was 0400, when all of the birds were safely hidden in the old abandoned airplane hangar. By 0500, all of the birds had been topped-off and all other mission essential task had been preformed. Dutch gathered everyone together in the Chinook and Alex addressed them, "Okay people, I want everyone to get at least ten hours sleep today. That's one of the reasons we've got the four men from the diesel crews standing watch today. Tonight is our first big night when we pick up our six pax in Vermont.

"We don't know what to expect yet. We don't know if there will be any violence in the area due to the gun confiscations that are happening all over the country. We'll make contact with our people there this evening to notify them of the pick up and get a current sit report of the area.

"At any rate, we've got to be ready for anything. When we fly, I want every swinging dick, uh, sorry Leiko, uh you know what I mean, everybody wearing their full body armor. Gunners, keep your eyes pealed and remember to report any questionable targets to your chain-of-command for authorization to fire. Any questions?"

The crew chief for the Chinook raised his hand and asked, "This first pick up doesn't have any ATVs coming onboard, does it?"

Alex said, "Good question. No, sir, we don't. Any other questions?"

Luis asked, "What if there are some feds in the area to collect some guns?"

Alex replied, "Well, Luis, we won't give them any of our guns, but we might give them a generous supply of our ammo."

You could have heard a gnat fart in that chopper. Luis stood there with his fly trap open. Then everyone busted out laughing. After the howling and laughter stopped, Luis said, "Oh sure, go ahead and laugh it up. I'll sick General Walker on ya'all to handle my light work." Once again the laughter ensued.

Finally, Alex closed the meeting. He told everyone to go and get that well deserved shut-eye. First call would come at 1800.

Then Leiko slid up beside Alex and asked him softly, "Would you like to come over to my sleeping bag for a little powwow, if ya get my meaning?"

He said, "I would love to, my dear, however, none of these other guys has that opportunity with their ladies, therefore, I won't take it. I want a rain check on that when we get home there, shorty."

She slid back away form him and said, "Aw well, we'll see, maybe, who knows? You don't know. I don't know, perhaps." They both started cracking up.

'OPERATION FREEDOM RUN'—EXTRACTIONS

10 JULY 2011
4ᵀᴴ NIGHT
HEADING NORTHEAST, NOE

At 1800 the guards were making sure that everyone was awake. Alex was already sitting in the cockpit of his Hughes. He had gotten up before everyone else. He pulled out his encrypted cell phone to Kenley and Raku in Vermont and made the call.

The couple was sitting on the couch in their living room watching the national news when the phone beside them rang. Raku literally jumped up off of the couch from being so startled. After all, neither of them had ever heard that phone ring before. Then Kenley answered the phone and said "Heeeello," as if he didn't know who might be at the other end.

Alex started laughing and said, "What's the matter, Kenley? You sound like you expected Elvis or ET to be on the other end of this line? Are you both together and alone?"

Kenley replied, "Yeah, man, you just took us by surprise, that's all."

Alex said, "Okay then, well tonight's the night. Look for that shooting star at about 10:00 p.m. Have either of you ever made a call on this phone before?"

Kenley answered, "No, sir, it's a brand new phone."

Then Alex asked, "Good, is there anything that will prevent you from talking to me later?"

He said, "No, sir, in fact you can talk to the whole family, all six of us."

Alex thought to himself that Kenley had done a good job of remembering the coded phrases he had taught him when Leiko and he were there during the recruitment phase. Then Alex said, "That sounds good. Now can you tell me, are there any stray dogs around there, and has there been any animal attacks around there lately?"

Kenley assured him, "No, man, not in either case."

Then Alex said, "Okay, I guess the report I heard was wrong. Anyway, can I say hey to Raku?" Kenley put her on the phone.

Raku said, "Hey, mister, how ya doing?"

Alex replied, "Oh, I'm doing fine. Are you ready to talk to your sister later on?"

She said, "Yes, sir, I've been wanting to talk to her for some time now."

Alex made his closing statement. "Okay, girl, tell everybody we'll talk to them later, see ya, bye."

After they hung up with Alex, they looked at each other and said, "The kids!" Then they scrambled for their other phone to call their children to bring the grandkids over for grandpa's surprise birthday party. They told them to be there at 8:00 p.m. sharp. Alex taught their kids the code phrases for the mission as well.

Precisely at 2155, Alex made his last call to Kenley and Raku. "Hello," Kenley answered.

Then Alex said, "Kenley, Alex, is everyone in the garage and ready for the party?"

Kenley replied, "Yes, sir, I can't wait."

Then Alex said, "All right then, you can open our package in five minutes, okay?"

Kenley said, "Okay, I can't wait to see it, talk to ya tomorrow, bye."

Alex said, "Bye, talk to ya tomorrow."

Kenley remembered Alex saying that they wouldn't see them until after they heard them. He and Raku had everything ready for them. The unidirectional beacon was set and activated and

Raku stood ready with the smoke grenade. Kenley was scanning the skyline with his NODs for helos. Their kids and grandkids were all kneeling down behind them.

A minute later, Kenley said, "I see them." Just then Cyclops went screaming over their heads.

Raku said, "That can't be them, how are we all going to fit in that thing!"

Kenley said, "That can't be them, I see two other birds over by the horizon. Raku, pull the pin on that smoke and throw it!"

About thirty seconds after she popped the smoke, the huge CH-47 popped up over the tree line from behind them. Raku yelled, "Yeah, that's more like it! Get ready to run, kids!" Kenley could now see the Chinook as it silhouetted it's self between them and the full moon.

As the huge CH-47 Chinook was landing just 50 feet from the family, they were being familiarized with the sand blasting rotor wash. Once all the rubber was on the deck Kenley saw a man, through his NODs, run off of the back of the ramp and started waving them over with his arms. So the six civilians started running toward the crew chief.

Kenley stumbled and fell because he hadn't taken off his NODs. He'd forgotten that he didn't have any depth perception with them on. As he looked up after falling, he saw two other helos flying around to the north and east of them. Then he pulled the NVGs off his face and got up.

Once they reached the end of the ramp the crew chief was directing them around the barrel of the ramp mounted 50 cal. We couldn't have them being flagged by that cannon and possibly preventing the gunner from firing if he had to. Finally, the crew chief showed the people the fuel lines from the small refueling tank for Cyclops and instructed them not to trip over them.

Once they were all in and strapped down, the crew chief notified Hunter on the comms and the huge beast started ascending back into the blackness again. Then the crew chief assisted

Kenley in donning a flight helmet so he could communicate with the cockpit. Once he had it on the crew chief looked at him and said, "Check, check, can you hear me?"

Kenley answered, "Yes, sir, loud and clear." Then the crew chief gave him a thumbs up and just sat down beside him.

Kenley could hear Alex speaking to him in his helmet. "Well, buddy, it's good to have you all onboard. I'd come back and greet you all, but I'm in another chopper right now. I'll see you in a few hours when we set down for the day. Now why don't you put your helmet on Raku and send her up to the cockpit. We've got a little surprise for her. See ya later, brother, out here."

So Kenley took the helmet off and placed it on Raku. After he had the chinstrap fastened, he told her to go up to the cockpit. Then the crew chief stood up before her and held out his hand to assist her. Once in the cockpit the crew chief plugged her comms cord into a hot jack.

Then Raku heard her sister Leiko say, "It's about time you got onboard with us." Raku looked around and said, "I can hear you sis but where are you?" Then Leiko turned her head around and said, "I'm flying this thing you knuckle head." If it weren't for Raku's chinstrap, her jaw would have hit the deck.

Raku questioned, "Is that you behind those goggles?"

"Yes, ma'am," Leiko assured her.

"It's me."

Leiko then commented, "This is Hunter beside me, Alex's dad."

Raku said, "Oh, ah, pleased to meet you, sir. I've heard a lot about you."

Hunter said, "Likewise, young lady, now you better go back with your family and don't distract your sister anymore. She looks for any excuse she can find to blame her questionable flight skills on, ha, ha, ha, haaaaa."

As soon as Raku was back seated with her family, she yanked the helmet off and yelled to them, "My sister is up there, flying this monster!" Everyone's mouth dropped open. Since they knew

Leiko better than the crew chief, he couldn't figure out if that was good or bad.

From that point onward, the flight was now on the outbound side of the mission. Alex came over the Titan net and announced, "All Titan call signs, assume outbound formation, how copy over?"

"Hades copy, over."

"Zeus copy, over."

"Pegasus copy, over."

Then Alex confirmed, "Cyclops, good copy, out."

10 JULY 2011
HEADING SOUTH, NOE

That leg of the flight was shorter than the rest. In fact, the refueling point for Cyclops was about the same distance as the ROD; therefore, they consolidated both into one. The squadron sat down about fifty miles east of Scranton, Pennsylvania. Once again their fuel cache was in two old hay barns.

Alex and Damon had agreed before the mission ever began that all birds would always top-off no further than 100 miles away before an extraction. That way all birds would have the maximum amount of fuel if anything ever went wrong near a target PZ. That's why some legs of the flight mission were different distances.

Once everyone was settled in for the day, Leiko had time to get with her family and talk. She answered all of their questions and told them of their wonderful new home in the west. Then she showed them some photos of Shadow Wolf Ranch on her iPad. Finally she had to send them all to bed so she could get some much needed rest. Flying at night on NODs for hours at a time would really smoke your eyes.

Over at the Hughes 500, Alex was thinking about his time in Kuwait during 'Operation Desert Storm'. That was a little country in the sand box where the big bully, Saddam, was trying to take their candy away. Well, with a million-man army it was a scuffle that required the attention of Uncle Sam. He gave his boys the word to go and get it done.

After weeks of US bombers kicking the crap out of Hussein's army, it took the sass out of them. Then after the mile of death, their will was broken. Still it was good experience for a combat soldier—tested and tried. Except for the dive mission on the Specter C-130 gunship that crashed in the gulf. They could thank the US Navy for screwing them, (US Army–SF Combat Divers) out of that combat mission. That was the kind of combat mission that a Combat Diver would train his whole career for.

As soon as the Specter gunship hit the drink, SOCOM (Special Operations Command) scrambled to find a unit that could conduct the recovery mission and blow the wreckage. Alex's A-team was the only SF unit in-country that had all of their dive gear with them for dive ops (operations). Therefore, SOCOM assigned the dive mission to them.

According to navy regulations, in order to conduct a dive of any sort, peace time or war time, a dive recompression chamber is required to be within a certain distance of the divers. They were in luck. There was a navy vessel that had a dive chamber on it that was located in the gulf, about fifty miles from the crash site.

After his team sent their request up through SOCOM for the support of the navy vessel, the navy informed SOCOM that their dive chamber was down—out of commission. When asked how long it would be down, the navy replied, "Indefinitely—we don't know."

Alex's team stayed ramped-up for the mission in the event that the dive chamber was repaired. Fourty-eight hours later, they were told to stand down. It seemed that a team of Navy Seals was in range to conduct the mission. Much to the navy's amazement, that ship's dive chamber had come back on line about the same time a seal team had been brought in from the open seas.

It was amazing that service branch rivalry went on even in a time of war. One would have thought that the dead Americans, black box, and classified aircraft would have taken priority instead of service rivalry and bragging rights. Alex said, "Some things never change." Then he drifted off to sleep.

11 JULY 2011
5TH NIGHT
HEADING SOUTH/SOUTHWEST, NOE

The task force lifted off at 2200. They were scheduled to have a very short flight tonight. It only took about twenty-five minutes to get within range for Alex to make his final cell call to Brooke, his sister. After the two spoke last night, they all decided to link-up at the alternate PZ near James' farm. She informed him that there had been some trouble in town with the feds taking weapons. There were even a couple of shootouts.

Since Brooke was under added tension with the shootings and all, Alex decided to speak in plane text to her over their encrypted cell phones. He called her five minutes out. She answered the phone, "Hello?"

Alex replied, "It's me, is everything okay there?"

Brooke replied, "As far as I can tell." Then Alex could hear her in the background asking James if he saw anyone through his goggles. Then she came back on the line and said, "We don't see anyone but we can hear some shooting a ways off."

Alex told Brooke, "Hold on."

Then Alex said over the squadron net, "Attention all Titan call signs, possible shots fired near the PZ, keep yer eyes open and scan with thermal as well, how copy, over?" Then he received acknowledgement from all birds.

Back on the phone Alex coached Brooke, "Okay, sis, we'll be there in about one minute. As soon as we hit the ground have James drive the ATV up the ramp and then you and the kids run up after him, okay?"

Brooke said, "Okay, I love you, Alex."

He replied, "Don't worry, little slimy worm, you'll be okay. Hang up now."

Then Alex called Pegasus and instructed the crew chief to be quick on deploying the small ramp for the ATV. The two

Huey gunships were taking up a defensive perimeter around the Chinook while Cyclops was searching the edge of the wood line with their thermal sights.

Just as the Chinook was landing, Cyclops discovered the cause of the gunfire. Alex barked out the following instructions. "All Titan call signs, we've got about 30 armed men heading our direction through the woods. Zeus, assist me from the west, Hades, escort Pegasus until their out of the area, how copy over?"

After the two Hueys confirmed their instructions, each gunship took off in its own direction. Alex told Dutch to hold his fire because he wasn't sure if they were civilians or feds. As they were breaking into the open, Alex hit his five-million candle power spotlight and lit em up. Then he could plainly see that they were indeed civilians with rifles and shotguns.

Alex said, "Zeus, Zeus, they're civilians. I repeat, they're civilians, over."

Dutch confirmed, "Copy, civilians, over."

Then Alex activated his bird's PA system and shouted, "We are not the police. We are civilians. Do not shoot. Do not shoot!" Well, that's when a few of them began shooting at Cyclops.

Alex knew at that point that they didn't have the time to try to reason with the people. That's when he decided to try to scare them into submission through superior firepower. Ethan looked over at Alex's hand as Alex flipped-up the red safety cover on the arming button for the two mini guns. Then Alex squeezed off a hundred round linear burst in the ground, right in front of their feet.

Alex's actions achieved two results. For a moment, the few stopped firing. Then they all started firing. Then Ethan said, "Screw that, let's try this!" Then he fired two 2.75 inch rockets to the left and right of them. All firing from the ground ceased.

Just then Cyclops received the call from Pegasus that they were up and away. Alex replied, "Copy, all birds break contact, break contact. How copy, over?" Everyone copied. Within moments all four helos were gone into the black night as quickly as they had come.

With that, the farmers and hunters all stood there just looking at each other, as if to say, what just happened? Then one by one they started whooping and a hollering at each other. It wasn't long before they started convincing themselves that the helicopters flew away because they were afraid of the Buckeyes. It was actually quite an amusing site. If they only knew the truth of how close they came to utter annihilation.

As the squadron assumed their standard heavy right formation, Dutch came over the air, "All Titan call signs, this is Zeus, ACE report (Report after enemy contact = Ammo, Casualties, and Equipment status), over."

"Zeus, Pegasus, all okay, over."

"Zeus, Hades, all okay, over."

"Zeus, Cyclops, Minus 100 rounds 7.62 and two rockets, over." This is Zeus, good copy on all ACE reports, out."

They flew to their next ROD, forty-five miles southwest of Harrisburg, Pennsylvania. This time their home for the day would be an old commercial garage for tractor trailers. It had eight truck bays, large enough for the four helos. Once all necessary tasks had been performed, Alex called a meeting in the Chinook.

Then he proceeded,

> Okay, my friends, let's talk about that extraction tonight. First and foremost of all, no one was hurt on either side. This mission we're on can be a very dangerous one, given the main fact that civilian people think we're the feds, and the feds think we're civilians or terrorist. Still, sometimes that can work in our favor.
>
> Tonight, about thirty or so locals thought we were the feds and started firing on us. With the grace of God, we didn't have to kill any of them. A little quick thinking on Ethan's behalf didn't hurt any either.
>
> For these reasons, we ask that anyone not part of the flight crew, please do exactly what we ask you, when we ask

you. If bullets are flyin' you won't have any time to think about it; just do it, even if it doesn't make any sense to you at the moment.

Flight crews, before you turn in, I want you to go over your birds with a fine-toothed comb. That small arms fire from those farmers could have struck our aircraft any-where. I want to ensure that there is no damage that we haven't repaired. Please give Dutch a status report before you crash. Good night, and that was a good job out there, people, thank you.

About an hour later while Alex was talking to his mom and dad, Dutch brought him the status report. Dutch said, "Well, brother, we came out of this one pretty lucky, my friend. Here it is, Pegasus took seven hits, all superficial. Hades took no hits. Zeus took five hits, all superficial. And you Mr. point man took twenty-seven hits, all somehow superficial. I think we should have named your bird Washington instead of Cyclops."

Dutch was making a subtle reference to the battle fought on July 9, 1755, on the Monongahela River, part of the French and Indian war near Fort Dequesne, now the city of Pittsburgh. A young George Washington was protected by the hand of God during a fierce battle where he received four bullet holes through his clothes and had two horses shot out from under him without harm to the future general and president.

Dutch continued with his status report. "Anyway, all systems are up and running. No injuries and as far as Gerard can tell, no overly interested parties in our flight activities so far."

Alex said, "Good job, Dutch. I don't see any reason to lay low tonight, do you?"

"No, sir" Dutch replied.

Alex replied, "Thanks, Dutch, have a good night." With that, Dutch headed back to his bird. They all always slept in or right next to their birds in the event they had to bug out at a moments notice.

12 JULY 2011
6ᵀᴴ NIGHT
HEADING SOUTHWEST/SOUTH, NOE

They were back in the air by 2100 and headed for West Virginia. Once again, another short flight. The night before, Alex's brother Stuart also reported no strange activity around his area. In the event they had any trouble such as they had in Pennsylvania, Hunter was prepared to handle it, here in his old hunting grounds.

As they were about ten minutes out from PZ-33, Hunter reminded his tail gunner and crew chief that the second ATV would be coming onboard. Then Alex called Stuart on his phone. As Stuart answered he heard his brother say, "Hey, buddy, is your motor running?"

Stuart replied, "Running and ready. I don't see you yet."

Alex said, "We're about three mikes out. As soon as you see us light your cigarette, okay?"

"Aye, Captain" Stuart said. "I'll be lit up like a Christmas tree." Then he hung up.

Since Stuart was driving the modified ATV, Sarah was scanning the horizon for any signs of aircraft. As soon as they heard the first bird they popped the smoke. Then about thirty seconds later, Sarah said, "I see them baby. O, there's another one and another one."

Then Stuart handed her some dust goggles and said, "Here, swap these out for your frog eyes."

Hunter landed right on top of their IR strobe. As soon as Pegasus touched down, Stuart had the ATV bouncing in their direction. After Stuart had driven up the ramp, the ATV became stuck on the fuel cell lines that ran across the deck of the bird. Then the crew chief came up behind Stuart and yelled, "Punch it, man. We gotta get out-da-here!"

Stuart revved the engine five times before the ATV broke loose, popped a wheelie and shot forward toward the cabin.

Luckily for everyone, the crew chief was prepared for that and had a cargo net stretched across their path. Just in case they needed little extra air brakes.

Then the crew chief yelled for James to assist Stuart in helping Sarah get seated. The two men scooped up Sarah and had her seated ten seconds later. Then the crew chief informed Hunter and Leiko that they were all good-to-go in the back. Then the Chinook was airborne once again. That extraction went off without a hitch.

Then the squadron was headed for its next ROD near Rocky Mount, North Carolina. This time their quarters would be an old tobacco farm with some large tobacco barns. The good thing about tobacco barns is that they are very high, to hang the tobacco from to dry. Of course, our diesel fuel crew had to make a few modifications for our helos.

By 0430 they were all tucked in and being fueled up. Each evening the task force stopped for the day we had more and more family and friends with us. It was like having a family reunion. While a lot of us were talking of old times, Gerard was watching times of new. He was tracking on the progress of the feds in collecting citizen's legal firearms.

At 0530, Alex walked over to Gerard's bird to watch some news with him. They saw some concerning reports coming out of Fayetteville, North Carolina; home to Fort Bragg. They had good cause to be concerned. Bragg was the location of their next extraction at PZ-44. Alex got on his cell phone and asked Dutch, Hunter, and Damon to come over to watch some TV.

13 JULY 2011
FAYETTEVILLE, NORTH CAROLINA

As they all watched the broadcast, it seemed as though FayetteNam was having some major turmoil in their streets. The main reason why; there were so many retired and active duty veterans there that weren't willing to surrender their weapons. Especially since this ban of Osama's went against the very constitution they all took an oath to defend.

The feds problem was that they were afraid of dragging the active duty troops into the fight when they came for the retirees. After all, the feds would encounter the same dilemma when they tried to take the retired law officers weapons as well. Then the newscast switched from the reporter in the studio to an early morning seen of a weapons confiscation operation being conducted in the middle of a Fayetteville street.

It seemed that there were three buddies living together in an apartment after they were all discharged from the military a month ago. They were former soldiers from the 82nd Airborne Division at Fort Bragg. Upon completing their last overseas tour in Iraq, they were all honorably discharged.

The press received a tip that the police and sheriff's departments were going to conduct an early morning raid on the apartment. Therefore, they had a reporter and cameraman standing by to record any possible protocol violations. They were not disappointed.

The law dogs knocked on the door and shouted, "Police, open up!" Not even a second later, they knocked the door off of the hinges with a battering ram and rushed into the apartment with weapons at the ready. Seconds later, they drug the three men out of their beds and slammed their faces into the street. They weren't even given a half second to comply and answer the door.

The entire military town of Fayetteville and all connected towns like Spring Lake and Hope Mills were a hotbed of activity. After all, these towns were full of active, retired, and former military servicemen and women. The civilian and military communities were woven together at a cellular level.

13 JULY 2011 - 7TH NIGHT
TWENTY-FIVE MILES EAST OF ROCKY
MOUNT, NORTH CAROLINA

Back in the old tobacco barn the news broadcast about FayetteNam ended. Damon looked around at the other men and said, "Now that has the potential to be a real hot PZ."

Gerard looked at Alex and said, "Maybe we ought to schedule the pick-up farther away or even for another time?"

Alex replied, "There's no time. It's got to be tonight. Anything else would be too risky for all involved."

Then Dutch added, "Yeah, Alex is right. That place is a powder keg waiting to blow."

Alex then said, "I'm getting ready to call all our people and tell them the pick-up is tonight. I'm also going to direct the SF guys to bring their weapons and ammo with them, if they think they can get away with it. That way if we are coming into a hot PZ, at least we'll have some supporting fire on the ground as well."

Damon agreed, "That's a sound idea. I've seen small amounts of friendly ground fire make or break a hot pick-up before."

While Alex notified all of the POCs (point of contact) being extracted, he also launched his HUMINT (human intelligence) resources so they could alert him of any problems coming down the road before he got there. That last extraction would come down to the wire.

At 2000, on the seventh night of 'Operation Freedom Run', everyone was in or at the ramp of the Chinook for the final mission brief before they conducted their last extraction and headed back west again. Dutch walked from the ramp, through the main cabin, and up to the cockpit and informed Alex that everyone was present.

Alex left Hunter and walked back to the middle of the chopper. Before he started to address everyone, he looked at all the faces looking back at him. From the elderly to the young, he really realized how much they were really relying on him. Then he regained his focus and said, "Hey, how's everybody doing tonight? I hope everyone got enough sleep today. Here's why." He began the brief,

Please hold all of your questions until I finish the entire briefing. Tonight is going to be a very long and hectic night before we lay our heads down to sleep again. Tonight we conduct the last extraction of our brothers and sisters before we all head for our new home out west.

All of our other extractions have been near small towns with no real authorities to speak of. Tonight, however, will be a whole different ballgame. Tonight, we step up to the major leagues. Why? Because we're going to be flying right up the front door of Fort Bragg and Simmons Army Airfield.

If we are perceived as a threat, they will launch military aircraft to challenge us in the air. That, on top of the fact that there are some major law enforcement engagements going on all over the city, will make for a very interesting flight indeed.

I spent fifteen years at Bragg. I've seen and known enough of those men there that I can tell you when the feds start knocking down doors and dragging these guys out of their beds at night, they will fight back. There is no limit as to what kind of ordinance these men can muster. I can testify to that fact. I've seen it for myself.

Now trust me. In a dynamic environment like that, anything that can go wrong, will go wrong. That's right. I'm talking about that SOB Murphy! Let's keep him pinned down tonight so he can do us no harm.

Passengers, I simply ask that you all stay strapped in your seats and do anything the flight crew may ask you to do. No more, no less. Even if you don't understand why you are being asked to do something, please just do it. Thank you all very much.

Flight crews, we need to be at the top of our game tonight. Everyone must keep their eyes peeled for anything that could affect us. That means aircraft, ground troops, hostile small arms fire from the ground, ground search lights, or just anything totally out of the norm.

Weapons teams, remember, if a bird goes down, we're going to do everything in our power to extract the downed crew. That's why you all will be in your rappel body-harnesses so you can rappel down to them if necessary. We also have all electric hoists ready for action. Your mission is to medically assist and protect them until we lift you all out. We must protect and keep this Chinook in the sky at all cost. If this big beast goes down, everyone looses, End of mission!

If the downed crew isn't injured and needs to bug out of the area ASAP, we also have the option to drop any of the six E & E trail bikes to you. They're all equipped with explosive opening chutes that will be fully inflated within twenty-five feet after deployment. If that happens, stay on your comms, and we will direct you where to go for a pick up. Every one of these bikes has a SAW and an M-14 attached to it.

Remember that our primary mission is to protect the civilian cargo on Pegasus. If we encounter enemy aircraft and it's at all possible, we'll let Damon's bird, Hades, engage them first or lead the attack. He's the only combat pilot among us. Don't misunderstand me though. If there's a threat, and it makes better sense for another bird to respond due to timing or proximity, do so.

One last thing. This could get real hairy real quick. Keep all the unnecessary chatter off the radio. If you hear repeated calls to a call sign and they're not answering, then relay for them.

All of the people being picked up were notified this morning and are all ready. The SF guys will have their own weapons on the ground incase they have to support us during the extraction. Take note, people, all friendlies on the ground will be wearing glint tape on their head and both shoulders. Ensure you are performing positive IDs on everyone you're firing at. Well, that's about it, people. Are there any questions?

The crew chief of Pegasus asked, "Are we ditching the small fuel cell used for refueling Cyclops?"

Alex replied, "Yes, sir, we're removing that right after this brief, and we'll rig the first pair of trail bikes in its place." Then Alex looked at Captain Probts and said, "If he has to deploy the bikes, you'll have to lock your ramp 50 down until the bikes and static lines have been cleared. We can't have them getting hung up on your gun." The captain just gave Alex a thumbs up.

The Pegasus crew chief raised his hand and said, "One more question, Alex. We've got this stretcher and med station set up here. Can you go over the med plan again?"

Alex said, "Yes, sir, no problem." Then he covered the med plan in detail. "Our first response for a medical emergency is self-and-buddy treatment. If that isn't sufficient, then Leiko, the copilot of the Chinook, can be freed up. She will assist. If she can't be spared in the cockpit, we'll have to make do ourselves until she can lend a hand. That's the plan until we pick up our next passengers.

"Once we get them aboard, we'll have an 18D medic and a medical doctor to handle all injuries. We've got enough supplies here for a small hospital. Pegasus will be our flying ambulance and hospital. Next question?"

Kenley raised his hand and Alex said, "Yes, Kenley, what do you have?"

Kenley replied, "I did four years in the navy. If you can use me anywhere, I would be glad to help."

Then Alex asked, "Can you fire a 50 cal, M-79 grenade launcher, or a sniper rifle?"

Kenley took a brief second to turn his head and look at the massive Browning 50 caliber machine gun that was mounted on the ramp of the Chinook. Then he turned his head back toward Alex and said, "Yes, sir, I could figure them out if I had to."

Alex grinned and said, "Great, the crew chief will use you if he needs you. Thank you for volunteering."

Luis then asked Alex, "Can you go over the different PZs again please?"

Alex said, "Yes, sir, good question."

Then Dutch looked at Alex and said, "I can cover that one for ya."

Alex replied, "Please do."

Dutch said, "All pilots please move in closer. Then he stretched out a map of Cumberland County and began,

- The Primary PZ is here, just south of Gray's Creek. Note its east of I-95. If nothing goes wrong, that is where we'll extract them. We want to stay east of I-95 so we don't alert Fort Bragg or Simmons Army Airfield to send up aircraft to challenge us.

- The Alternate PZ is here, just east of Eastover. Once again, it also is east of I-95 for the same reason. If something would go wrong and we couldn't pick them up at the primary, then they would drive up I-95 to the alternate for extraction. Take note, this is where Doctor Kellerman's office and home are.

- The Emergency PZ is here, just south of Rockfish. If the other two PZs aren't suitable for pick-up and we need a closer PZ to the majority of the people, we'll dictate this one. Take note; this PZ is west of I-95. Therefore, if we have to use this one, we will probably attract some unwanted attention. That covers the three PZs, folks.

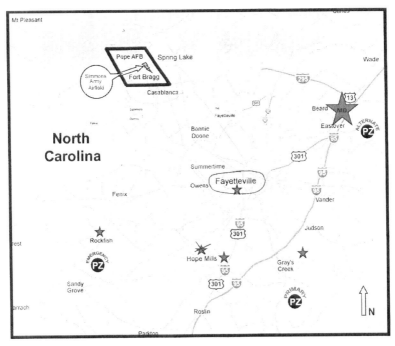

Alex asked if there were any other questions. No one had anything for him so he said, "Okay then, just as soon as the first two E & E bikes are rigged on the ramp we'll blast off. Dutch, would you please send a small patrol around the perimeter for one last check before we lift off?"

Dutch looked at Alex and said, "WILCO." Then Alex closed the meeting with a prayer.

By 2100, the squadron was ready to depart. Cyclops was the first in the air so he could perform a five mile radius check with his thermal sights. Once Alex was satisfied that it was safe for the remainder of the squadron to lift off, he gave the word and provided over watch.

After the Hueys were in the air the Chinook lifted off and took its position in the formation. A moment later the dust settled and the area was silent again. The only thing that remained was the fuel truck and small fuel tank from the CH-47, possibly for a follow on mission.

As the Titan Task Force flew over Eastover, North Carolina, they saw a huge firefight in progress. The feds were enforcing a weapons siege and even had a five mile stretch of I-95 blocked. That was one advantage that the squadron had by being able to get eyes on the alternate PZ. They then knew they wouldn't be able to use it.

Alex came over the comms and said, "All Titan call signs, Alpha is no longer an option, how copy over?"

Everyone acknowledged his transmission. Then Ethan said to Alex, "I sure hope our other two PZs are clear."

Alex replied, "Ya gotta have a little faith, brother."

As the squadron was flying just to the east of Vander, North Carolina, Alex received a call on his encrypted cell phone. It was John Birch, one of the SF guys to be picked up. Alex answered, "Yes, John, what is it?"

John said, "Hey, Alex, I've got Danner Sanderson here with me and I've got to let ya know that we can't get to the primary PZ; there's road blocks everywhere."

Just then, Alex's other line rang, and he looked at the caller ID. It was Logan Blayteck. Alex said, "John, hang on. I've got Logan on the other line."

John replied, "Standing by."

Then Alex switched over to the other line. He said, "Yeah, Logan, what-da-ya got?"

Blayteck said, "I'm at the PZ. We've got everyone accept John and Danner."

Alex replied, "Yeah, I know, they can't get there because of all the road blocks. Stand-by." Alex switched back to John and said, "That's Logan on the other end. Everyone else is at the primary. Can you guys make it to the emergency PZ?"

John looked at Danner and said, "What da ya think? Can we make it there?"

Danner pointed his HK-91 (7.62mm, shoulder fired, magazine fed, select fire rifle) toward the ceiling of the Dodge dually and jacked a round into the chamber and said, "Hell, yeah! I'm not staying in this country any longer."

John got back on the phone and said to Alex, "We'll be there in thirty mikes."

Alex said, "We'll be there. Keep us informed of any changes, okay, brother?"

John replied, "You got it, brother, out here."

Then Alex switched lines again and told Logan that they were on the way to get them at the primary PZ and then they would go to pick up John and Danner at the emergency PZ. Logan assured Alex that they were ready for extraction.

As the squadron was ten mikes away from the primary PZ, Cyclops informed the rest of the birds that he was going on ahead to recon the PZ. He left Dutch in charge of the squadron. Dutch knew that meant Alex would give him an all clear before he was to bring the remainder of the squadron in to the PZ.

As Cyclops neared the PZ, Ethan was on thermals while Alex was still on NODs. Alex identified Logan's unidirectional IR strobe light and all expected bodies on the ground. Ethan saw nothing out of the norm on the ground or in the air. Then Alex made the call.

He radioed, "Zeus, Zeus, this is Cyclops, over."

"Cyclops, this is Zeus, send it, over."

"Zeus, its supper time, come and get it, over."

"Copy Cyclops, we're coming for chow, Out." Meanwhile, Cyclops had assumed a hovering position in a stand of trees where he could over watch the entire PZ as well as the nine pax they were picking up.

As soon as Pegasus cleared the tree line Hunter immediately picked up on the IR strobe and headed for it. That's when Logan looked at Tanner, the MD, and told him to toss the smoke. Cyclops maintained his concealed position while Zeus and Hades assumed defensive over watch positions.

As soon as Hunter and Leiko set the big Chinook down, Alex saw the nine pax running toward the tail of Pegasus. About halfway there he saw one of the silhouettes go into the prone position. Then several of them stopped for about ten seconds and then continued on to the bird.

Then Alex asked Pegasus for a status report on the new passengers. It turned out that Logan Blaytecks son fell in a groundhog hole and broke his leg. Not to worry though, Doctor Kellerman and Galvin Norstrum were working on the boy.

The rotor wash covered the small PZ as the Chinook lifted off and joined the rest of the squadron already airborne. Then Alex came over the net. "All Titan call signs, this is Cyclops, we have two more pax at Echo, how copy, over?" Everyone acknowledged.

As the squadron flew over I-95, Alex told Ethan to keep his eyes pealed. Ethan censed the tension in Alex's voice. He knew he was expecting the worse. Then Alex got back on the radio. "Zeus, Zeus, Cyclops, over."

"Cyclops, send it, over."

"Zeus, make sure you're skinning that rabbit, over."

"Cyclops, WILCO, out." Gerard knew that Alex wanted him monitoring the frequency hopping system as he listened for any sign that Simmons Army Airfield had launched any aircraft to investigate them.

Then it happened. Three minutes after passing Hope Mills, the ramp gunner on the Chinook saw two helos in trail. He reported the sighting to Hunter, who in turn sent the word out to the entire squadron. "All Task Force Titan call signs, this is Pegasus, we've got two bogies on our tail, over." Then Alex asked Hunter if they could ID the birds.

Hunter asked Captain Probts if he could ID them. The captain could not; they were too far away. Then Hunter told him to combine his spotting scope with his NODs for a telescopic effect. That did the job. They were two Blackhawk gunships. Hunter then informed Alex of the bird's true demeanor. That was all Alex needed to know.

"Hades, Zeus, Cyclops here, those are Blackhawk gunships, break"

"Break off and intercept, we'll continue on to Echo, over."

"Cyclops, Zeus, WILCO, over. As both Hueys broke off and spun around on an intercept course, Cyclops took up the direct lead for Pegasus.

As the two Hueys were headed for the two Blackhawks, Damon told Luis to join his spotting scope to his NODs and tell him what kind of armament they had. Luis reported that he saw no external weaponry on the aircraft; only door gunners with machine guns. Then Damon sent his instructions on to Dutch.

"Zeus, Hades, we've got them out gunned, so if this goes bad, we need to wack em fast. I'm going to make contact first, break. Simmons Army Blackhawks, this is North Carolina Air National Guard helos, over."

"NC Air Guard, this is Simmons aircraft–A348W, what is your call sing, over."

Damon replied, "This is NC Air Guard W883N, over." Then the Blackhawk pilot requested the nature of their business. Damon replied, "We're conducting practice PZ missions. We even have some of those 82nd boys to play our VIPs we're picking-up, over."

By now all four aircraft had come to a complete hover 100 meters opposite each other. The Blackhawk pilots could see that they were hopelessly out gunned. Their two crews were discussing why the two old National Guard Hueys were so heavily armed.

Then Damon came back on the radio and told the Blackhawk pilots that they had to get back to the planned exercise. Then he added that General Walker had given express instructions for all non-exercise aircraft to hold a five mile exclusionary zone for the drill. Then the Blackhawk pilot said, "Copy, standby for further instructions, over."

That's when Damon got on Dutch's net and said, "Screw this Dutch, we've gotta get back to Pegasus. Do a 180 and we'll get out of here. If they fire on us we can spin around and smoke em before they can hurt us." The two Hueys proceeded to slowly turn around and head in the direction that Cyclops and Pegasus had gone.

The two Blackhawks proceeded to follow the two Hueys, while ordering the Hueys to stop and land. As Hades and Zeus continued flying, one of the door gunners in the lead Blackhawk sent a burst of 7.62 tracers across the bow of Damon's bird. Then Damon came over the radio and told Dutch, "Zeus, let's take em out, they're not going to stop!"

Both Hueys spun around in a heart beat and simultaneously fired their 2.75 inch rockets at the Blackhawks. Since they were about ninety meters apart, the Blackhawk pilots had no reaction time. Both birds went down in a fireball. The Hueys turned tail and hauled ass back toward the other half of their squadron at maximum speed.

As they were approaching their fellow Titans, Dutch informed Alex that they had to smoke the two aircraft and they would probably have some hostile company in a short time. At least they were only five minutes from the PZ. Alex phoned the guys on the PZ and updated them on what had happened.

John said, "Watch your ass. There's been a couple of Blackhawks flying around here. I was just getting ready to call you and give you a heads up. They look like they're looking for something."

Alex replied, "Hang tight, we're a couple minutes out. Go ahead and pop your smoke. Get off this cell phone and go to the radio we gave you."

John said, "Copy, WILCO, out."

Alex found himself wondering if the two birds around the PZ were with the two birds that the boys had to take out. Surely their command had to know by then that they were gone. One thing was for sure. When they found out they would send a whole squadron to avenge their brethren.

When Task Force Titan was one minute out, one of the Blackhawks went screamin' over the PZ and saw the smoke and IR strobe light. John Birch got on his radio and yelled, "Cyclops, Cyclops, Echo, enemy helo over the PZ, how copy over?"

"Copy Echo, Salute report, over."

"Cyclops, one Blackhawk gunship, one hundred feet AGL, heading northeast, over."

"Copy Echo, one mike out, over."

"Copy. One mike, out."

Just as the squadron was preparing to break over the tree line of the PZ, five armored Humvees broke through the wood line and headed straight for John and Danner, bringing death and destruction with them. John said over the radio, "Cyclops, Echo, we've got hostile ground vehicles headed our way!" While John was busy chit-chatting on the radio, Danner had engaged the vehicles with his HK-91.

Then John yelled into the mic, "Hot LZ, Hot LZ!"

Then the gunners in the Humvee cupolas opened fire on the two men, forcing them to pull back and take cover behind the engine block of the dually. John said, "We need heavier fire power than that HK," as he pulled a LAW (light antitank weapon 66mm, high explosive, single shot, shoulder fired weapon) from his duffel bag. It took him about five seconds to extend, arm, and fire it at the lead Hummer.

A direct hit to the engine compartment stopped it dead in its tracks. That was enough to make the other four, pause and rethink their direct charge tactic. Then two of the four gunners reoriented their main guns on Pegasus as he came over the tree line. Then Danner reengaged the hummers with his rifle while John was busy removing his M-60 machinegun from his bag of tricks. The two were under direct fire from the Hummers as John employed his good ole 60.

Just as the birds of the squadron were assuming their defensive positions to over watch while Pegasus landed, one of the Blackhawks showed up out of no where. Just as Hunter was directing his twin 50 cals toward the Blackhawk, they fired upon him. The Chinook received a line of fire from the crew chiefs port side window all the way to the open ramp. The sniper in that window received a fatal wound and fell limp to the deck.

By then Hunter had squeezed off a fifty-round burst from his Ma Duces at the Blackhawk. He had missed his mark. The M-79 gunner had unhooked his harness from the starboard side window and slid over to the port side door and anchored off. Then he saw the two men on the ground fighting for their lives and decided to assist them. He pumped three 40mm grenade rounds at the four Humvees.

As debris rained down on the troops in the Hummers, their gunners opened fire upon the birds in the air. That's when Alex instructed Pegasus to withdraw until they could neutralize the air and ground threats. Just then Hades unleashed four rockets on the Hummers.

Zeus was on the opposite side of the PZ looking for the Blackhawks. Cyclops had led Pegasus off the PZ while providing cover for them. Now that the Humvees were out of the mix, the remaining immediate threat was the two Blackhawks.

Alex knew that he had to get his people out of the AO, ASAP. Therefore he gave the order for the Chinook to extract the men with their SPIES rig. At the same time he instructed the other birds to form a defensive perimeter around Pegasus to provide possible cover fire while the men hooked-up.

As soon as John and Danner were connected to the line, one of the Blackhawks popped up out of a small clearing and opened up on Zeus with his M-240. Cyclops and Zeus saw him at the same time. Dutch yelled, "Bogie, two hundred meters north of the water tower!" While Alex was sending the Blackhawk a four hundred round burst of 7.62 millimeter AP (Armor Piercing Ammunition) from his mini guns, Dutch unleashed a rocket to deal with them.

Moments later the Blackhawk gunship exploded in the air and went down flaming. Then Alex received a call from Hunter, "Cyclops, Pegasus, cargo connected, over."

"Copy Pegasus, we've still got one bogie around here with more on the way. We gotta go now!"

"Copy Cyclops, let's go, over."

All Titan birds took their que from that transmission. They formed up in their heavy right formation and headed southeast. Their goal was to get back on the eastern side of I-95 and then head toward Florence, South Carolina. However, there was still the matter of John and Danner hanging below the Chinook.

The men at Shadow Wolf Ranch tried to think of every contingency possible when they rigged the birds before the mission. They rigged the SPIES line from the ceiling of the Chinook; right beside the ten-thousand-pound ceiling winch they installed. That way, if they had someone on the SPIES line and they couldn't set down to retrieve them, they could winch them in right through the floor while on the go.

Danner was hooked up above John; therefore, he was the first man reeled in. Danner had a difficult time transferring his body weight from the SPIES line to the winch hook because Pegasus was hauling ass with the squadron. That line transfer technique was meant to be preformed from a hover up to 50 knots. Task Force Titan was screamin' at 150 knots; NOE.

Danner was in a hard spin as he was nearing the trap door in the belly of Pegasus. He was spinning so hard that when he came up to the door he hit his head on the door frame and was knocked unconscious.

The loadmaster looked over at Kenley and yelled, "Hey, man, help me get him inside!" Kenley quickly unbuckled his seat belt and got down on his knees to assist getting him in.

The loadmaster then advised Kenley, "Watch your ass, man, you're not hooked up. It's easy to get sucked right out of this hole!" Kenley gave him a nod of acknowledgement and the two of them drug Danner inside.

Once they had him lying on the deck, the Doc and Galvin carried him over to their med station and started working on his head injury. Then the loadmaster sent the winch cable back down to John Birch. He was about to connect the winch hook to the

D-ring on his harness when the last Blackhawk bushwhacked the squadron.

It seemed as though the Blackhawk popped up out of a clearing in the wood line and unloaded both of its M-240s on the squadron as they flew by. Captain Probts was the first one to see them from Pegasus' ramp and he didn't hesitate to return fire with his 50 cal., while alerting all Titan call signs.

Hades came on the net and said, "Cyclops, Hades, I'll engage, over."

"Copy Hades, watch your six, over." Then Damon banked his Huey to the port side and raced toward the Blackhawk. When the loadmaster heard the big 50 cal. barking behind him, he turned his head to see what was happening. When he turned back around and looked back down at John Birch, he noticed he was motionless like a rag doll, just flapping in the wind.

Then Kenley looked at the loadmaster and asked, "Is he okay, he's not moving anymore?"

His reply, "I think he's hit, probably from that Blackhawk. I'm gonna winch him up anyway." As he started retrieving the winch cable he suddenly stopped and yelled, "Damn it, he never switched lines."

The loadmaster looked at Kenley and said, "I gotta go down and get him. You gotta operate the winch and bring us both up."

Kenly said, "No, sir, you're too valuable to this aircraft. I'll go down and get him. I need a harness." The loadmaster realized that he was right, so he got him a monkey harness out of his kit.

Once Kenley had the harness and a flight helmet on, the loadmaster told him what to do. "Once ya get to him, ya gotta connect this short line to his harness before you disconnect him from the line he's on now. If you forget that, he'll fall when you cut his main line. Got it?"

Kenley's eyes were as big as baseballs when he said, "Yes, sir, I got it. Let's go!"

Meanwhile, the Blackhawk had just dodged the second rocket that Damon had fired at him. Since the 2.75 inch rockets were line-of-sight and not wire or laser guided, a quick reacting air-craft and a good pilot could avoid one if he had enough time and saw it coming.

Damon said to Luis, "Okay, time to quit dickin' around with this guy!" Then Damon fired two more rockets at him with a two-meter spread. He knew that the pilot would bank to his starboard side to avoid them. Therefore, Damon laid on his mini guns so when he banked to avoid the rockets he would fly right into the wall of lead from the mini guns. It seemed as though the old Vietnam pilot knew some tricks that the Gulf War pilot didn't.

Onboard the Chinook, Kenley had made the switch over and was waving his left arm at the loadmaster to reel them up. After they squeezed through the trap door, the Doc and Galvin once again carried the wounded man over to the med station. The two had their work cut out for them this time.

Once they conducted their BATS (Bleeding, Airway, Tension Pnenmothorax, and Shock–Initial medical check and care), they found that he had been shot three times. He took 7.62 rounds in his right lung, right shoulder, and left calf. He was lucky to still be alive. With the grace of God, one MD, and an 18-Delta he'd pull through.

After the last Blackhawk bit the dust, Hades reassumed his position within the squadron. After thirty minutes of hard flying, Task Force Titan had crossed the state line into South Carolina. Once the squadron was adjacent to Charleston, South Carolina, they assumed a new heading. Now it would be a straight shot to the national border near Joplin, Missouri. Hopefully the Titans could make it there without further interference.

'OPERATION FREEDOM RUN'——OUTBOUND

14 JULY 2011
GEORGIA

It was 0445 when the Squadron arrived at their next ROD location. They were hooching in an old crop duster hangar for the day. It was located about fifteen miles west of the Georgia state line. Everyone was ready for some well needed rest. The list of injuries for the night included a man with multiple gun shots, a man with a serious concussion, a boy with a broken leg, and one man dead from a bullet wound to the throat.

Once all security was posted, birds were fueled, and all status reports were in, Alex ordered a meeting before everyone tended to their own personal needs. Since the wounded couldn't be moved from their cots, the meeting was held inside Pegasus. After everyone was settled down, Alex began,

> First of all, I want to say that God has indeed had His protective hand upon us all tonight. We faced some pretty surmountable odds tonight and the Lord brought all but one of the fifty-four of us through the night.
>
> Let's all bow our heads for a word of thanks and a word for the fine young man that gave his life tonight in the pursuit of freedom. Lord, we commit this young man, Tim Richardson, to You as he lies here tonight. I personally knew him to be a Christian and a child of Yours, Lord. Please welcome him home, and don't let his sacrifice be in vain. Thank you for watching over us this far, and please see us safely to our new home out west, remembering that

it is only our temporary home until You bring us to our eternal home on high with You, Father. Amen.

As you all can see, we have the highest commitment to bring you all safely home with us. We've paid a high price here tonight to keep that dream of freedom alive. When we all get back to Shadow Wolf Ranch, we're going to build a memorial that will always remind us of the sacrifices that were made by free men and women during 'Operation Freedom Run'.

Remember, my friends, we're not home free yet. The worst may yet be ahead of us. Be brave, and please continue to do as we may ask of you. I want to recognize a man here tonight that did just that when he was asked to tonight. Kenley, please come forward.

Kenley worked his way through the people standing around the ramp of the Chinook and walked up beside Alex. Then Alex put his left hand on Kenley's shoulder and began to explain, "Here's what happened tonight, people. As some of you witnessed yourselves, when this big helicopter was attacked from behind, the attackers shot John Birch to pieces. He was hanging beneath this very bird awaiting his turn to be hoisted aboard.

"Being unable to help himself, he would have died without assistance. Kenley volunteered and went down that cable himself to help a man he didn't even know. All he knew was that a man's life was in the balance and someone had to do something.

"He did indeed save John Birch's life tonight. So you see, my friends, this mild-mannered man is a true American hero. Let's give him our thanks and a round of applause."

Everyone there gave him a standing ovation, all accept Sarah and the wounded. She would have as well if she hadn't been bound to that damn wheelchair. Then Alex concluded his meeting. "Okay, everyone, we've had a long night. Let's get some chow and some shut-eye. Tomorrow night will be a very anxious night. Oh, and everyone, please keep your body armor on when in the air. I know it's uncomfortable, but it could save your life. Good night, everybody."

What the Titan Task Force didn't know that day while they were resting was the US Army had launched a large scale search for whoever had taken out four of their helos and five of their Humvees. Fort Bragg-North Carolina, Fort Campbell-Kentucky, Fort Rucker-Alabama, and Hunter Army Airfield-Georgia all had patrols in the air and on the ground. It was a massive manhunt.

14 JULY 2011
WASHINGTON, D.C.

Meanwhile, in Washington President Osama was setting a plan in motion. He wanted much tighter control on the new national border and he wanted an end to all the gun owners. He thought that if he could pit key government agencies against the American gun owners, he could wipe out all of the gun holdouts in a mater of days. Then he told FBI Director Miller that he would assist him with that mission; whether he liked it or not. Osama had too much on him for him to refuse.

He arranged a classified meeting between himself, Miller, and the secretary of Homeland Security, Jacky Napoleonic. The two persuaded her that the NRA was funding, training, and equipping the nation's psycho gun owners against the federal government. They convinced her that the DHS was needed to assist in a nationwide effort to defeat the NRA and all of the domestic terrorist that they were supporting to defy the federal government. Once the top government judicial offices were on board, things moved quickly.

In 2009, DHS ordered 2,500 GLS (Gesellschaft Fur Logistischen Service = MRAP) armored vehicles designed for combat. Since DHS ordered those war machines and not DOD, they were purchased to be used on the streets of America. Those vehicles along with 450 million 40 cal. bullets, 100 million 12 ga. shotgun rounds, and 350 million 5.56mm rounds they ordered, would give them the means to put America under siege to accomplish their evil goals.

In 2009 FEMA (Federal Emergency Management Agency) had also graduated their first class of 231 recruits. They were all ages 18 to 24 and recruited from the president's AmeriCorps volunteers. They were the first wave of DHS's paid Youth Corp Army across the country. To date, they had five thousand of those brainwashed troops. They sort of reminded people of Hitler's Youth Corp, in an eerie sort of way.

This Osama plan wouldn't be that hard to put into motion with the new federal power that FEMA had been given, thanks to him. The mission already even had a name. It was called, 'Operation Garden Plot'. A highly unknown federal law that gave the federal government the authority to imprison threatening Americans in concentration camps throughout America.

So now the federal government was going to make its move— one that they had been planning for years. The DHS along with the support from the other federal agencies would put 'Operation Garden Plot' into effect. Martial law had been invoked throughout the United States of America. The military had been moved up to the border in force. The entire country was thrust into civil unrest.

14 JULY 2011
8TH NIGHT
HEADING NORTHWEST, NOE

Just after everyone's breakfast at 2100, Alex has his preflight briefing with everyone. Once again they all gathered in and around the Chinook. Then he asked, "Can everybody hear me okay?" They all nodded their heads north to south. He said, "All right then, I'll get started" and the briefing began.

- As you all know, last night we had to shoot some choppers down and kill some men to defend our very lives. Well, the United States government isn't happy about that, and they're trying their best to find those responsible.

- Well, I don't particularly want to be found by those people who don't even uphold the Constitution any more. I can only imagine what kind of justice we'd receive at the hands of those socialist commies.

- Gerard has heard over the military airways that the government has declared martial law, and they have reinforced the federal border that we've got to cross tonight. Well, my friends, we're going to give it our all to get across that border, even if we've got to call in some favors.

- The possibility is there that we could see some heavy action tonight. If we do, I once again ask you all to do as we ask, as soon as we ask, and don't ask any questions. In combat, we don't have time to answer any questions. In the time it takes to answer a question, you could be killed for not having already done what you were asked to do in the first place. Everyone keep your body armor on and fastened.

Then Alex looked at Doc and said, "Tanner, make sure all your patients are firmly strapped down. I foresee some rough air ahead."

Tanner replied, "I've got my patients covered. Just try not to give me any more, okay?" Alex gave him a silent nod, yes.

Alex continued, "All right, you seasoned air crew know the drill. Stay sharp, keep calm, and think before you act. Captain Probts, did you get Mr. Richardson replaced with one of your diesel troops?

The captain replied, "Yes, sir, Tony Allard has taken his place," as he pointed to him.

Alex looked at Mr. Allard and said, "Thank you, sir," as he gave him a nod.

Alex continued, "Air crews, make sure you're topped off all the way. We'll have to sit down one more time between here and the border to top off. Then hopefully, we'll have a safe, straight shot across our border. Well, there's only one thing left to do: Pray."

Alex looked at Hunter and said, "Dad, would you lead us in prayer?" Everyone bowed their heads as Hunter began,

> Oh, Heavenly Spirit in the sky, please watch over us, Your people, tonight. Give us eyes of the owl, wings of the eagle, and armor of the armadillo. If we must defend ourselves from these lying white men, let our arrows fly as straight and as swift as Your judgment. And if they're still coming at us, let our big guns do the talkin' for us. Amen.

Everybody said *amen* and started laughing. Looking him in the eye, Alex walked past his dad and said, "I love you, Dad." Only Hunter could give an inspiring prayer like that. With that, they all headed for their aircraft.

By 2200, Task Force Titan was in the air and headed west. They flew without incident to their next refueling location about seventy-five miles northeast of Memphis, Tennessee. The whole operation took about two hours and they were back in the air. Along with their helo fuel at every ROD location, they also had ordinance of every kind to replace any spent ordinance along the way. The squadron was headed for the border armed to the tooth.

The squadron was in Arkansas, over HWY 67 between the towns of Jonesboro and Popular Bluff when Captain Probts reported two aircraft on their six. After further identification he was able to tell Hunter that they were two Blackhawk gunships. Not like the Blackhawks they engaged over Bragg with M-240s. They were real gunships with rocket pods and mini guns, and they were closing fast.

The Titans pushed their aircraft to the limits and gave it everything they had. They were topping out at 150 knots. However, the newer, faster Blackhawks eventually closed the gap and challenged the squadron over the radio.

"Army westbound helos, this is US Army attack helos from Fort Campbell, Kentucky, identify yourselves, over."

Alex came over the Titan net and said, "All Titan call signs, these guys have rockets, be ready on your flairs and chaff. Hades, ease back to cover Pegasus; Zeus, be prepared to assist. I'll keep pressing on with Pegasus, how copy, over?" All call signs acknowledged their instructions.

Then the call came over their radio again. "Westbound helos on heading two-eight-zero degrees, seven-five-feet AGL, this is US Army attack helo AH160W, identify yourselves, or we will fire upon you, over."

By then Hades had slipped back to the portside rear of Pegasus, and Damon replied, "AH160W, this is Arkansas Air National Guard 384TP, what's the problem, over?" Then there was silence for about fifteen seconds. Damon told Luis that they were running their call sign through their HQ, just like a cop did when he pulled a car over. That was all right with Damon because every second that passed, the squadron was getting closer to the border. Finally their reply came.

"Roger, 384TP, this is AH160W, we have no record of your call sign or flight mission. What is your business, over?"

Immediately, Damon responded, "AH160W, this is 384TP, we have generals Wesley, Goodman, and Donavan on board that we're taking to the border to evaluate our border troops ASAP, over."

Damon, Dutch, Hunter, and Alex had done their homework and researched and printed lists of all high ranking US Army and USAF military commanders. They knew such a list could come in most helpful when trying to run a successful ruse on enemy pilots or ground forces. Especially when the enemy was hearing that those VIP's were onboard. Then the verification process would get a whole lot longer and more certain before anyone fired a round.

The enemy pilots recognized the generals' names and were waiting for their HQ to confirm or deny their claim that they were in fact onboard. That bluff bought Task Force Titan valuable time as they continued westward. The Squadron was nearly at Branson, Missouri when the army helos contacted them again. All Titan helos heard the call.

" 384TP, this is AH160W, land all of your aircraft now, or we will blow you out of the sky! You have sixty seconds to comply, Out." Just then, the Titans received another incoming call.

"Six aircraft heading two-eight-zero degrees, seven-five feet AGL, this is FSA Army border forces, do not attempt to cross this border, or you will be fired upon. I say again, six aircraft heading two-eight-zero degrees, seven-five feet AGL, this is FSA Army border forces, do not attempt to cross this border, or you will be fired upon!"

Dutch called Alex and said, "I think it's time to make that call, brother."

Alex replied, "I'm already on the phone, my friend." It seemed that the SFCPF boys still had an ace up their sleeve. As Alex's phone stopped ringing, an old familiar voice answered.

Clint Stanley said, "Yes, Alex, is it that time?"

Alex said, "Yes, sir, make the call, now!"

Clint replied, "Godspeed, Alex, bye."

As it turned out, Clint Stanley used to be Rich Pevey's attorney. He was, however, still his long-standing good friend. Mr. Pevey always did trust Clint's opinion and his word. Alex and Clint had prearranged for Clint to call Governor Pevey, the Free States' provisional leader if they were having issues getting back across the border, especially if Osama invoked martial law or the civil war kicked off.

Since the attack on Dyess Air Force Base, Mr. Pevey had always carried an emergency cell phone that only a few trusted officials had the number to. Clint Stanley just happened to be one of those trusted few. Even though it was 0538 in Texas, Clint didn't hesitate to call the governor on behalf of his friends.

After fumbling with three different phones, Governor Pevey finally answered the one that was ringing. "Hello, who is this?"

"Rich, this is Clint Stanley, Listen closely! This is a life or death situation." Then he proceeded to explain the situation and that the troops on his side needed to permit the four helos to cross his border. Before Rich could give Clint his reply, the phone went dead.

As task force Titan was getting dangerously close to the border, the trailing Blackhawks opened fire and each launched a Sidewinder missile at the two Hueys. Captain Probts yelled, "Incoming missiles, target Hueys!" Then he opened up on both birds with his 50 cal. while yelling, "Door gunners, get those mini guns smoking!"

While Captain Probts was barking out orders, both Hueys popped their flairs and chaff. They avoided destruction that round; however, they'd probably run out of flairs and chaff before the Blackhawks ran out of missiles.

The trailing Blackhawks were taking a lot of heat as the 50 cal. and both mini guns on Pegasus were melting their barrels down. As both Hueys conducted simultaneous left and right banks to do 180 turns so they could fire on the trailing helos, the Blackhawks each fired a missile right at Captain Probts. None the less, he continued firing at them with his five thousand-round belt of ammo.

Since the Chinook crew knew that they'd always have a ramp gunner on the mission, they ensured that he could fire the bird's flairs and chaff from his gun position, as well as the cockpit. The captain was so focused that he fired his missile counter measures without missing a beat on his Ma Duce.

As the old Hueys were banking hard, the sound of thick chopping air could he heard by all; the way only a Huey could sound. Once again a Titan bird escaped destruction from enemy missiles. After the smoke cleared from the exploding missiles, both Hueys let em have the whole can of whoop-ass.

The Hueys each fired rockets at both birds and cut loose with their mini guns. Normally the responsive Blackhawks could have evaded the rockets and maybe dodged the wall of lead; however, since the Hueys were right in their face, that didn't pan out so well for them.

It was daylight by now and after the smoke from the exploding Blackhawks disseminated, Damon and Dutch saw six more fast approaching US Army gunships; and these were Apaches. Hades and Zeus immediately did another 180 and hauled ass behind Pegasus, trying to catch up. Then Dutch called Alex again.

"Cyclops, Zeus, over."

"Zeus, send it, over."

"Cyclops, did you get through to Clint?"

"Affirmative, Zeus."

Then Dutch gave Alex the bad news, "Good, Cyclops, we've got six Apaches closing fast from our six, how copy? Over."

Then Alex asked, "How far out, over?"

Dutch simply replied, "Two mikes out!"

Then Alex put out a net call, "All Titan call signs, enemy rear two mikes out, border front one-mike out. Let's run for the gauntlet, everything ya got. Let's go!" The squadron flew like angels en-rout for Armageddon.

Just as Task Force Titan was approaching the border, they saw the USA infantry troops on the Missouri side and the FSA AD troops on the Kansas side. Just then Hunter flipped on the PA system inside Pegasus and yelled, "Take off your body armor and sit on it—-quickly!"

Ten-seconds later they were over the infantry troops and all the pilots and copilots saw the infantry troops raise their rifles and open fire on the helos. All four birds took hits from the grunts on the ground.

As the squadron had cleared the USA side and was preparing to cross the FSA side, the air crews once again saw the troop's weapons systems rising toward them. This time they were the FSA's air defense big guns; four VADS (Vulcan Air Defense Systems) and two Avenger AD systems. Most of the flight crews thought that was the end of the mission?

Alex was surprised to even see the VADS at all. He knew that the US took them out of service in 1994, three years after

Desert Storm. However, after the USA and FSA split, the western states had to bring all of their obsolete equipment out of storage. Irregardless, the Vulcan was still an effective weapon against helos and ground troops. In Alex's opinion, they should never have retired the burp guns in the first place.

Alex and Damon came over the Titan net at the same time and said; "Hold your fire, Titans!" as the squadron screamed over the FSA positions. The AD unit did not fire on Alex and his birds. Quickly trailing the Titan Task Force were the six USA Apaches and they weren't stopping either.

The FSA troops gave several radio calls for the Apaches to cease and desist, with no response. Therefore, the commander of the unit ordered one of his Vulcans to send a hundred round burst of twenty mike mike across their bow. Then Major Dollar, the commander of the Apache attack squadron ordered his birds to open fire upon the FSA troops on the other side of the national border. This was the act that started America's second civil war.

Therefore, Colonel Heiser, the Ad commander, had no choice. He ordered his unit to open fire and open fire they did. They sent sixteen Stinger missiles, in volleys of four, so they couldn't avoid them all. Then they followed that up with 12,000 rounds of armor piercing 20mm. Needless to say, there were no survivors.

The Vulcans were firing four-in-one tracers. Just like Puff, that gave the weapon system a futuristic look; like a laser burst. Colonel Heiser insisted on his Vulcans using four-in-one so that in the event they ever lost their hi-tech automated radar targeting system, the gunners could still walk their rounds in on the target.

Once the squadron was three clicks past the FSA defensive line on the border, Dutch sent out his Mayday. "Cyclops, Zeus, *Mayday, Mayday,* I gotta set her down, I'm losing power and smoking bad, over!"

"Copy, Zeus, break, Pegasus, kick two packs now, over." Hunter then immediately instructed his loadmaster to deploy two sets of trail bikes.

The four-man crew would have to ride the E & E bikes far enough away that Pegasus could have time enough to land and pick them up. It was way too risky to land that behemoth just three clicks away from the FSA troops. They saw the badly damaged and smoking Huey fly over. They were sure to send a unit to try to capture it when it sat down or crashed.

Dutch and his crew knew that was the only way because there wasn't enough room on Hades and Cyclops to get them. Then Alex had instructions for Damon. "Hades, Cyclops, once they're clear of Zeus, sterilize it and rejoin the squadron, how copy over?"

"Cyclops, Hades, WILCO, over." Damon knew that Alex didn't want him flying escort over them. That would be an overhead beacon for the FSA troops to follow.

Then Alex gave Dutch his final marching orders. "Zeus, Cyclops, maintain present heading for ten miles, how copy, over?"

"Cyclops, Zeus, WILCO, out." Dutch knew that meant their tentative PZ was ten miles ahead on their current heading.

Zeus set down before the two pallets of bikes did. Therefore, Hades spotted them for the grounded crew. "Zeus, Hades, your package is 650 meters ahead of you, over."

"Copy Hades, we're clear and mobile, thanks, out."

The only thing the crew grabbed was their personal weapons and they were on the run. Once they were 500 meters away, Hades took care of their unfinished business. He fired four consecutive rockets into the Huey. It actually brought a tear to his eye. It was like shooting one of his fellow troops. After all, Damon had been flying and fighting in the Hueys for over 40 years. They were a good workhorse.

Then Hades flew close to the flaming wreckage to ensure he achieved total destruction. As usual he had. By now the four men had finished de-rigging the bikes and were cranking them to life. Once Damon and Luis saw all four bikes moving, Hades blasted overhead and toward the rest of the squadron. They had about five minutes to catch up.

Well, one thing seemed certain to the Titan Task Force. Mr. Pevey didn't let his old friend or the fifty-five citizens of his nation down. The governor was the only explanation why the FSA troops didn't fire on them, but blasted the USA helos out of the sky. Alex thought to himself that he owed the good governor and Clint Stanley a Texas Rib-eye when they got back.

After the FSA AD unit blasted the six USA Apaches, all hell broke loose. The Big Red 1 (First Infantry Division) across from the AD unit opened fire on them, and they were well equipped with TOWs (BGM-71; Tube-launched, Optically-tracked, Wire guided missiles) and Javelins (FGM-148; Shoulder fired, portable anti-tank weapon). Both units slugged it out for an hour before the firing ceased.

Since the AD unit was preoccupied with trying to save their own skins, they never gave chase to the helos or the four men on trail bikes. By then Pegasus had picked up the Zeus crew and was halfway across Kansas when they reached their next refueling location. Task Force Titan was well overdue for their ROD.

Once all three helos were safely tucked away in their wheat barns, Alex requested a status report on all personnel and aircraft. Meanwhile, Doc, Galvin, and Leiko had their hands full with the wounded. It seemed that 13 people were wounded during the volatile border crossing. Leiko really earned her pay; even before she started helping to tend to the wounded.

Hunter took three 5.56 rounds through his right calf and left elbow as Pegasus flew over the grunts on the ground. Therefore, Leiko had to take the helm and bring Pegasus in the rest of the way. It turned out that they both were the heroes of the day. Hunter's quick decision to instruct all of his passengers to sit on their body armor had prevented nine people from sustaining fatal wounds from the small arms barrage from below.

After Alex had checked out all of the damage on the birds, topped them off, and visited all of the wounded, he got up with Gerard to check out the news. He feared that today's activities could have profound consequences for everyone. Especially since it had been a week since Osama had unleashed his federal army on his nation's population; in the name of legal gun control.

By the end of the sit report that Dutch handed him, Alex officially knew that as a result of the border crossing, they had one dead, three critical, and ten walking wounded. All three birds were still air worthy with repairs and they still had a full combat load of ammo; even though, Alex was sure they wouldn't have to fire another round before they reached Shadow Wolf Ranch.

CIVIL WAR
IS FORCED AGAIN

14 JULY 2011
CENTRAL KANSAS

Alex had gathered Dutch, Damon, and Gerard as they all watched a CBS live report. It was President Osama announcing that the United States of America had been attacked by the Free States of America. He claimed for that reason, and because they were aiding and abetting domestic and international terrorist concerning the national gun ban, they had to be stopped. He even had the balls to claim that FSA troops downed six helos on the border without provocation.

President Osama got straight to the point:

> My fellow Americans, as you all know, we have been fighting a war on guns in this country for years now. We have had countless Americans in this country needlessly killed by civilian firearms. However, since I signed the national gun ban into effect, my administration has been able to take tens of thousands of dangerous guns of the streets and keep our children safe under my direction.

> Ever since the FBI discovered that the NRA has been funding, training, and supplying these domestic terrorist to resist the national firearms ban and fight against the US government, we have been in an armed conflict with this rabble.

> We have known for some time now that the FSA has also been harboring and supporting these domestic terrorist,

thus making them international terrorist. Today, the FSA shot down six of our helicopters that were flying routine patrols along our side of the border. Then, without provocation, they engaged our army ground troops that we have protecting our western border.

It is my opinion that we must force the removal of the FSA's radical provisional leader, Governor Rich Pevey. He's the one responsible for eighteen of our western states breaking away from us. He's also the one directly responsible for the attack on Dyess Air Force Base. He forced my hand for the security of this nation.

I am formally announcing that all civilian movement between the United States of America and the Free States of America is hereby ended. Any USA civilians caught trying to cross our national border, one direction or the other, will be tried for treason and hung. We cannot tolerate any defiance against this executive order.

As of this moment, there is a fifty-thousand-dollar reward for information on anyone trying to transit our western border. If you have such information, call your nearest law enforcement agency to be a hero for justice. You will be paid once the terrorist are apprehended and hung.

In closing, these are trying times America. We will do whatever it takes to keep you save from Governor Pevey and all of the radical extremist that are following and supporting him. Good night, and keep your eyes open, America.

That was the end of President Osama's address to America and the rest of the world. He thought he had it all tied up in a nice, neat package. He also believed that Americans would swallow every word he shoveled them. Well, he had a surprise coming and very soon.

Governor Pevey came over the airways right after *The (Osama) View*. Pevey was speaking live from Austin, Texas. He was on *FOX News*; however, every major news franchise in the industry was running with the story. This time, Governor Pevey ensured that the new flag of the Free States of America was present to show the world what they stood for and what they would fight for. It was high above his head and un-obscured so everyone could read every word. He was even going to show the world the preverbal smoking gun.

Governor Pevey, the provisional leader of the Free States of America began his address with a brief history lesson.

> Never forget, my friends, that on 7 February 2011, President Bakr Houssam Osama killed 666 Americans in the unemployment riots when he ordered the National Guard to fire on unarmed American men, women, and children throughout America.
>
> Always remember, my fellow Americans, that on April 20 2011, President Bakr Houssam Osama ordered the United States military to attack the state of Texas and kill fellow American civilians and military personnel. He committed that heinous crime without provocation or warning. Like a thief in the night, they struck while he and his administration watched the atrocity live in the White House, like some Tuesday-night sitcom.
>
> Afterward, he claimed that he had to attack Texas and kill innocent civilians and military people in the name of national security. President Osama killed over eight hundred Americans that night, both from the USA and the FSA.
>
> Americans of the Free States and the United States, I come to you all today with a very heavy heart. The burden has fallen on me to tell you all the truth of what transpired at our national border in Kansas and Missouri today near the

town of Joplin, Missouri. The burden of truth has fallen in my lap because President Bakr Houssam Osama has told you all many flat-out lies with only one intent—to justify his actions for starting another civil war.

He told us all many lies in his address today. I'm going to address every single lie he spoke today and give the United States citizens the proof they need to remove him from office and try him for the criminal that he is. I will present his statements just as he said them.

First, President Osama said that the FBI discovered that the NRA has been funding, training, and supplying these domestic terrorist to resist the national firearms ban and fight against the US government. This is a lie! US citizens, demand unequivocal proof of this allegation, official documents, witnesses, bank accounts, etc.

Second, President Osama said that the FSA has also been harboring and supporting these domestic terrorist. This is a lie! US citizens, demand unequivocal proof of this allegation, passport documentation, videos, witnesses, etc.

Third, President Osama said that the FSA shot down six of our helicopters that were flying routine patrols along our side of the border. That is a lie! Those armed gunships were flying straight for the national border of the Free States of America. FSA ground troops radioed the gun ships to turn around. They refused to turn around, therefore, FSA troops fired a warning shot across the bow of the gun ships.

Then the six Apache gunships opened fire on our FSA border troops. The FSA ground troops fired upon the six hostile USA gunships and destroyed them in self defense. Please watch this official FSA military video. It is much like a video in the dash of a police patrol car.

Then Governor Pevey showed the world the video clip from the FSA's first radio warnings to the USA's helos destruction. There was absolutely no doubt in anyone's mind that was exactly what happened. It proved that President Osama had lied. Once the clip was finished, the screen switched back to Governor Pevey, and he continued,

> Forth, President Osama said that they engaged our army ground troops that we have protecting our western border with no provocation. That is a lie! No one fired on the First Infantry Division until after they had fired upon the FSA AD unit.

Once again, Governor Pevey showed the world the video clip of the FSA's final rounds being fired at the six attacking gunships to the Big Red One, initiating fire on the FSA AD unit. Once again, there was no doubt that Osama had lied. Then Mr. Pevey continued,

> Fifth, President Osama said that I, Governor Rich Pevey, was the one responsible for eighteen of our western states breaking away from us. That is a lie! All eighteen states seceded from the union because President Osama wouldn't uphold the United States Constitution and the Second Amendment.
>
> In fact, he is trying to abolish the Second Amendment by signing and enforcing a national gun ban. He knows that once the American public has been disarmed, they will have no means to resist him or his federal storm troopers.
>
> I, on the other hand, support the Second Amendment to the fullest of my ability and my dying breath. I am smart enough to view history and acknowledge the fact that every country in the world that has ever allowed its self to be disarmed has fallen victim to whatever dictator wanted to rule them. I will not let that happen to the Free States of America!

Sixth, President Osama said that I was the one directly responsible for the attack on Dyess Air Force Base. That is a lie! President Bakr Houssam Osama is the one who ordered and signed the top secret classified operations order that sent the 1/75th ranger battalion descending on Texas to kill innocent civilians and military Americans.

Lastly, President Bakr Houssam Osama formally announced that all civilian movement between the USA and the FSA is hereby ended. Any USA civilians caught trying to cross the national border, one direction or the other, will be tried for treason and hung. This is immoral and unjust! I, Rich Pevey, the provisional leader of the Free States of America am making an official announcement to the civilians of the United States of America.

Anyone, whom wishes to come to the Free States of America to escape the tyrannical rule of your socialist dictator Bakr Houssam Osama is welcome. If you get to the border and cross over to us, we will provide you with protection to ensure the US government does not drag you back to their side and hang you as President Osama swore he would do.

Just then all of the people in the audience and the press crews themselves started clapping and cheering to the governor's words. Once they stopped, he continued,

What you can expect from the Free States of America, is a fair and moral government with fair and reasonable taxes. We support and are governed by the entire US Constitution. We have put our Christian God back into our government and nation, the way our founding forefathers intended this great nation to be. We truly believe in a smaller federal government and more control given back to the states. After all, who better knows how to run that state than its own people.

The one and only official language spoken here is English. All school and government test are written only in English. If you want to live here and become a citizen of this country, you are required to speak, read, and write English, just the way our ancestors coming thru Ellis Island did.

Unlike the 2008 elections that were riddled with widespread fraudulent voting practices like ACORN, our voting process requires 100 percent voter ID in order to vote. This will put an end to voting scams.

What you cannot expect is a corrupt government with crazy laws that don't make any sense. We do not sponsor welfare or affirmative action; however, we do enforce strict immigration laws. Therefore, if you come to our nation, be prepared to pull your own weight in society and live a life free from government oppression. We are putting the common sense back into government! And lastly, we are going to clear the NRA's good name and prove that they have done none of the things that President Osama claims.

That, my friends, is what we can offer you if you desire to have a better life. Thank you all for your valuable time, and God bless you all. In God we trust. Good day.

Gerard got up and closed the lid on the laptop, turned around to face the other men, and said, "Wow, Governor Pevey handed Osama his ass."

Dutch said, "Yeah, pretty much."

Then Alex replied, "I bet Mr. Pevey would make one hell-of-a excellent defense attorney. He slammed Osama on every lie he threw out there. Governor Pevey's got my vote for president."

Then Alex stood up and said, "Okay, gents, let's get some shuteye. We've got one more long night of flying ahead of us. I'm going to go look in on dad, and then I'm hitting the hay. Good night." Everyone headed their own way and bedded down.

***

Meanwhile, while Task Force Titan was sleeping, there were hostile border skirmishes all up and down the national border. Things were definitely heating up between the USA and FSA. It seemed as though there were plenty of families willing to take the risk to get to the western side of the border. Some made it and some didn't.

15 JULY 2011
9TH NIGHT
HEADING WEST, NOE

By 2100, the squadron was back in the air headed for their next course change near Alamosa, Colorado where they would assume a northerly heading. Much to everyone's delight, the flight was non-eventful. Once they made their course change it was one straight shot up to Shadow Wolf Ranch.

Since Hunter was out of commission and Dutch didn't have a bird, he took over in the cockpit of Pegasus. Leiko was much relieved because she didn't dig being the only pilot in that big beast. It was a daunting task for one person; especially under their circumstances.

Near Leadville, Colorado the squadron was preparing to land for their last refueling stop before reaching Shadow Wolf Ranch. Their fuel cache was in an old ski lodge maintenance bay. They weren't even going to hide the birds before topping off. Fill em and fly; that was their intent. They couldn't get back home to the safety of their underground hangars soon enough.

Ninety minutes later they were airborne again. By Alex's calculations, they should reach the ranch just before dawn. That would be great because they couldn't afford to have anyone report to the authorities that they saw a squadron of helos land on Alex Boulder's ranch. That would make for a whole lot of unnecessary questions by the law.

15 JULY 2011,
SHADOW WOLF RANCH
END OF MISSION

The time was 0500 and Task Force Titan had just flown over the southern border of Shadow Wolf Ranch. As Alex looked out his starboard side window he saw the slightest slivers of pink and orange over Cheyenne, Wyoming. He whispered to himself, "Thank you Lord for bringing us home safely." Ethan said, "What did ya say Alex? I didn't catch that." Alex replied, "Never mind buddy, we're home now." Then Alex started barking out orders over the radio.

"Hades, Hades, Cyclops, over."

"Cyclops, Hades, send it."

"Hades, you go to the south, Pegasus and I will go to the north, how copy, over?"

"Cyclops, Hades, WILCO, over."

"Hades, Cyclops, copy, out."

"Cyclops, this is Pegasus, I copy direct, over."

"Copy Pegasus, I'll go in last so I can provide over watch, out here."

Hades dropped off from the other two birds and began their descent to the surface hangar that covered the blast door over the sub-surface hangar shaft. They were sitting on the hangar deck with rotors stopped by the time the other two helos reached their hangar fifteen miles to the north.

Once Pegasus' rotors had stopped turning, Cyclops hovered in beside them and shut her down. Ten minutes later their hangar platform was down to bunker level and all overhead blast doors were secured. As soon as Alex got out of the Hughes 500, he went over to the ramp of the Chinook.

Alex walked up to Captain Probts, shook his hand, and said, "How are you doing, my friend? You did a great job up there, brother. Would you please call in your off-duty shift to help us down here?"

The captain replied, "Yes, sir, it would be my pleasure."

When Alex walked up to his father, Dutch was already by his side talking to him. Hunter said to Alex, "Well, we made it, boy."

Alex replied with, "Yeah, well, no thanks to your flying. You got us all shot up!"

Then they all started laughing and Hunter said, "Yeah, well, I still got yas home, didn't I?"

Alex looked at him with a smile and said, "Yes, sir, you did, and we all thank you for that. Well, all accept Leiko, she said, 'You put a pain in her ass, and she had to take up your slack!'"

Then the Doc stepped in and said, "Don't you boys get my patient laughing too hard. If he busts those stitches, I'm going to put you all on KP (kitchen police; performing menial task in the facility's kitchen). Alex and Dutch split without another word.

Over the next twelve hours, all of the injured were setup in the bunker's small hospital. That med unit had fifty beds and was even equipped with an OR (Operating Room). The Huey on the Colorado side was disarmed and the bullet holes repaired, so it could pass an unannounced visit from the FAA or the feds. All of the new community members were presented with their new homes.

23 JULY 2011
FREE STATES OF AMERICA

All the while 'Operation Freedom' Run was going on. The four candidates for election were still campaigning on the FSA side. The red-and-blue political machines were in overdrive.

The popularity polls were definitely looking good for the Republicans. One week before Election Day and the Pevey/Payne ticket was far ahead of the Scissor/Gregtree ticket at 69 percent to 31 percent. It seemed that Governor Pevey's firm stance with President Osama was an extremely popular and positive boost for his campaign.

This was to be the first of its kind as presidential elections went. This would be the first time in American history that both presidential tickets consisted of a man and a woman. One thing was for certain. A woman would be the Vice President of the Free States of America in 2011, no matter which party won.

The only question was, if Governor Pevey won, how hard would it be for him to leave his beloved Texas for four years and live in Denver, Colorado? The government of the FSA had already announced that they were not going to call the president's home the White House. Instead they were going to call it the People's House. In fact, that building was already one quarter completed. The construction crews had been working 24/7 around the clock. They started construction on it right after they elected Denver as their new capital city.

27 JULY 2011
FREE STATES OF AMERICA

Three days before Election Day, President Osama and his administration thought that they could discredit Governor Pevey just before the FSA elections. They believed this one statement would bring him down. President Osama made a public accusation on live national television.

President Osama, with the use of his teleprompter, was straight to the point:

> People of the Free States of America, I would like to enlighten you on the honesty and integrity of your provisional leader, Governor Pevey. He has been lying to you and to the entire world.

> Governor Pevey said that I was the one who directed and signed the orders that sent the 1/75th Ranger Battalion to Texas to attack Dyes Air Force Base. That is simply just not true. It was the joint chiefs-of-staff and the secretary

of defense who gave the military their marching orders. I did not conceive or orchestrate such plans.

The good citizens of the Free States of America, you must not give Governor Pevey any further opportunity to lead your country by voting for him in three days. You must send him the clear message that you will not tolerate him making any more bad policies and sending you good folks any farther down the road to destruction. That is exactly where you are headed if you continue to attack the United States of America.

It's a simple choice you have to make on election day. Vote Republican for Mr. Pevey or Democrat for national peace. The choice is yours. Thank you and good night.

Then the *CNN News* commentator came on the screen and started to regurgitate what the president had just said.

* * *

Since President Osama and the JCOS had directed the 'Operation Condor Repo' air crews to collect and shred the only copies of the OPORD, they all assumed that there were none left in existence. Osama was betting everything on that fact.

Meanwhile, Governor Pevey was in high gear with the elections only three days away. He was just getting off his campaign bus when Osama's propaganda was hitting the airways.

Governor Pevey had just stopped in Colorado Springs for a campaign rally. This would prove to be a very powerful rally indeed. Former President Greg W. Booth was his guest speaker. That same day Sahara Payne was speaking at a rally in California.

Once Mr. Booth and Mr. Pevey were backstage in their dressing room, one of the governor's aides showed the two men President Osama's broadcast. At its end, Booth asked the secret service agents and Pevey's aides to leave the room.

Once the room was clear, Booth looked at Pevey and said, "Do you believe that lying socialist, SOB? I can't believe he'd stoop to such dastardly deeds. I can't believe that he thinks the people of this fine nation would be so gullible as to believe his traitorous lies."

Then Governor Pevey calmly said, "Its okay, Greg, we've got him by the balls!"

"What-da-ya mean, Rich?" the former president asked.

Then Mr. Pevey explained, "Well, Mr. President, it's like this. After the battle of Dyess, while taking all of the remaining 1/75th soldiers into custody, one of their officers surrendered a very special top secret document to us. It was the ranger's military operations order personally signed by President Bakr Houssam Osama himself. It even has his authenticating thumbprint on it.

"When Colonel Oakley asked Captain Harmonski why he had voluntarily surrendered the document, this is what he said. He knew there was something fishy about the way the aircrew would only print one copy, and they wanted it back before the mission began. To him, it looked like the top brass in Washington was trying to cover up an illegal order given to American troops. Captain Harmonski wanted proof for the history books, exactly who ordered Americans to attack Americans." Therefore, he surrendered it, instead of destroying it. In fact, we have this whole conversation recorded for the history books."

Then Pevey showed him the electronically scanned copy of the infamous OPORD on his encrypted note pad. After Mr. Booth had finished looking at the classified document, he looked up at Pevey and said, "They don't know that you have this, do they?"

The Governor replied, "No, sir, they think all aircraft copies were destroyed after the rangers jumped in. We were waiting to use this smoking gun after our presidential elections to set history straight."

President Booth looked Governor Pevey straight in the eye and said, "Well, son, I'd say he's got a big sharp knife to your nuts right now!"

Pevey replied, "Yes, sir, and I don't like it. We're preparing to stomp him right now, just after you announce your endorsement for me and Sahara."

Mr. Booth said, "Let's do it, Rich. I'm tired of that piss ant, bringing America down and trying to shove his socialist crap down our throats!"

Then the two headed out on stage to do battle.

27 JULY 2011
SHADOW WOLF RANCH

Alex, Leiko, and all the flight crews were visiting Hunter in the hospital when Osama spouted his poison on *CNN*. Afterward, Gerard got up and said, "Let's see what *FOX* has to say about this nonsense," as he grabbed the remote and switched the station. When the *FOX* channel appeared, the correspondent was introducing Governor Pevey and former President Greg W. Booth to the stage in Colorado Springs.

The image showed both men walking down the stage toward the podium. Mr. Booth was dressed casually; probably a welcomed feel after eight years in a suit as the most powerful man in the world. Mr. Pevey had a blazer on without a tie; probably so it wouldn't stifle him while slamming Osama.

After reaching the podium and giving all necessary greetings and introductions, Governor Pevey began,

> People of Colorado Springs, the Free States of America, and the United States of America, I want to once and for all, put the nail in President Osama's coffin. I am going to produce the smoking gun that should put an end to his political career; that is if his Congress, Senate, and the American people have any standards left.

> Several days ago, President Osama told America and the world that I was the one responsible for the attack on Texas. Just moments ago, he made that same accusation

again, and this time, he swore that he had nothing to do with the signing of those military orders.

Well, my friends, if you all direct your attention to the screens before you and above you, I am going to show the entire world that President Bakr Houssam Osama is a bold-faced liar. What you all see before you is an authentic copy of the military operations order that sent the 1/75th ranger battalion to attack and kill Americans in the state of Texas.

This authentic document has President Bakr Houssam Osama's personal signature and his right thumb print on it, signifying presidential authorization and approval.

This document was taken from one of the captured US Army Ranger officers after the attack on Dyes Air Force Base. If there are any doubts as to the authenticity of this classified military document, the FSA would be willing to let the USA examine it under the supervision of a neutral country. Now, without further adieu, it is my great pleasure to introduce to you, former US President Greg W. Booth.

(CLASSIFIED)

(TOP SECRET)

OPORD for:

"OPERATION CONDOR REPO"

UNITED STATES ARMY

1st Battalion, 75th Ranger Regiment

This operations order is not in standard

U.S. Army OPORD format.

- Conduct a combat jump to perform an airfield seizure on Dyess Air Force Base, Abilene, Texas. *This is not a training exercise!!! You will encounter hostile forces that will try to destroy you! The 1/75th Ranger Battalion must not fail!!!*

The security of our nation depends on the successful completion of this urgent and necessary mission.

By order of the President of the United States of America

and Commander-in-Chief of the Armed Forces;

04/20/2011, 2000 Hrs EST.

Presidential Signature: *Bakr Houssam Osama*

- Your unit will jump in at 500 Feet AGL and secure the runway, tarmac, all B-1 Bombers and all F-15 Fighters.

As Mr. Booth stepped up to the microphone, he received the standing ovation of a roaring crowd. Americans were truly pleased to see him in the limelight again. Once the people finally quieted down, he began to speak,

> People of Colorado Springs, the Free States of America, the United States of America, and the entire world, it is truly good to be here before you all again. I would like to start off by saying that this is my official endorsement for Governor Rich Pevey and Sahara Payne.

He's a long time friend that I have seen mature in the political arena over the years. He is a good Christian man of good conscience, morals, and ethics, and he has a true patriotic sense of what this nation needs to be a great God-fearing Christian nation again. He can do for the Free States of America what he did for the great state of Texas. I will support him and Sahara Payne to the utmost of my ability.

Now, as for President Bakr Houssam Osama, I believe he has finally gotten the just attention he deserves. Instead of a Nobel Peace Prize or award from all of his Hollywood supporters, today the world has seen him for the true criminal that he really is.

President Osama, your time has come! I have good faith in the American people over there that they will boot you out of their White House and try you for the many crimes that you have committed against their nation and the Free States of America.

I truly love the United States of America with all of my heart. I always have. It crushes my soul to see you under such poor governmental leadership that you as a people are paying such a dear price. I pray that with the unequivocal proof that Governor Pevey has shown you and the rest of the world, you will finally take action. The Free States of America will pray for you all. Thank you and good day. God bless you all.

With that, the station switched to the *FOX News* commentator and Dutch turned the TV off. Everyone kind of just looked at each other in amazement. Then Alex said, "I don't think we could ask for anything more in a good government, as far as what Pevey is telling us we can expect out of his administration."

Hunter said, "Yeah, it sounds pretty good."

Damon said, "I'll believe it when I see it."

Leiko looked at Damon, rolled her eyes and said, "You got that right, buddy!" As always, they could rely on Leiko to break it up.

NEW HOPE FOR A NATION

30 JULY 2011
FREE STATES OF AMERICA

By 11:45 MST (Mountain Standard Time) the final results were in. It had taken longer than expected to tally the landslide results because the polling authorities had to work through the bugs of a new system with eighteen states instead of fifty. However, this time there was no voter fraud to deal with.

It was confirmed; the first President and Vice President of the Free States of America would be Mr. Rich Pevey from Texas and Mrs. Sahara Payne of Alaska. This was truly a great day for this new nation. President Pevey had just finished their acceptance speech when one million pieces of confetti fell from the ceiling of the convention center. President Pevey, Vice President Payne, and her daughter Pippin were covered with the rainbow of paper.

30 JULY 2011
WASHINGTON, D.C.

Meanwhile, the top dogs in the Osama administration were watching the election coverage on *FOX News* in the situation room in the White House. President Osama was loosing his mind. He couldn't believe Governor Pevey had won. Now he was really sweating it because he knew that President Pevey would surely be gunning for him, since he had so much dirt on him. A thousand schemes were going through Osama's mind as to how to best cover his own ass.

03 AUGUST 2011
SHADOW WOLF RANCH

It was 1035 MST and Alex's cell phone rang. It was Clint Stanley's personal number. Alex answered, "Good morning Clint, how ya doing?"

Clint replied, "I'm doing fine Alex but I've got quite a surprise for you."

"Oh yea," Alex questioned, "What would that be?"

Clint said, "I'm about fifteen minutes out in a chopper and I'm bringing President Pevey with me. We're in an unmarked helo to keep a very low profile. He wants to meet you and have a parley. Is that all right with you?" There was silence on the phone for several moments and then Alex said, "Yes of course, I just wish you had given me a little more notice to clean up, that's all."

Alex said, "Have them land the chopper on our helo pad out by the big metal building. Clint, what does he want?"

"Well, Alex, all I can say is President Pevey has quite an amazing proposal for you, young man. Be prepared to be shocked!"

Alex Boulder will serve his nation and her people again…

The next book in this civil war trilogy is; PATRIOT MISSION, bringing a tyrant to justice…

LIST OF ACRONYMS AND ABBREVIATIONS

- 18A ————————————————-Special Forces Detachment Commander (Captain, O-3; in command of a 12-man Army Special Forces (A) team)

- 18B ————————————————-Special Forces Weapons Sergeant (E-6/E-7; Trained in small arms, crew serve weapons, heavy weapons, and special tactics)

- 18C ————————————————-Special Forces Demolitions Sergeant (E-6/E-7; Trained in explosives and engineering/construction skills)

- 18D ———————————————- Special Forces Medic (E-6/E-7; the most advanced/skilled medics in the US Military with surgical and dental skills)

- 18E ————————————————-Special Forces Communications Sergeant (E-6/E-7; Trained in all forms of short and long range communications and Morse code)

- 18F ————————————————-Special Forces Operations and Intelligence Sergeant (E-7; Trained in intelligence, target, and threat analysis, and ID and fingerprinting)

- 18Z ————————————————-Special Forces Operations Sergeant (E-8; Operations Sergeant; NCO in-charge of a 12-man Army Special Forces (A) team)

- 180A ———————————————-Special Forces XO (WO-1 and 2; Executive Officer of a 12-man Army Special Forces (A) team)

ARMY MILITARY RANK (ENLISTED AND OFFICER)

ELISTED

- PVT —————-Private E-1
- PV2 —————-Private E-2
- PFC —————-Private First Class E-3
- SPC —————-Specialist E-4
- CPL —————-Corporal E-4
- SGT —————-Sergeant E-5
- SSG —————-Staff Sergeant E-6
- SFC —————-Sergeant First Class E-7
- MSG —————Master Sergeant E-8
- 1SG —————-First Sergeant E-8
- SGM —————Sergeant Major E-9
- CSM —————Command Sergeant Major E-9

OFFICER

- WO-1 —————-Warrant Officer-1
- CW-2 —————- Chief Warrant Officer-2
- CW-3 —————-Chief Warrant Officer-3
- CW-4 —————-Chief Warrant Officer-4
- CW-5 —————-Chief Warrant Officer-5
- 2LT —————-Second Lieutenant O-1
- 1LT —————-First Lieutenant O-2
- CPT —————Captain O-3
- MAJ —————Major O-4

- LTC ————————Lieutenant Colonel O-5
- COL ————————Colonel O-6
- BG ————————Brigadier General O-7
- MG ————————-Major General O-8
- LTG ————————Lieutenant General O-9
- GEN ————————General O-10
- COS ————————Army, Chief of Staff = General O-10

US TIME ZONES

- EST ———————————— Eastern Standard Time
- CST ———————————— Central Standard Time
- MST ————————————-Mountain Standard Time
- PST ————————————Pacific Standard Time
- AKST ————————————Alaska Standard Time
- HST ———————————— Hawaii-Aleutian Time

- 2.75 inch Rockets ————————-Mighty Mouse; [FFAR] Forward Firing Aircraft Rockets, 70mm, air-to-ground, speed: 1,500 fps, range: 3,400 meters
- 32 auto ——————————————-.32 Caliber, semi-automatic pistol
- 7.62 Mini Gun ————————7.62 mm medium, rapid fire automatic electric Gattling gun, with 6 ea. barrels that fires 3,000 rounds per minute
- 50 Cal. ——————————————-Browning .50 caliber, heavy automatic machine gun, belt fed
- AAF ——————————————Army air field

- AC-130H Pave Spectre ———AC-130 gunship with massive amounts of fire power, for ground support (Same as Puff, Spectre, or Spooky)
- ACC ————US Air Force, Air Combat Command
- ACE Report ————Report after enemy contact = Ammo, Casualties, and Equipment status
- ACF ——————— Access control facility
- ACORN ————Association of community organization for reform now
- AD ——————Air defense
- AFB ——————Air Force Base
- AFSOC ——————Air Force Special Operations Command
- Aft ——————The rear of a water vessel, aircraft, or wheeled vehicle
- AGL ——————Above ground level
- AIRTEK ——————-A fictional, rotary-wing flight school in Sanford, Florida
- AIT ——————-Advanced individual training
- AK-47 ——————7.62 mm, shoulder fired, magazine fed battle rifle
- AMC ——————-US Air Force, Air Mobility Command
- AO ——————Area of operation
- AP ——————Armor piercing ammunition

- Apache Gunship ——————AH-64 Longbow; USA, a four-blade, twin-engine attack helichopter with a tandem cockpit for a two-man crew, 30mm chain-gun, 2.75 inch rockets, and Hellfire misslies

- ARFF —————————- Aircraft rescue fire fighters

- ASAP —————————As soon as possible

- ASOT ————————— Advanced special operations techniques (an SF school)

- AT-4 ————————84 mm, unguided, portable, single-shot recoilless smoothbore weapon

- A-Team ————————— US Army Special Forces, 12-man team

- ATCT ————————Air traffic control tower

- ATF ————————Federal bureau of Alcohol, Tobacco, and Firearms

- ATV ————————All terrain vehicle

- Avenger AD System ————- Humvee Air Defense; 360-degree gunner operated, 50 cal. and 8-pack Stinger FIM-92; [SAM] Surface-to-air missile, heat seeking, speed: Mach 2.2, range: three-miles

- B-1 Bomber ————————B-1B Lancer; USAF, supersonic, four-engine, variable-sweep wing, strategic long range bomber with a crew of four

- Batt. ————————Battalion (Same as Bn.)

- BATS ————————Bleeding, Airway, Tension Pnenmothorax, and Shock–Initial medical check and care

- BFT ——————————Blue force tracker; satellite tracking module

- Binos ——————————-Binoculars

- Blackhawk Gunship ————AH-60: Gunship; USA/USAF, four-bladed, twin turbine, medium helicopter with pilot operated 7.62mm mini guns, 2.75 inch rockets, and Sidewinder air-to-air missles with a four-man crew

- Black-out-drive ——————-No lights

- B-Team ——————————— US Army Special Forces, Company level HQ

- Bn. ——————————— Battalion

- Bona-fides ———————————-A set of pre-coordinated phrases to confirm a contacts identity

- B & W ——————————Black and White

- C-5 Cargo/Troop Jet ————-M–Super Galaxy; the US's largest cargo transport jet aircraft designed to provide strategic airlift for deployment and supply of combat troops

- C-17 Cargo/Troop Jet ————Globemaster III; a large military transport jet aircraft used for rapid strategic airlift of troops and cargo. (It replaced the prop, C-130 cargo/troop transport)

- Cache ——————————-To hide something or a hiding place

- CB ——————————————Citizens band radio

- CCT ——————————Air Force, air traffic combat control team

- CCTV ——————————Closed circuit television
- CDL ——————————Commercial driver's license
- CDR ——————————Commander
- CDS ——————————Chase Defensive System; sprays oil behind vehicle and can drop road spikes. At night has powerful rearward flood lights to blind pursuers.
- Chinook——————————CH-47 Chinook, a twin-engine, tandem rotor, heavy-lift helichopter with crew of 2 to 4
- CIA ——————————-Central Intelligence Agency
- CJCS ——————————- Chairman of the Joint Chiefs of Staff
- Click ——————————1 Kilometer = 1,000 meters/1,093 yards
- CMH ——————————- Congressional Medal of Honor
- CNIC ——————————-Commander, Navy Installations Command
- *CNN* ——————————Cable News Network or (The Communist News Network)
- CO ——————————Commanding officer
- COB ——————————Close of business
- COC ——————————Chain-of-Command

- Combat Diver ——————-Underwater Combat Diver; SCUBA (Compressed Air) and Closed Circuit (Oxygen Re-breather; INFIL/EXFIL) (an SF school)
- COS ——————————Chief of Staff
- CPA —————————— Certified public accountant
- CSAR ——————————Combat search and rescue
- CST ——————————Central stand-ard time
- CST ——————————-Construction surveillance technician
- DA —————————— Direct Actions (offensive operations)
- DDM ————————— Designated Defensive Marksman = (Same as Sniper)
- Delta Force ——————-A US Army Special Operations force that specializes in counter-terrorism and special DA missions
- DFAC ——————————Dining facility
- DHS —————————Department of Homeland Security
- DOD —————————Department of Defense
- DOS —————————Department of State
- DOT —————————Department of Transportation
- Dunage ————————— Cargo packing materials; pallets, 4 x 4's, ratchet straps, etc.

- DX ——————————— Discard / Throw away / Exchange
- DZ ————————————————Drop Zone
- ECM ————————————— Electronic Counter Measures; to jam all radio frequencies of the enemy
- EEZ ——————————————-- Exclusive Economic Zone = twelve to two hundred miles off shore of a nation
- E & E ————————Escape and Evasion
- Ele. ———————————-Elevation
- EMP ———————————————— Electromagnetic Pulse; the abrupt pulse of electromagnetic radiation usually results from certain types of high energy explosions
- EMT ———————————Emergengy Medical Technician
- ERFS————————————-Extended Range Fuel Systems–II Robinson tanks
- ETS ————————————-Estimated time of separation–get out of the military
- EXFIL ———————————Exfiltration from an area
- F-14 Fighter Jet ——————-D – Super Tomcat; USN, supersonic, twin-engine, two-seat, variable-sweep wing fighter
- F-15 Fighter Jet ——————-E–Strike Eagle; USAF, supersonic, single seat, twin engine, all weather, tactical fighter

- F-22 Fighter Jet —————————-Raptor; USAF, supersonic, single seat, stealth fighter
- FAA —————————————Federal Aviation Administration
- FARE ————————————— Forward Area Refueling Equipment
- FAV ————————————————Fast Attack Vehicle
- FayetteNam —————————-Fayetteville, North Carolina
- FBI ——————————————Federal Bureau of Investigations
- FEBA —————————————Forward Edge of Battle Area
- FEMA ————————————-- Federal Emergency Management Agency
- FID ——————————————-- Foreign Internal Defense
- FO ——————————————————-Forward Observer; one that calls in fire support from sea, air, or land
- FRAGO ————————————————-Fragmentary order; used to send timely changes of existing orders to subordinate troops and supporting commanders
- FRIES ———————————————-Fast Rope Insertion/Extraction System
- FSA ——————————————————-Free States of America

- Garrote ————————————Weapon Designed for Strangulation, constructed of steel wire, filament cord, or high strength fishing line
- Glock-30 ————————————- .45 Caliber, semi-automatic pistol
- GLS ————————————Gesellschaft Fur Logistischen Service–armored vehicles (Same as MRAP)
- GOA ————————————Guns of America; domestic terrorist organization fabricated by President Osama
- GPS ————————————-Global Positioning System
- HAAF ————————————Hunter Army Airfield
- HALO ————————————High Altitude Low Opening parachute jump (an SF school)
- HAZ-MAT ————————————Hazardous Materials; such as fuel, ammunition, or chemicals
- Head ————————————Bathroom
- Hellfire Missile ————————-AGM-114; [A.S.M.] Air-to-surface missile, semi-active laser homing, speed: Mach 1.3, range: five miles
- HK-91 ————————————7.62mm, shoulder fired, magazine fed, select fire rifle
- HQ————————————Head Quarters
- Huey ————————————Same as, UH-1H Iroquois, a single blade, single engine, medium utility or gunship, helicopter with crew of 1 to 4

- Hughes 500 —————————A four blade, single engine, light utility or gunship, helicopter with crew of 1 to 2
- HUMINT ————————————Human intelligence
- Hundred-mile-an-hour Tape————————Duct Tape
- Humvee ————————————(HMMWV) High Mobility Multipurpose Wheeled Vehicle
- ID ————————————-Identify or Identification
- INFIL ————————————Infiltrate into an area
- INTAC ————————————- International Terrorist Awareness Course (an SF school)
- IR ————————————-Inferred
- Javelin ———————————— FGM-148; shoulder fired, portable anti-tank weapon with a tandem warhead for explosive reactive armor
- JCS ————————————-Joint Chiefs of Staff for the army, air force, navy, and Marines
- Jedi ————————————Trained in special operations and tactics to issue-out the entire can of Whoop-Ass, and Feared by all (an SF school)
- JP-4 ————————————-One type of jet fuel (Highly explosive)
- KP ————————————Kitchen Police; performing menial task in the facility's kitchen
- kph ———————————— Knots per hour

- LAT/LONGs ——————— Latitude and Longitude
- LAW ——————————- Light Anti-tank Weapon; 66mm, high explosive, single shot, shoulder fired weapon
- LED ——————————Light Emitting Diode
- Leg ——————————Military, Non-Airborne qualified personnel
- Link-up ——————————-Coordinated Meeting
- Loaded ——————————Encrypted
- LP/OP ——————————Listening Post/ Observation Post
- LZ ——————————Landing Zone
- M-1 Super 90 ——————12 gauge, shoulder fired, magazine-tube fed, semi-auto shotgun
- M-4 ——————————- 5.56 mm, shoulder fired, magazine fed, select fire rifle
- M-14 —————————— 7.62 mm, Shoulder fired, magazine fed, select fire Rifle
- M-60A3 ——————————7.62 mm medium machine gun, belt fed, shortened length
- M-79 ——————————40 mm, single shot, grenade launcher
- M-82A1 Barrett ——————-.50 caliber BMG, recoil-operated, semi-automatic sniper system
- M-203 ——————————40 mm, single shot grenade launcher that mounts under a primary rifle

- M-240 —————————————7.62 mm medium machine gun, belt fed
- Ma Duce ————————————-(Same as .50 cal.)
- MASS TAC ——————————-USAF airborne operation = more than three aircraft dropping paratroopers
- Mikes —————————————-Minutes
- Mini-MUTES radar sites ——(AN/MST-T1 (V) = An electronic warfare training system that simulates enemy air defense systems
- Mods ———————————-Modifications
- MRAP ————————————Mine Resistant Ambush Protected vehicles
- MP-5 —————————————-9 mm, shoulder fired sub-machine gun
- Murphy's Law ————————Anything that can go wrong, will go wrong
- NASA —————————————National Aeronautics and Space Administration
- NASFWJRB ————————Naval Air Station Fort Worth, Joint Reserve Base
- NAV ————————————— Navigations
- NCA ——————————— National Command Authority
- NCO ——————————— Non-Commissioned Officer
- NCOIC ——————————-Non-Commissioned Officer in Charge
- NODs ————————————-(Same as NVG's)

- NOE ———————————————Nap-of-the-earth; flying a very low-level type of flight course used to avoid detection and attack by an enemy when in a high-threat environment. (Rotary or fixed wing aircraft)

- NORAD ———————————North American Aerospace Defense Command; inside Cheyenne Mountain, the Rockies

- NRA ———————————National Rifle Association

- NVG's ———————————Night Vision Goggles

- O & I——————— Operations and Intelligence Sergeant's Course = 18F (E-7; Trained in intelligence, target, and threat analysis, and ID and fingerprinting) (an SF school)

- OPS ———————————-Operations

- OPORD ————————————Operations Order; A directive issued by a commander to subordinate commanders for the purpose of effecting the coordinated execution of an operation

- OP/SEC ———————————Operational Security

- OR ———————————Operating Room

- PA ———————————-Physician's Assistant

- PA ————————————-Public Address system

- PA ———————————Public Affairs

- Pax ———————————Personnel

- Phalanx —————————MK-15; Close-In weapons system; fires between 3,000–4,500 20mm cannon rounds per minute, either autonomously or under manual command, as a last-ditch defense against incoming missiles and other targets

- Phoenix Missile —————————-AIM-54C: [AAM]- Air-to-air-missile, long range, radar guided, speed: Mach-5, range: 100 miles

- Pinger ————————————— Underwater hydrophone listening amplifier and acoustic alarm

- PJ —————————————-Air Force Para-Rescue/special operations airman

- POC —————————————Point of contact

- Port side —————————————-Left side of a water vessel, aircraft, or vehicle

- POW —————————————-Prisoner of War

- PSG —————————————Platoon Sergeant

- PT————————————-- Physical Training

- Puff/Spectre —————————-AC-130 gunship with massive amounts of fire power, for ground support

- PZ —————————————- Pick-up Zone

- Q-Course —————————-US Army Special Forces qualification course (Same as SFAS) (an SF school)

- Qual ————————————— Qualification

- RAPCON ——————————— Air Force base, radar approach control

- Real Time —————————-Live

- Recon ——————————Reconnaissance, to look for
- RIP ——————————-Ranger Indoctrination Program
- RN ——————————Registered Nurse
- ROD ——————————Rest over day stop
- RON ——————————Rest over night stop
- RP ——————— ——-Reference Point, aids in navigation
- RV ——————————— Recreational vehicle
- Ruse ——————————Trick or deception
- Sally Port ——————————ACF Vehicle Gate; a vehicle trap
- SALUTE ——————————-Report = Size, Activity, Location, Unit, Time, and Equipment
- SAT ——————————Satellite
- SAW ——————————Squad Automatic Weapon–5.56 mm light machine gun, belt or magazine fed
- SCAR ——————————5.56 mm, shoulder fired, magazine fed, SF service rifle, FHN-USA
- SEC SAT COMM ———SecureSatellite Communications (Encrypted/Decrypted)

- SERE ——————————————-Survival, Evasion, Resistance, and Escape (an SF school)
- SF —————————————————-- US Army Special Forces, the Green Berets
- SFAS —————————————— Special Forces Assessment and Selection (an SF school)
- SFG ——————————————-Special Forces Group
- Sidewinder Missile ——————-AIM-9X; [AAM] Air-to-air missile, medium range, heat seeking, speed: Mach 2.5, range: twenty-too miles
- Sit Report ——————————————Situation Report
- SFOD-A ——————————————-Special Forces Operational Detachment–Team Alpha (Same as A-Team)
- SFCPF ——————————————-Special Forces Citizen Protection Force; a force that comprises of God fearing, patriotic Americans and former Special Forces soldiers (Stationed at Shadow Wolf Ranch)
- SFQC ——————————————-Special Forces Qualification Course (same as Q-course) (an SF school)
- SL ——————————————————-Squad Leader
- SLAMER Missile ——————-AIM-120C; [AMR] advanced medium-range air-to-air missiles, semi-active radar guided, speed: Mach 4, range: fifty-seven miles
- SMG ——————————————Sub-Machine Gun
- S.O.B. ——————————————Son of a Bean Eater

- SOCOM ————————————————-Special Operations Command

- Sparrow Missile ————————AIM-7R; [AAM] air-to-air missile, medium range, semi-active radar homing, speed: Mach-4, range: thirty-one miles

- Spectre ————————————-AC-130H Pave Spectre; a C-130 gunship with massive amounts of fire power, for ground support (Same as Puff or Spooky)

- SPIES ————————————Special Patrol Infiltration/Exfiltration System

- SR ————————————————Special Reconnaissance

- SRT ————————————————Special Response Team

- Starboard Side ————————Right side of a water vessel, aircraft, or vehicle

- Stinger Missile ————————FIM-92; [SAM] Surface-to-air missile, short range, heat seeking, speed: Mach 2.2, range: three-miles

- Storm Trooper ————————Cloned human; one of many, limited in skills and training, and unable to operate without instruction and guidance

- SWAT————————————————Special Weapons and Tactics

- SWR ————————————————Shadow Wolf Ranch

- SWTC————————————— Special Warfare Training Center (Same as USAJFKSWC)

- TCs ————————————-- Truck Commanders

- Tech/s —————————————Technician/s
- Thompson SMG —————————.45 Caliber, automatic, magazine or drum fed, sub-machine gun
- TL —————————————————Team Leader
- TOC —————————————Tactical Operations Command
- TOW Missile ————————BGM-71; Tube-launched, Optically-tracked, Wire guided missile
- TRP ————————————-Target Reference Point
- T/S —————————————————Top Secret
- USAJFKSWC ————————————-United States Army John F. Kennedy Special Warfare Center
- USASOC —————————————United States Army Special Operations Command
- UW—————————————————-Unconventional Warfare
- VADS ————————————————Vulcan Air Defense Systems = An M-113 personnel carrier with a 20mm cannon that can fire three thousand rounds per minute (Same gun as in an MK-15 Phalanxs)
- VC ————————————Viet-Cong = North Vietnamese
- Vo-tec —————————————Joint vocational school = Trade school; carpentry, auto-body, welding, drafting, etc.
- WILCO ———————————— Will Comply
- XO —————————————Executive Officer–2nd in charge = 2IC